SHOGEKI,
SHOJO!!☆

2

story & art by
Kumiko Saiki

Contents

5
OO3

6
O37

7
O77

8
118

Special
Thanks
159

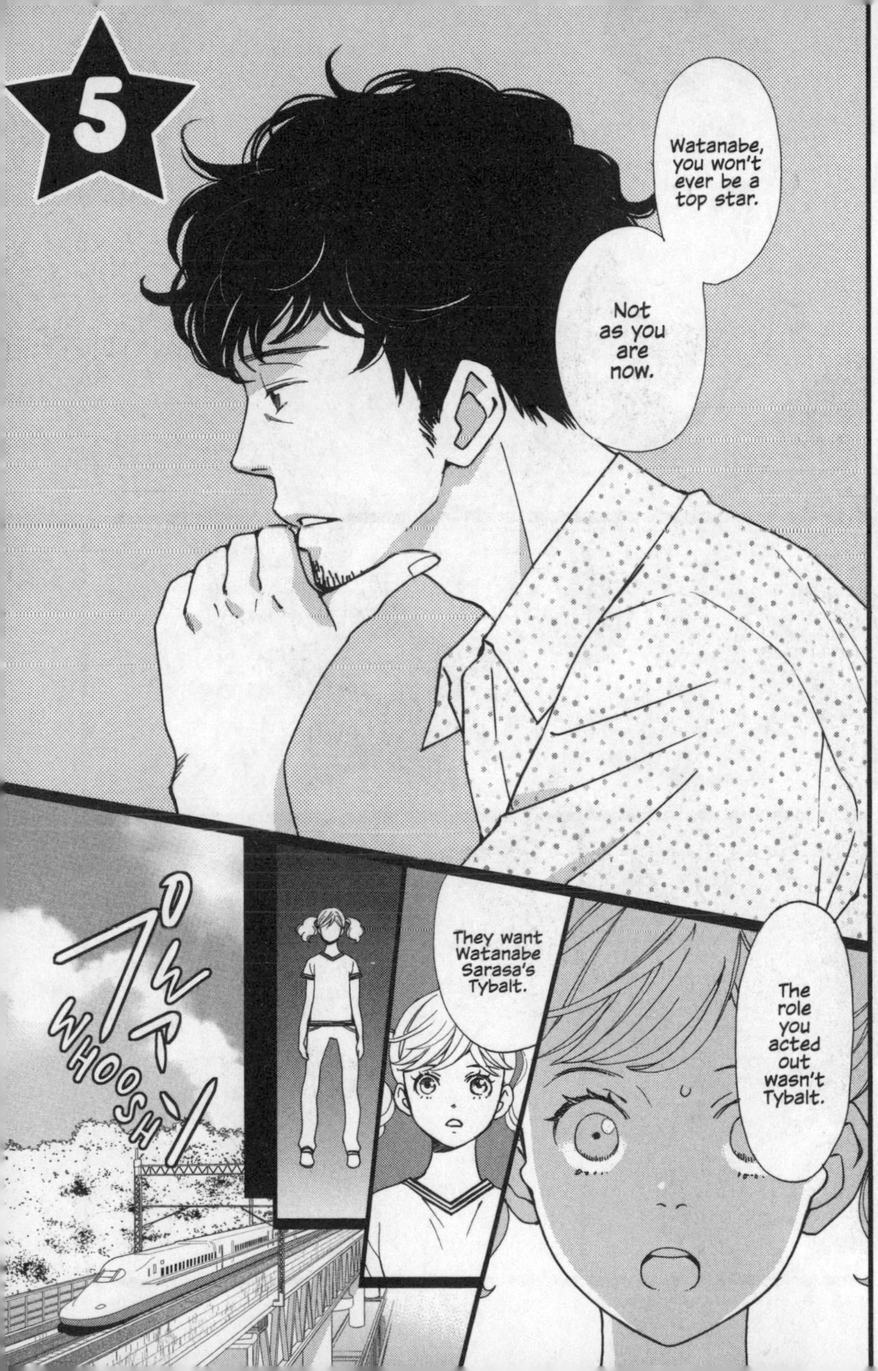
5
Watanabe, you won't ever be a top star.
Not as you are now.
The role you acted out wasn't Tybalt.
They want Watanabe Sarasa's Tybalt.
プワァーン
WHOOSH

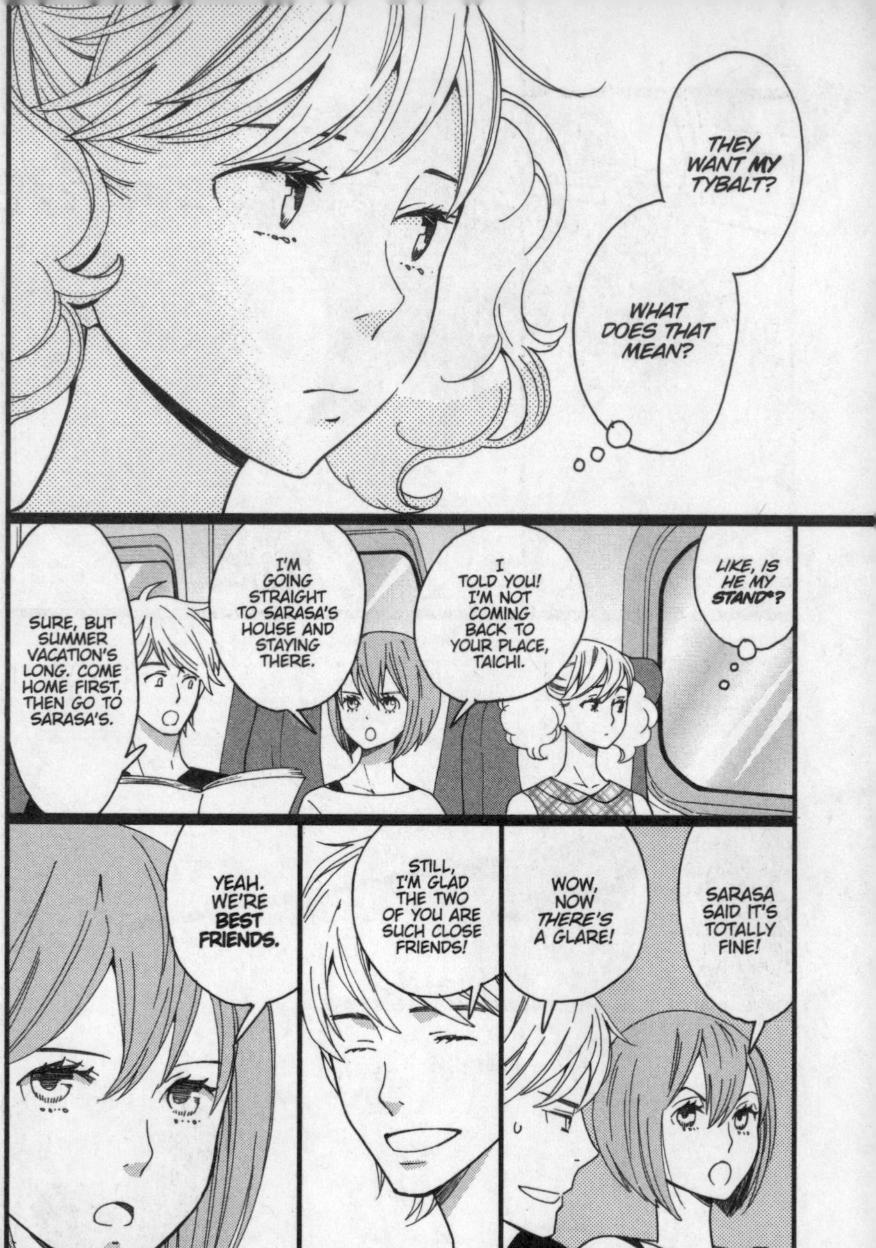
THEY WANT MY TYBALT?
WHAT DOES THAT MEAN?
LIKE, IS HE MY STAND*?
I TOLD YOU! I'M NOT COMING BACK TO YOUR PLACE, TAICHI.
I'M GOING STRAIGHT TO SARASA'S HOUSE AND STAYING THERE.
SURE, BUT SUMMER VACATION'S LONG. COME HOME FIRST, THEN GO TO SARASA'S.
SARASA SAID IT'S TOTALLY FINE!
WOW, NOW THERE'S A GLARE!
STILL, I'M GLAD THE TWO OF YOU ARE SUCH CLOSE FRIENDS!
YEAH. WE'RE BEST FRIENDS.

*A Jojo's Bizarre Adventure *reference.*

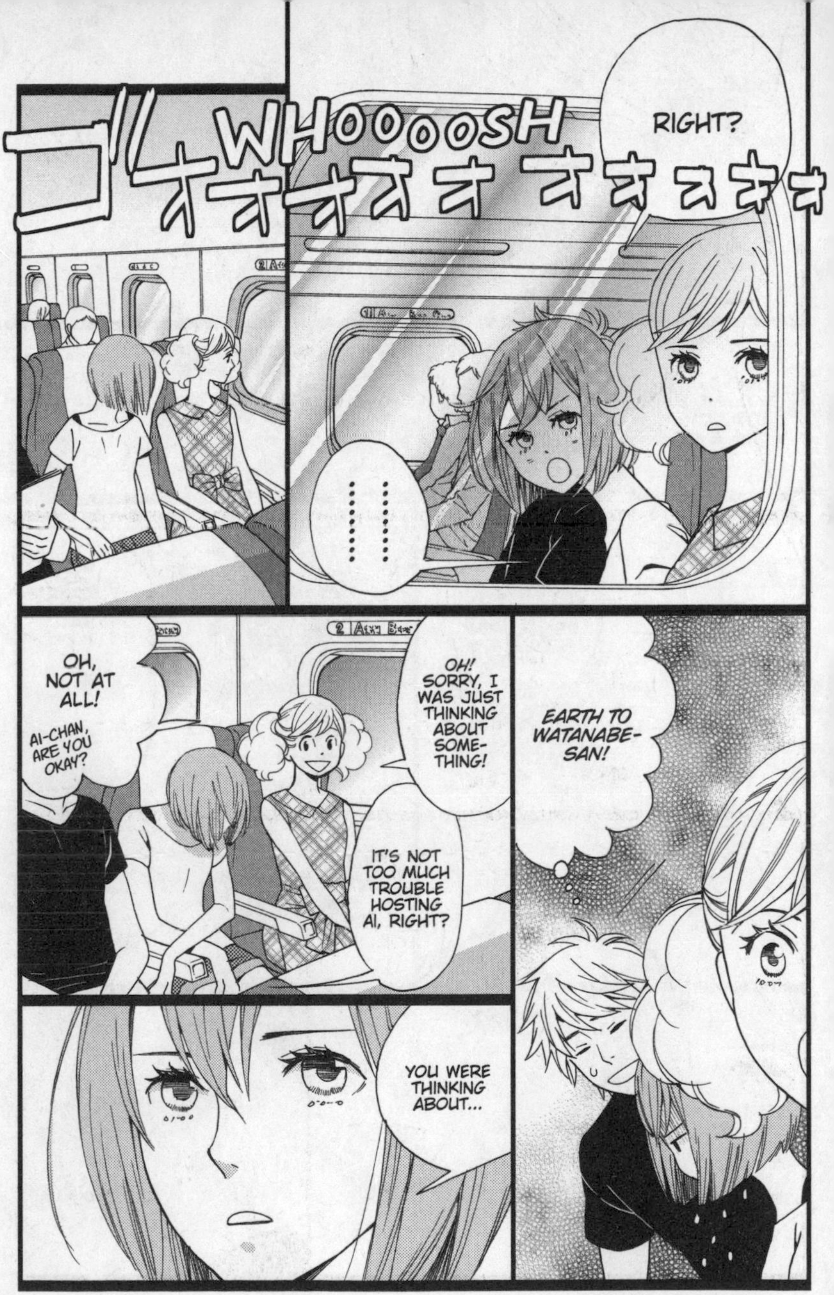
RIGHT?
WHOOOOOSH
ゴオオオオオ オォォォォ
......
EARTH TO WATANABE-SAN!
OH! SORRY, I WAS JUST THINKING ABOUT SOME-THING!
IT'S NOT TOO MUCH TROUBLE HOSTING AI, RIGHT?
OH, NOT AT ALL!
AI-CHAN, ARE YOU OKAY?
YOU WERE THINKING ABOUT...

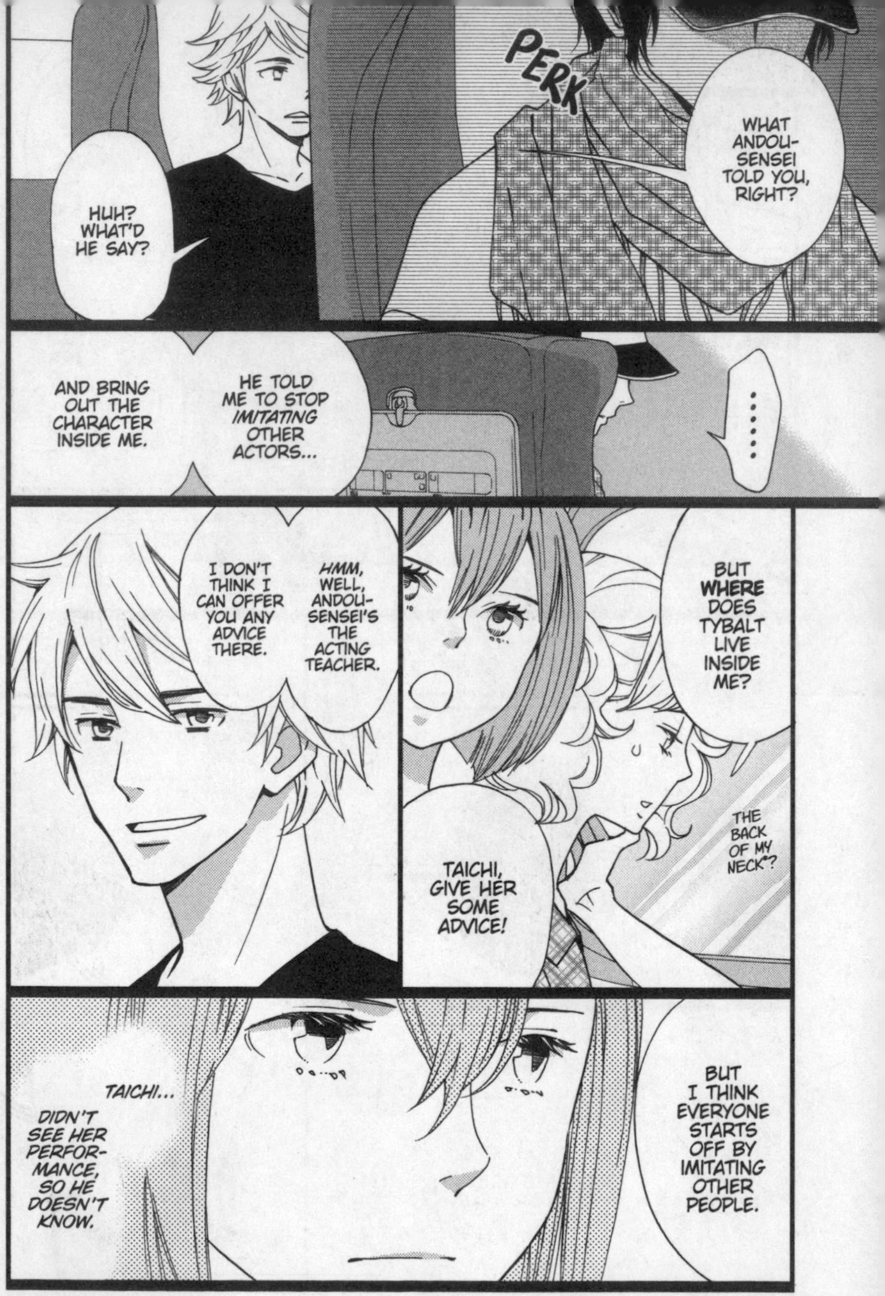
PERK
WHAT ANDOU-SENSEI TOLD YOU, RIGHT?
HUH? WHAT'D HE SAY?
......
HE TOLD ME TO STOP *IMITATING* OTHER ACTORS...
AND BRING OUT THE CHARACTER INSIDE ME.
BUT **WHERE** DOES TYBALT LIVE INSIDE ME?
THE BACK OF MY NECK*?
TAICHI, GIVE HER SOME ADVICE!
HMM, WELL, ANDOU-SENSEI'S THE ACTING TEACHER.
I DON'T THINK I CAN OFFER YOU ANY ADVICE THERE.
BUT I THINK EVERYONE STARTS OFF BY IMITATING OTHER PEOPLE.
TAICHI...
DIDN'T SEE HER PERFORMANCE, SO HE DOESN'T KNOW.

*An Attack on Titan *reference.*

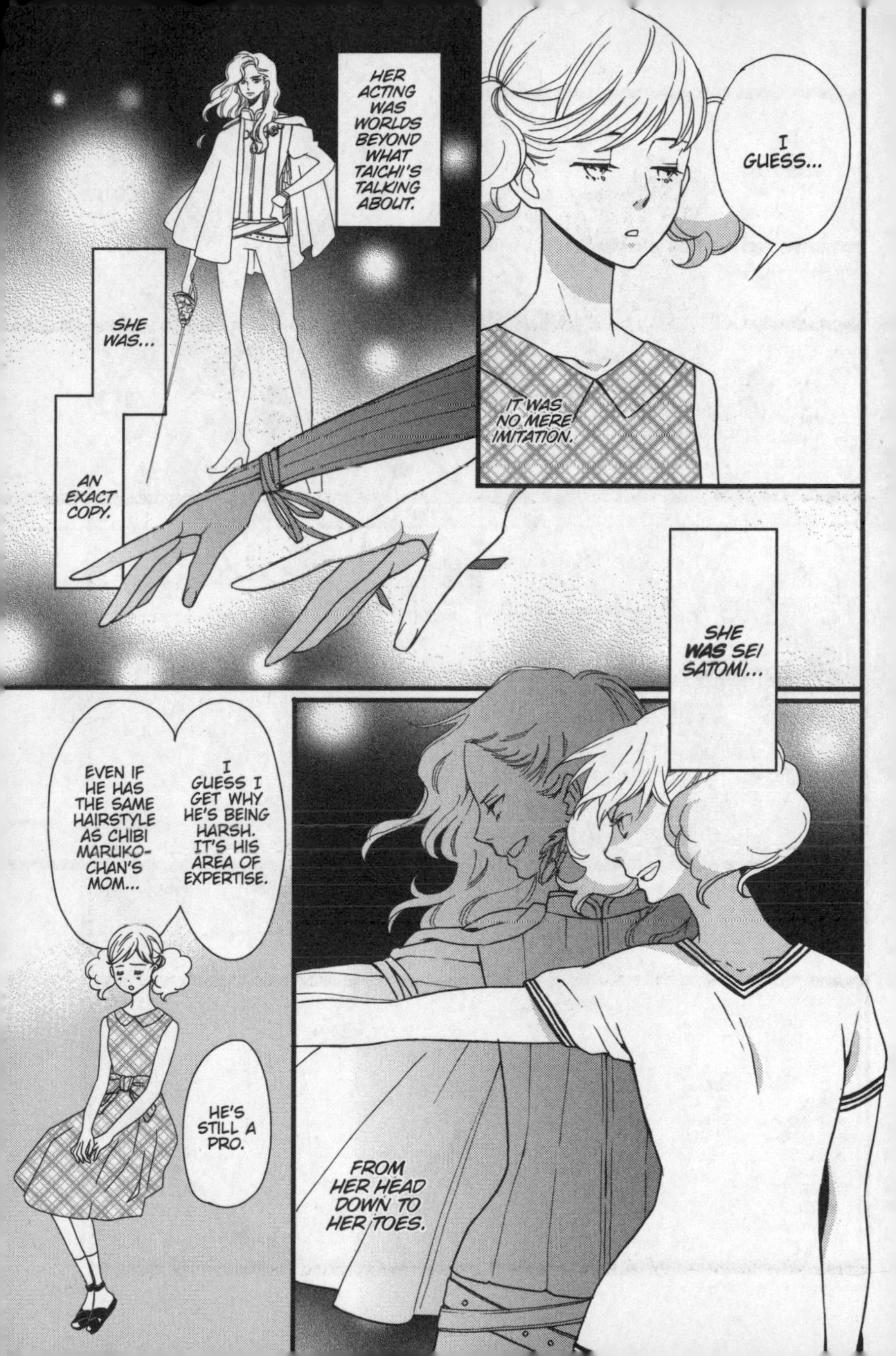
I GUESS...
IT WAS NO MERE IMITATION.
HER ACTING WAS WORLDS BEYOND WHAT TAICHI'S TALKING ABOUT.
SHE WAS...
AN EXACT COPY.
SHE WAS SEI SATOMI...
FROM HER HEAD DOWN TO HER TOES.
I GUESS I GET WHY HE'S BEING HARSH. IT'S HIS AREA OF EXPERTISE.
EVEN IF HE HAS THE SAME HAIRSTYLE AS CHIBI MARUKO-CHAN'S MOM...
HE'S STILL A PRO.

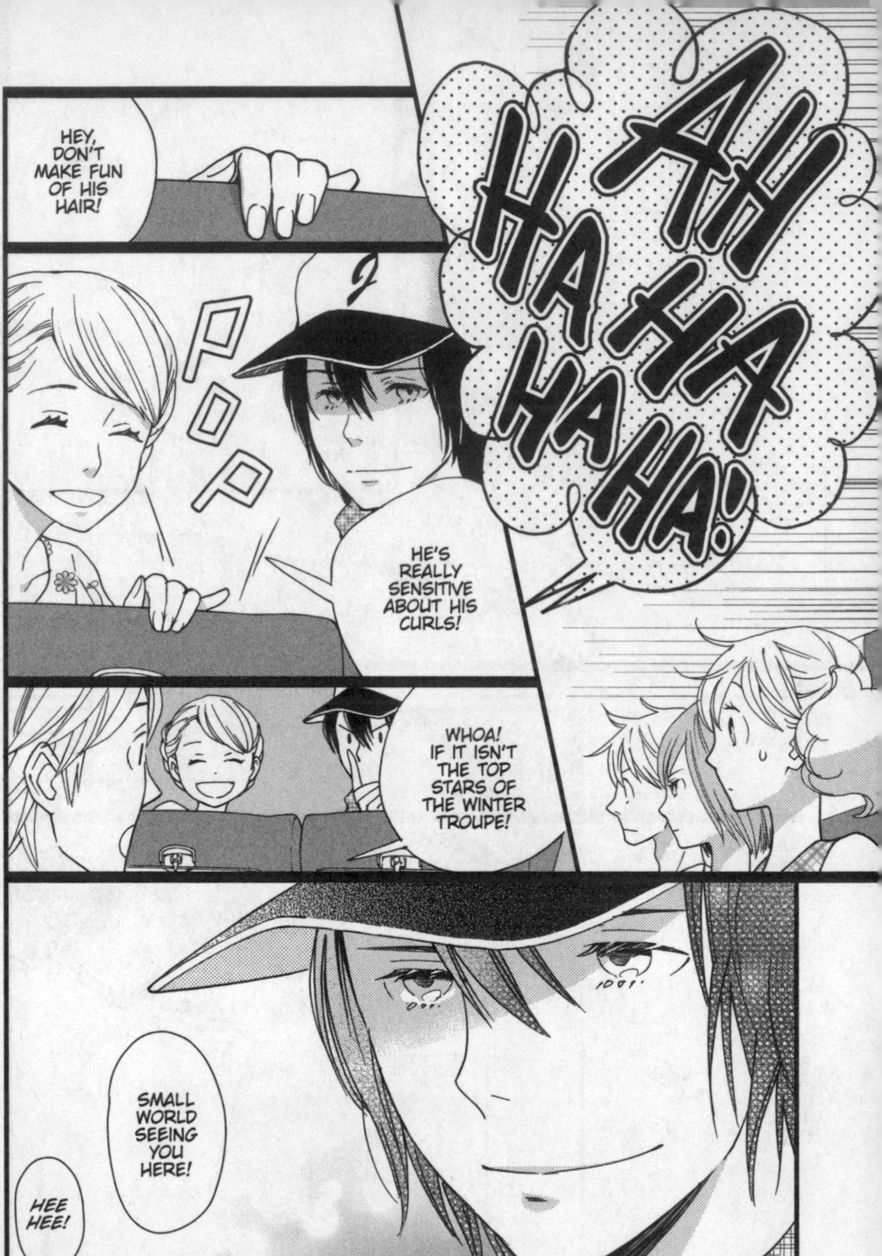
AH HA HA HA HA HA!
HEY, DON'T MAKE FUN OF HIS HAIR!
POP
HE'S REALLY SENSITIVE ABOUT HIS CURLS!
WHOA! IF IT ISN'T THE TOP STARS OF THE WINTER TROUPE!
SMALL WORLD SEEING YOU HERE!
HEE HEE!

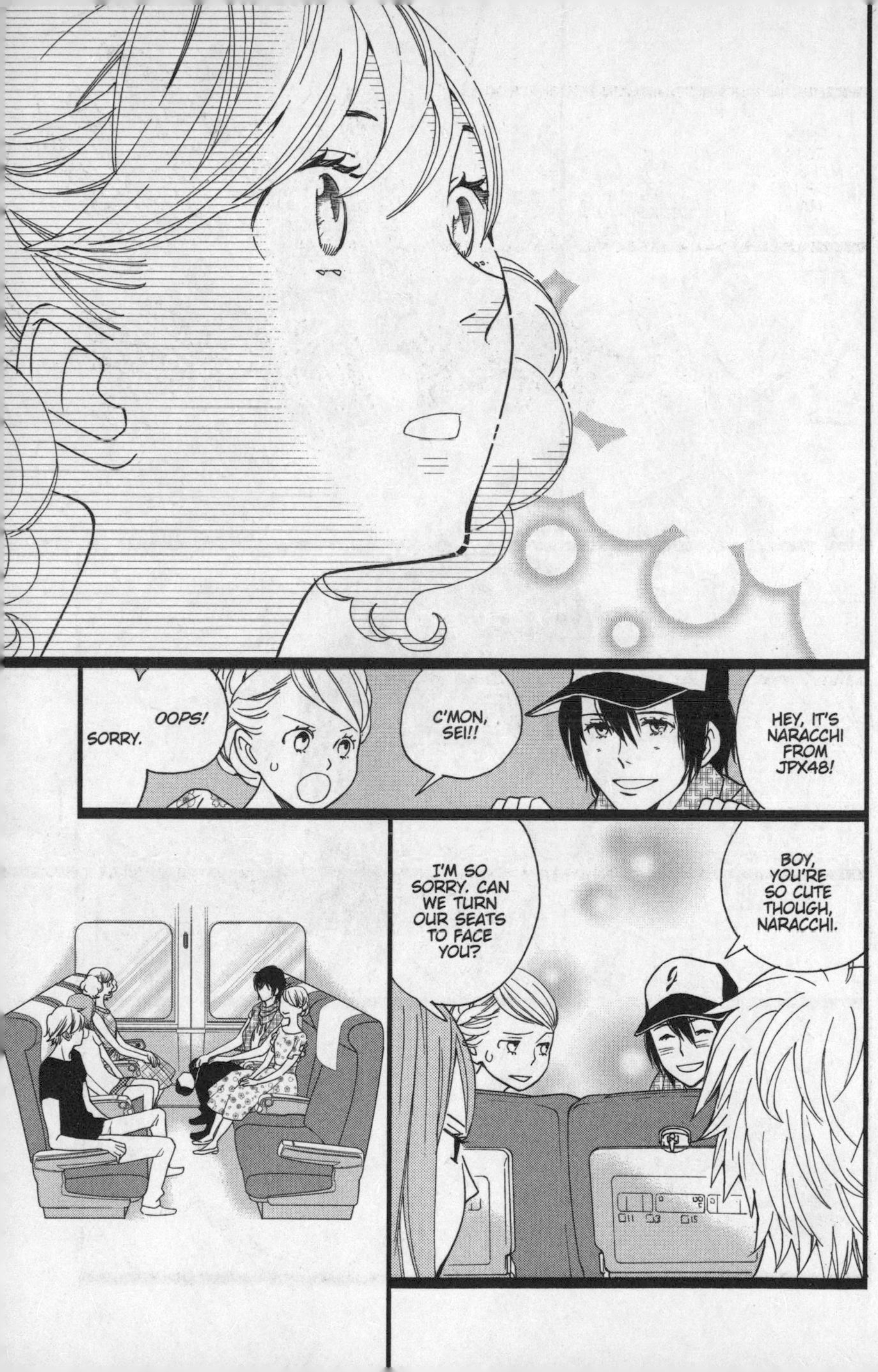
HEY, IT'S NARACCHI FROM JPX48!
C'MON, SEI!!
OOPS!
SORRY.
BOY, YOU'RE SO CUTE THOUGH, NARACCHI.
I'M SO SORRY. CAN WE TURN OUR SEATS TO FACE YOU?

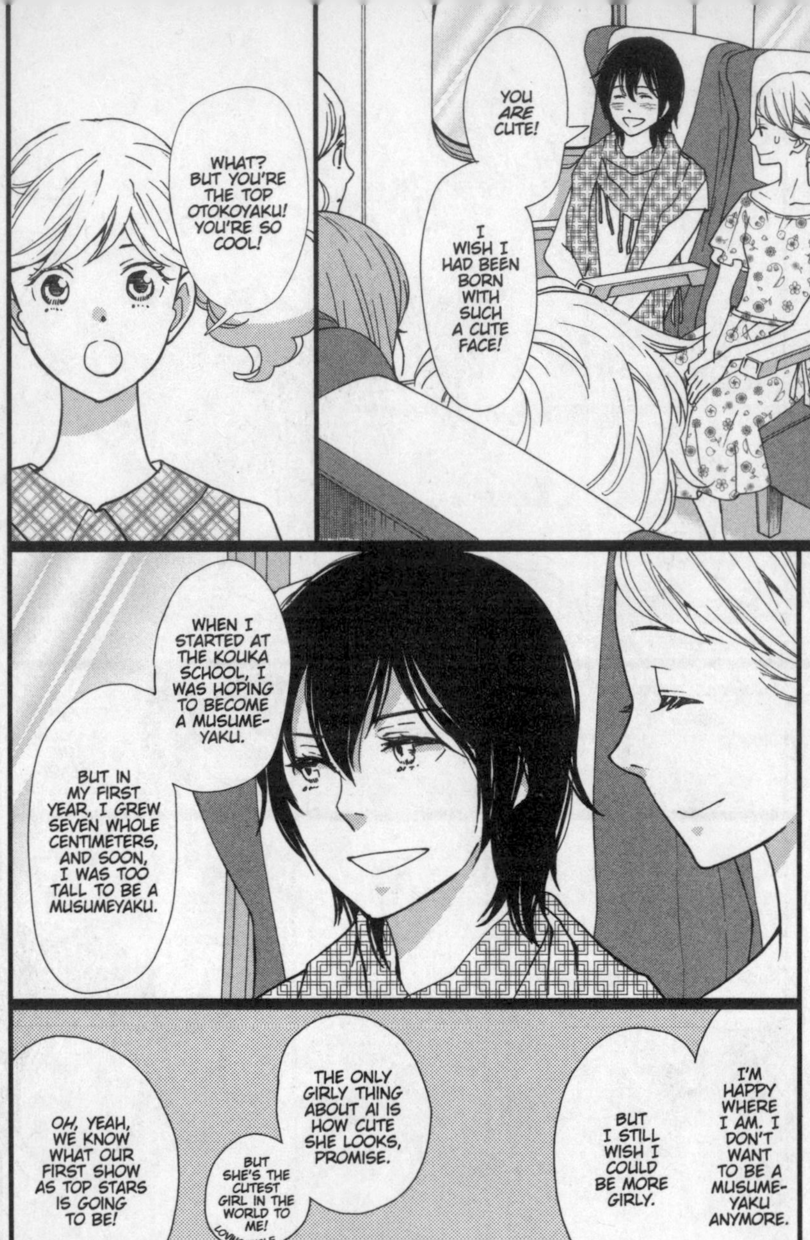
YOU ARE CUTE!
I WISH I HAD BEEN BORN WITH SUCH A CUTE FACE!
WHAT? BUT YOU'RE THE TOP OTOKOYAKU! YOU'RE SO COOL!
WHEN I STARTED AT THE KOUKA SCHOOL, I WAS HOPING TO BECOME A MUSUME-YAKU.
BUT IN MY FIRST YEAR, I GREW SEVEN WHOLE CENTIMETERS, AND SOON, I WAS TOO TALL TO BE A MUSUMEYAKU.
I'M HAPPY WHERE I AM. I DON'T WANT TO BE A MUSUME-YAKU ANYMORE.
BUT I STILL WISH I COULD BE MORE GIRLY.
THE ONLY GIRLY THING ABOUT AI IS HOW CUTE SHE LOOKS, PROMISE.
BUT SHE'S THE CUTEST GIRL IN THE WORLD TO ME!
LOVING UNCLE
OH, YEAH, WE KNOW WHAT OUR FIRST SHOW AS TOP STARS IS GOING TO BE!

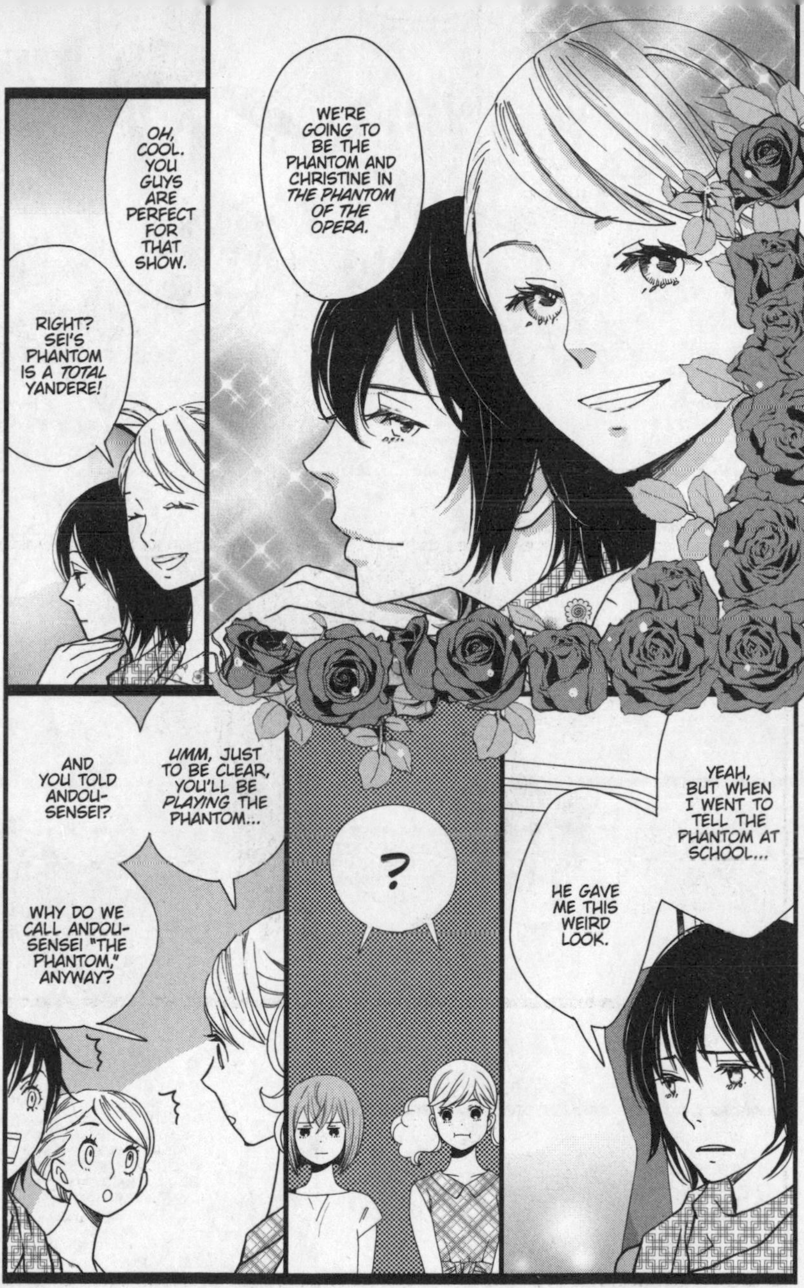
WE'RE GOING TO BE THE PHANTOM AND CHRISTINE IN *THE PHANTOM OF THE OPERA*.
OH, COOL. YOU GUYS ARE PERFECT FOR THAT SHOW.
RIGHT? SEI'S PHANTOM IS A *TOTAL* YANDERE!
YEAH, BUT WHEN I WENT TO TELL THE PHANTOM AT SCHOOL...
HE GAVE ME THIS WEIRD LOOK.
?
UMM, JUST TO BE CLEAR, YOU'LL BE *PLAYING* THE PHANTOM...
AND YOU TOLD ANDOU-SENSEI?
WHY DO WE CALL ANDOU-SENSEI "THE PHANTOM," ANYWAY?

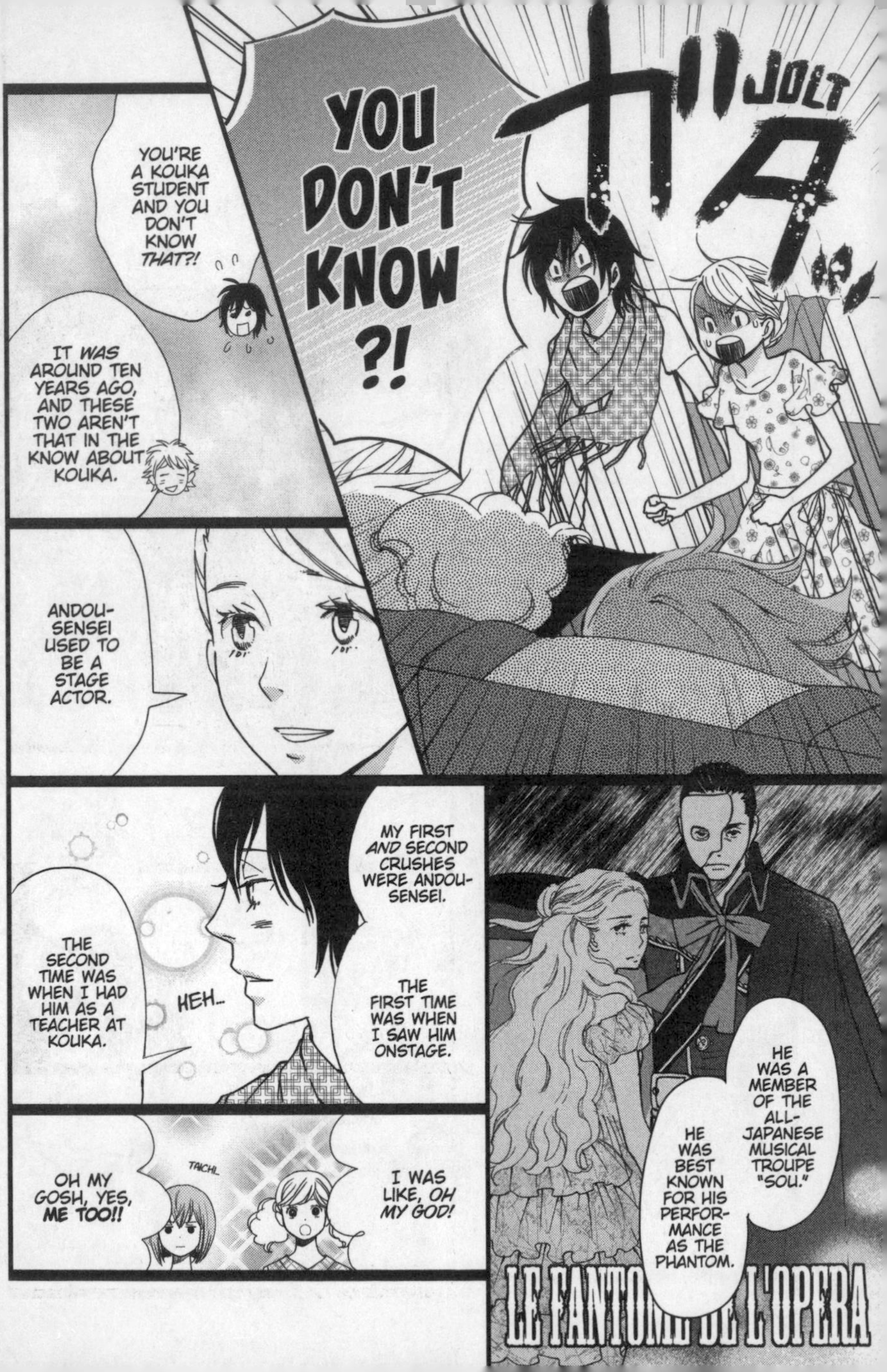

JOLT
YOU DON'T KNOW ?!
YOU'RE A KOUKA STUDENT AND YOU DON'T KNOW *THAT?!*
IT *WAS* AROUND TEN YEARS AGO, AND THESE TWO AREN'T THAT IN THE KNOW ABOUT KOUKA.
ANDOU-SENSEI USED TO BE A STAGE ACTOR.
HE WAS A MEMBER OF THE ALL-JAPANESE MUSICAL TROUPE "SOU."
HE WAS BEST KNOWN FOR HIS PERFORMANCE AS THE PHANTOM.
LE FANTOME DE L'OPERA
MY FIRST *AND* SECOND CRUSHES WERE ANDOU-SENSEI.
THE FIRST TIME WAS WHEN I SAW HIM ONSTAGE.
HEH..
THE SECOND TIME WAS WHEN I HAD HIM AS A TEACHER AT KOUKA.
I WAS LIKE, *OH MY GOD!*
TAICHI...
OH MY GOSH, YES, **ME TOO!!**

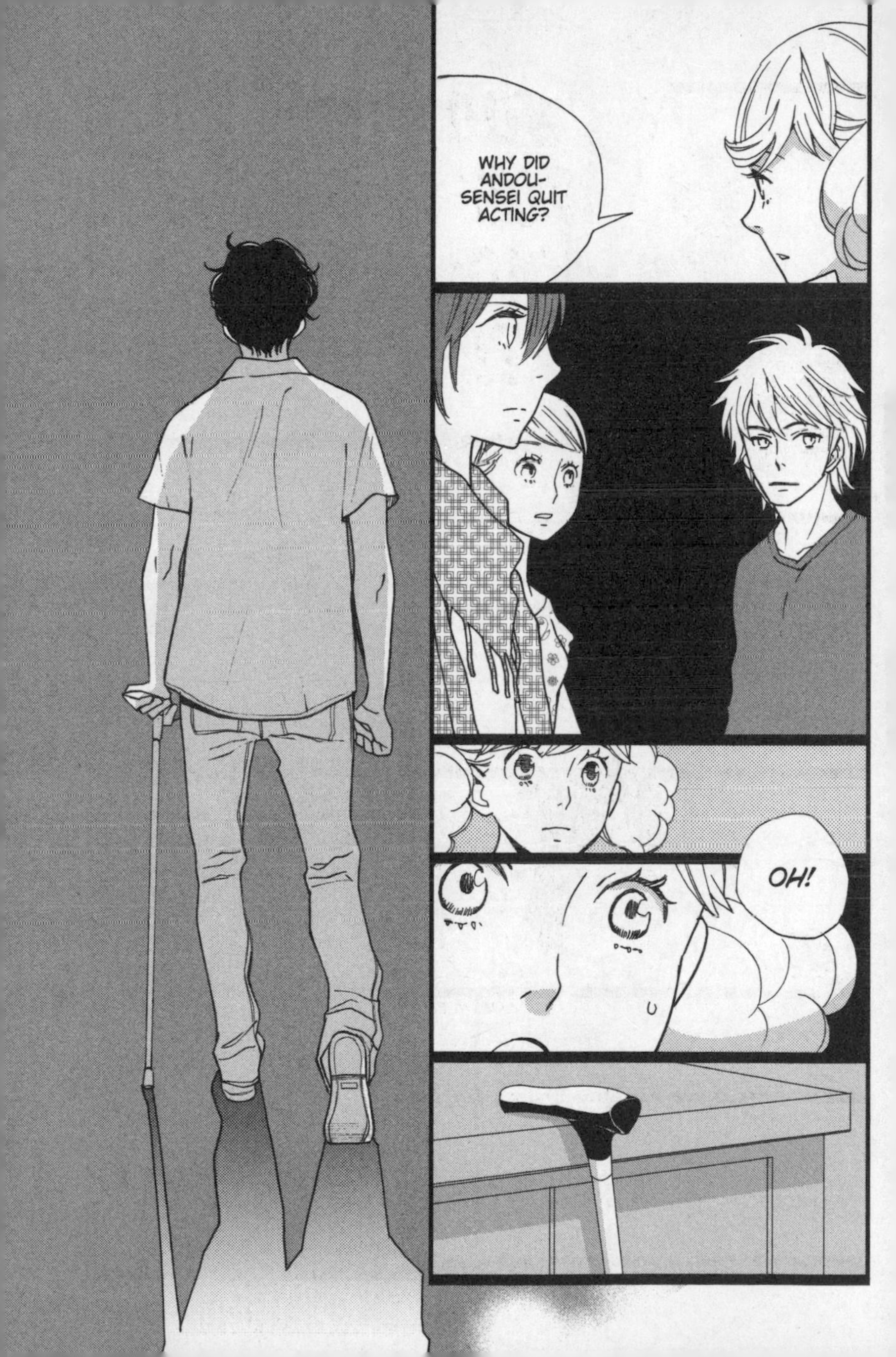
WHY DID ANDOU-SENSEI QUIT ACTING?
OH!

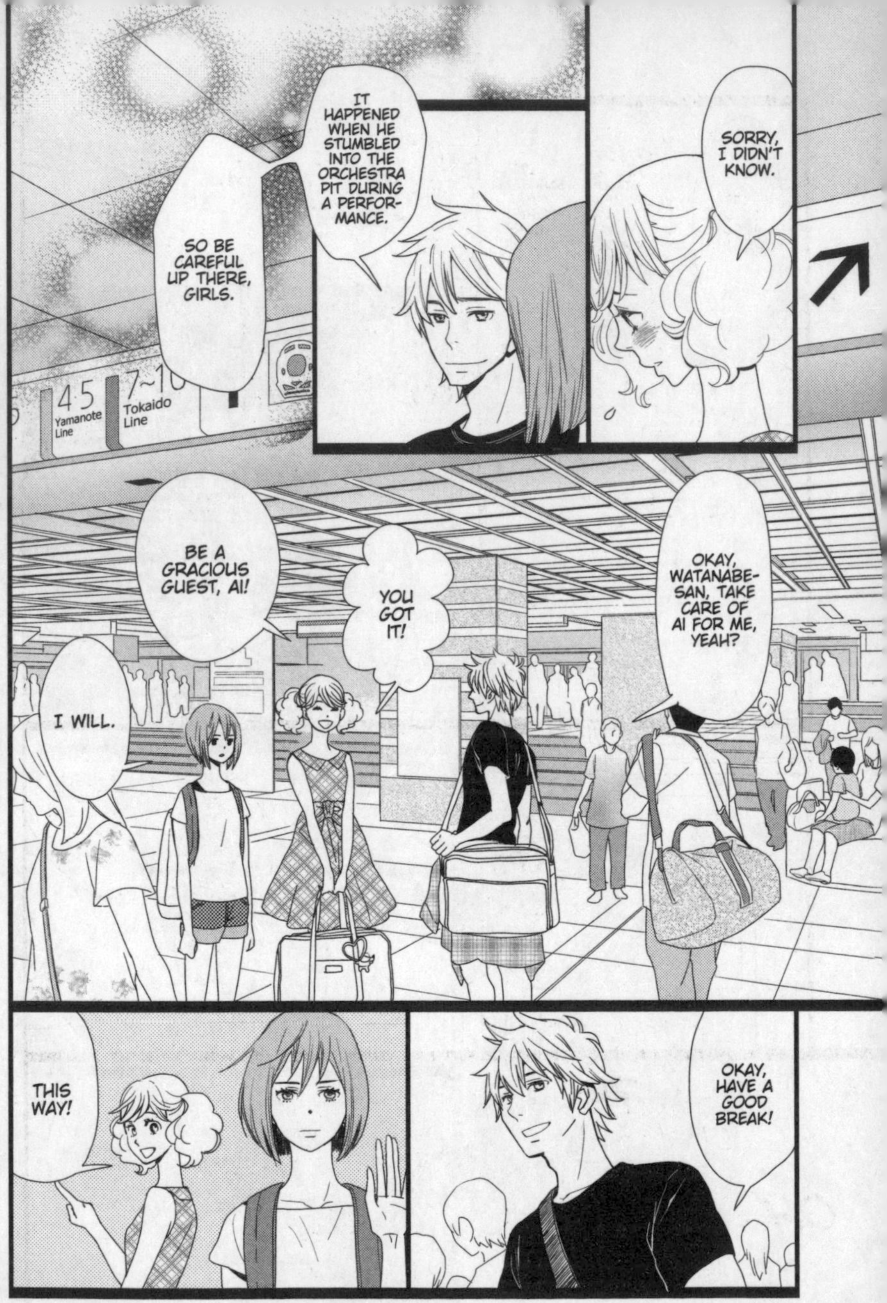
SORRY, I DIDN'T KNOW.
IT HAPPENED WHEN HE STUMBLED INTO THE ORCHESTRA PIT DURING A PERFOR-MANCE.
SO BE CAREFUL UP THERE, GIRLS.
4·5 Yamanote Line
7~10 Tokaido Line
OKAY, WATANABE-SAN, TAKE CARE OF AI FOR ME, YEAH?
YOU GOT IT!
BE A GRACIOUS GUEST, AI!
I WILL.
OKAY, HAVE A GOOD BREAK!
THIS WAY!

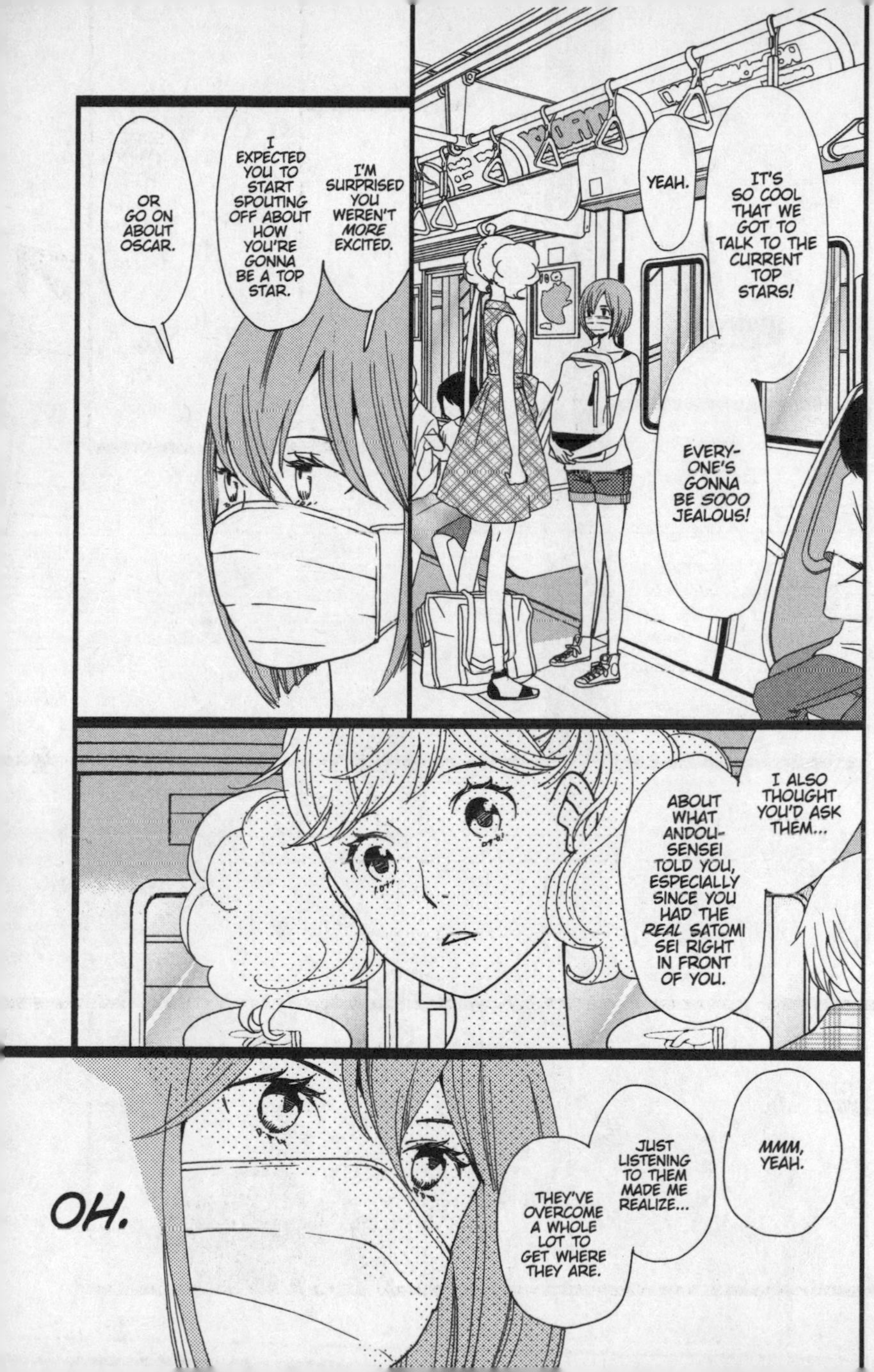
IT'S SO COOL THAT WE GOT TO TALK TO THE CURRENT TOP STARS!
YEAH.
EVERY-ONE'S GONNA BE *SOOO* JEALOUS!
I'M SURPRISED YOU WEREN'T *MORE* EXCITED.
I EXPECTED YOU TO START SPOUTING OFF ABOUT HOW YOU'RE GONNA BE A TOP STAR.
OR GO ON ABOUT OSCAR.
I ALSO THOUGHT YOU'D ASK THEM...
ABOUT WHAT ANDOU-SENSEI TOLD YOU, ESPECIALLY SINCE YOU HAD THE *REAL* SATOMI SEI RIGHT IN FRONT OF YOU.
MMM, YEAH.
JUST LISTENING TO THEM MADE ME REALIZE...
THEY'VE OVERCOME A WHOLE LOT TO GET WHERE THEY ARE.
OH.

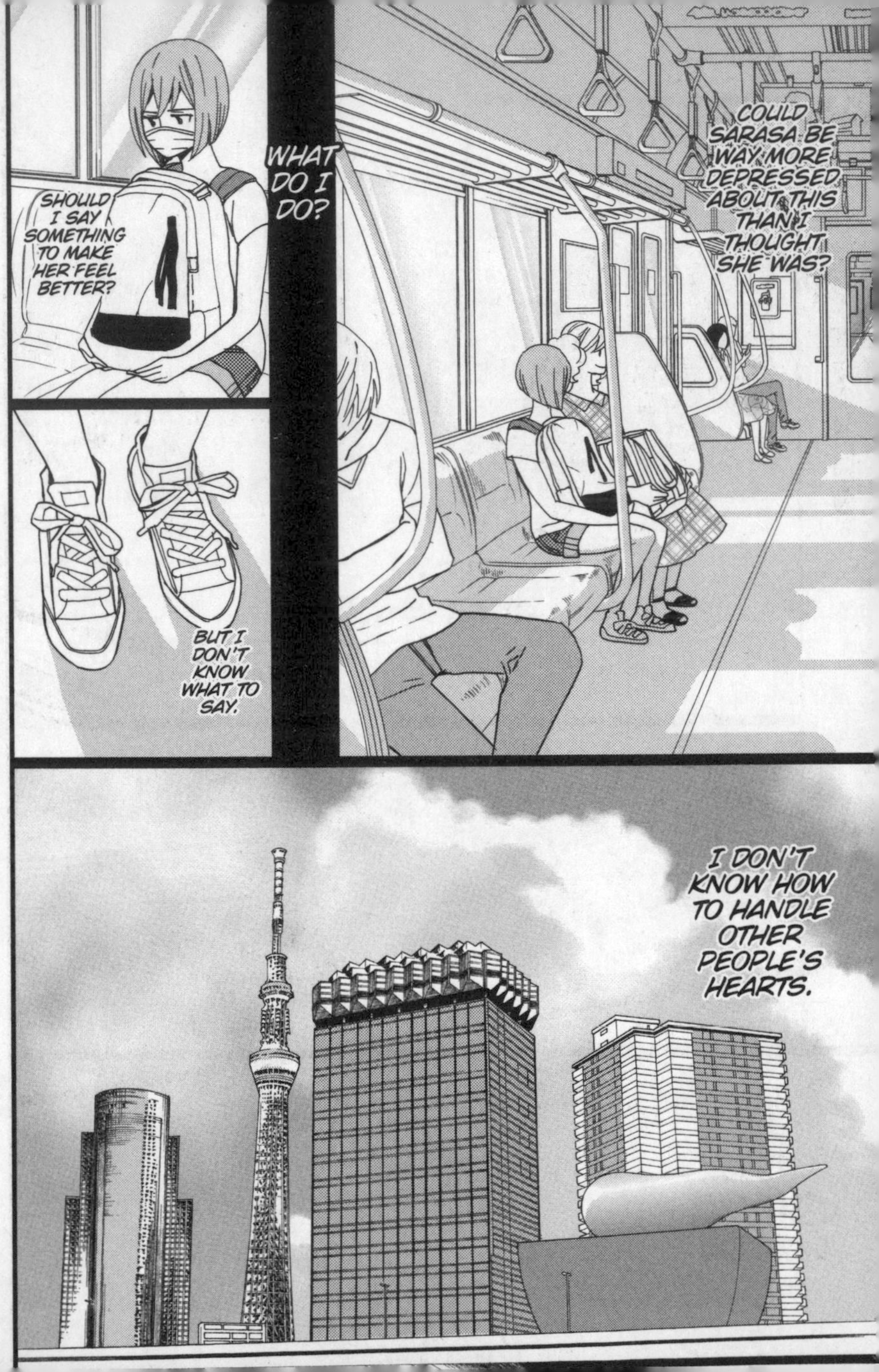
COULD SARASA BE WAY MORE DEPRESSED ABOUT THIS THAN I THOUGHT SHE WAS?
WHAT DO I DO?
SHOULD I SAY SOMETHING TO MAKE HER FEEL BETTER?
BUT I DON'T KNOW WHAT TO SAY.
I DON'T KNOW HOW TO HANDLE OTHER PEOPLE'S HEARTS.

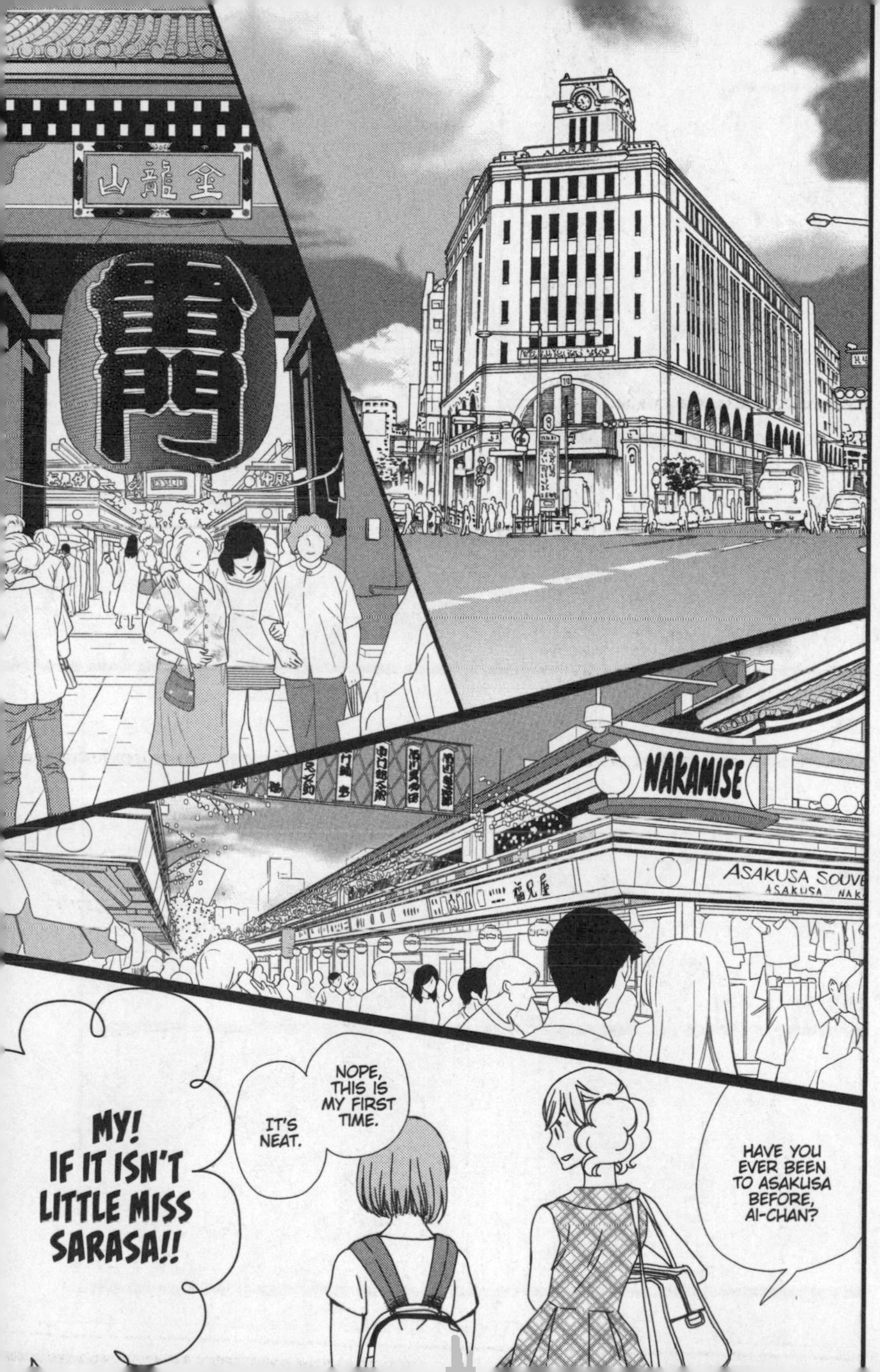
金龍山
雷門
NAKAMISE
HAVE YOU EVER BEEN TO ASAKUSA BEFORE, AI-CHAN?
NOPE, THIS IS MY FIRST TIME.
IT'S NEAT.
MY! IF IT ISN'T LITTLE MISS SARASA!!

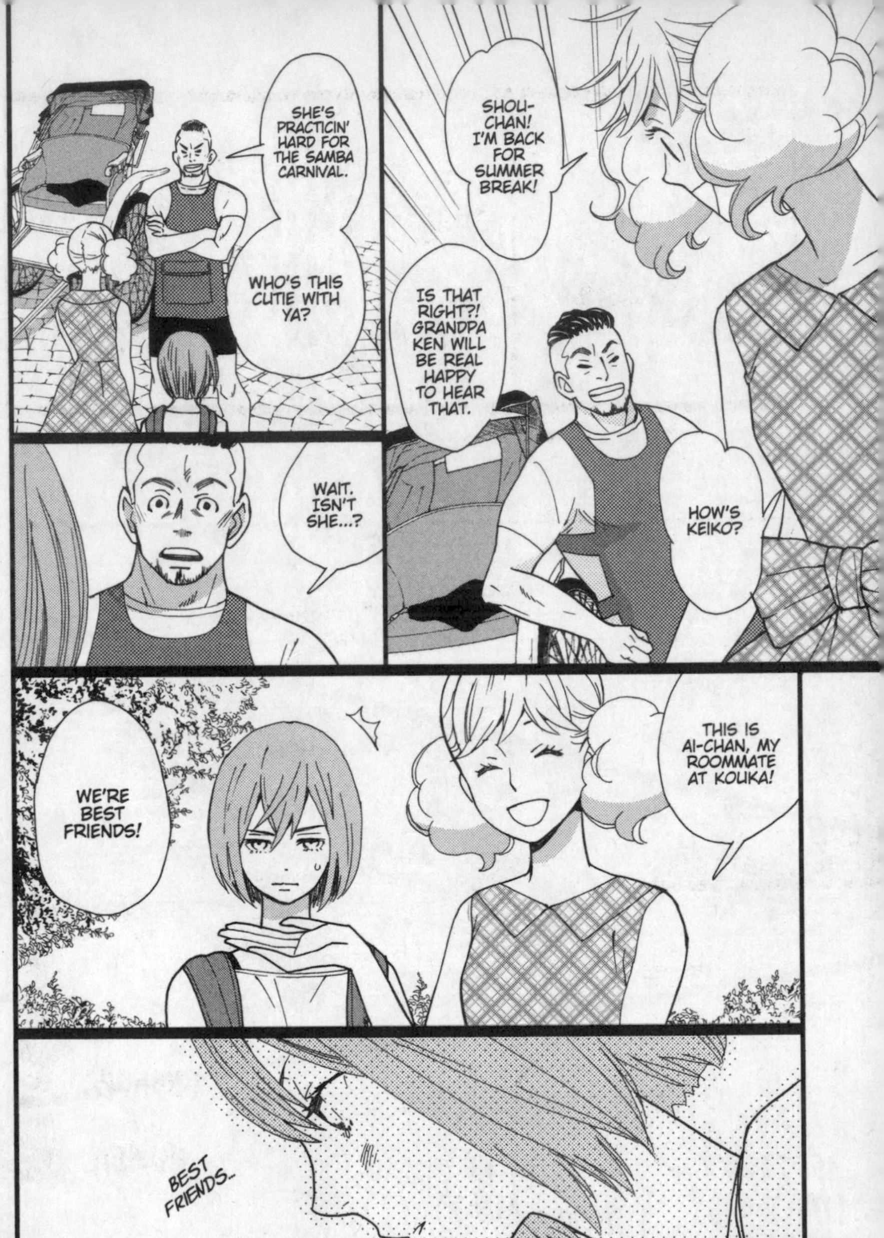
SHOU-CHAN! I'M BACK FOR SUMMER BREAK!
IS THAT RIGHT?! GRANDPA KEN WILL BE REAL HAPPY TO HEAR THAT.
HOW'S KEIKO?
SHE'S PRACTICIN' HARD FOR THE SAMBA CARNIVAL.
WHO'S THIS CUTIE WITH YA?
WAIT. ISN'T SHE...?
THIS IS AI-CHAN, MY ROOMMATE AT KOUKA!
WE'RE BEST FRIENDS!
BEST FRIENDS...

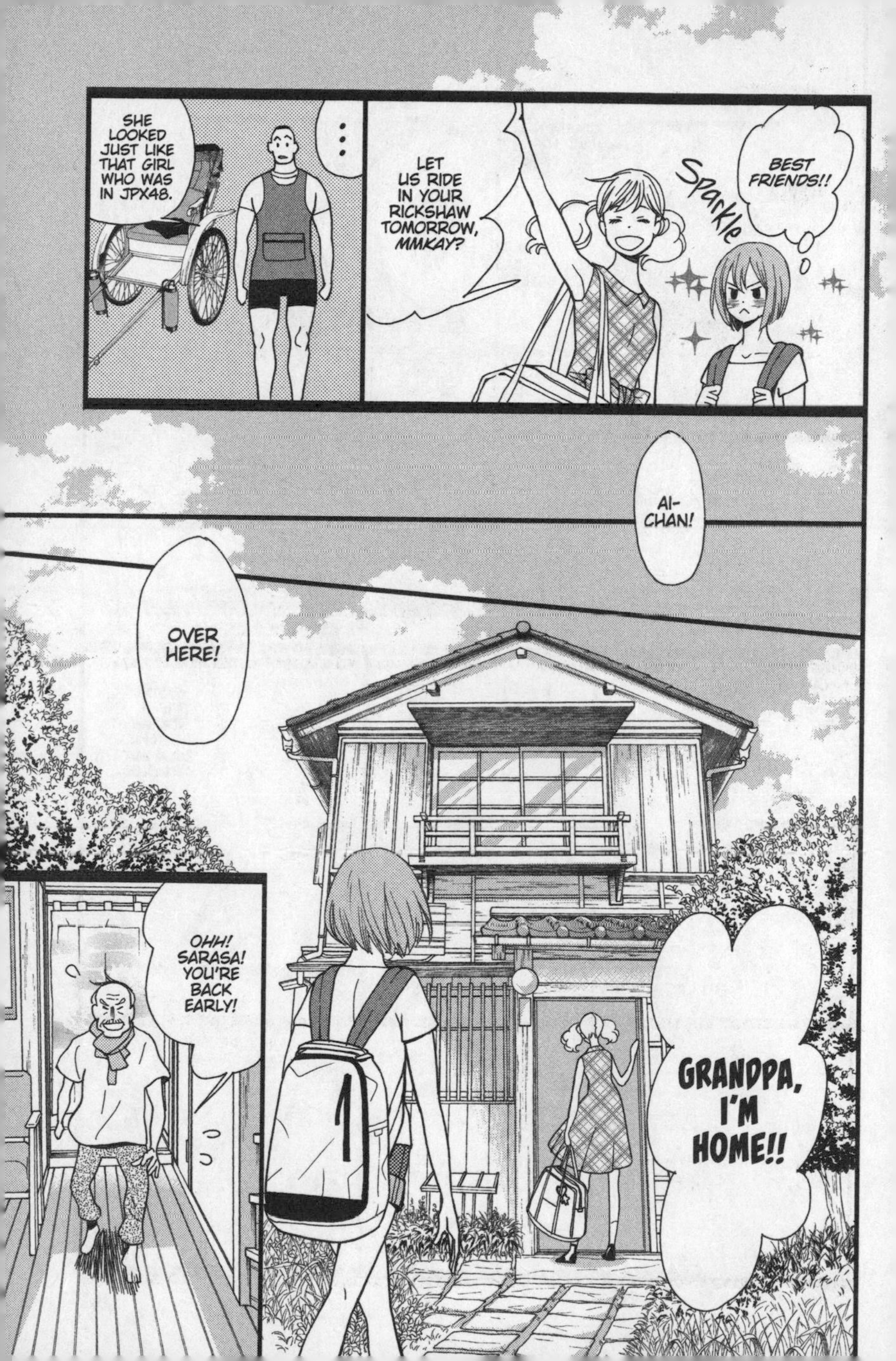
BEST FRIENDS!!
Sparkle
LET US RIDE IN YOUR RICKSHAW TOMORROW, MMKAY?
...
SHE LOOKED JUST LIKE THAT GIRL WHO WAS IN JPX48.
AI-CHAN!
GRANDPA, I'M HOME!!
OVER HERE!
OHH! SARASA! YOU'RE BACK EARLY!

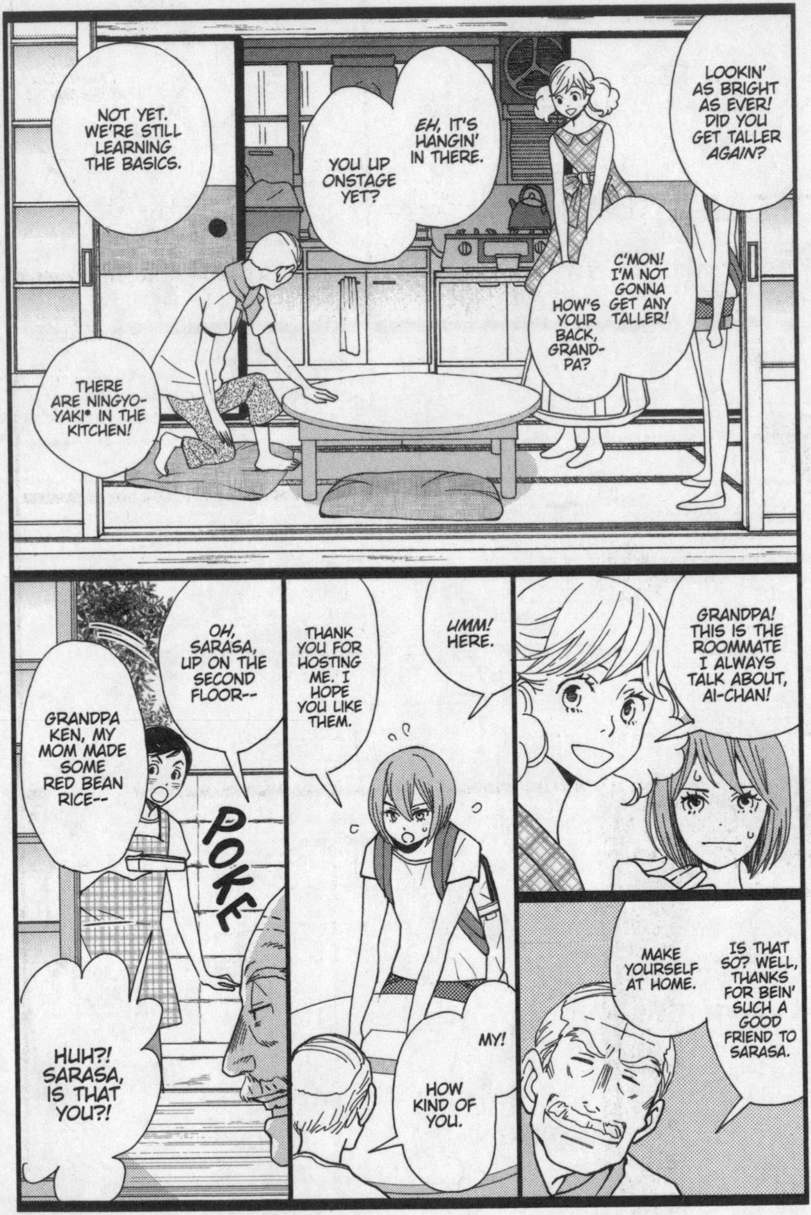
LOOKIN' AS BRIGHT AS EVER! DID YOU GET TALLER *AGAIN?*
C'MON! I'M NOT GONNA GET ANY TALLER!
HOW'S YOUR BACK, GRANDPA?
EH, IT'S HANGIN' IN THERE.
YOU UP ONSTAGE YET?
NOT YET. WE'RE STILL LEARNING THE BASICS.
THERE ARE NINGYO-YAKI* IN THE KITCHEN!
GRANDPA! THIS IS THE ROOMMATE I ALWAYS TALK ABOUT, AI-CHAN!
IS THAT SO? WELL, THANKS FOR BEIN' SUCH A GOOD FRIEND TO SARASA.
MAKE YOURSELF AT HOME.
UMM! HERE.
THANK YOU FOR HOSTING ME. I HOPE YOU LIKE THEM.
MY!
HOW KIND OF YOU.
OH, SARASA, UP ON THE SECOND FLOOR--
GRANDPA KEN, MY MOM MADE SOME RED BEAN RICE--
POKE
HUH?! SARASA, IS THAT YOU?!

Ningyo-yaki: A traditional snack popular in Asakusa.

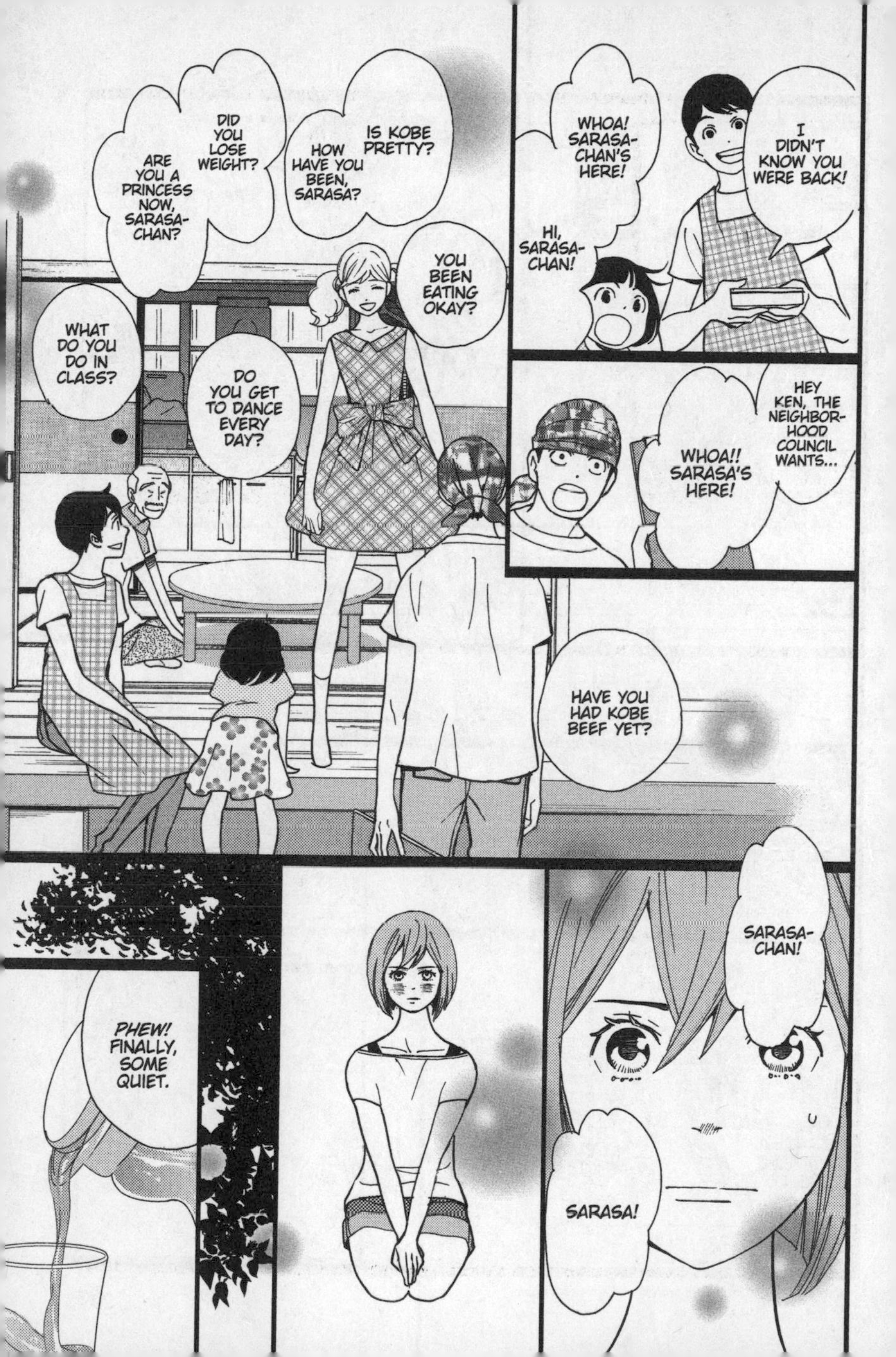
I DIDN'T KNOW YOU WERE BACK!
WHOA! SARASA-CHAN'S HERE!
HI, SARASA-CHAN!
HEY KEN, THE NEIGHBOR-HOOD COUNCIL WANTS...
WHOA!! SARASA'S HERE!
IS KOBE PRETTY?
HOW HAVE YOU BEEN, SARASA?
DID YOU LOSE WEIGHT?
ARE YOU A PRINCESS NOW, SARASA-CHAN?
YOU BEEN EATING OKAY?
DO YOU GET TO DANCE EVERY DAY?
WHAT DO YOU DO IN CLASS?
HAVE YOU HAD KOBE BEEF YET?
SARASA-CHAN!
SARASA!
PHEW! FINALLY, SOME QUIET.

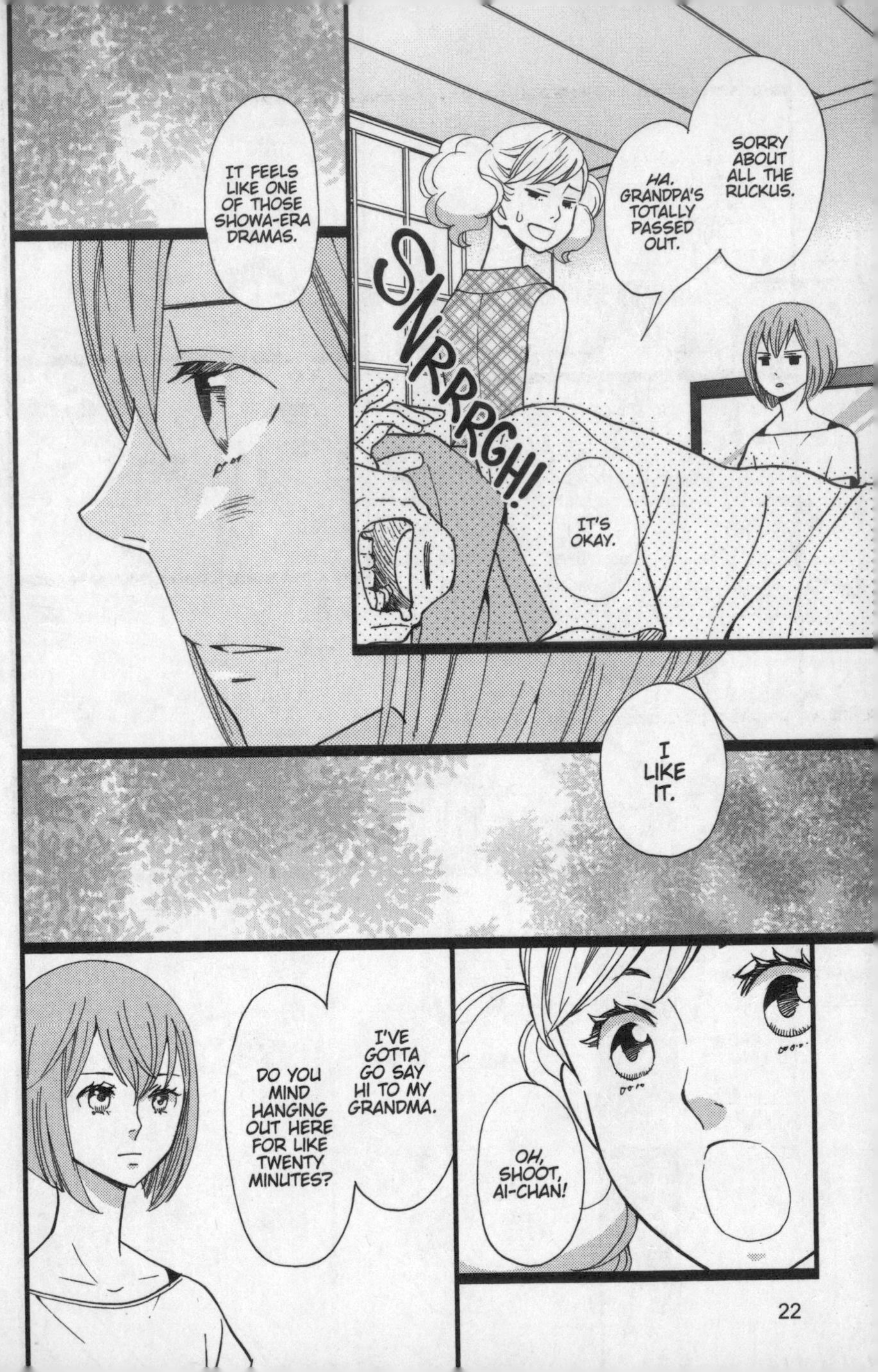

SORRY ABOUT ALL THE RUCKUS.
HA. GRANDPA'S TOTALLY PASSED OUT.
SNRRRGH!
IT'S OKAY.
IT FEELS LIKE ONE OF THOSE SHOWA-ERA DRAMAS.
I LIKE IT.
OH, SHOOT, AI-CHAN!
I'VE GOTTA GO SAY HI TO MY GRANDMA.
DO YOU MIND HANGING OUT HERE FOR LIKE TWENTY MINUTES?

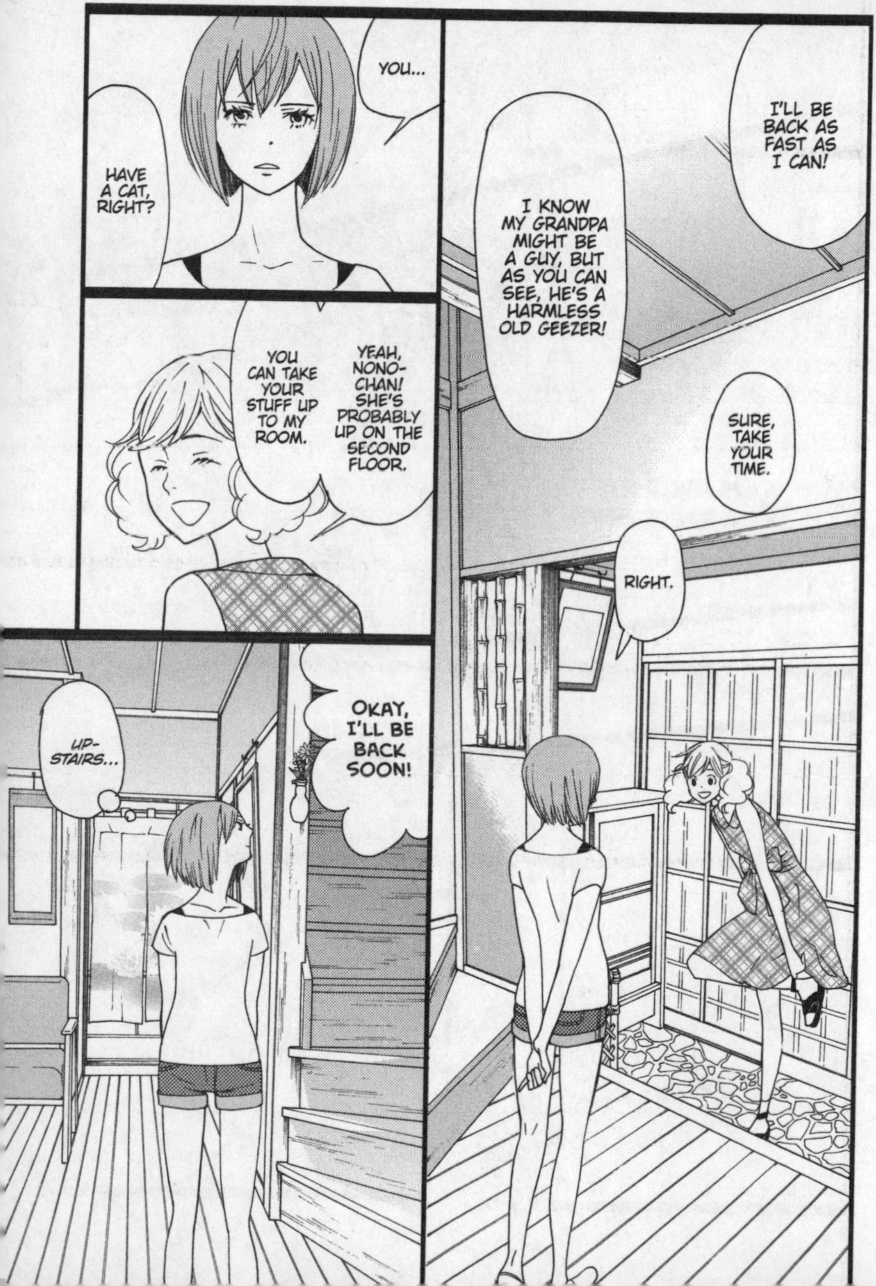
I'LL BE BACK AS FAST AS I CAN!
I KNOW MY GRANDPA MIGHT BE A GUY, BUT AS YOU CAN SEE, HE'S A HARMLESS OLD GEEZER!
SURE, TAKE YOUR TIME.
RIGHT.
YOU...
HAVE A CAT, RIGHT?
YEAH, NONO-CHAN! SHE'S PROBABLY UP ON THE SECOND FLOOR.
YOU CAN TAKE YOUR STUFF UP TO MY ROOM.
OKAY, I'LL BE BACK SOON!
UP-STAIRS...

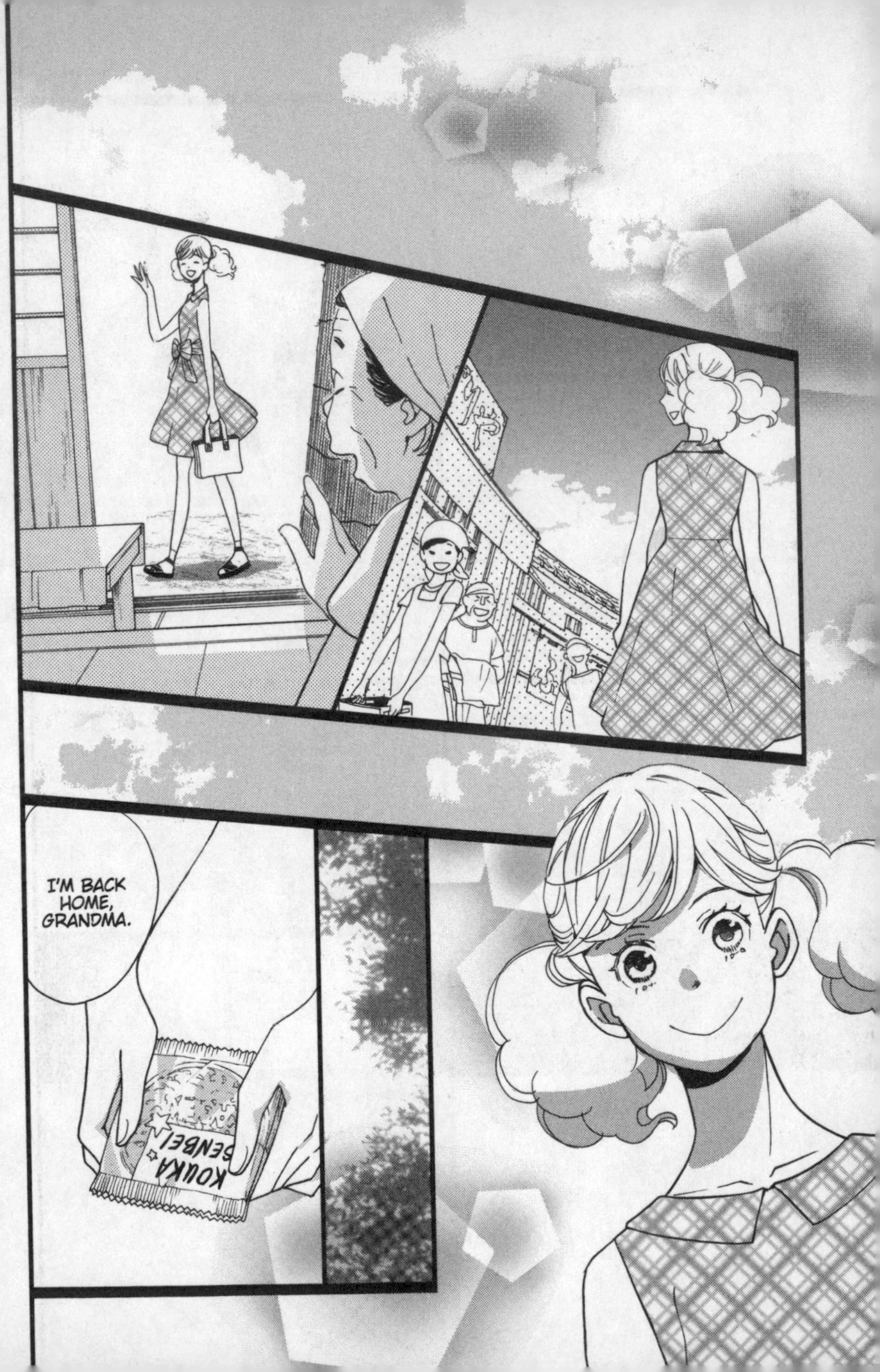
I'M BACK HOME, GRANDMA.
KOUKA SENBEI

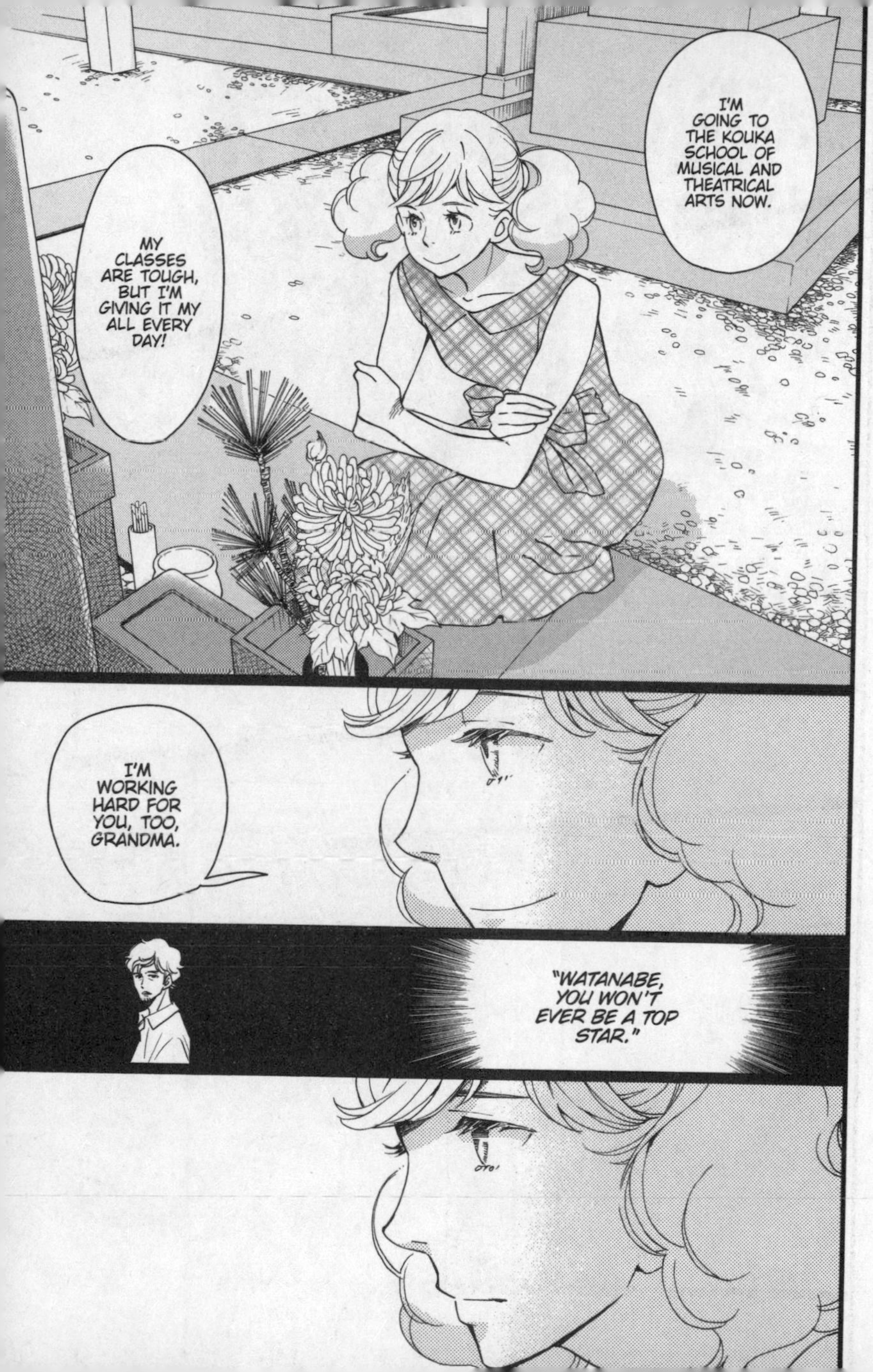
I'M GOING TO THE KOUKA SCHOOL OF MUSICAL AND THEATRICAL ARTS NOW.
MY CLASSES ARE TOUGH, BUT I'M GIVING IT MY ALL EVERY DAY!
I'M WORKING HARD FOR YOU, TOO, GRANDMA.
"WATANABE, YOU WON'T EVER BE A TOP STAR."

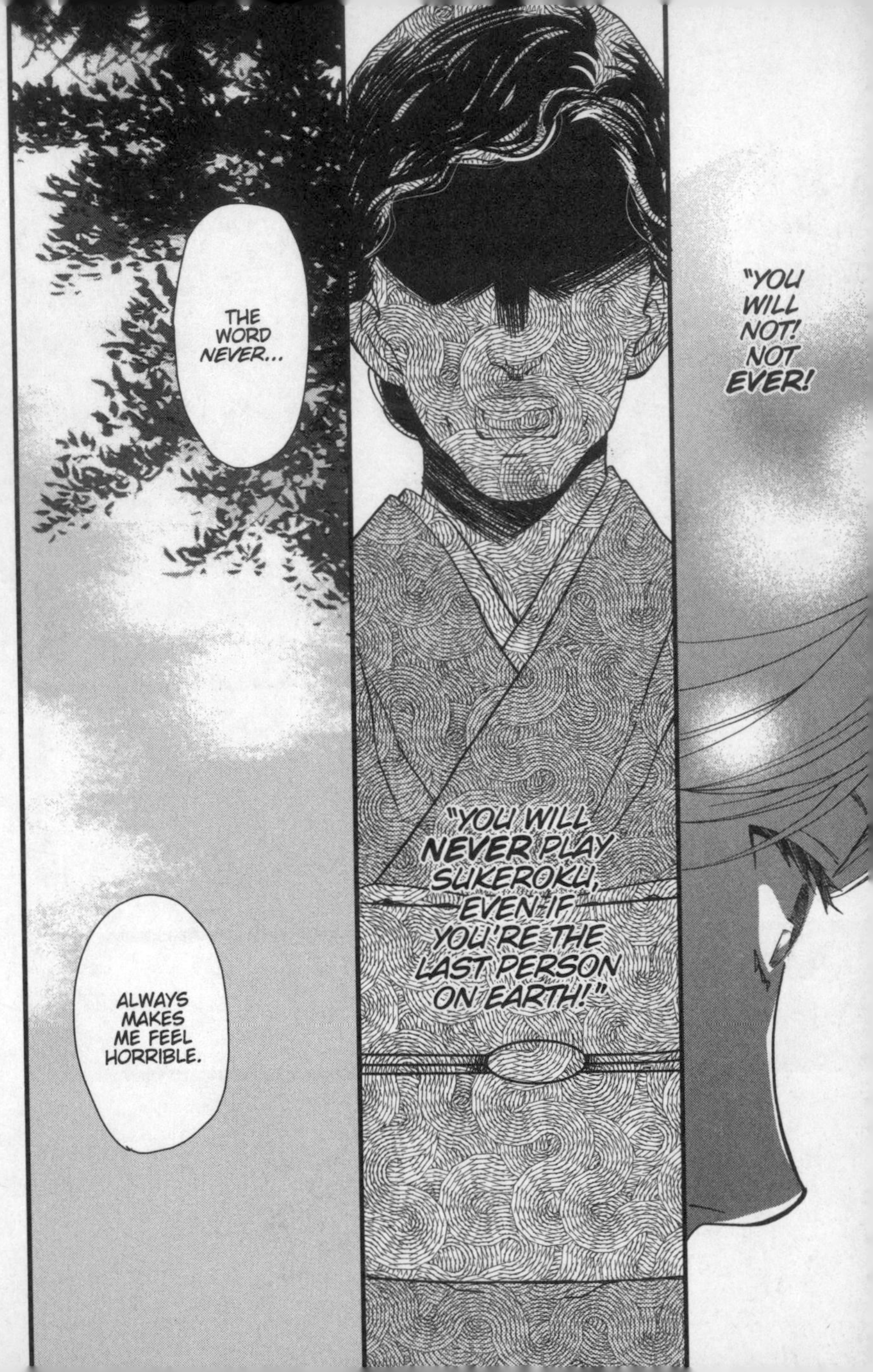
"YOU WILL NOT! NOT EVER!
"YOU WILL NEVER PLAY SUKEROKU, EVEN IF YOU'RE THE LAST PERSON ON EARTH!"
THE WORD NEVER...
ALWAYS MAKES ME FEEL HORRIBLE.

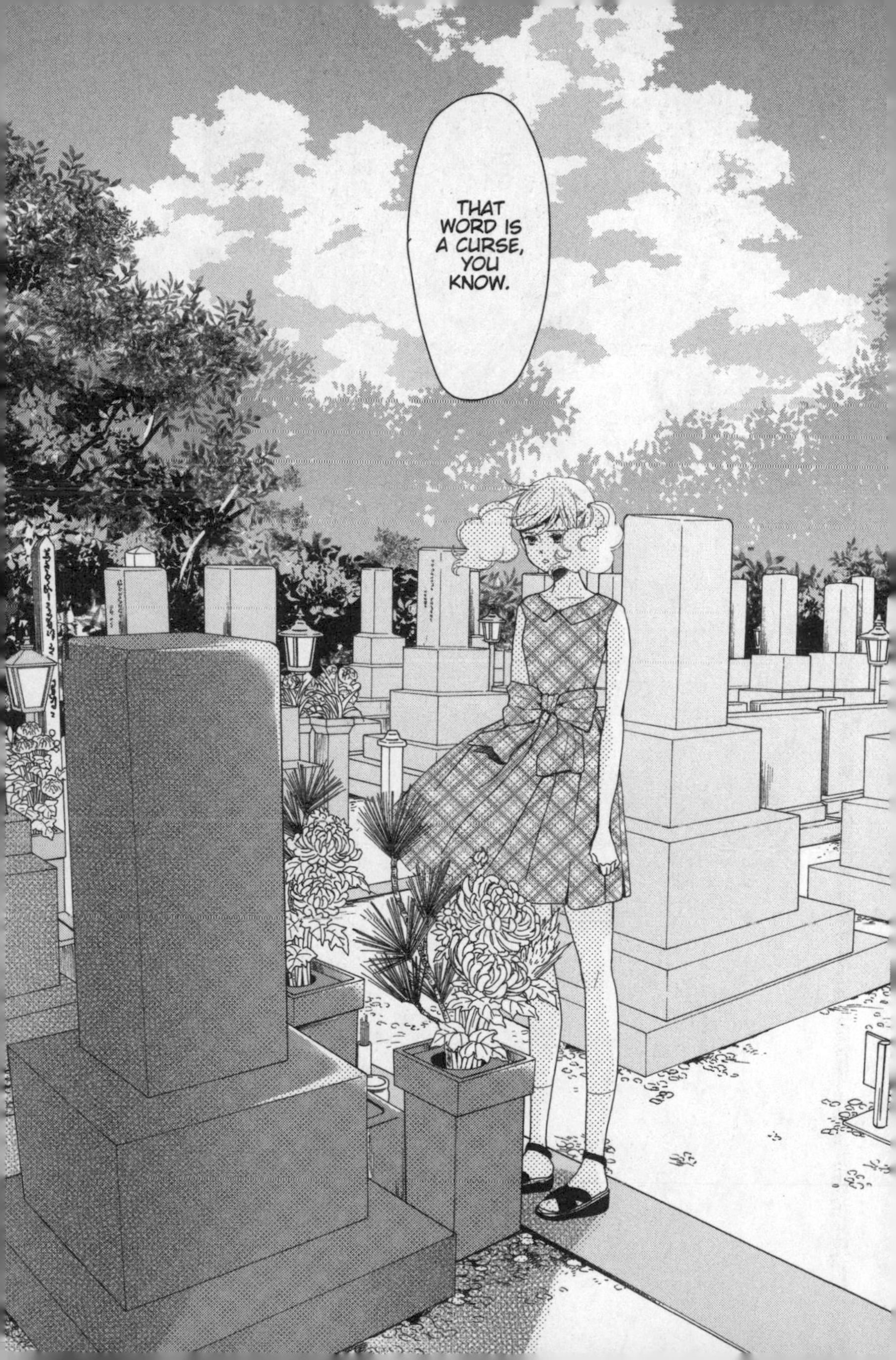
THAT WORD IS A CURSE, YOU KNOW.

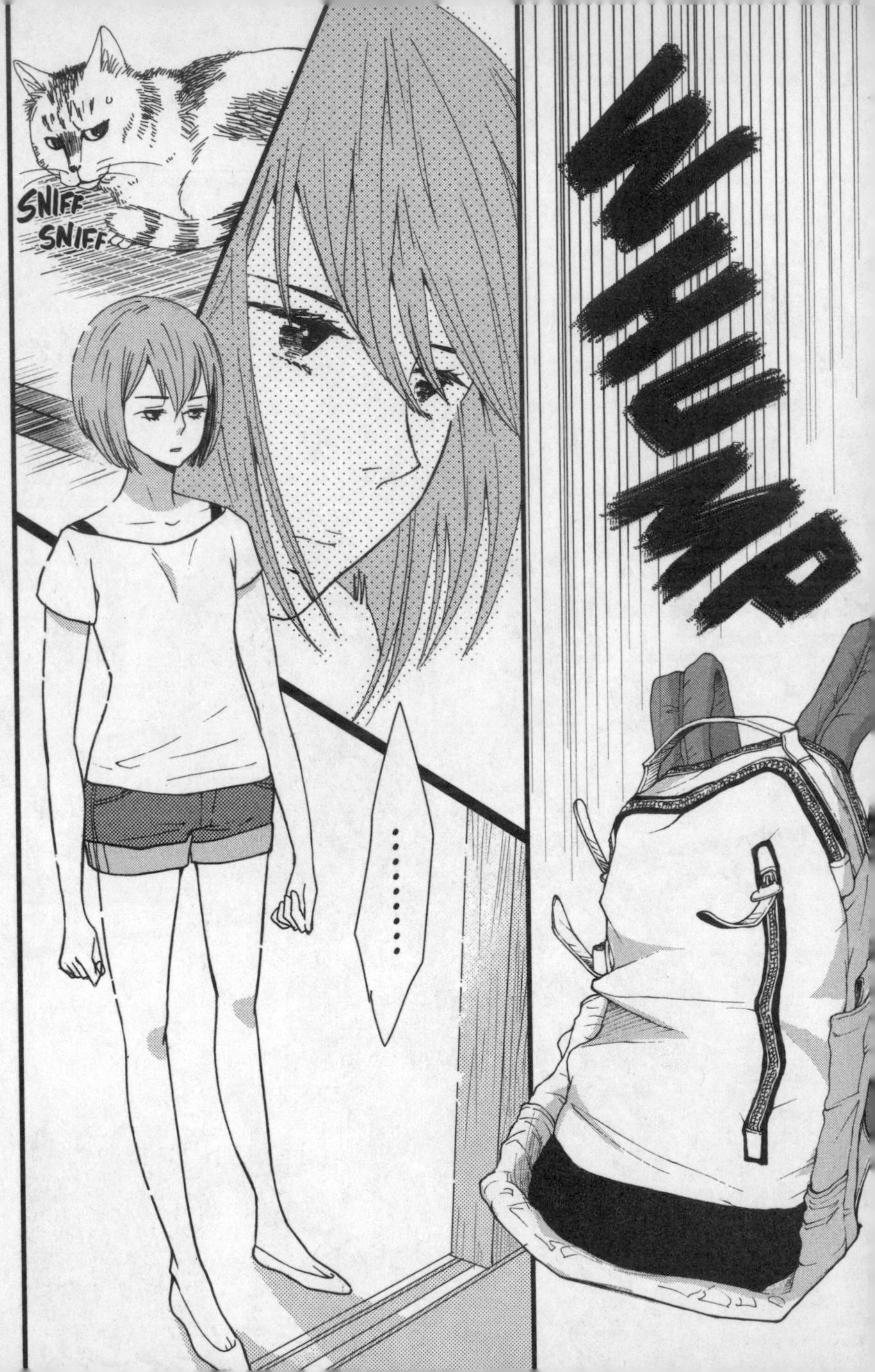
WHUMP
SNIFF SNIFF
......

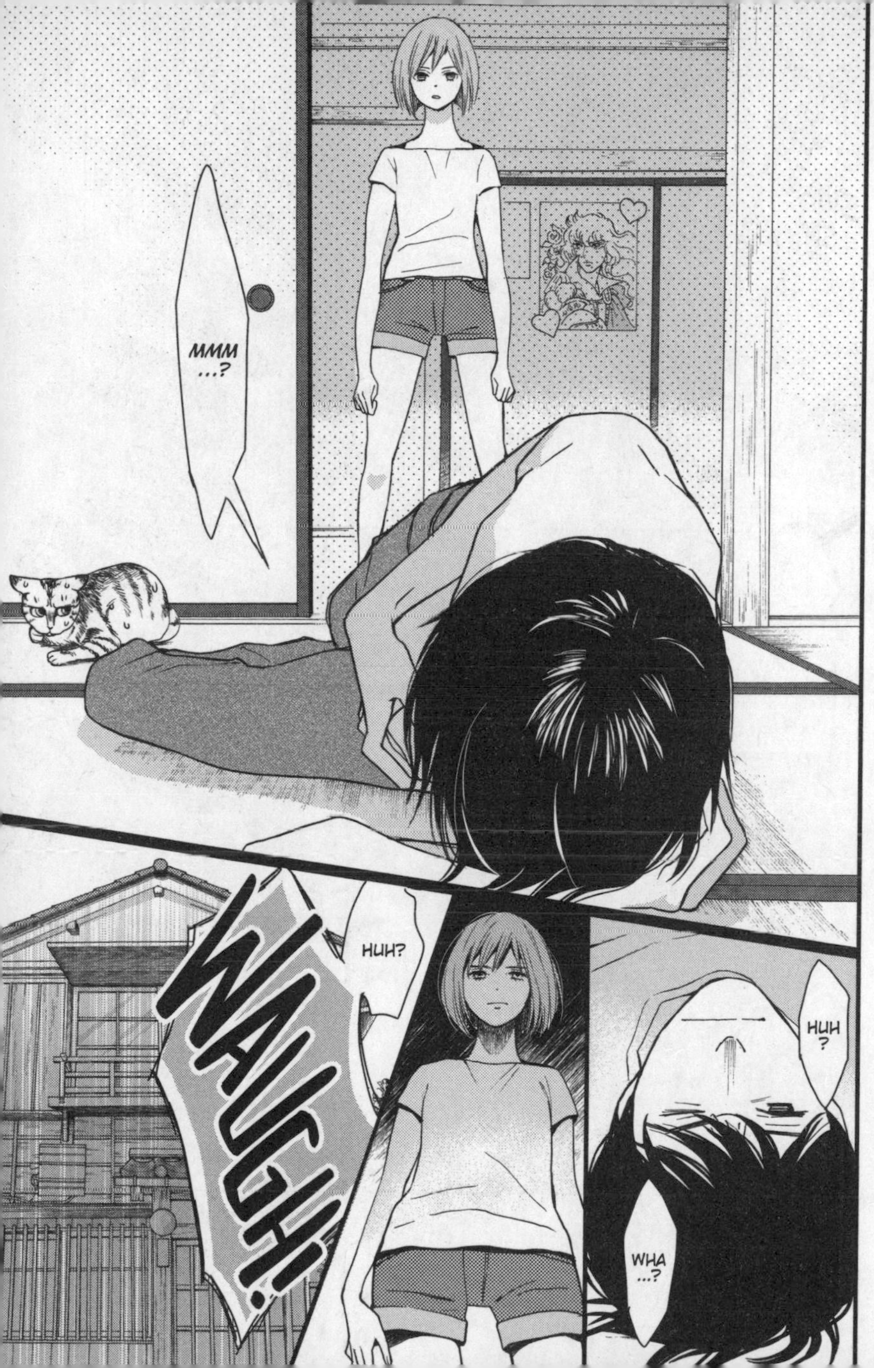
MMM ...?
HUH ?
WHA ...?
HUH?
WAUGH!

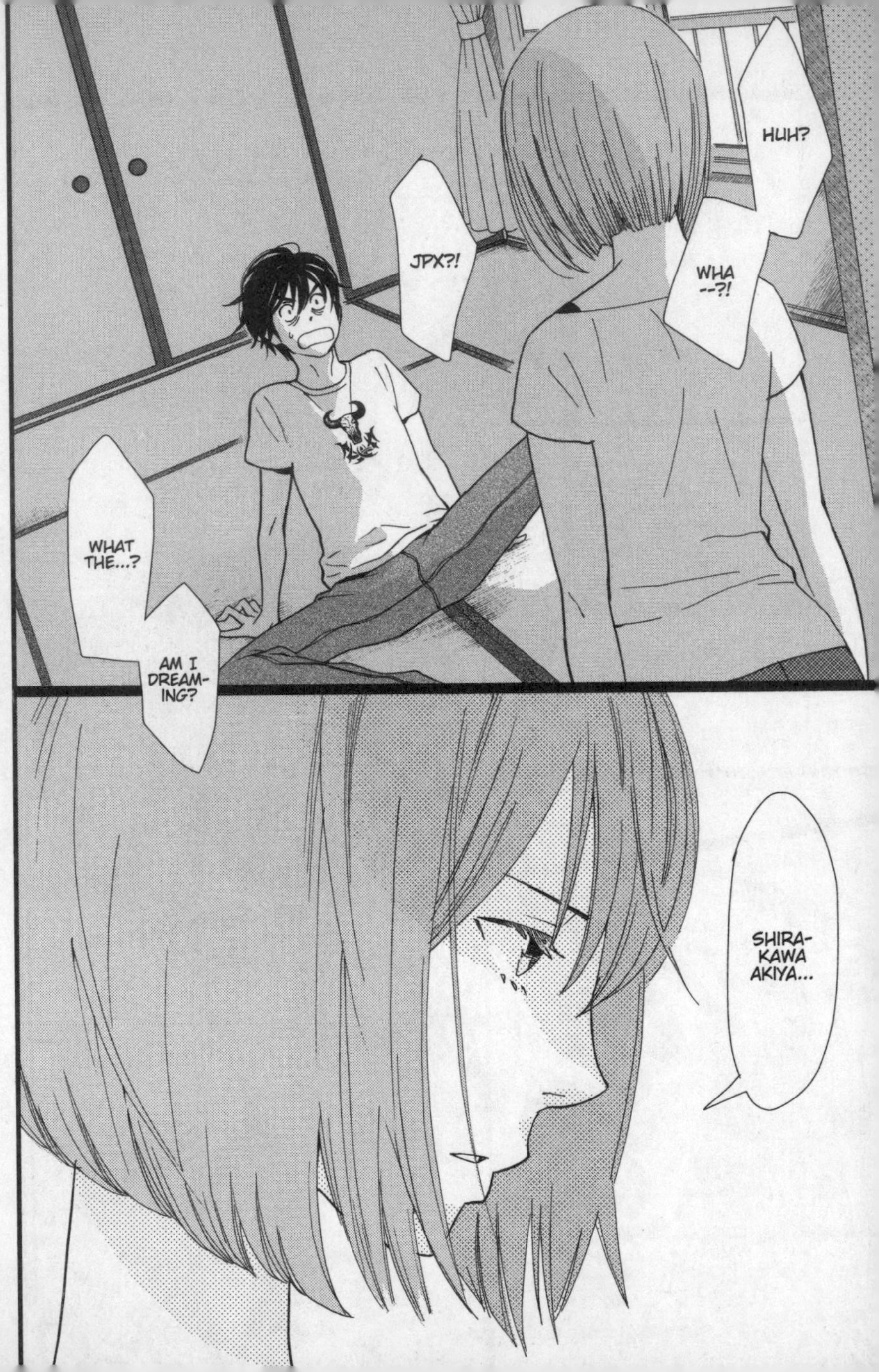
HUH?
WHA --?!
JPX?!
WHAT THE...?
AM I DREAMING?
SHIRAKAWA AKIYA...

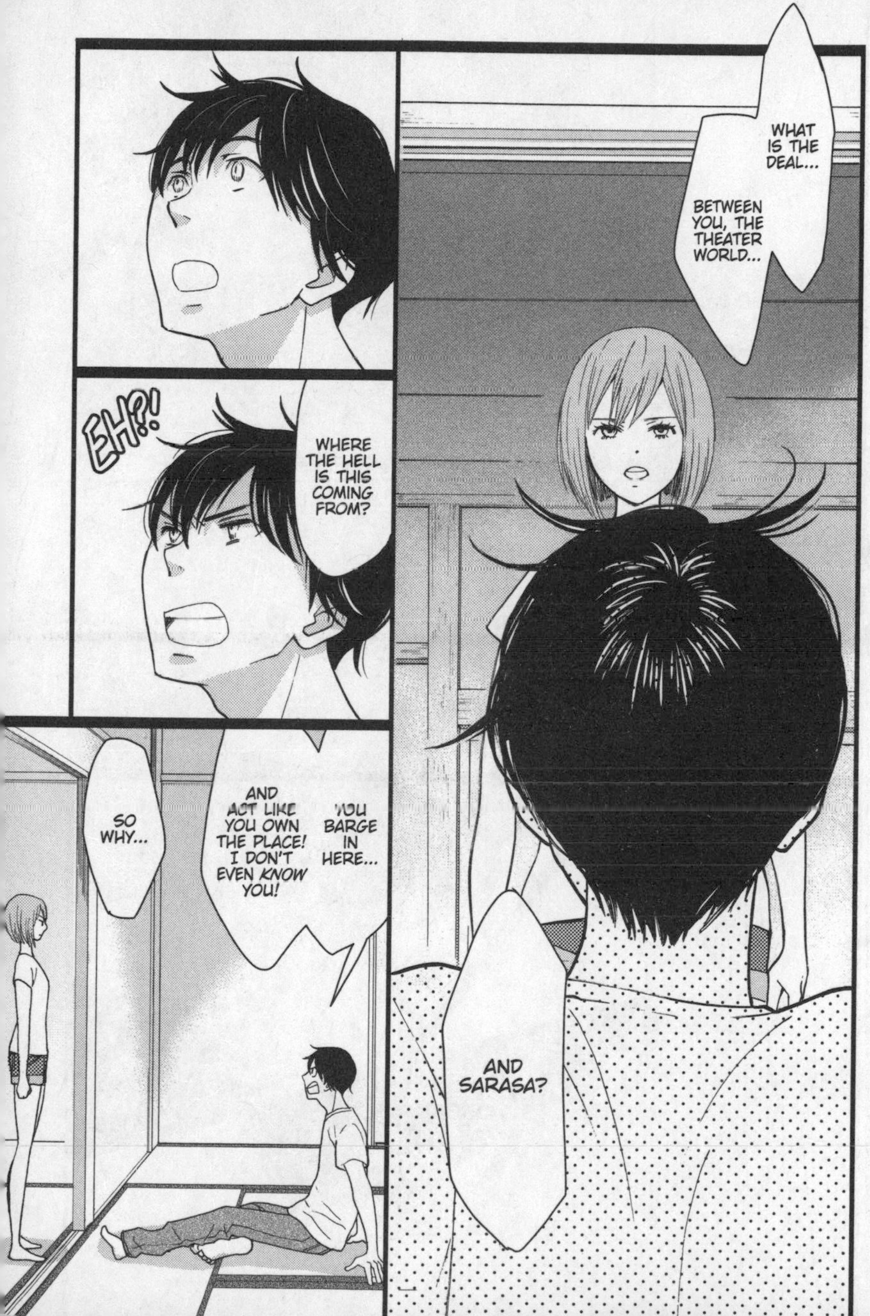
WHAT IS THE DEAL...
BETWEEN YOU, THE THEATER WORLD...
AND SARASA?
EH?!
WHERE THE HELL IS THIS COMING FROM?
YOU BARGE IN HERE...
AND ACT LIKE YOU OWN THE PLACE! I DON'T EVEN KNOW YOU!
SO WHY...

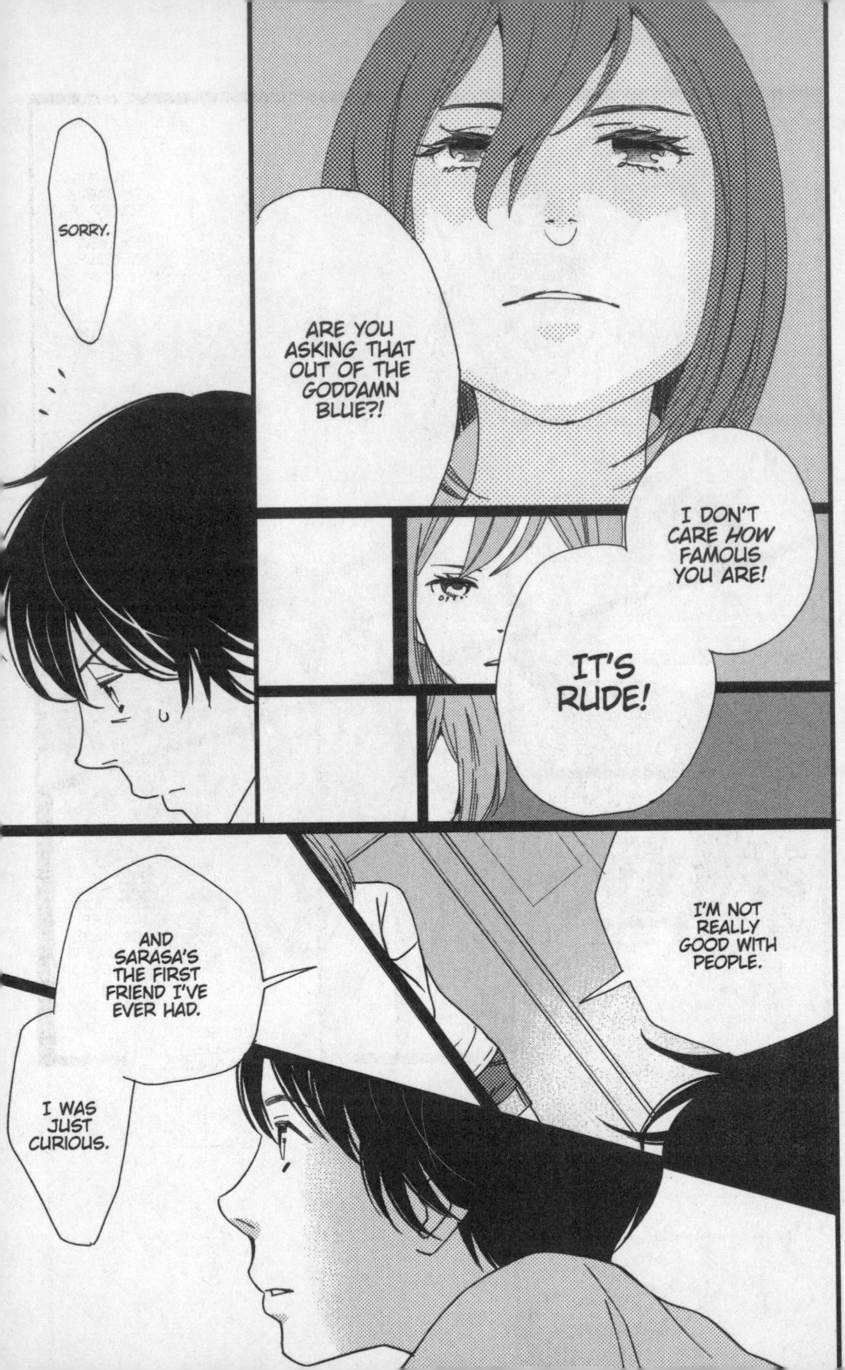
ARE YOU ASKING THAT OUT OF THE GODDAMN BLUE?!
I DON'T CARE *HOW* FAMOUS YOU ARE!
IT'S RUDE!
SORRY.
I'M NOT REALLY GOOD WITH PEOPLE.
AND SARASA'S THE FIRST FRIEND I'VE EVER HAD.
I WAS JUST CURIOUS.

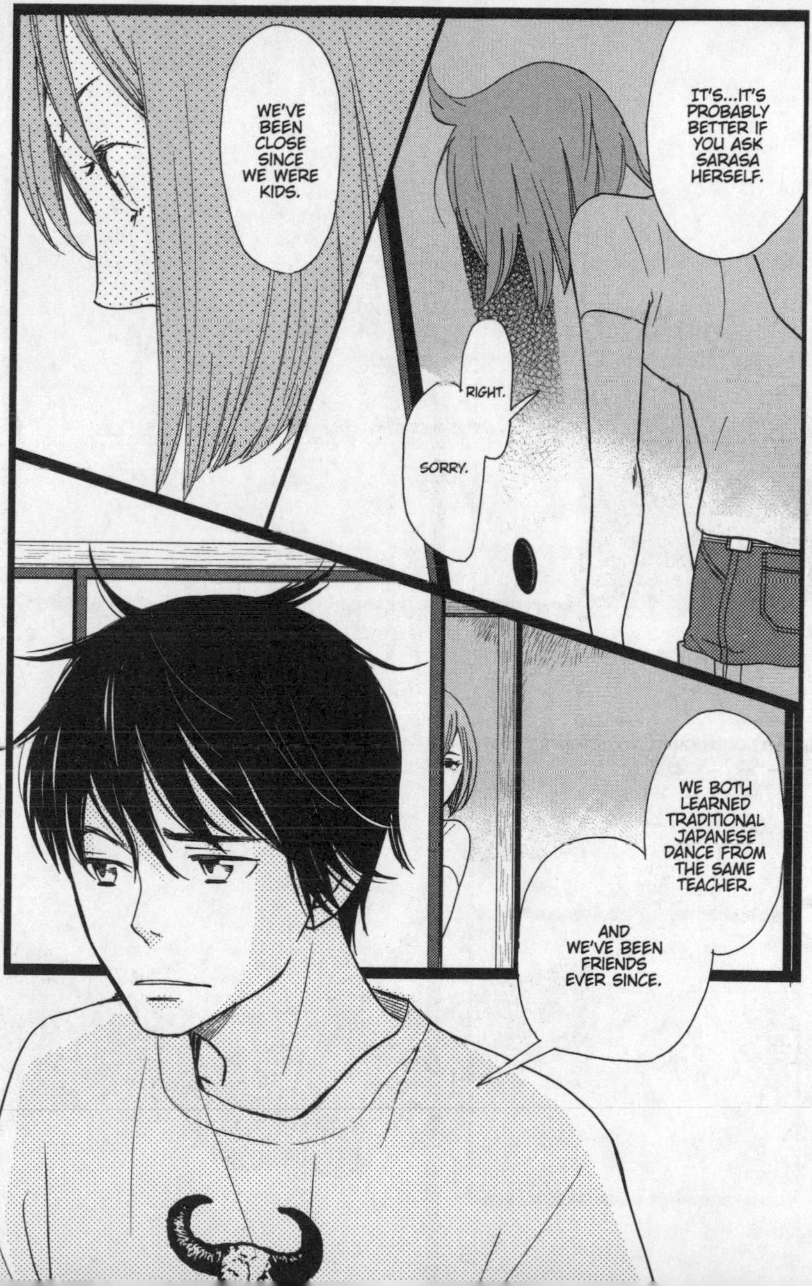
IT'S...IT'S PROBABLY BETTER IF YOU ASK SARASA HERSELF.
RIGHT.
SORRY.
WE'VE BEEN CLOSE SINCE WE WERE KIDS.
WE BOTH LEARNED TRADITIONAL JAPANESE DANCE FROM THE SAME TEACHER.
AND WE'VE BEEN FRIENDS EVER SINCE.

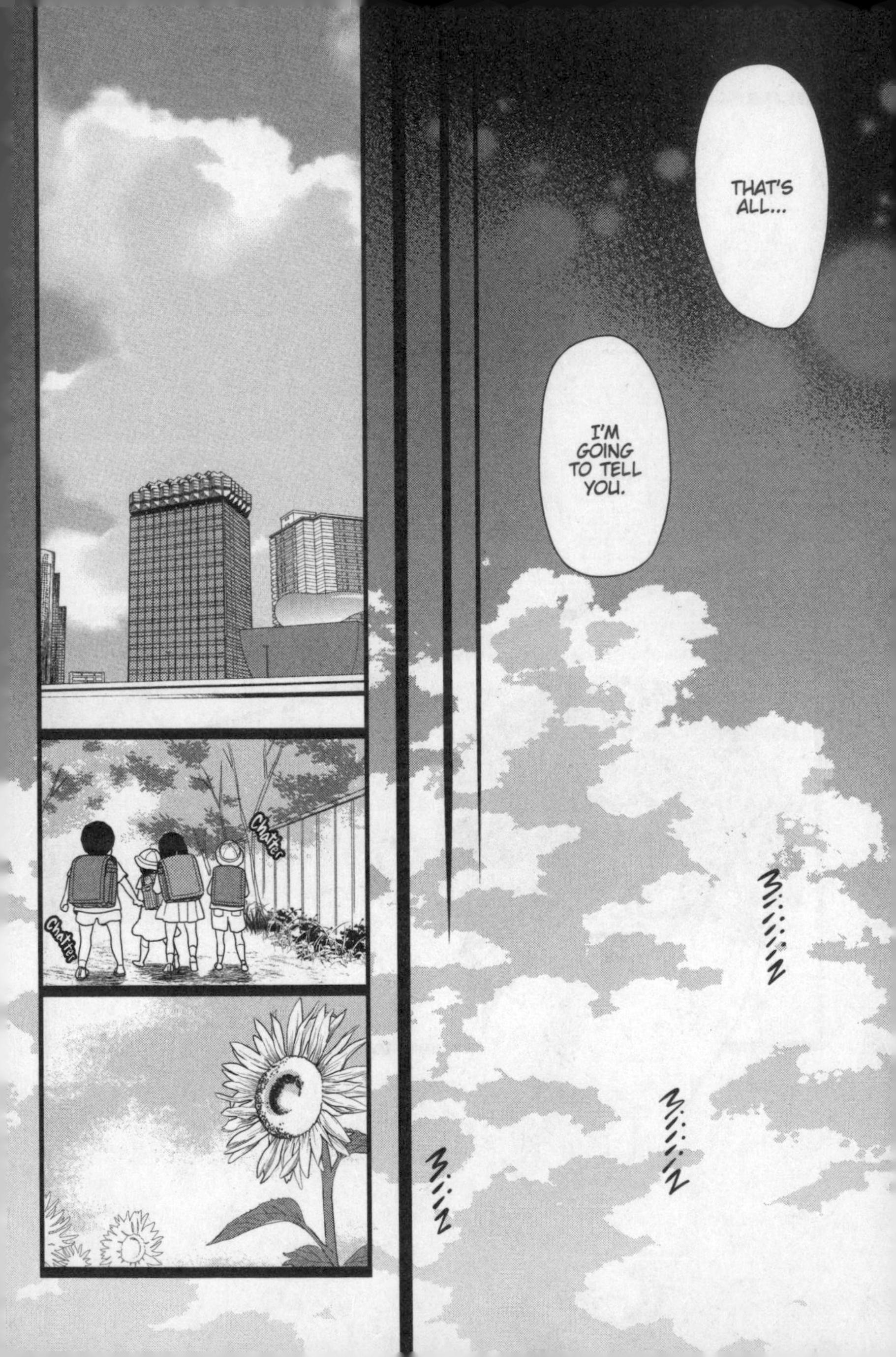
THAT'S ALL...
I'M GOING TO TELL YOU.
Miiiiin
Miiiin
Miin
Chatter
Chatter

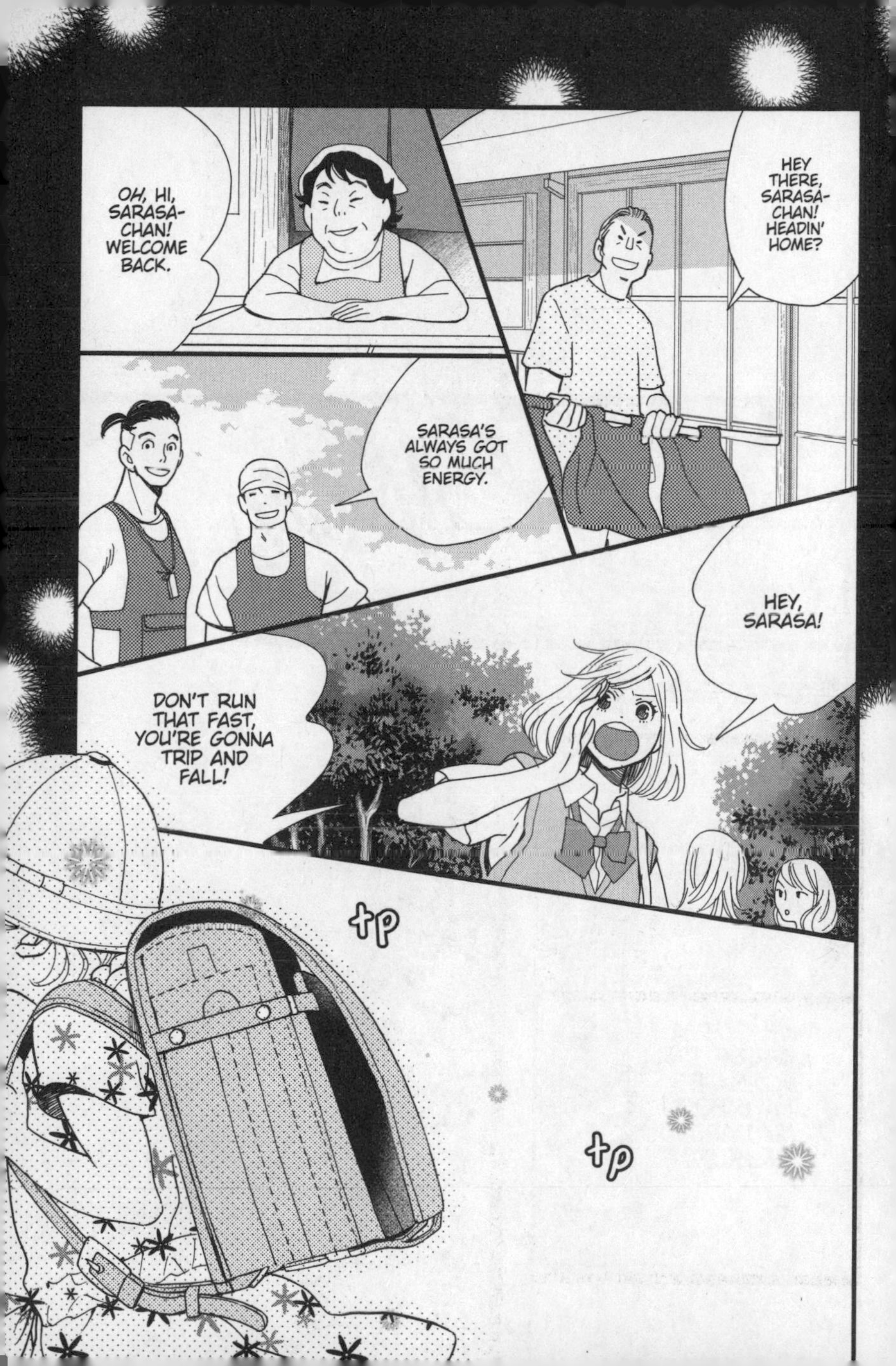
HEY THERE, SARASA-CHAN! HEADIN' HOME?
OH, HI, SARASA-CHAN! WELCOME BACK.
SARASA'S ALWAYS GOT SO MUCH ENERGY.
HEY, SARASA!
DON'T RUN THAT FAST, YOU'RE GONNA TRIP AND FALL!
tp
tp

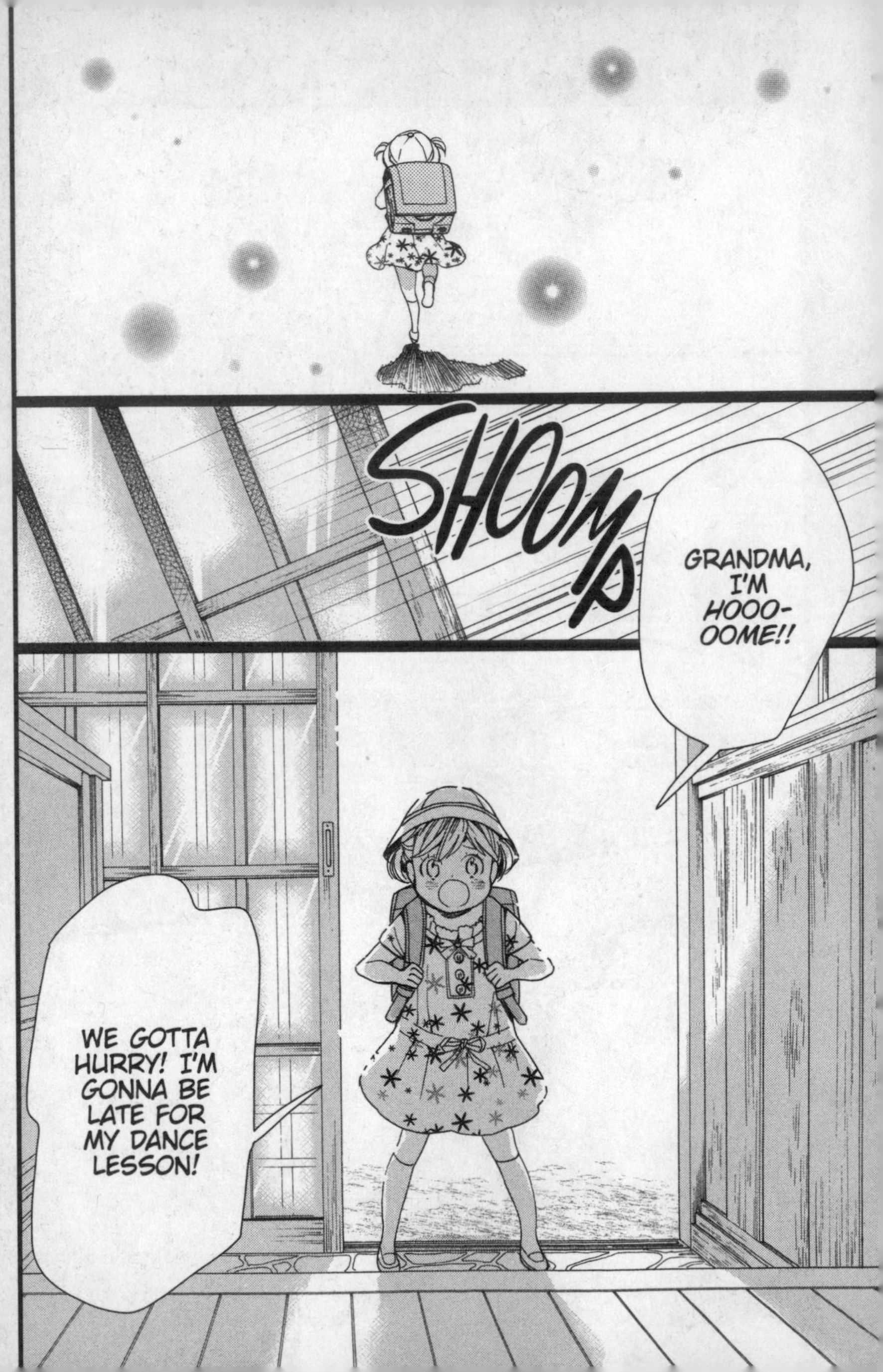
GRANDMA, I'M HOOOO-OOME!!
SHOOMP
WE GOTTA HURRY! I'M GONNA BE LATE FOR MY DANCE LESSON!

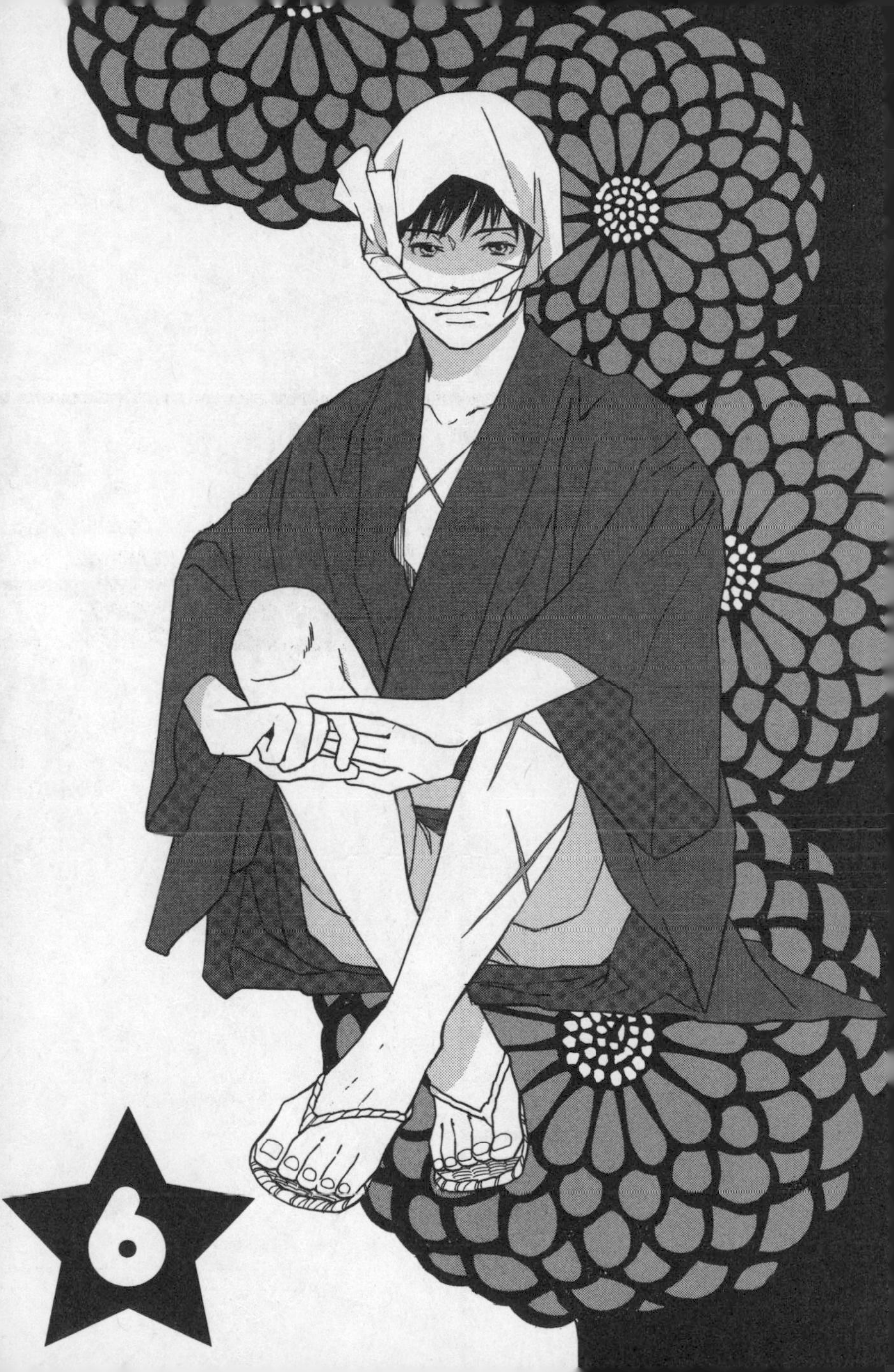
6

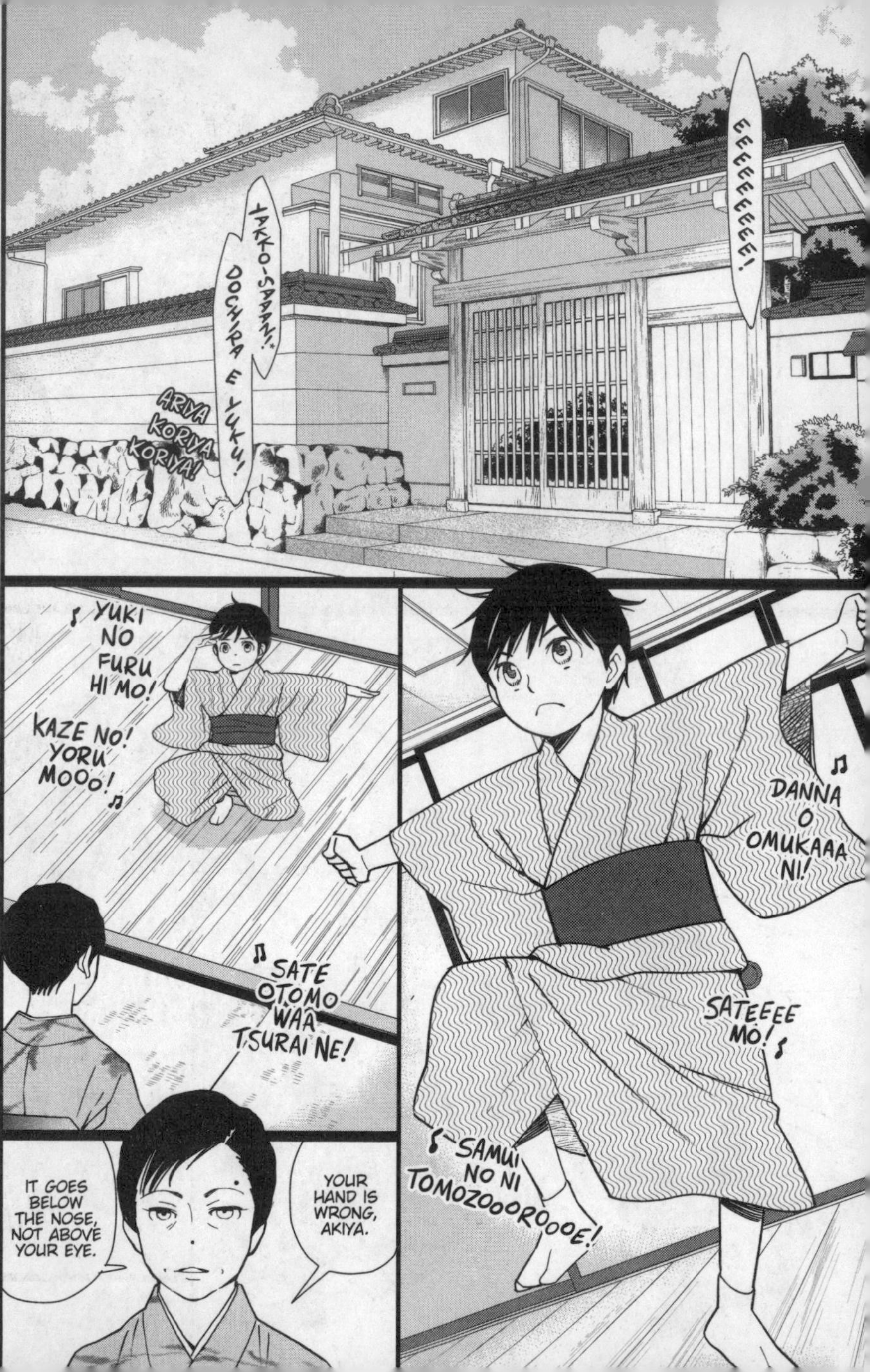
EEEEEEEEE!
YAKKO-SAAAN!* DOCHIRA E YUKU!
ARIYA KORIYA KORIYA!
DANNA O OMUKAAA NI!
SATEEEEE MO!
SAMUI NO NI TOMOZOOOROOOE!
YUKI NO FURU HI MO!
KAZE NO! YORU MOOO!
SATE OTOMO WAA TSURAI NE!
YOUR HAND IS WRONG, AKIYA.
IT GOES BELOW THE NOSE, NOT ABOVE YOUR EYE.

*"Yakko-san" is a folk song from the late Edo period about a servant's devotion to their master.

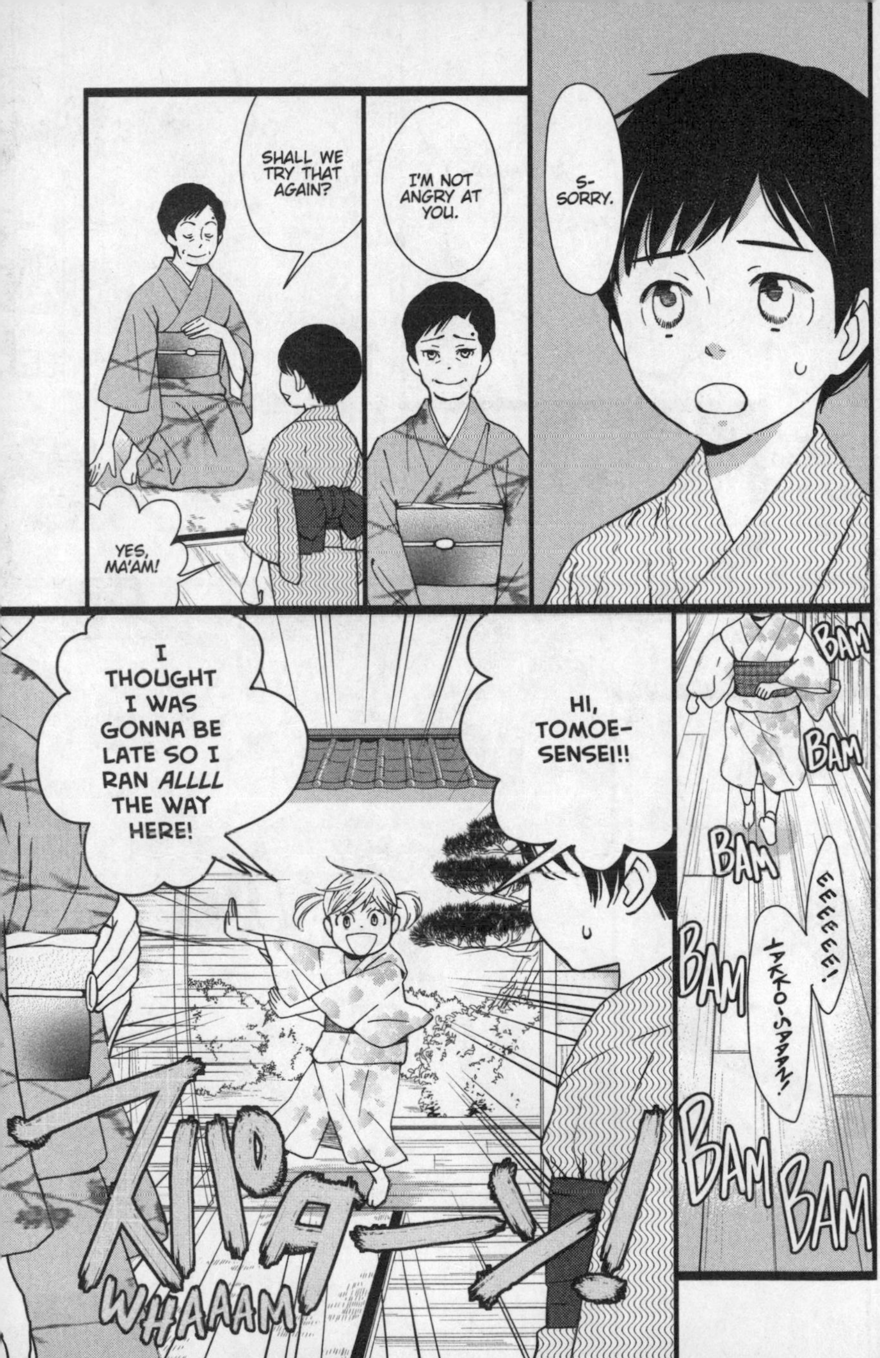
S- SORRY.
I'M NOT ANGRY AT YOU.
SHALL WE TRY THAT AGAIN?
YES, MA'AM!
BAM
BAM
BAM
BAM
BAM
BAM
EEEEEEE!
YAKKO-SAAAN!
HI, TOMOE-SENSEI!!
I THOUGHT I WAS GONNA BE LATE SO I RAN ALLLL THE WAY HERE!
WHAAAM

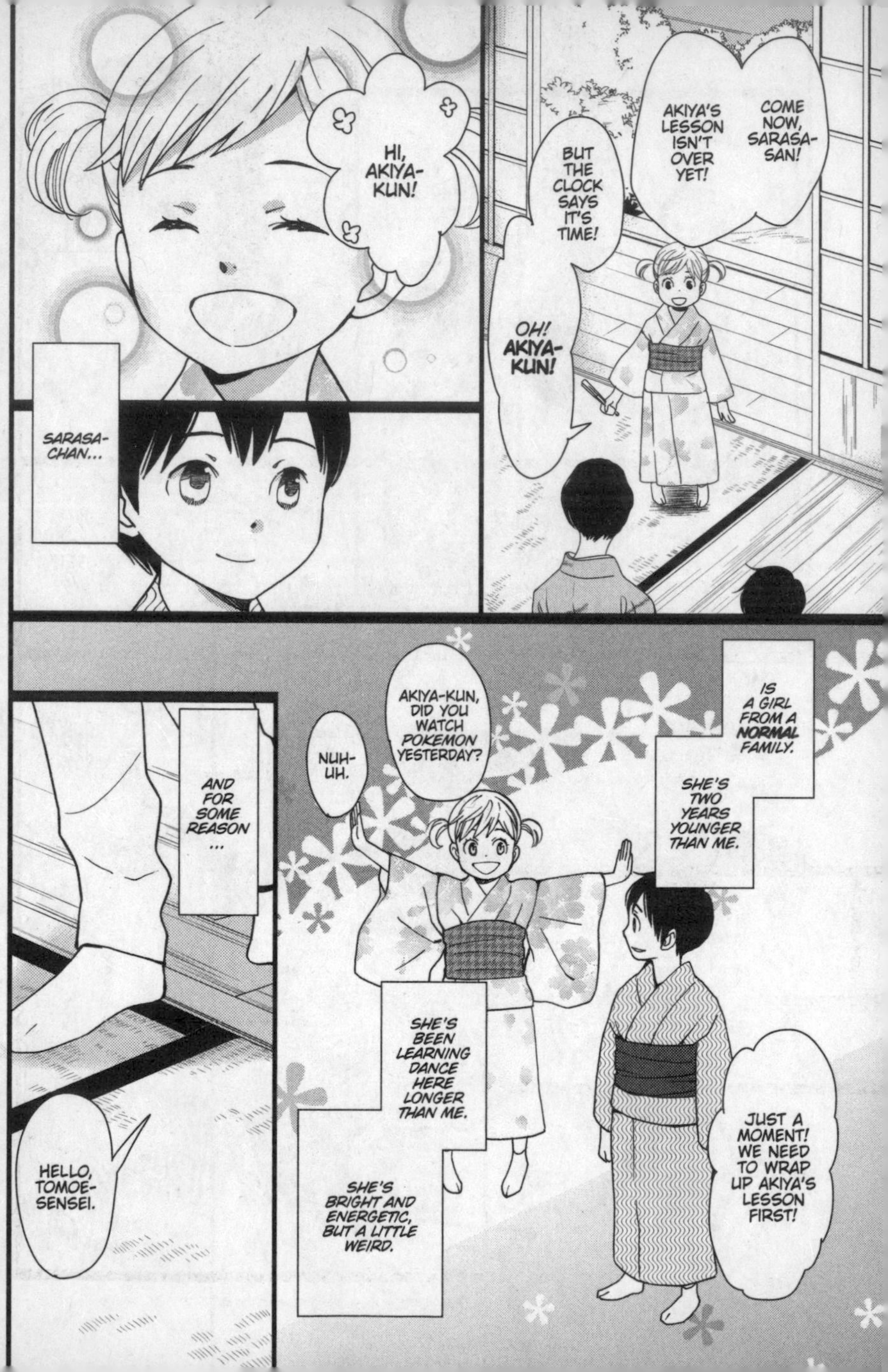
COME NOW, SARASA-SAN!
AKIYA'S LESSON ISN'T OVER YET!
BUT THE CLOCK SAYS IT'S TIME!
OH! AKIYA-KUN!
HI, AKIYA-KUN!
SARASA-CHAN...
IS A GIRL FROM A NORMAL FAMILY.
SHE'S TWO YEARS YOUNGER THAN ME.
AKIYA-KUN, DID YOU WATCH POKEMON YESTERDAY?
NUH-UH.
JUST A MOMENT! WE NEED TO WRAP UP AKIYA'S LESSON FIRST!
SHE'S BEEN LEARNING DANCE HERE LONGER THAN ME.
SHE'S BRIGHT AND ENERGETIC, BUT A LITTLE WEIRD.
AND FOR SOME REASON ...
HELLO, TOMOE-SENSEI.

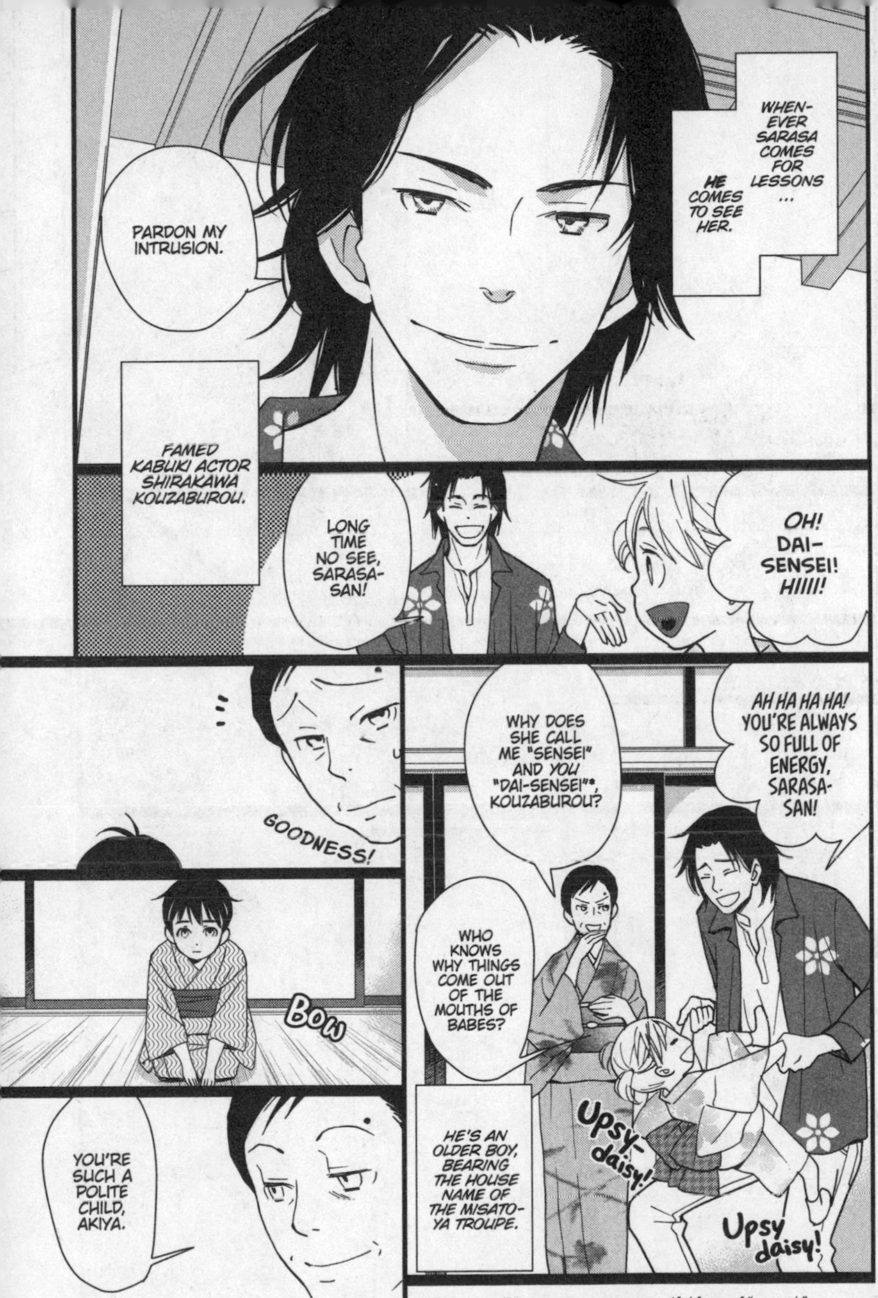
WHEN-EVER SARASA COMES FOR LESSONS ...
HE COMES TO SEE HER.
PARDON MY INTRUSION.
FAMED KABUKI ACTOR SHIRAKAWA KOUZABUROU.
OH! DAI-SENSEI! HIIII!
LONG TIME NO SEE, SARASA-SAN!
AH HA HA HA! YOU'RE ALWAYS SO FULL OF ENERGY, SARASA-SAN!
WHY DOES SHE CALL ME "SENSEI" AND YOU "DAI-SENSEI"*, KOUZABUROU?
WHO KNOWS WHY THINGS COME OUT OF THE MOUTHS OF BABES?
Upsy-daisy!
Upsy daisy!
HE'S AN OLDER BOY, BEARING THE HOUSE NAME OF THE MISATO-YA TROUPE.
GOODNESS!
Bow
YOU'RE SUCH A POLITE CHILD, AKIYA.

*"Dai-sensei" is an even more respectful form of "sensei."

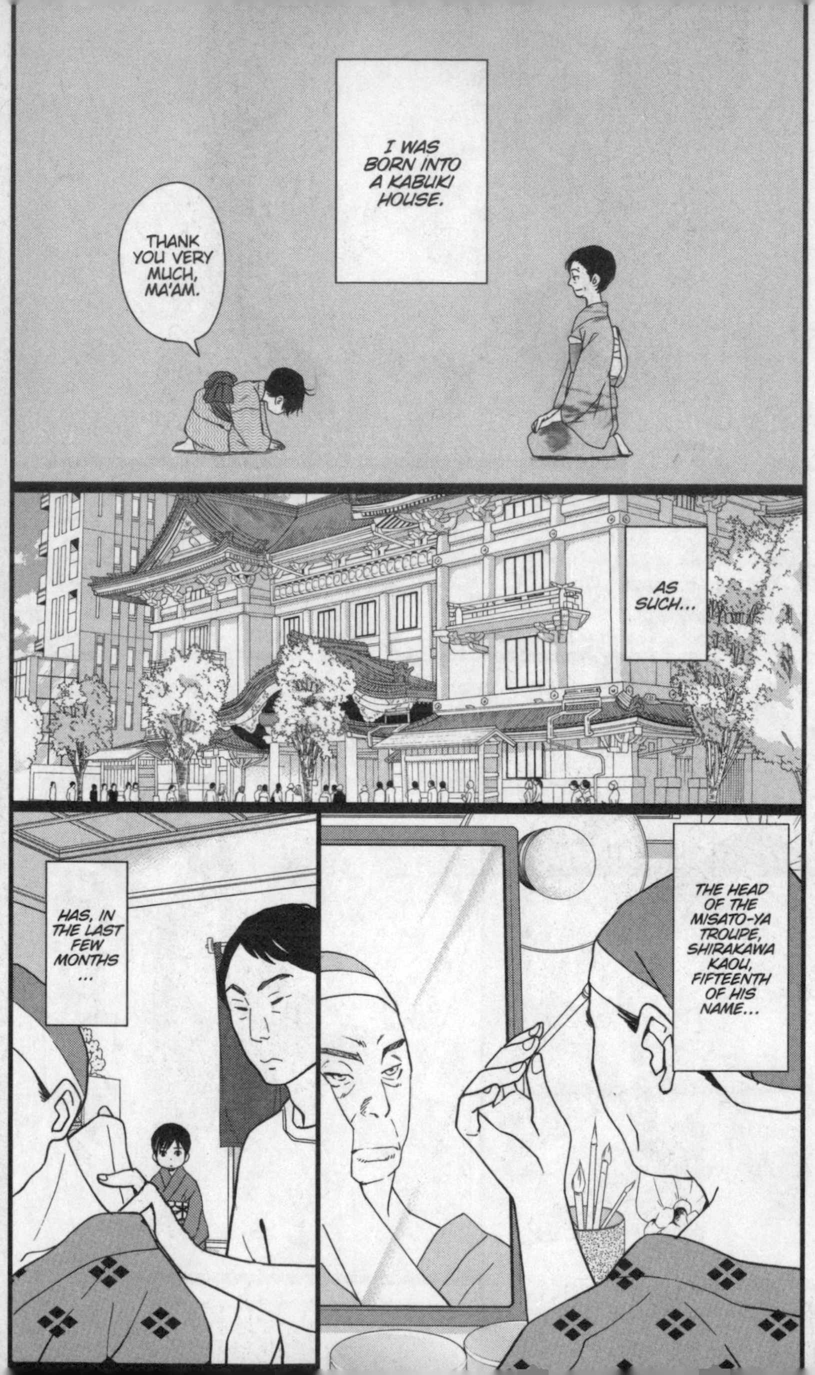
I WAS BORN INTO A KABUKI HOUSE.
THANK YOU VERY MUCH, MA'AM.
AS SUCH...
THE HEAD OF THE MISATO-YA TROUPE, SHIRAKAWA KAOU, FIFTEENTH OF HIS NAME...
HAS, IN THE LAST FEW MONTHS ...

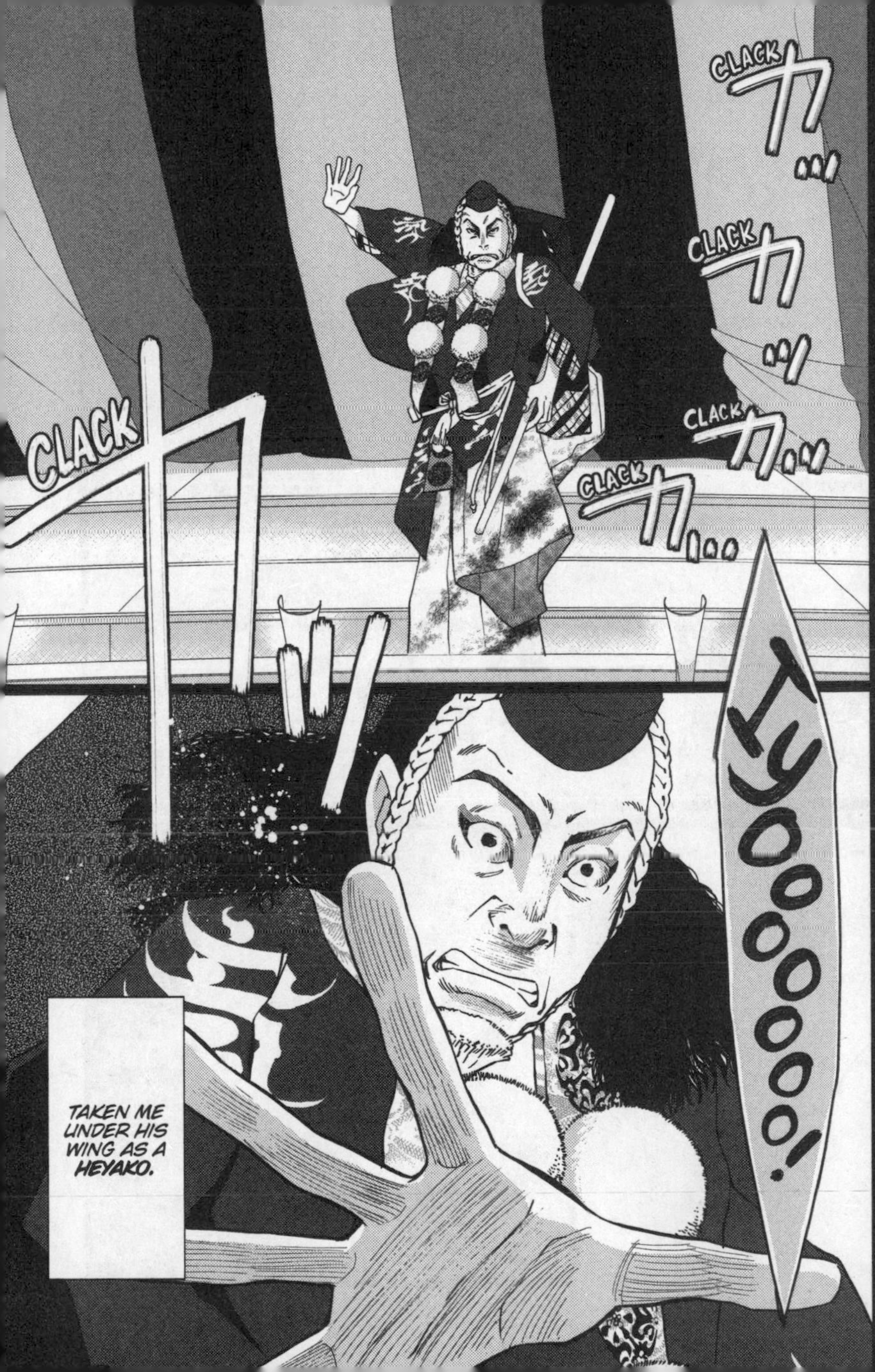
CLACK
CLACK
CLACK
CLACK
CLACK
IYOOOOOOO!
TAKEN ME UNDER HIS WING AS A **HEYAKO.**

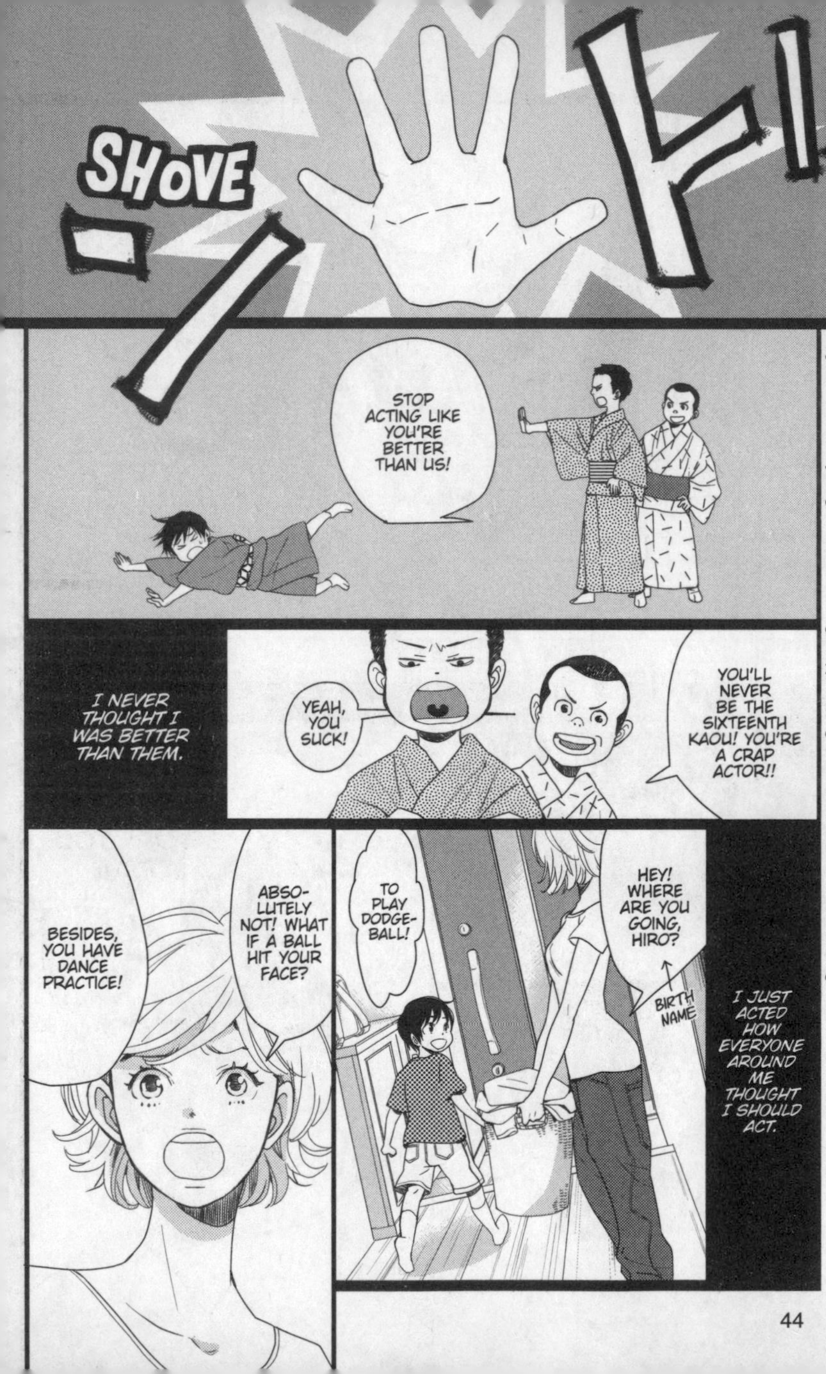
SHOVE
STOP ACTING LIKE YOU'RE BETTER THAN US!
YOU'LL NEVER BE THE SIXTEENTH KAOU! YOU'RE A CRAP ACTOR!!
YEAH, YOU SUCK!
I NEVER THOUGHT I WAS BETTER THAN THEM.
I JUST ACTED HOW EVERYONE AROUND ME THOUGHT I SHOULD ACT.
HEY! WHERE ARE YOU GOING, HIRO?
BIRTH NAME
TO PLAY DODGE-BALL!
ABSO-LUTELY NOT! WHAT IF A BALL HIT YOUR FACE?
BESIDES, YOU HAVE DANCE PRACTICE!

Heyako: *A child or young actor who has begun apprenticing with a kabuki actor. Literal meaning: "child of the room."*

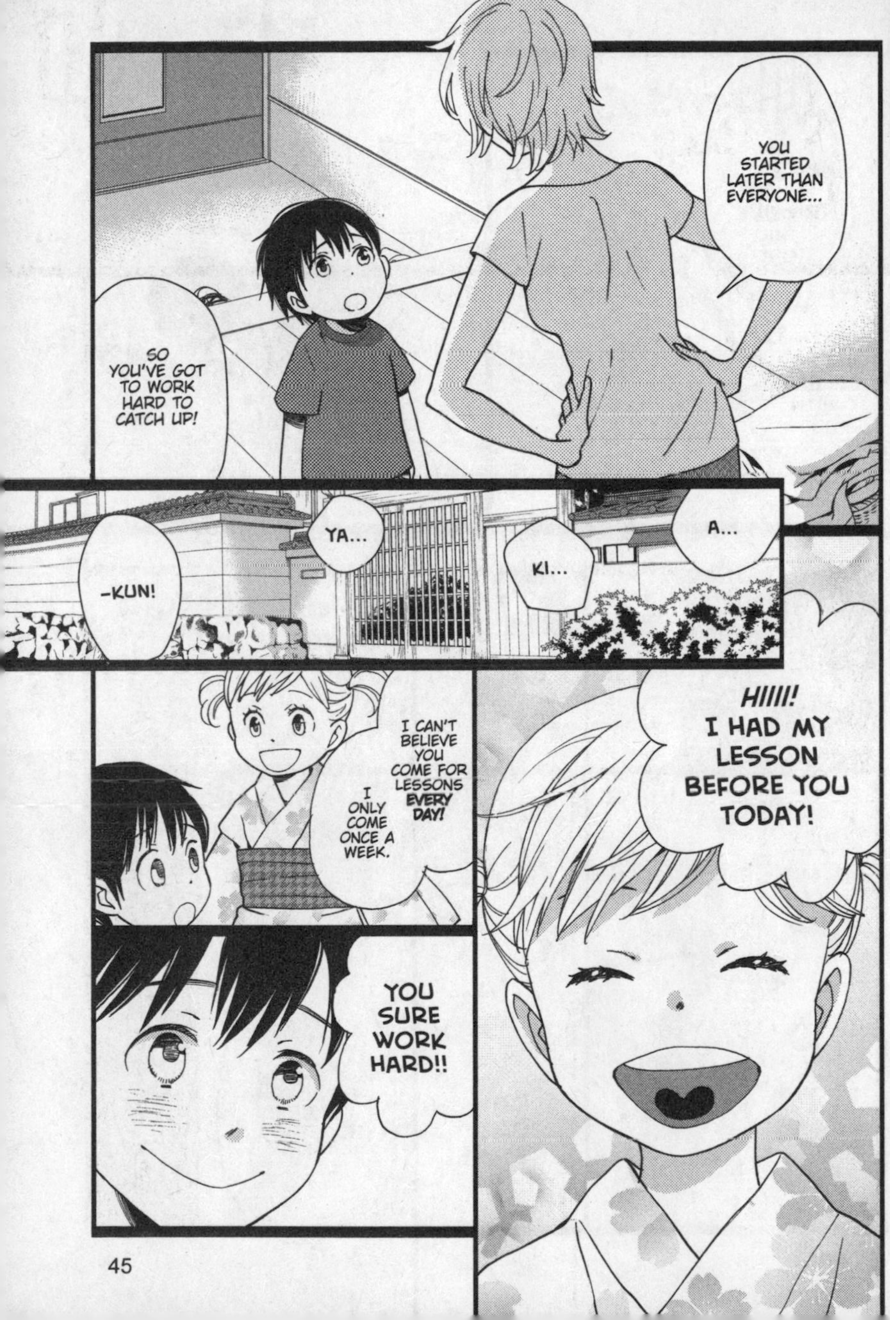
YOU STARTED LATER THAN EVERYONE...
SO YOU'VE GOT TO WORK HARD TO CATCH UP!
A...
KI...
YA...
-KUN!
HIIII! I HAD MY LESSON BEFORE YOU TODAY!
I CAN'T BELIEVE YOU COME FOR LESSONS EVERY DAY!
I ONLY COME ONCE A WEEK.
YOU SURE WORK HARD!!

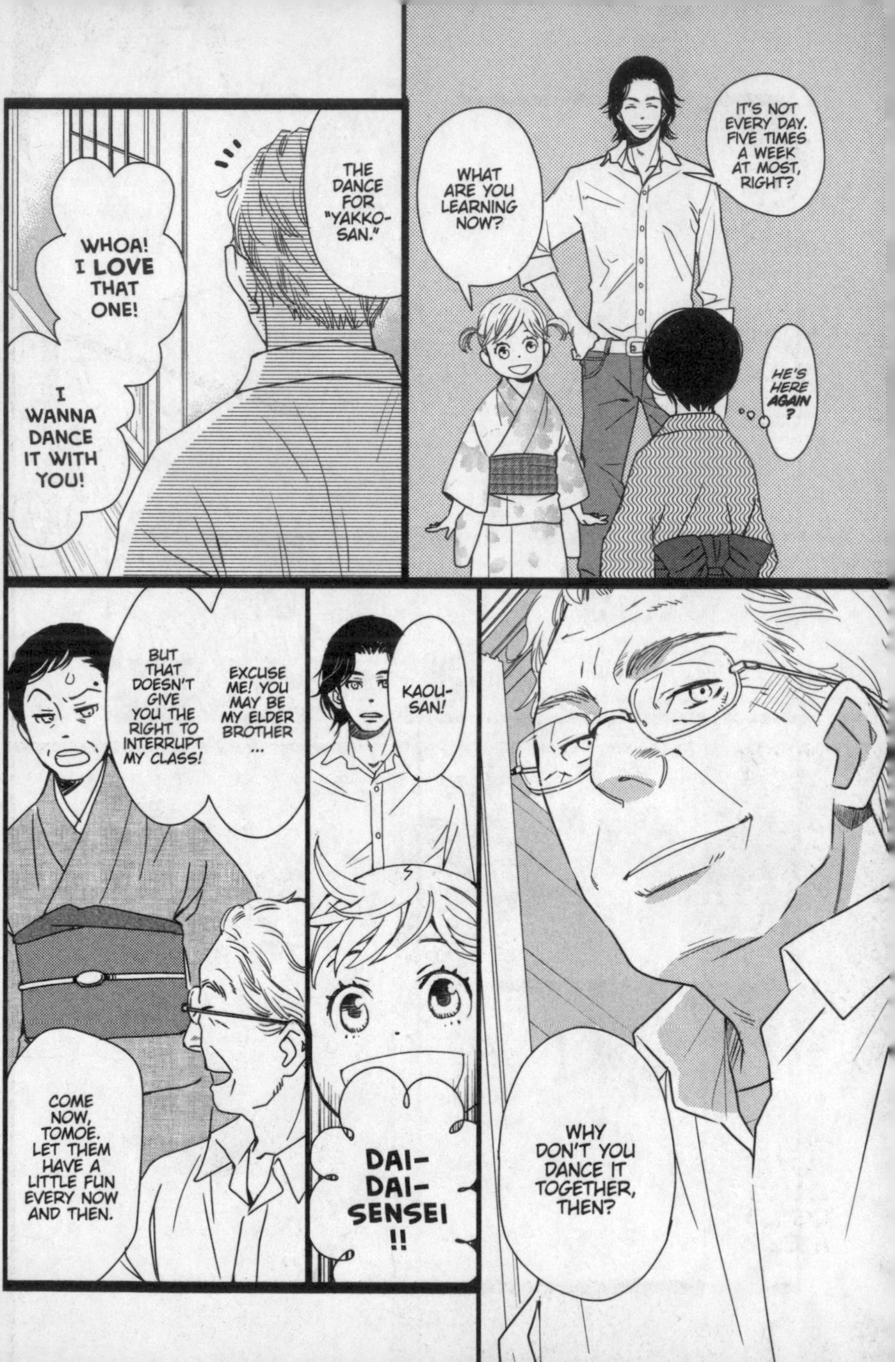
IT'S NOT EVERY DAY. FIVE TIMES A WEEK AT MOST, RIGHT?
WHAT ARE YOU LEARNING NOW?
HE'S HERE AGAIN?
THE DANCE FOR "YAKKO-SAN."
WHOA! I LOVE THAT ONE!
I WANNA DANCE IT WITH YOU!
WHY DON'T YOU DANCE IT TOGETHER, THEN?
KAOU-SAN!
DAI-DAI-SENSEI!!
EXCUSE ME! YOU MAY BE MY ELDER BROTHER ...
BUT THAT DOESN'T GIVE YOU THE RIGHT TO INTERRUPT MY CLASS!
COME NOW, TOMOE. LET THEM HAVE A LITTLE FUN EVERY NOW AND THEN.

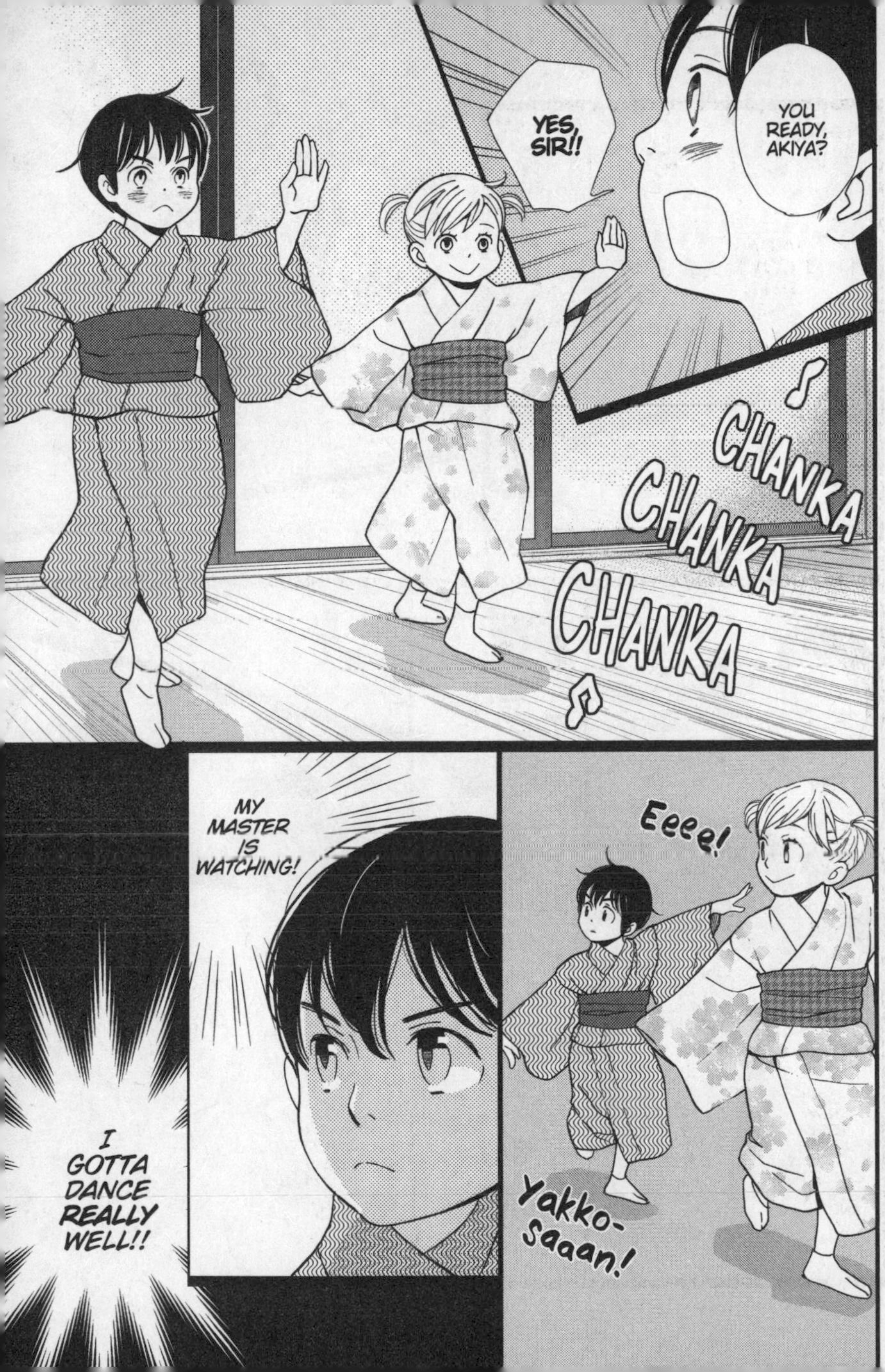
YOU READY, AKIYA?
YES, SIR!!
CHANKA CHANKA CHANKA
Eeee!
Yakko-Saaan!
MY MASTER IS WATCHING!
I GOTTA DANCE REALLY WELL!!

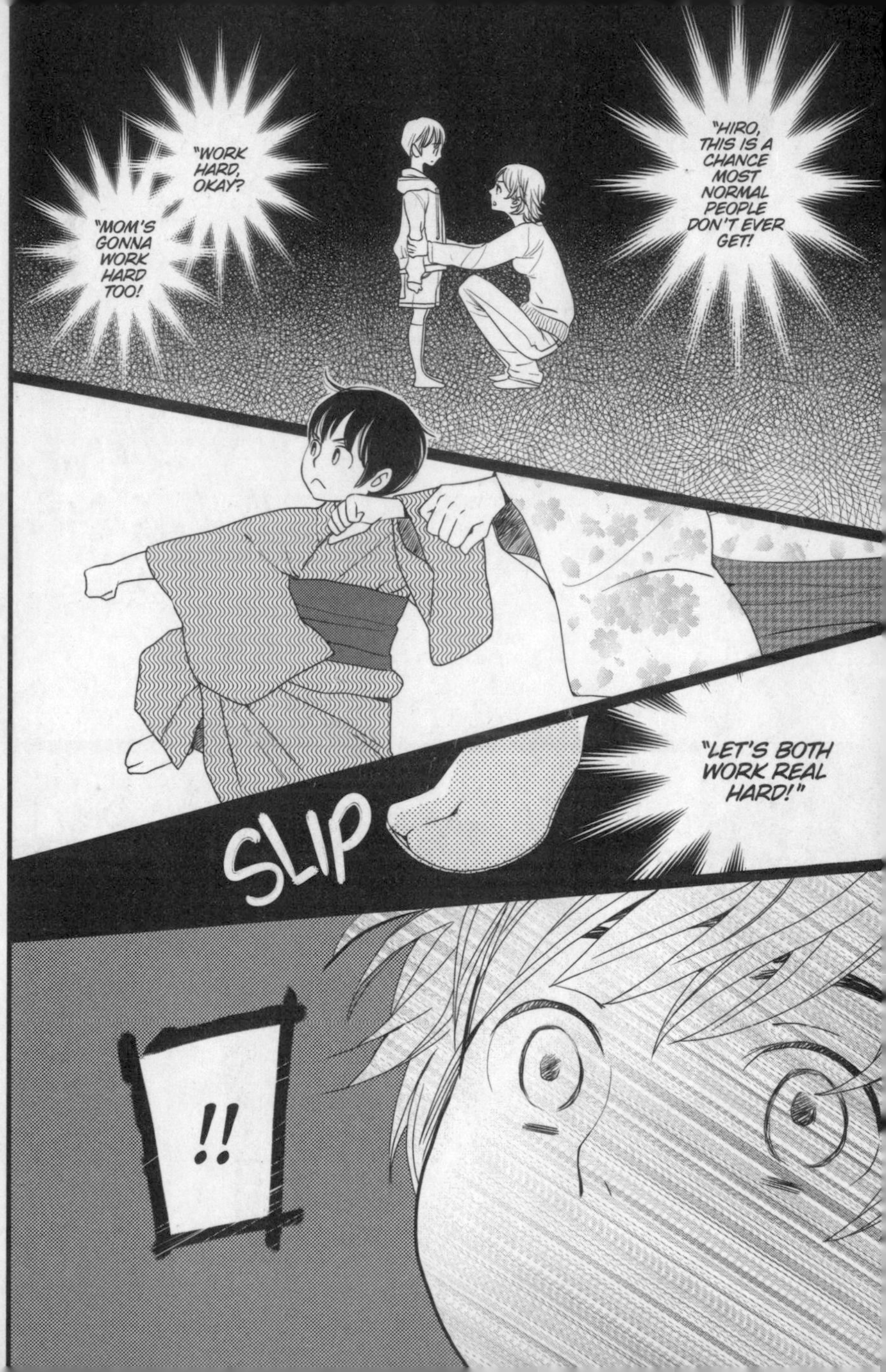
"HIRO, THIS IS A CHANCE MOST NORMAL PEOPLE DON'T EVER GET!
"WORK HARD, OKAY?
"MOM'S GONNA WORK HARD TOO!
"LET'S BOTH WORK REAL HARD!"
SLIP
!!

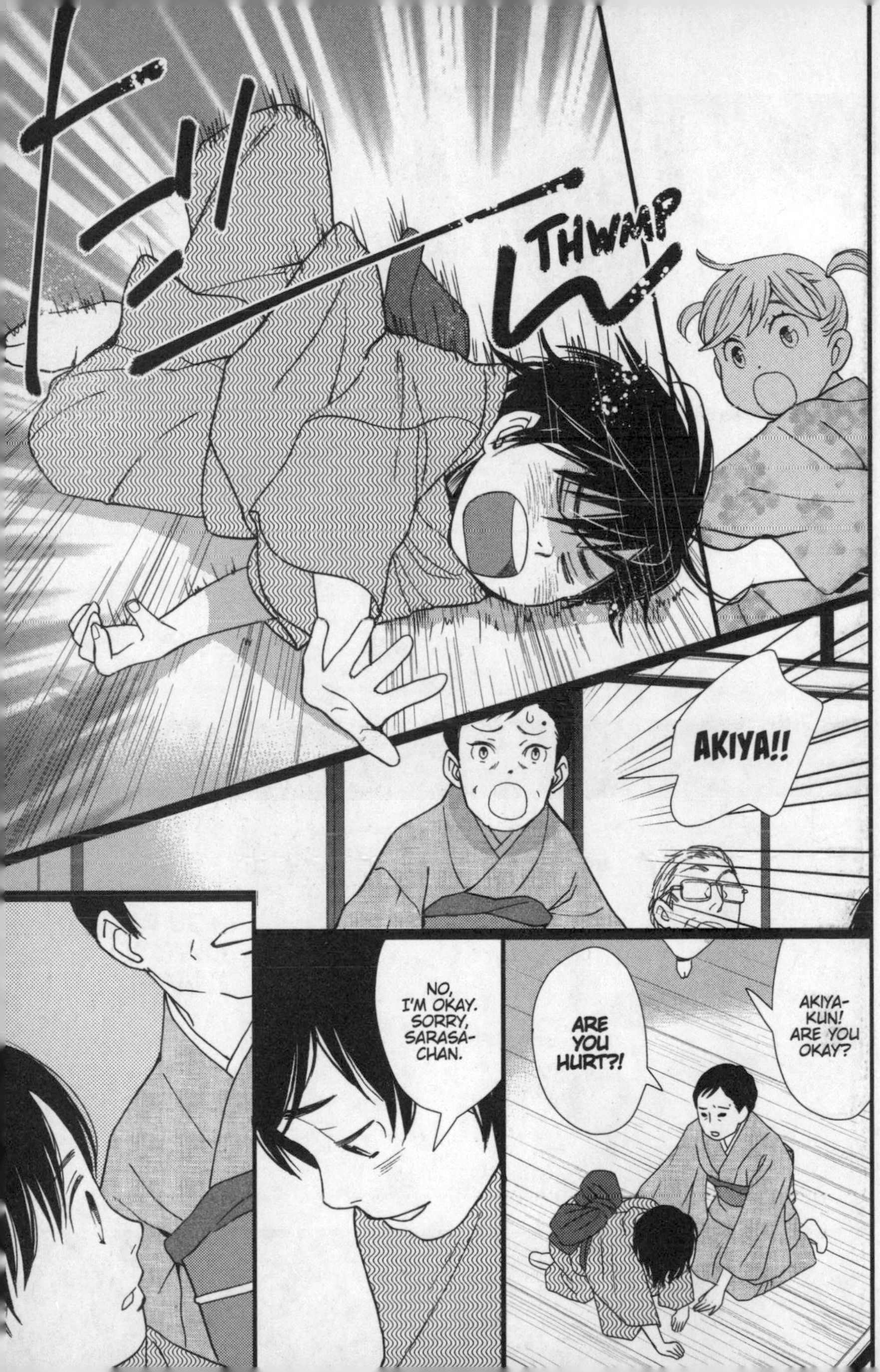
THWMP
AKIYA!!
AKIYA-KUN! ARE YOU OKAY?
ARE YOU HURT?!
NO, I'M OKAY. SORRY, SARASA-CHAN.

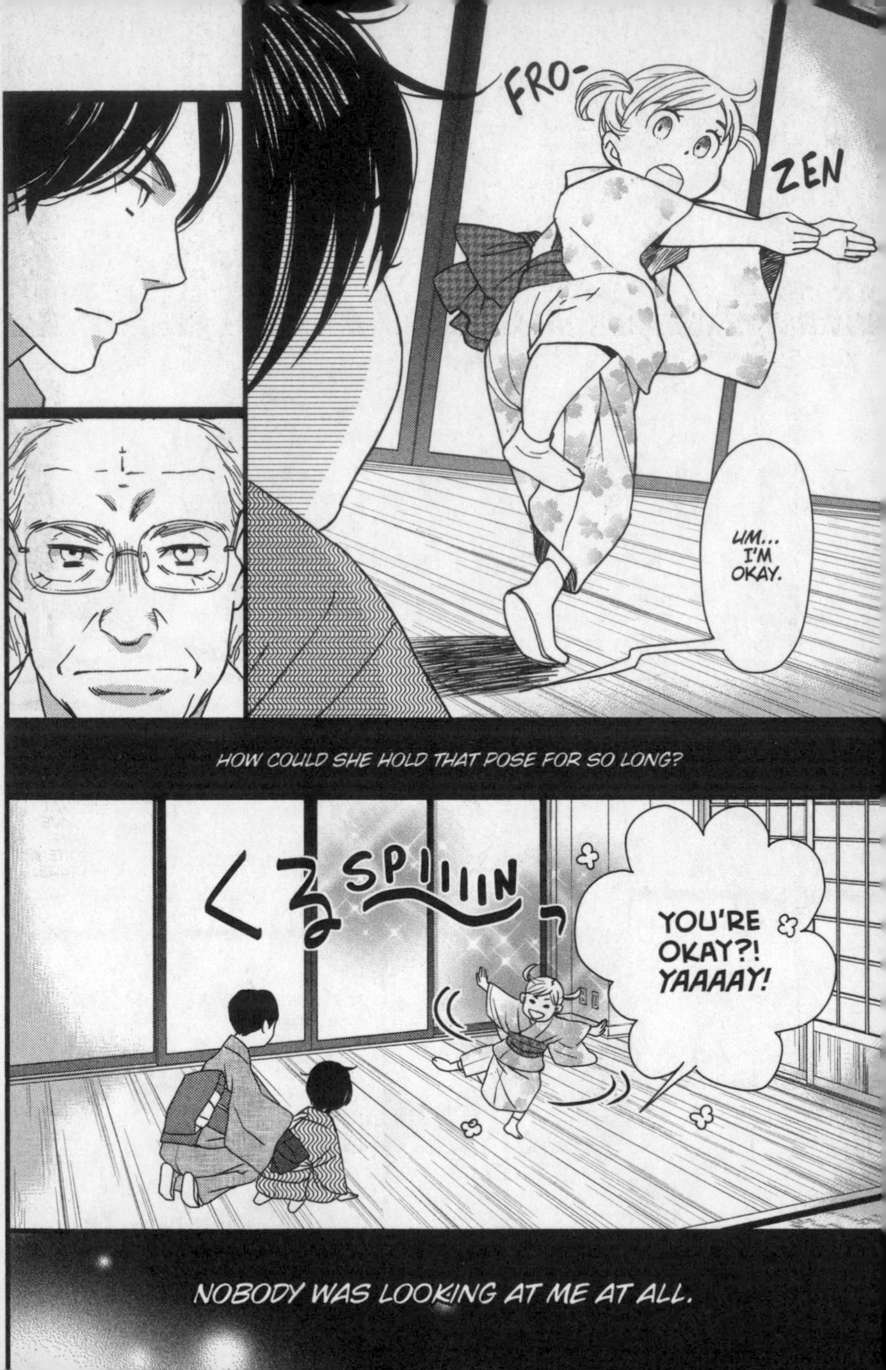
FRO-
ZEN
UM... I'M OKAY.
HOW COULD SHE HOLD THAT POSE FOR SO LONG?
YOU'RE OKAY?! YAAAAY!
くる
SPIIIIN
NOBODY WAS LOOKING AT ME AT ALL.

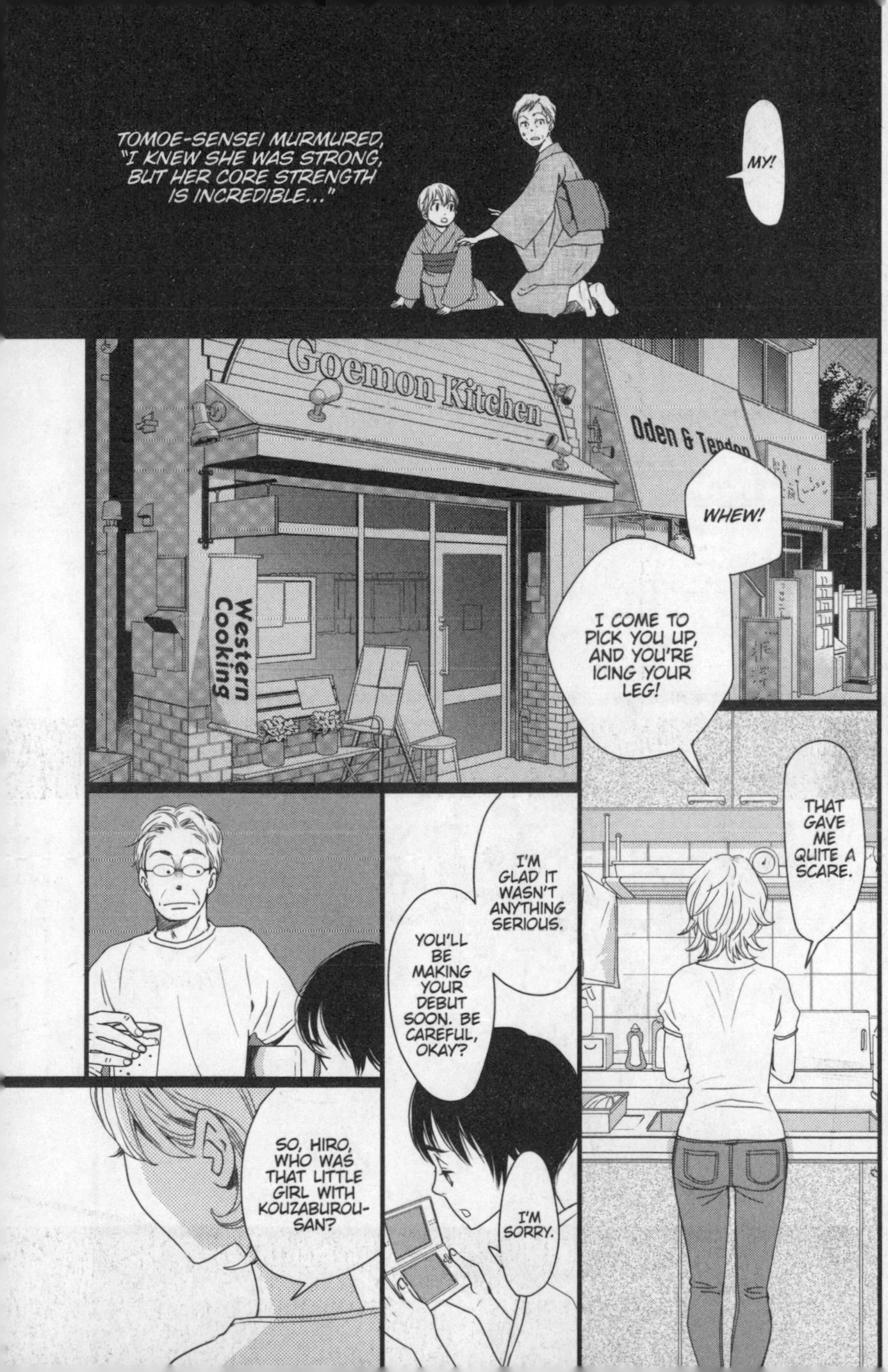
MY!
TOMOE-SENSEI MURMURED, "I KNEW SHE WAS STRONG, BUT HER CORE STRENGTH IS INCREDIBLE..."
Goemon Kitchen
Oden & Tendon
Western Cooking
WHEW!
I COME TO PICK YOU UP, AND YOU'RE ICING YOUR LEG!
THAT GAVE ME QUITE A SCARE.
I'M GLAD IT WASN'T ANYTHING SERIOUS.
YOU'LL BE MAKING YOUR DEBUT SOON. BE CAREFUL, OKAY?
I'M SORRY.
SO, HIRO, WHO WAS THAT LITTLE GIRL WITH KOUZABUROU-SAN?

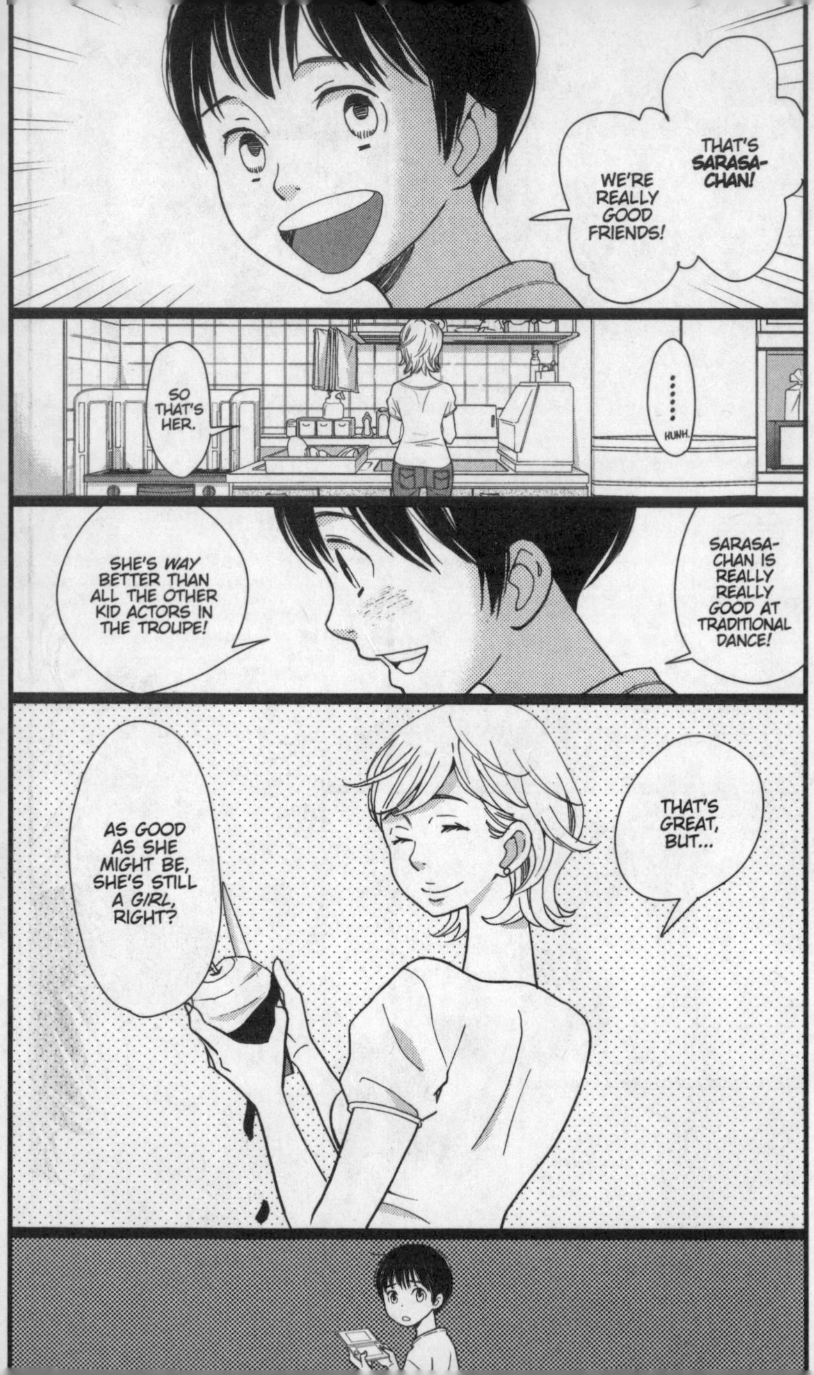
THAT'S SARASA-CHAN!
WE'RE REALLY GOOD FRIENDS!
...... HUNH.
SO THAT'S HER.
SARASA-CHAN IS REALLY REALLY GOOD AT TRADITIONAL DANCE!
SHE'S *WAY* BETTER THAN ALL THE OTHER KID ACTORS IN THE TROUPE!
THAT'S GREAT, BUT...
AS GOOD AS SHE MIGHT BE, SHE'S STILL A *GIRL*, RIGHT?

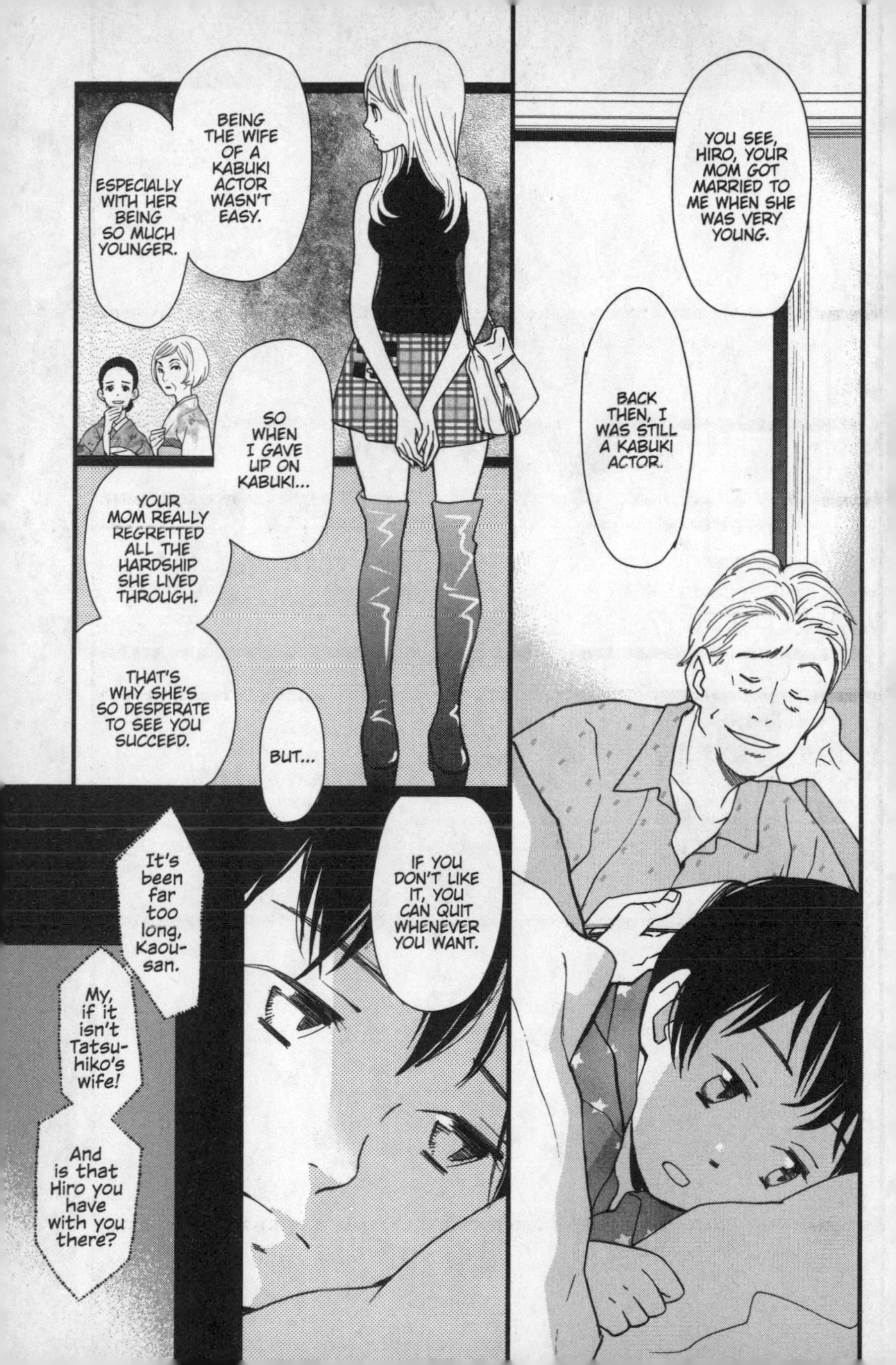
YOU SEE, HIRO, YOUR MOM GOT MARRIED TO ME WHEN SHE WAS VERY YOUNG.
BACK THEN, I WAS STILL A KABUKI ACTOR.
BEING THE WIFE OF A KABUKI ACTOR WASN'T EASY.
ESPECIALLY WITH HER BEING SO MUCH YOUNGER.
SO WHEN I GAVE UP ON KABUKI...
YOUR MOM REALLY REGRETTED ALL THE HARDSHIP SHE LIVED THROUGH.
THAT'S WHY SHE'S SO DESPERATE TO SEE YOU SUCCEED.
BUT...
IF YOU DON'T LIKE IT, YOU CAN QUIT WHENEVER YOU WANT.
It's been far too long, Kaou-san.
My, if it isn't Tatsuhiko's wife!
And is that Hiro you have with you there?

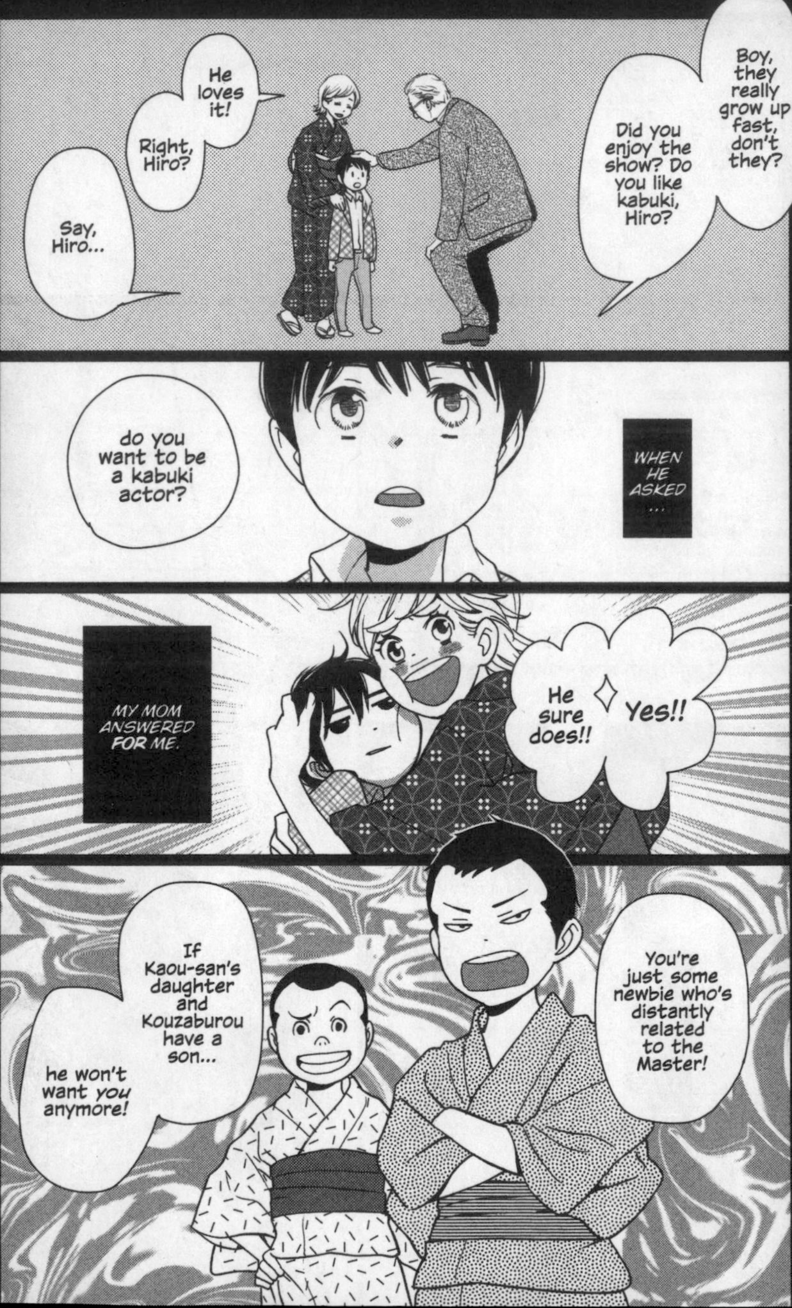
Boy, they really grow up fast, don't they?
Did you enjoy the show? Do you like kabuki, Hiro?
He loves it!
Right, Hiro?
Say, Hiro...
WHEN HE ASKED ...
do you want to be a kabuki actor?
Yes!!
He sure does!!
MY MOM ANSWERED FOR ME.
You're just some newbie who's distantly related to the Master!
If Kaou-san's daughter and Kouzaburou have a son...
he won't want you anymore!

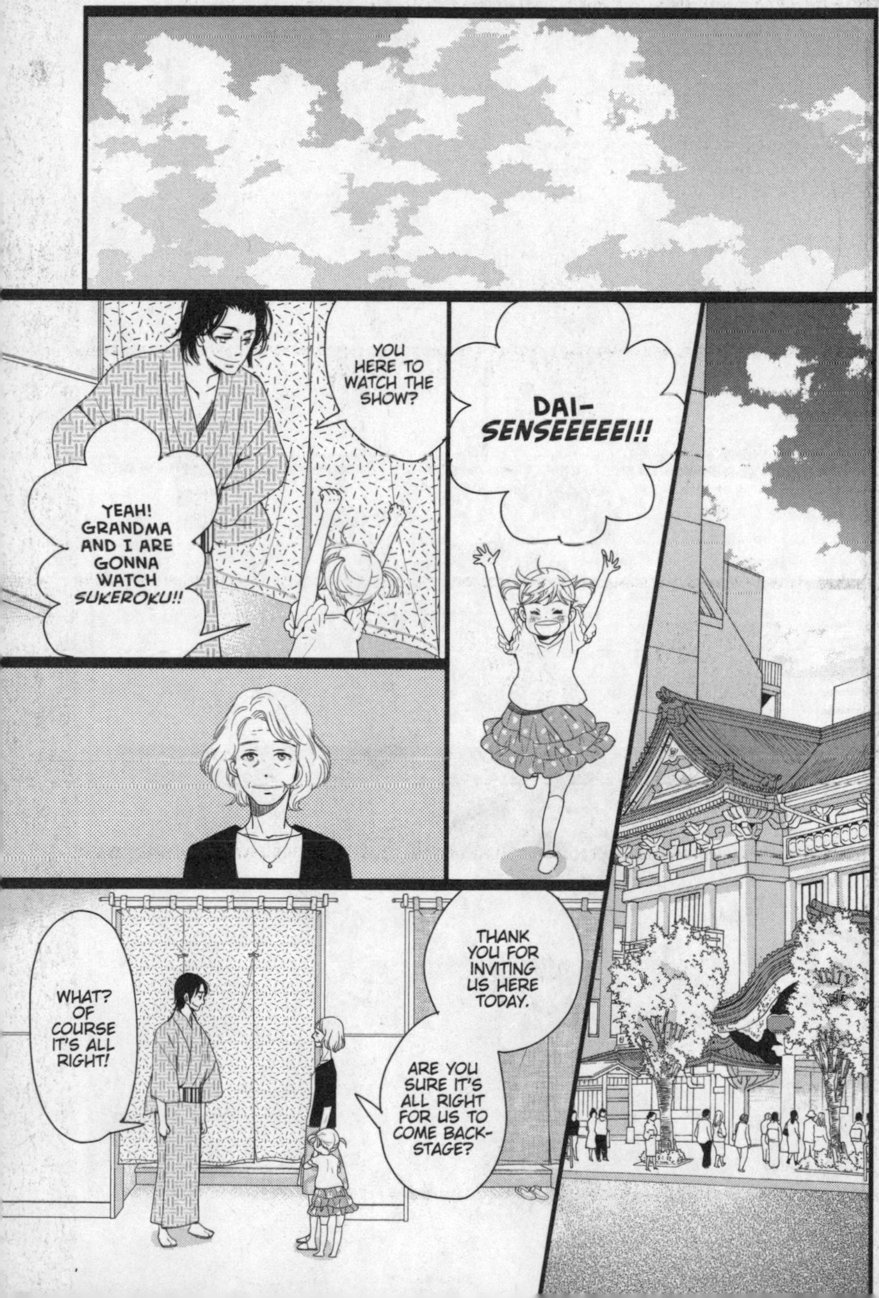
DAI-SENSEEEEEI!!!
YOU HERE TO WATCH THE SHOW?
YEAH! GRANDMA AND I ARE GONNA WATCH SUKEROKU!!
THANK YOU FOR INVITING US HERE TODAY.
ARE YOU SURE IT'S ALL RIGHT FOR US TO COME BACK-STAGE?
WHAT? OF COURSE IT'S ALL RIGHT!

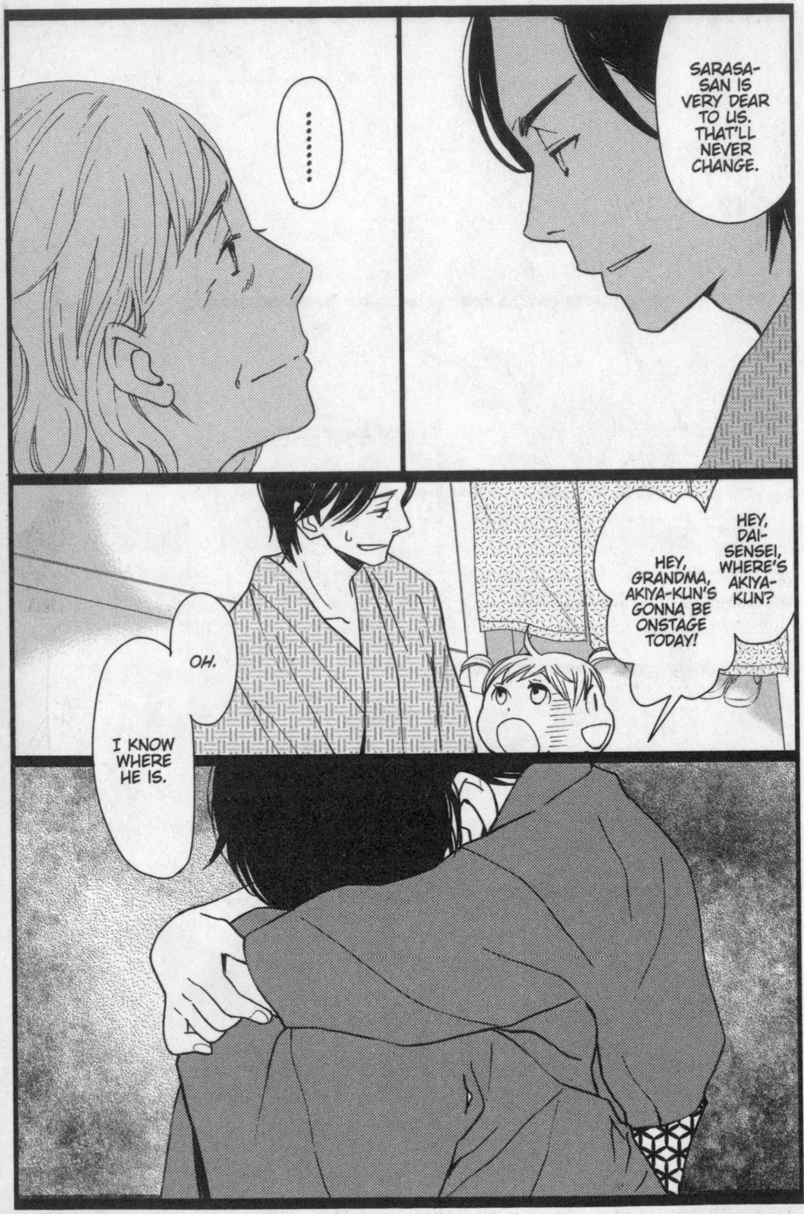
SARASA-SAN IS VERY DEAR TO US. THAT'LL NEVER CHANGE.
....
HEY, DAI-SENSEI, WHERE'S AKIYA-KUN?
HEY, GRANDMA, AKIYA-KUN'S GONNA BE ONSTAGE TODAY!
OH.
I KNOW WHERE HE IS.

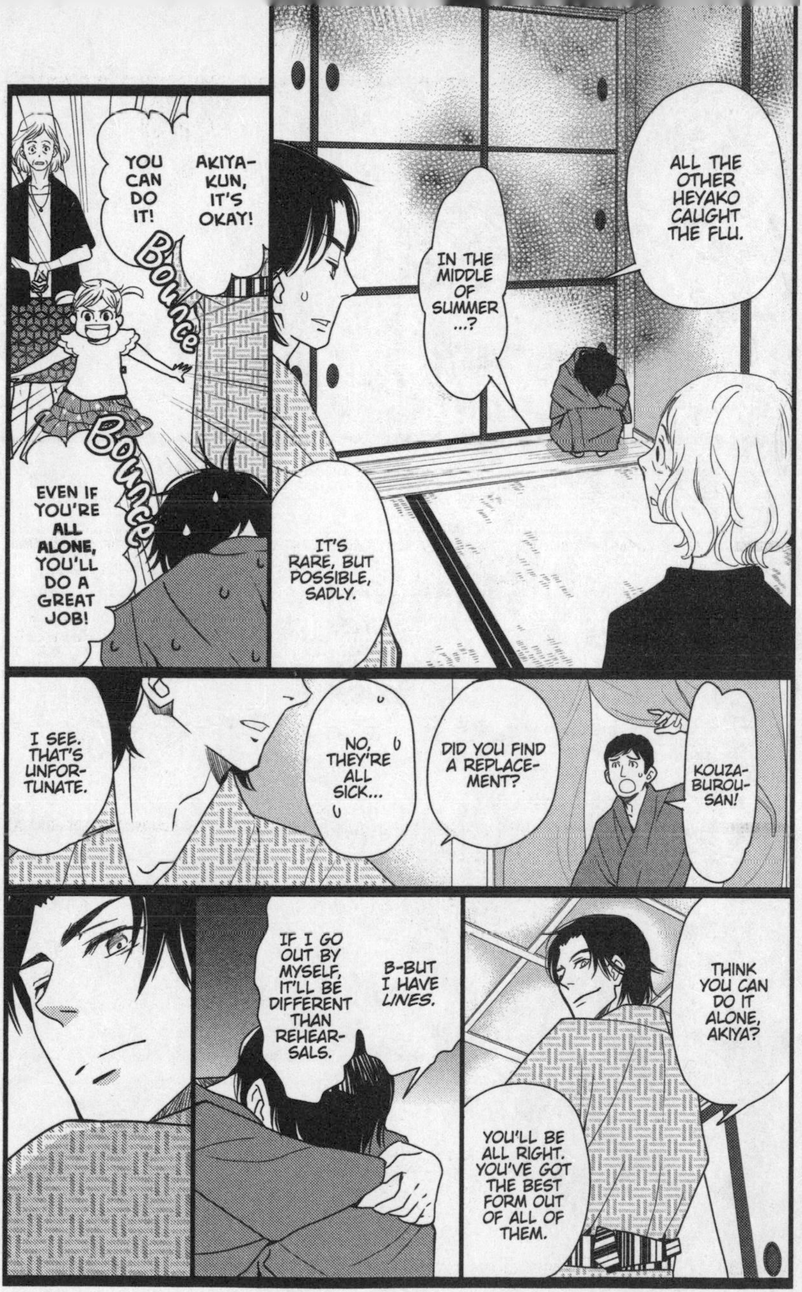
ALL THE OTHER HEYAKO CAUGHT THE FLU.
IN THE MIDDLE OF SUMMER ...?
IT'S RARE, BUT POSSIBLE, SADLY.
AKIYA-KUN, IT'S OKAY!
YOU CAN DO IT!
Bounce
Bounce
EVEN IF YOU'RE ALL ALONE, YOU'LL DO A GREAT JOB!
KOUZABUROU-SAN!
DID YOU FIND A REPLACEMENT?
NO, THEY'RE ALL SICK...
I SEE. THAT'S UNFORTUNATE.
THINK YOU CAN DO IT ALONE, AKIYA?
YOU'LL BE ALL RIGHT. YOU'VE GOT THE BEST FORM OUT OF ALL OF THEM.
B-BUT I HAVE *LINES.*
IF I GO OUT BY MYSELF, IT'LL BE DIFFERENT THAN REHEARSALS.

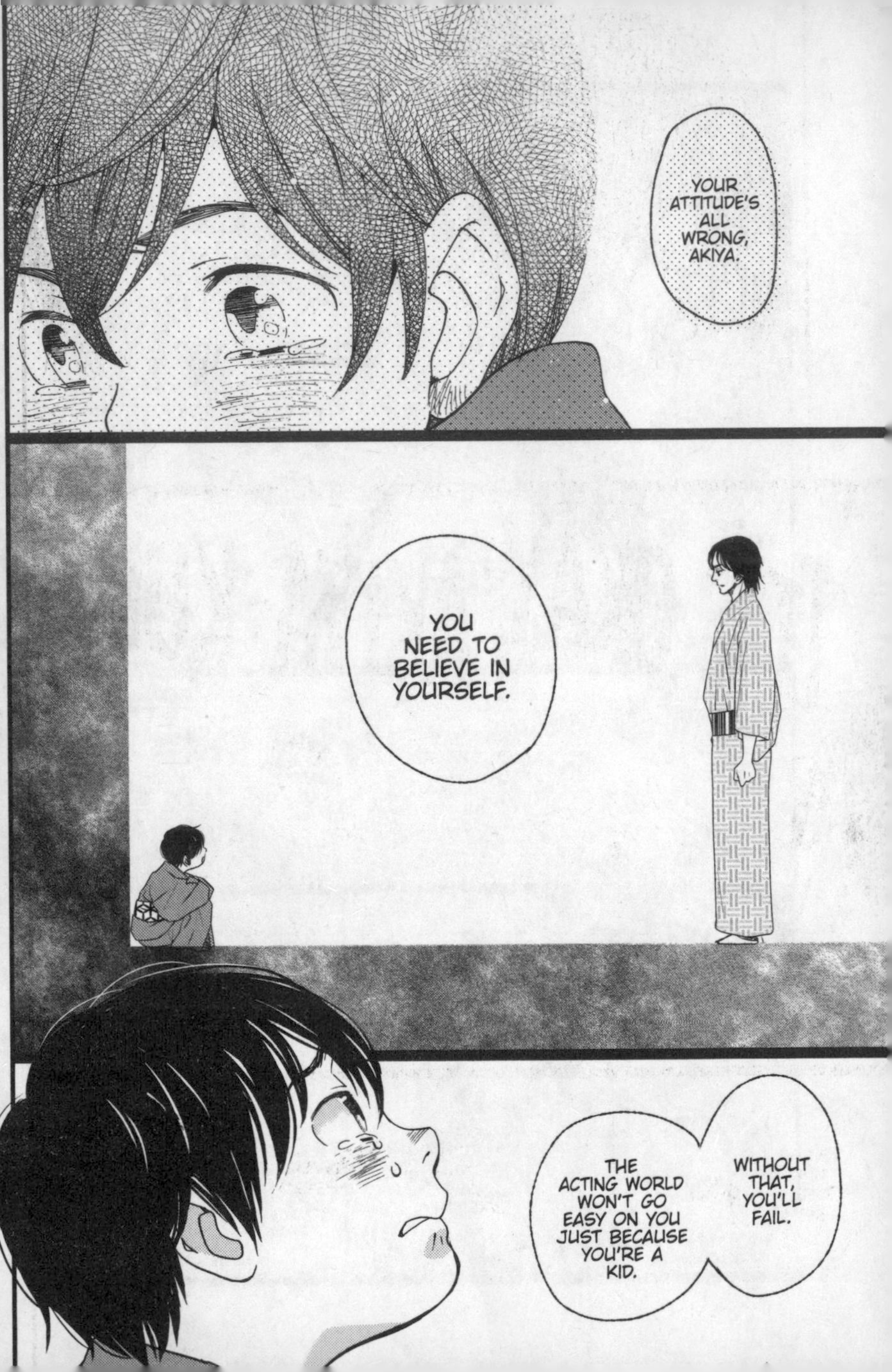
YOUR ATTITUDE'S ALL WRONG, AKIYA.
YOU NEED TO BELIEVE IN YOURSELF.
WITHOUT THAT, YOU'LL FAIL.
THE ACTING WORLD WON'T GO EASY ON YOU JUST BECAUSE YOU'RE A KID.

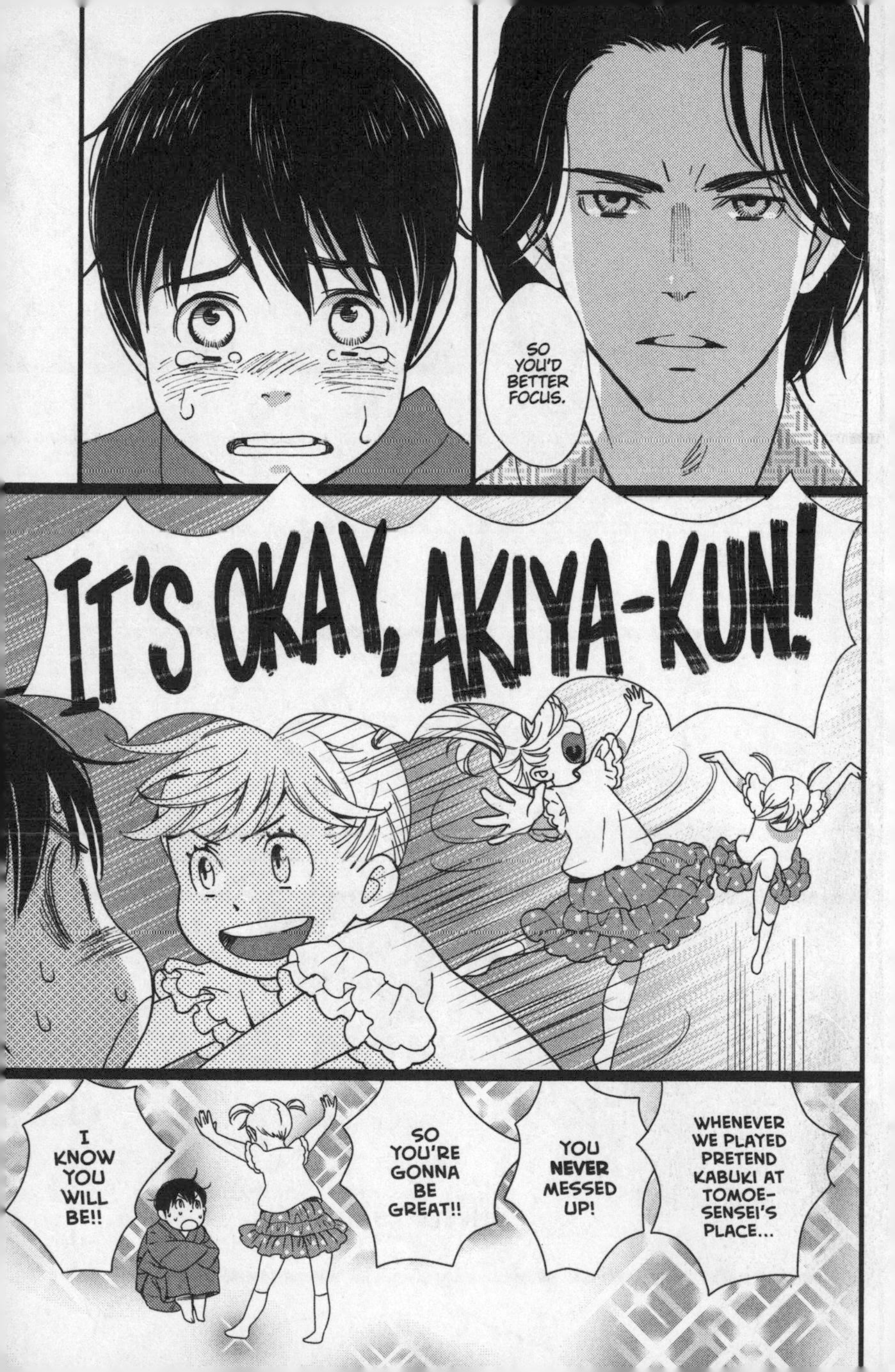
SO YOU'D BETTER FOCUS.
IT'S OKAY, AKIYA-KUN!
WHENEVER WE PLAYED PRETEND KABUKI AT TOMOE-SENSEI'S PLACE...
YOU **NEVER** MESSED UP!
SO YOU'RE GONNA BE GREAT!!
I KNOW YOU WILL BE!!

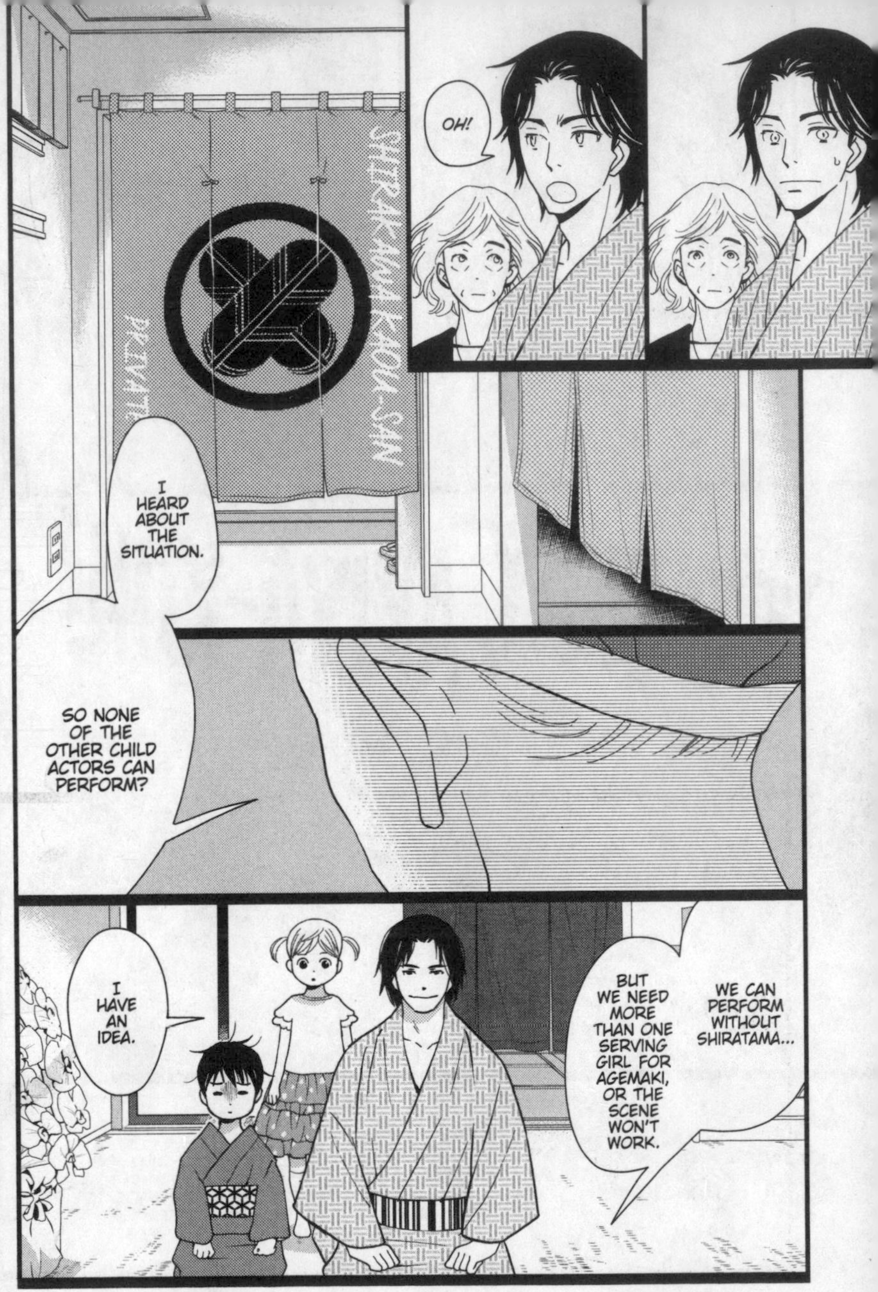
OH!
SHIRAKAWA KAOU-SAN
PRIVATE
I HEARD ABOUT THE SITUATION.
SO NONE OF THE OTHER CHILD ACTORS CAN PERFORM?
WE CAN PERFORM WITHOUT SHIRATAMA...
BUT WE NEED MORE THAN ONE SERVING GIRL FOR AGEMAKI, OR THE SCENE WON'T WORK.
I HAVE AN IDEA.

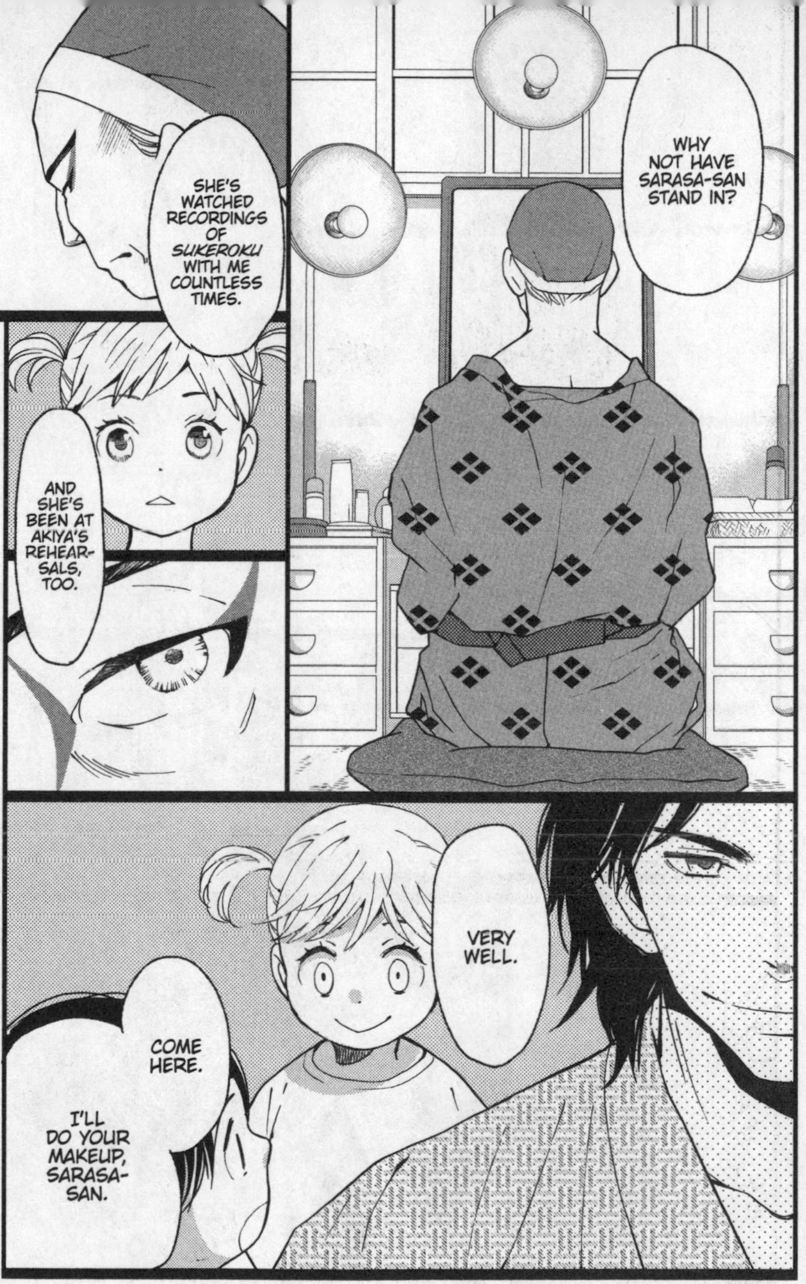
WHY NOT HAVE SARASA-SAN STAND IN?
SHE'S WATCHED RECORDINGS OF *SUKEROKU* WITH ME COUNTLESS TIMES.
AND SHE'S BEEN AT AKIYA'S REHEARSALS, TOO.
VERY WELL.
COME HERE.
I'LL DO YOUR MAKEUP, SARASA-SAN.

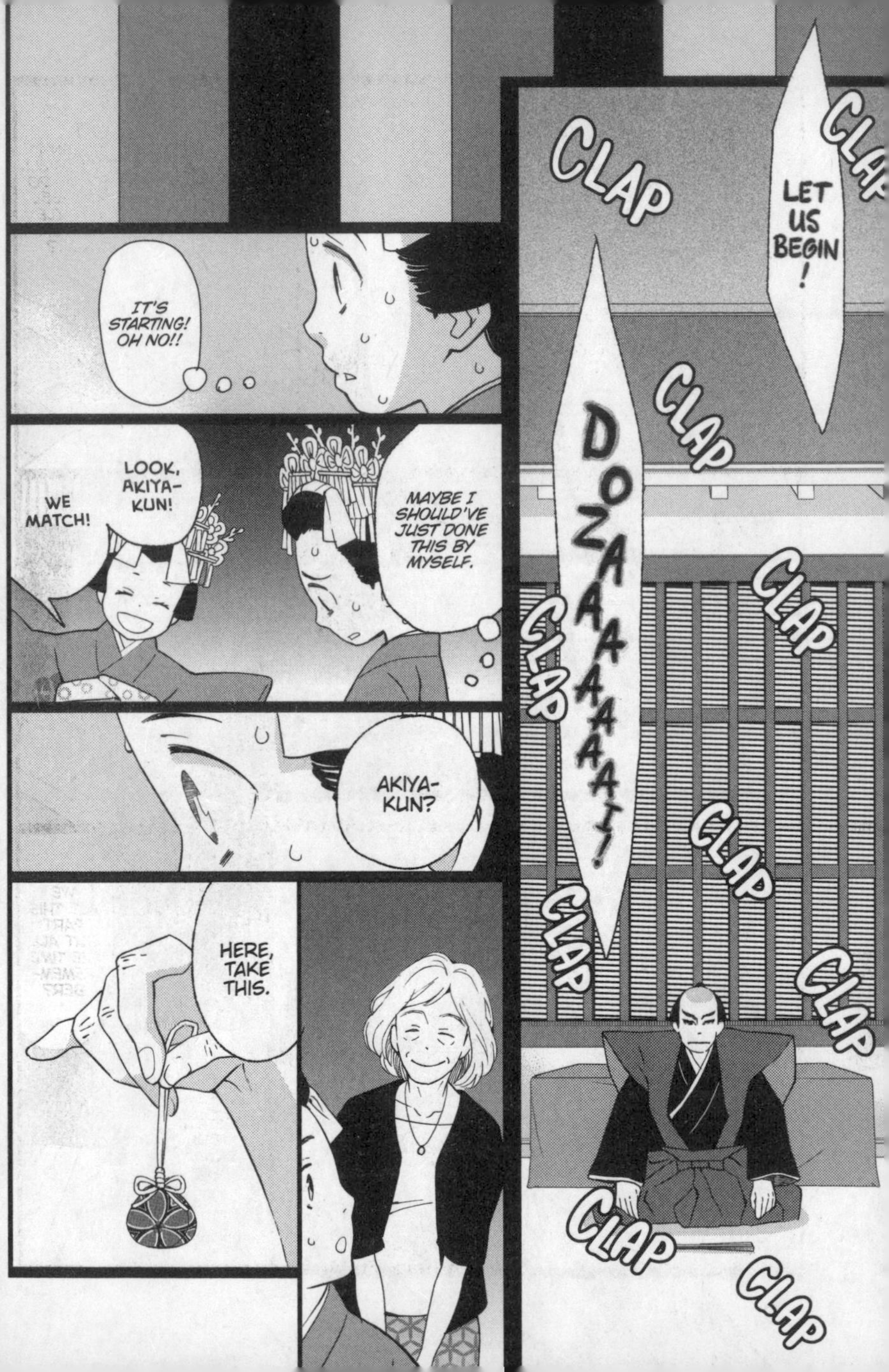
CLAP
LET US BEGIN!
CLAP
DOZAAAAAAAT!
CLAP
CLAP
CLAP
CLAP
CLAP
CLAP
CLAP
CLAP
IT'S STARTING! OH NO!!
MAYBE I SHOULD'VE JUST DONE THIS BY MYSELF.
LOOK, AKIYA-KUN!
WE MATCH!
AKIYA-KUN?
HERE, TAKE THIS.

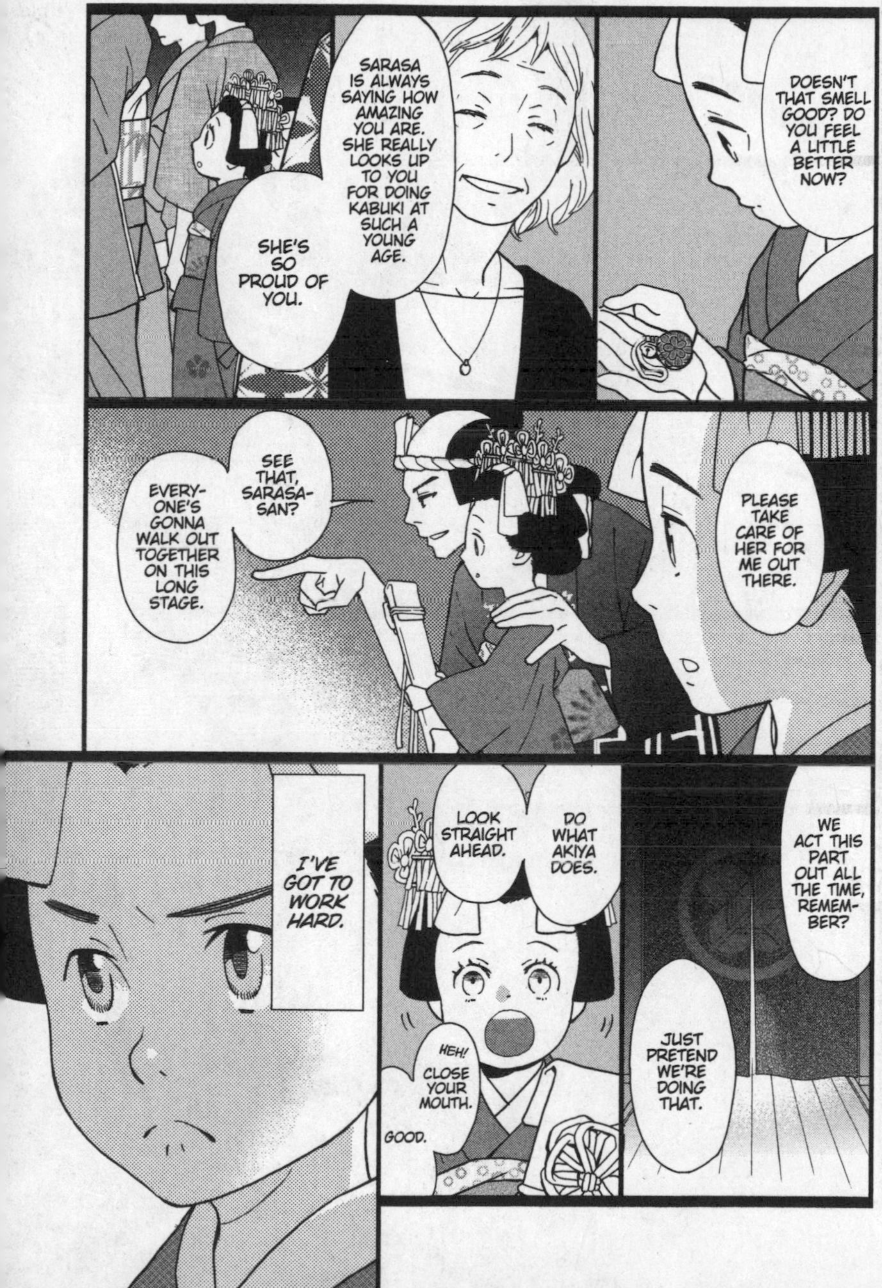
DOESN'T THAT SMELL GOOD? DO YOU FEEL A LITTLE BETTER NOW?
SARASA IS ALWAYS SAYING HOW AMAZING YOU ARE. SHE REALLY LOOKS UP TO YOU FOR DOING KABUKI AT SUCH A YOUNG AGE.
SHE'S SO PROUD OF YOU.
PLEASE TAKE CARE OF HER FOR ME OUT THERE.
SEE THAT, SARASA-SAN?
EVERYONE'S GONNA WALK OUT TOGETHER ON THIS LONG STAGE.
WE ACT THIS PART OUT ALL THE TIME, REMEMBER?
JUST PRETEND WE'RE DOING THAT.
DO WHAT AKIYA DOES.
LOOK STRAIGHT AHEAD.
HEH! CLOSE YOUR MOUTH.
GOOD.
I'VE GOT TO WORK HARD.

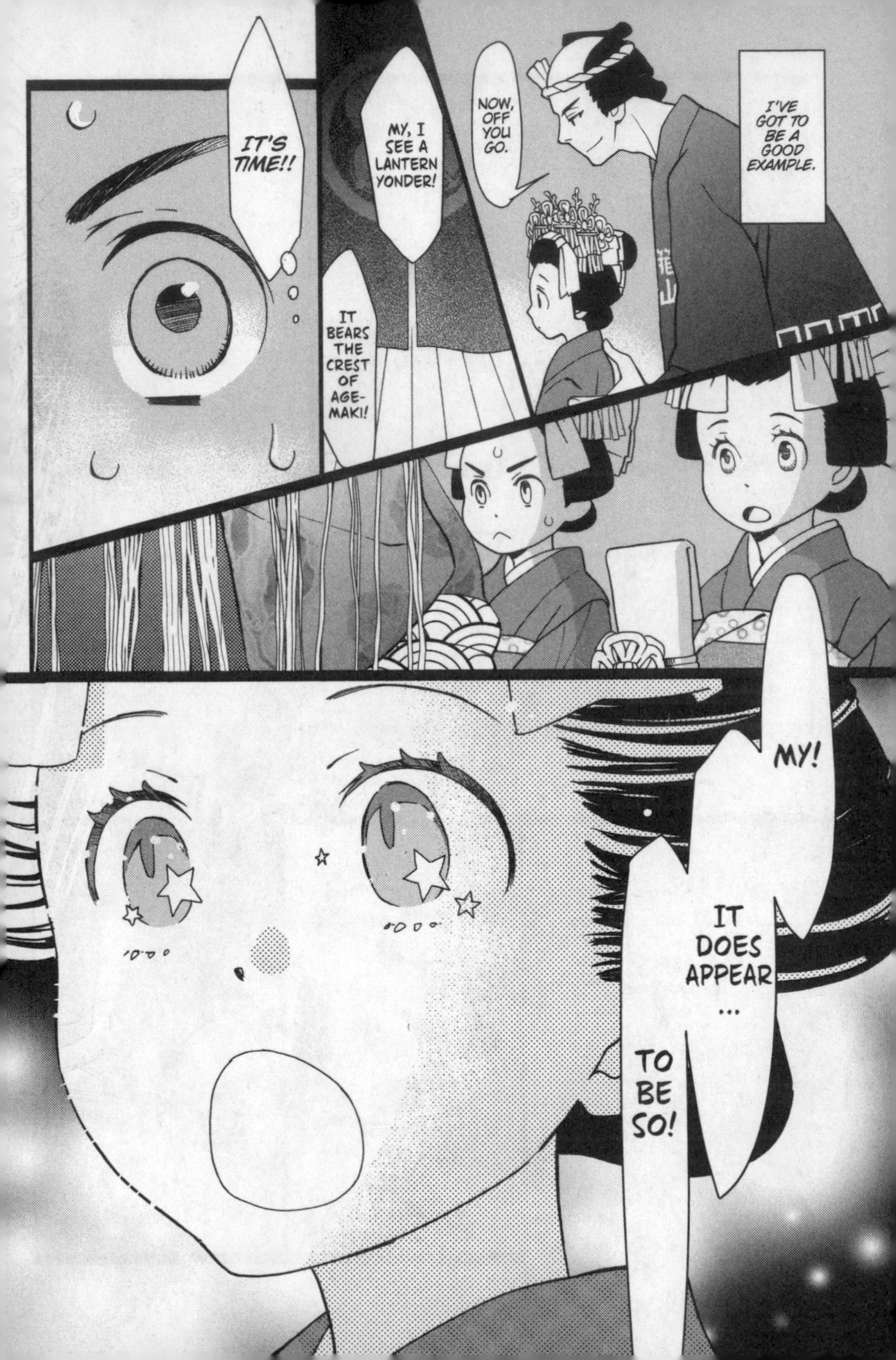
I'VE GOT TO BE A GOOD EXAMPLE.
NOW, OFF YOU GO.
MY, I SEE A LANTERN YONDER!
IT BEARS THE CREST OF AGE-MAKI!
IT'S TIME!!
MY!
IT DOES APPEAR...
TO BE SO!

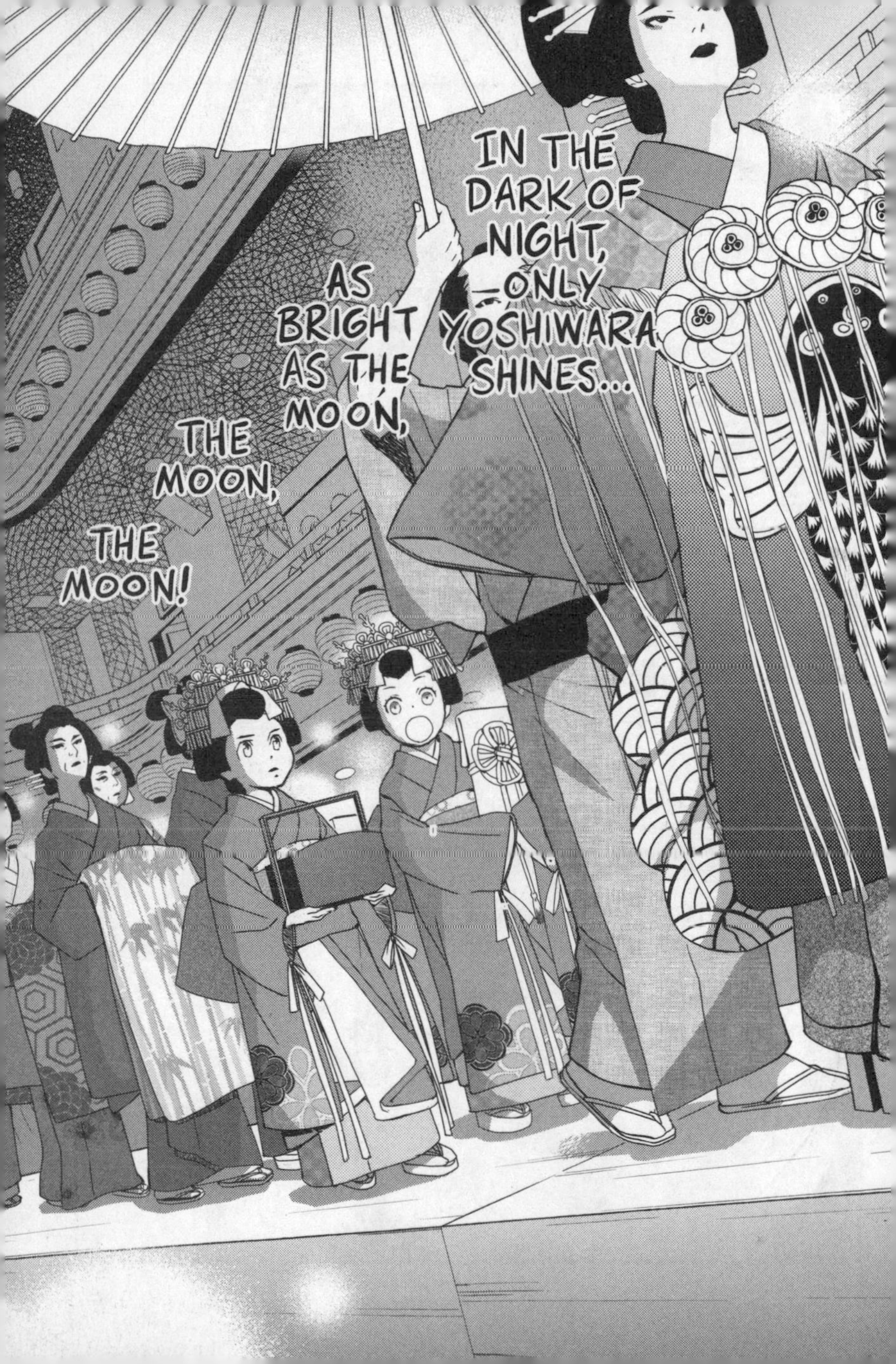
IN THE DARK OF NIGHT, ONLY YOSHIWARA SHINES...
AS BRIGHT AS THE MOON,
THE MOON,
THE MOON!

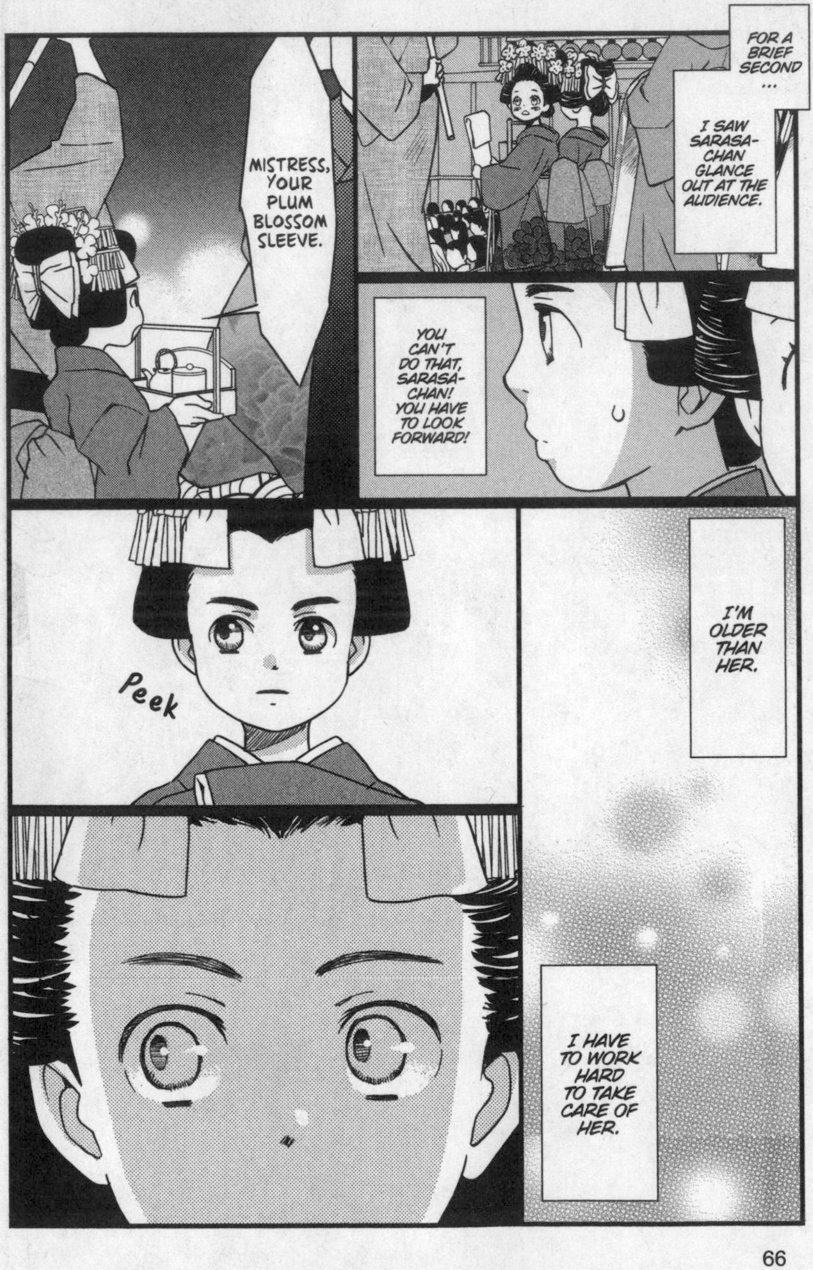
FOR A BRIEF SECOND ...
I SAW SARASA-CHAN GLANCE OUT AT THE AUDIENCE.
YOU CAN'T DO THAT, SARASA-CHAN! YOU HAVE TO LOOK FORWARD!
MISTRESS, YOUR PLUM BLOSSOM SLEEVE.
I'M OLDER THAN HER.
I HAVE TO WORK HARD TO TAKE CARE OF HER.
Peek

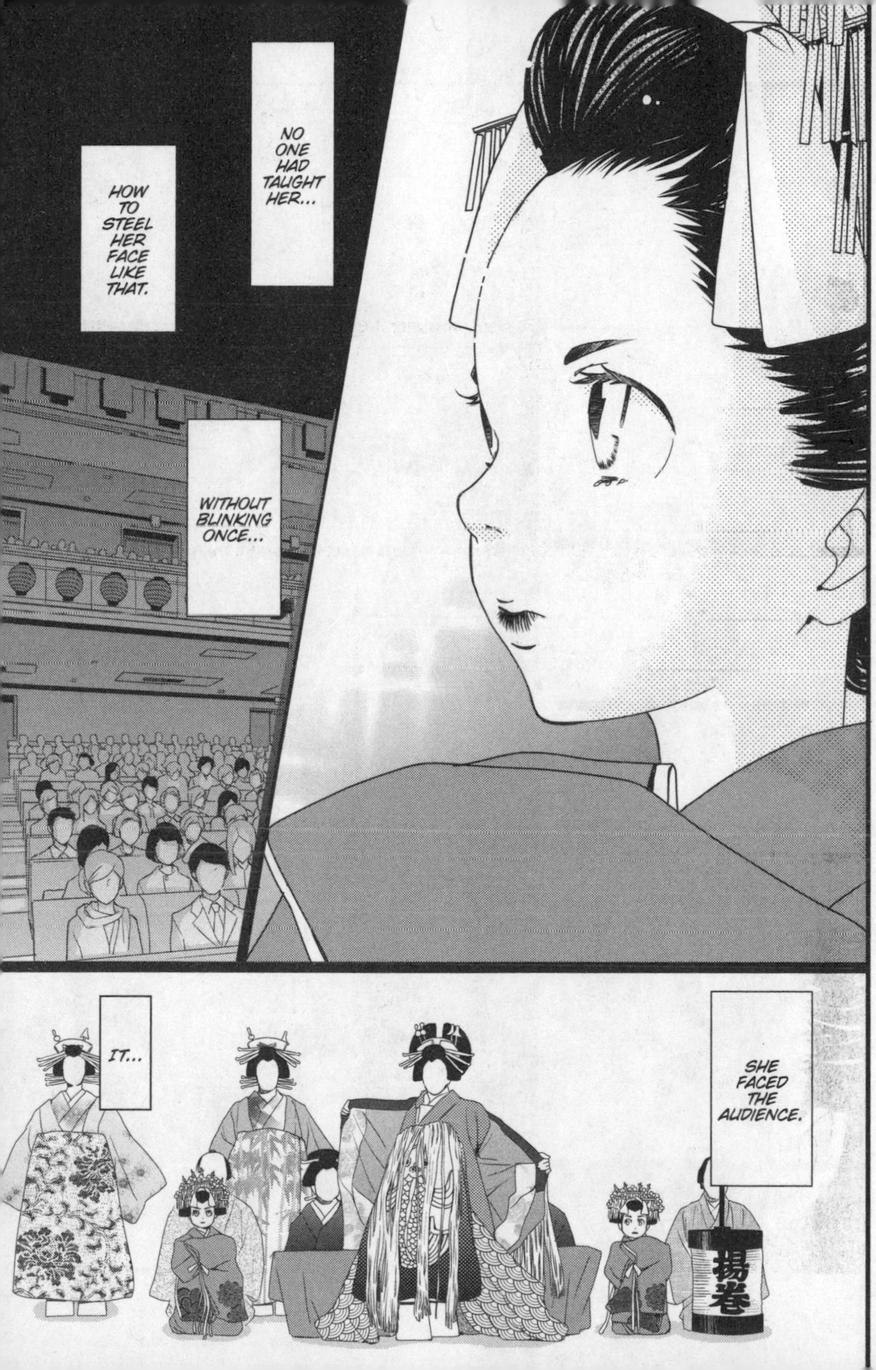
NO ONE HAD TAUGHT HER...
HOW TO STEEL HER FACE LIKE THAT.
WITHOUT BLINKING ONCE...
SHE FACED THE AUDIENCE.
揚巻
IT...

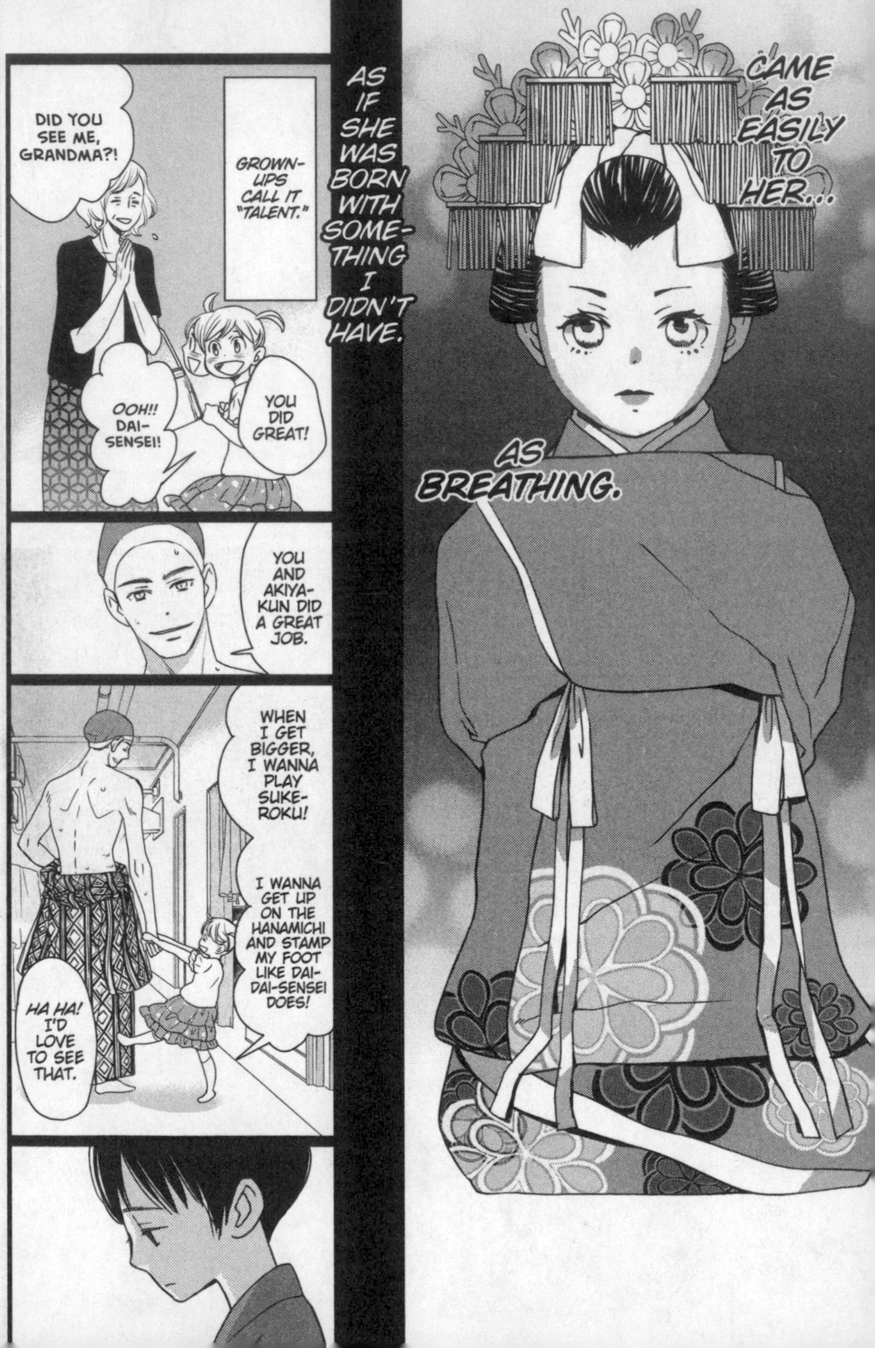
CAME AS EASILY TO HER...
AS BREATHING.
AS IF SHE WAS BORN WITH SOMETHING I DIDN'T HAVE.
GROWN-UPS CALL IT "TALENT."
DID YOU SEE ME, GRANDMA?!
YOU DID GREAT!
OOH!! DAI-SENSEI!
YOU AND AKIYA-KUN DID A GREAT JOB.
WHEN I GET BIGGER, I WANNA PLAY SUKE-ROKU!
I WANNA GET UP ON THE HANAMICHI AND STAMP MY FOOT LIKE DAI-DAI-SENSEI DOES!
HA HA! I'D LOVE TO SEE THAT.

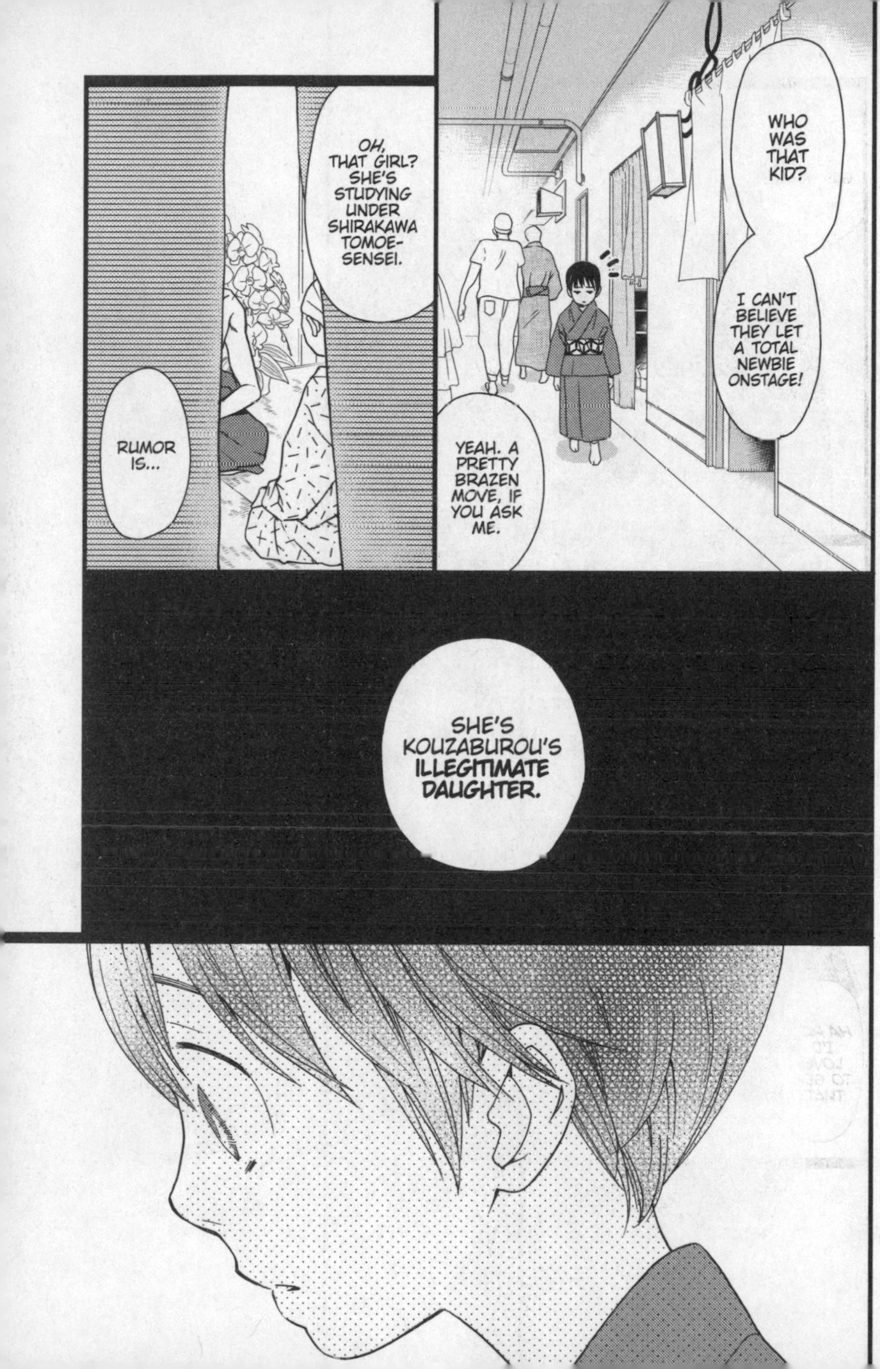
WHO WAS THAT KID?
I CAN'T BELIEVE THEY LET A TOTAL NEWBIE ONSTAGE!
YEAH. A PRETTY BRAZEN MOVE, IF YOU ASK ME.
OH, THAT GIRL? SHE'S STUDYING UNDER SHIRAKAWA TOMOE-SENSEI.
RUMOR IS...
SHE'S KOUZABUROU'S **ILLEGITIMATE DAUGHTER.**

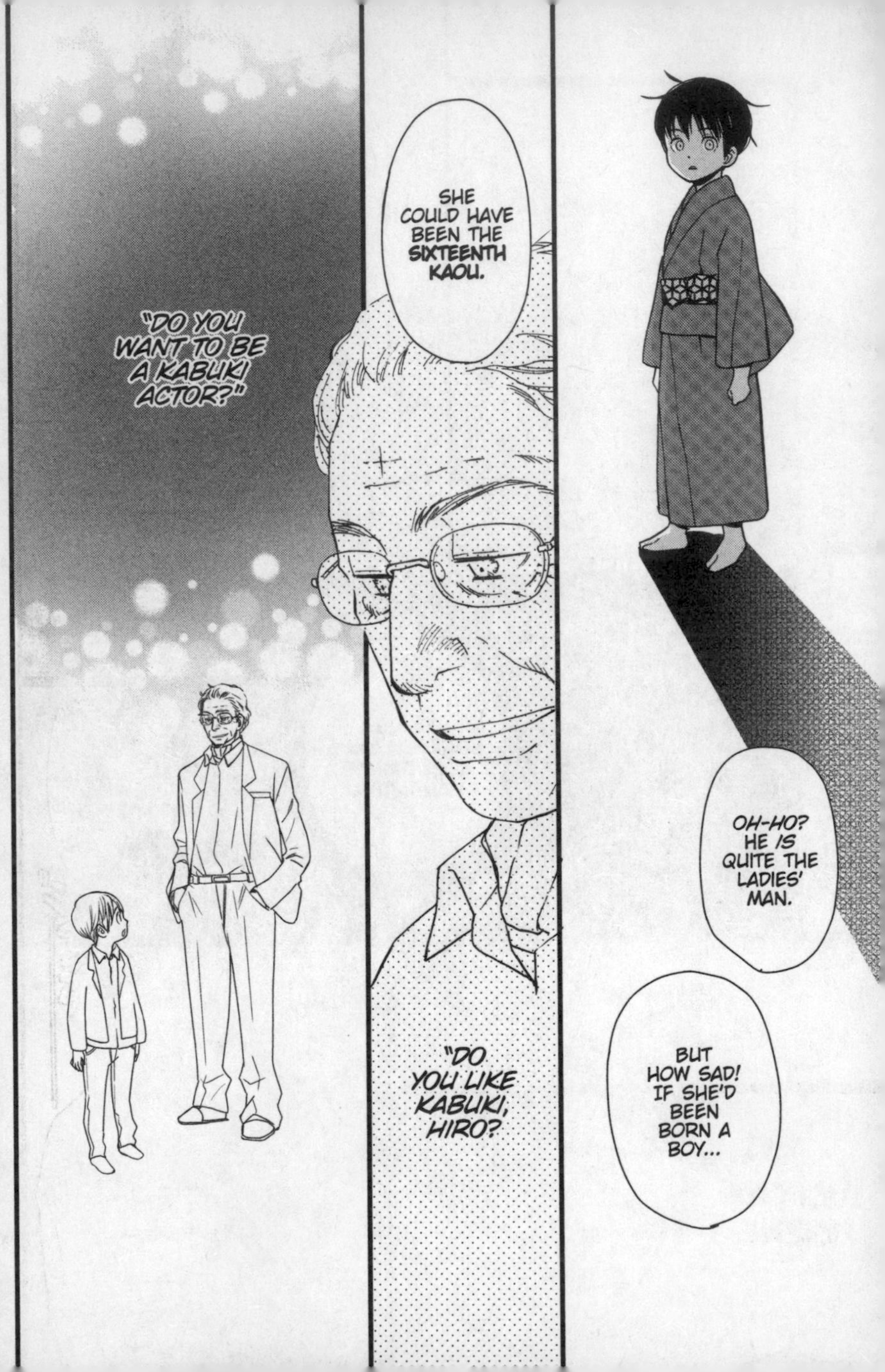
OH-HO? HE IS QUITE THE LADIES' MAN.
BUT HOW SAD! IF SHE'D BEEN BORN A BOY...
SHE COULD HAVE BEEN THE SIXTEENTH KAOU.
"DO YOU LIKE KABUKI, HIRO?
"DO YOU WANT TO BE A KABUKI ACTOR?"

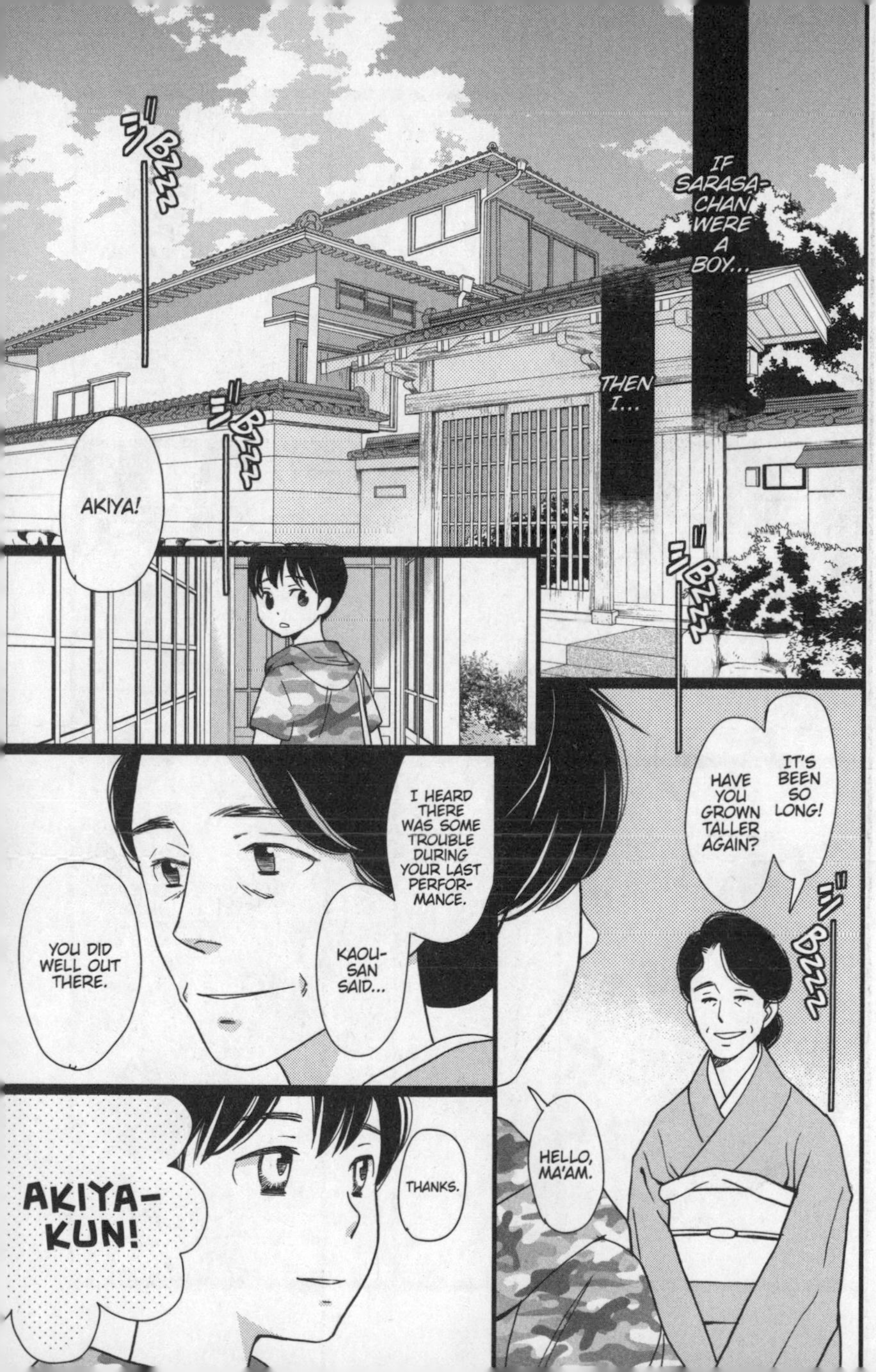
IF SARASA-CHAN WERE A BOY...
THEN I...
BZZZ
BZZZ
BZZZ
AKIYA!
IT'S BEEN SO LONG!
HAVE YOU GROWN TALLER AGAIN?
BZZZ
HELLO, MA'AM.
I HEARD THERE WAS SOME TROUBLE DURING YOUR LAST PERFORMANCE.
KAOU-SAN SAID...
YOU DID WELL OUT THERE.
THANKS.
AKIYA-KUN!

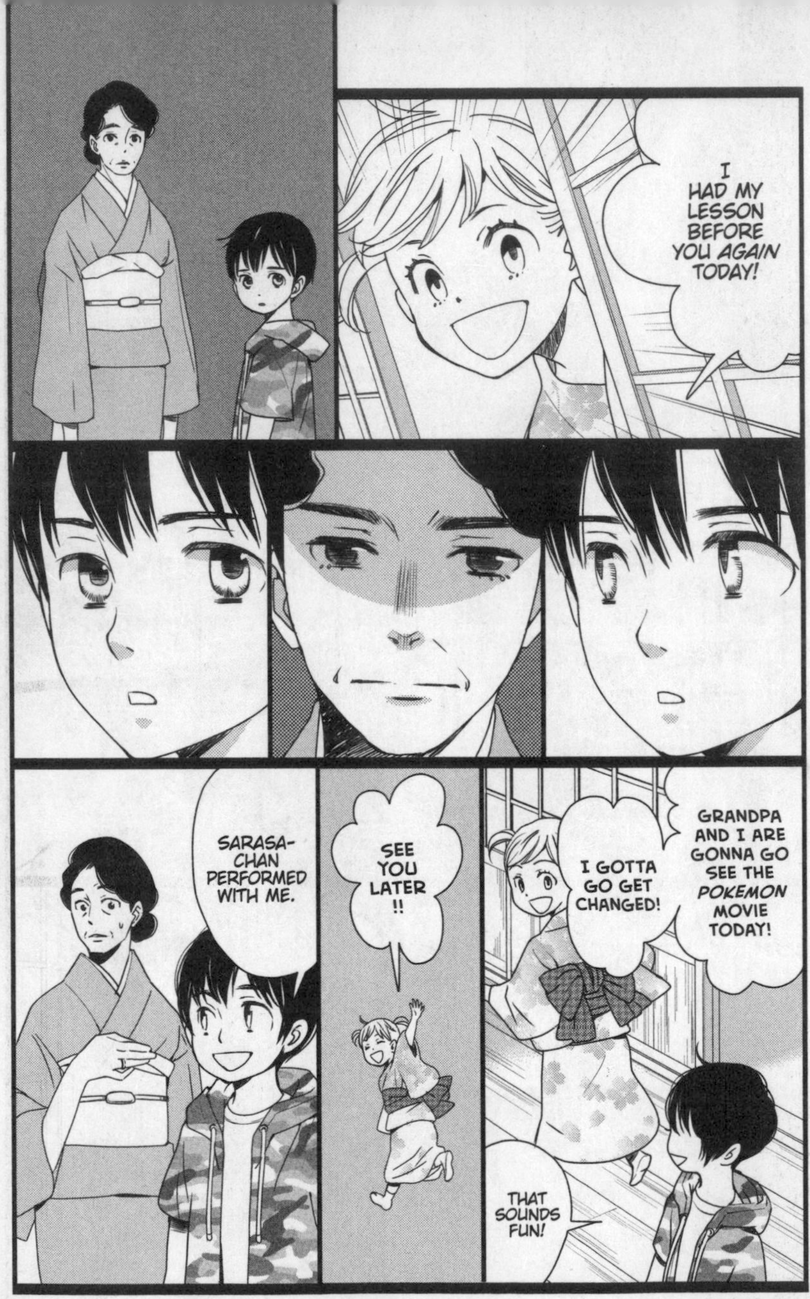
I HAD MY LESSON BEFORE YOU *AGAIN* TODAY!
GRANDPA AND I ARE GONNA GO SEE THE *POKEMON* MOVIE TODAY!
I GOTTA GO GET CHANGED!
THAT SOUNDS FUN!
SEE YOU LATER !!
SARASA-CHAN PERFORMED WITH ME.

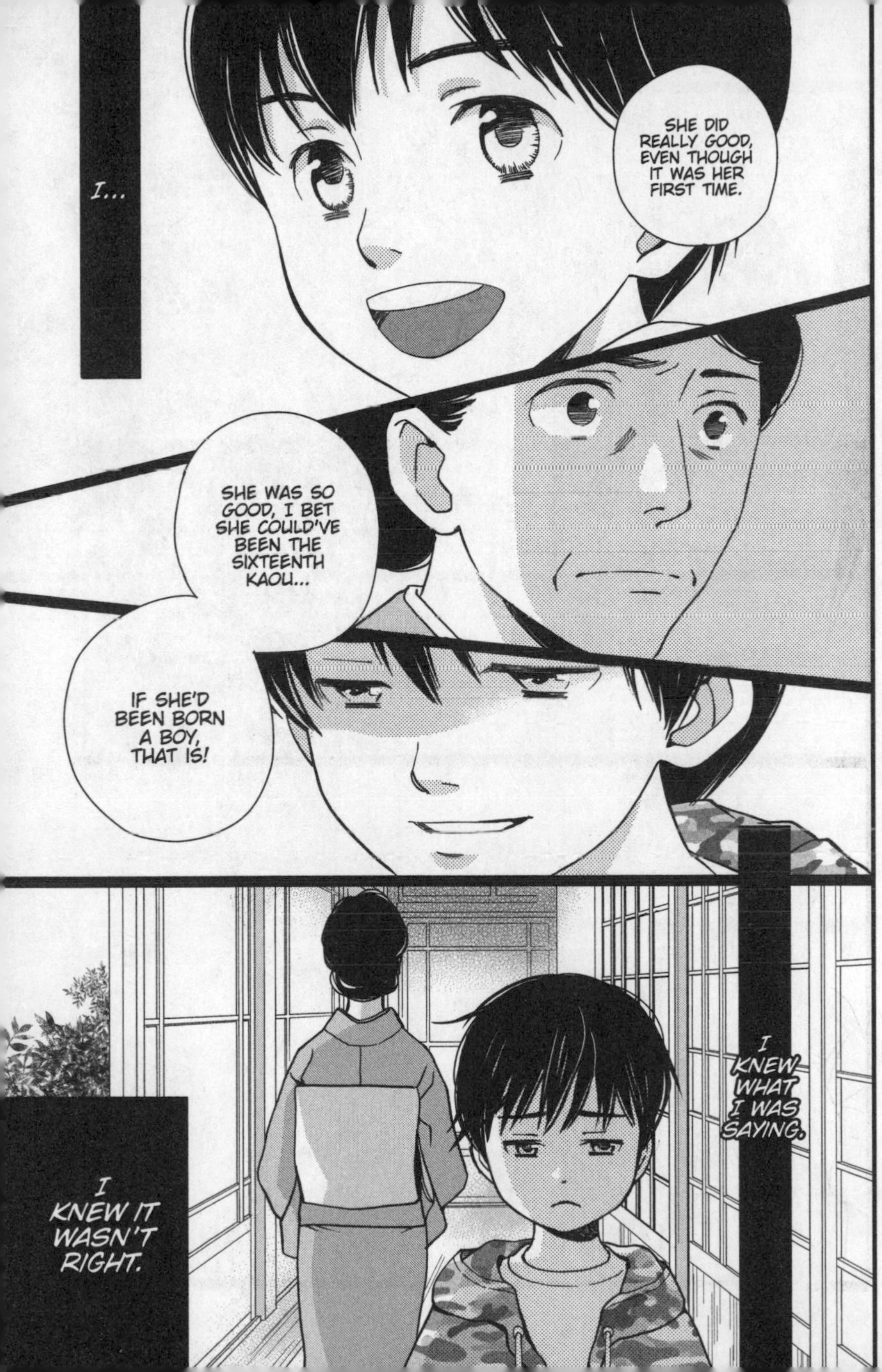
SHE DID REALLY GOOD, EVEN THOUGH IT WAS HER FIRST TIME.
I...
SHE WAS SO GOOD, I BET SHE COULD'VE BEEN THE SIXTEENTH KAOU...
IF SHE'D BEEN BORN A BOY, THAT IS!
I KNEW WHAT I WAS SAYING.
I KNEW IT WASN'T RIGHT.

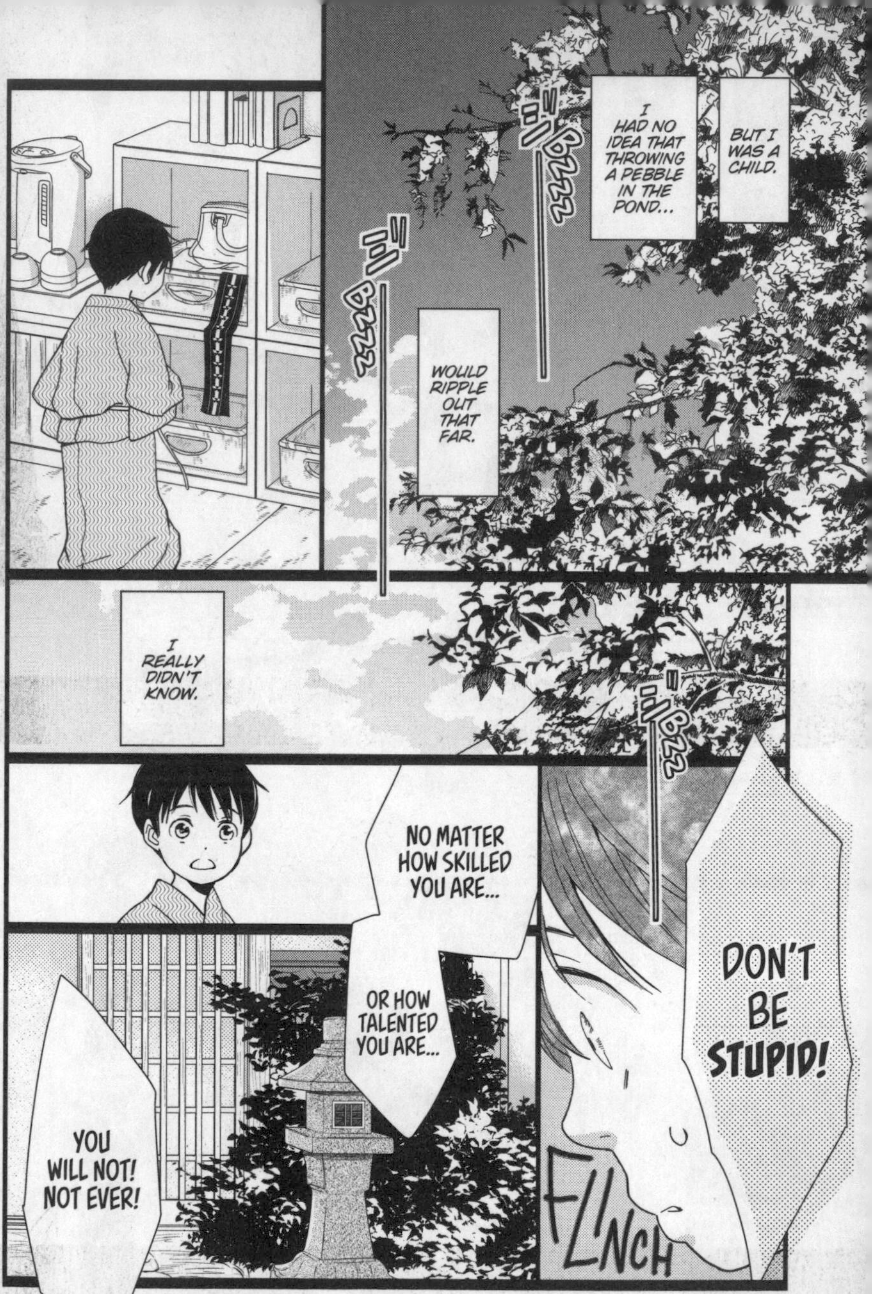
BUT I WAS A CHILD.
I HAD NO IDEA THAT THROWING A PEBBLE IN THE POND...
BZZZ
BZZZ
WOULD RIPPLE OUT THAT FAR.
I REALLY DIDN'T KNOW.
BZZ
DON'T BE STUPID!
FLINCH
NO MATTER HOW SKILLED YOU ARE...
OR HOW TALENTED YOU ARE...
YOU WILL NOT! NOT EVER!

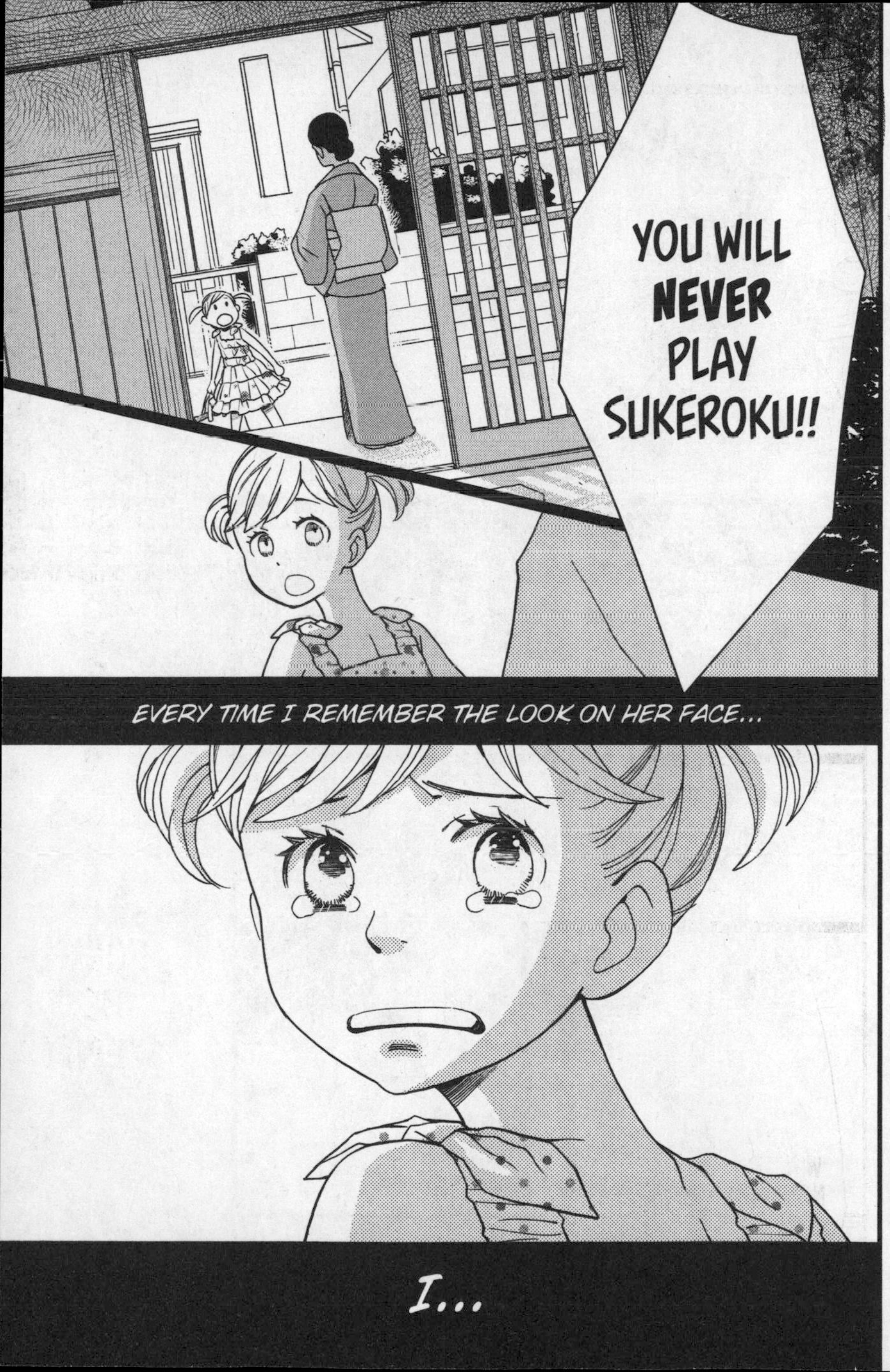
YOU WILL NEVER PLAY SUKEROKU!!
EVERY TIME I REMEMBER THE LOOK ON HER FACE...
I...

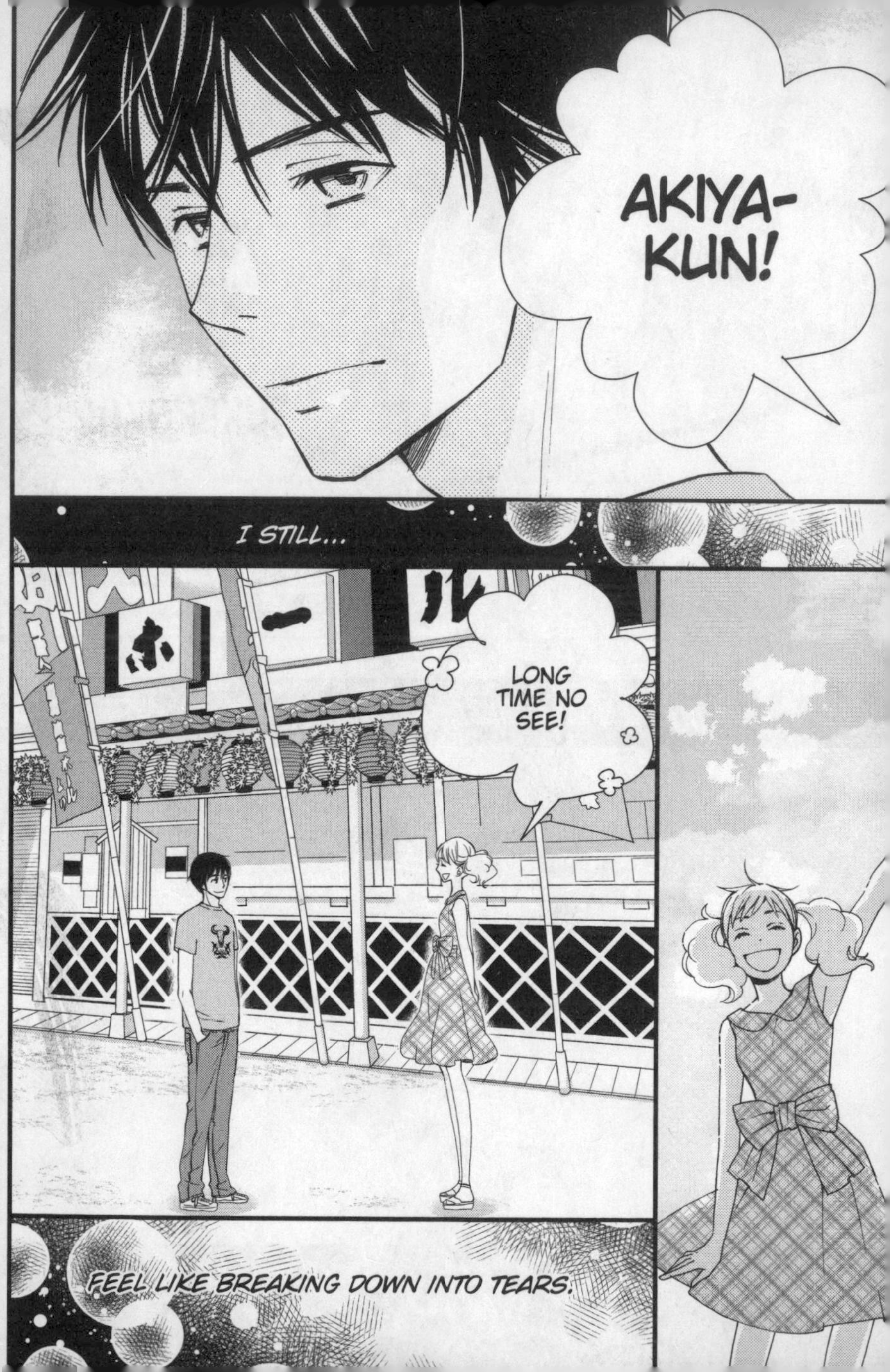
AKIYA-KUN!
I STILL...
LONG TIME NO SEE!
FEEL LIKE BREAKING DOWN INTO TEARS.

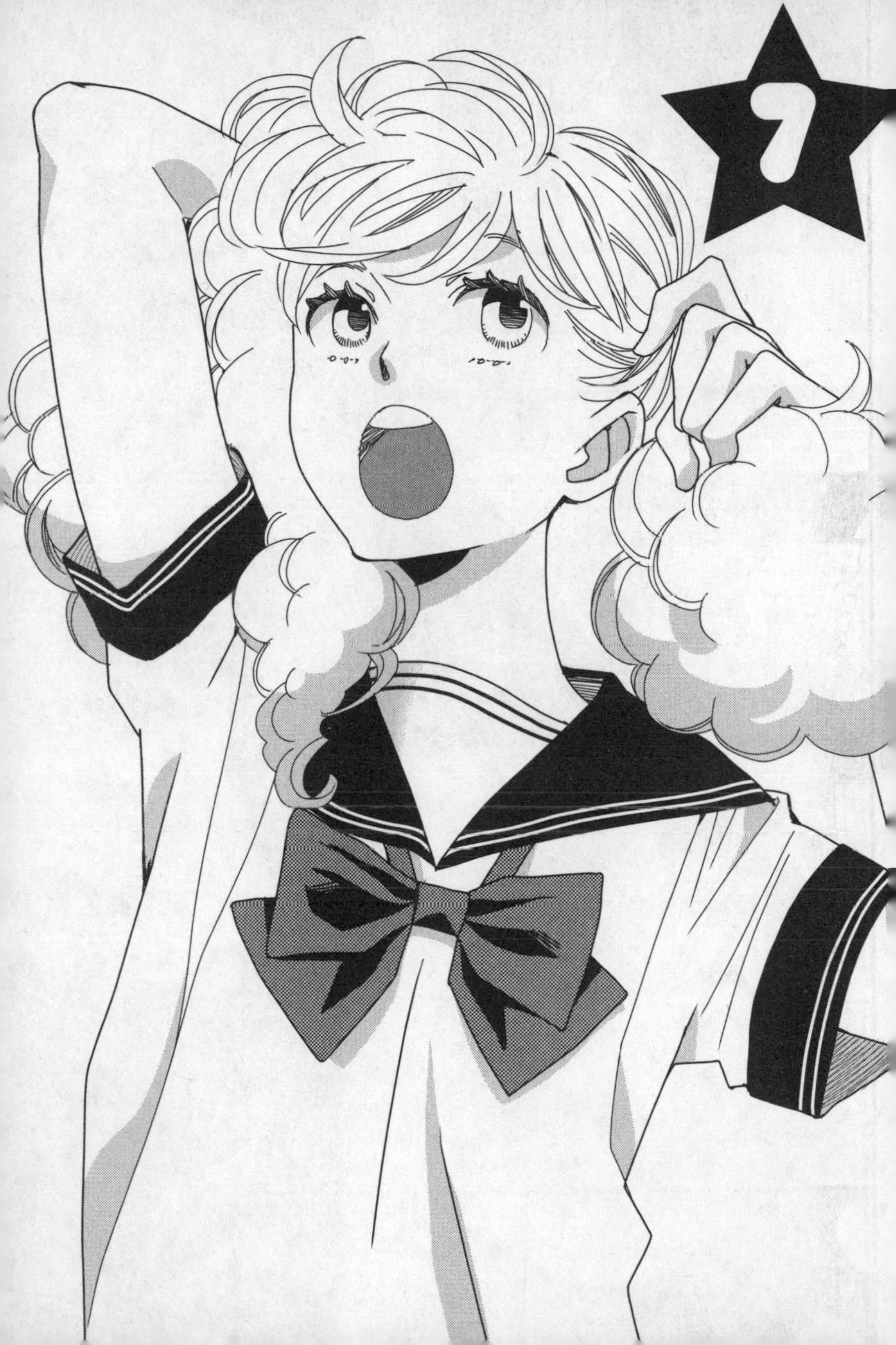
7

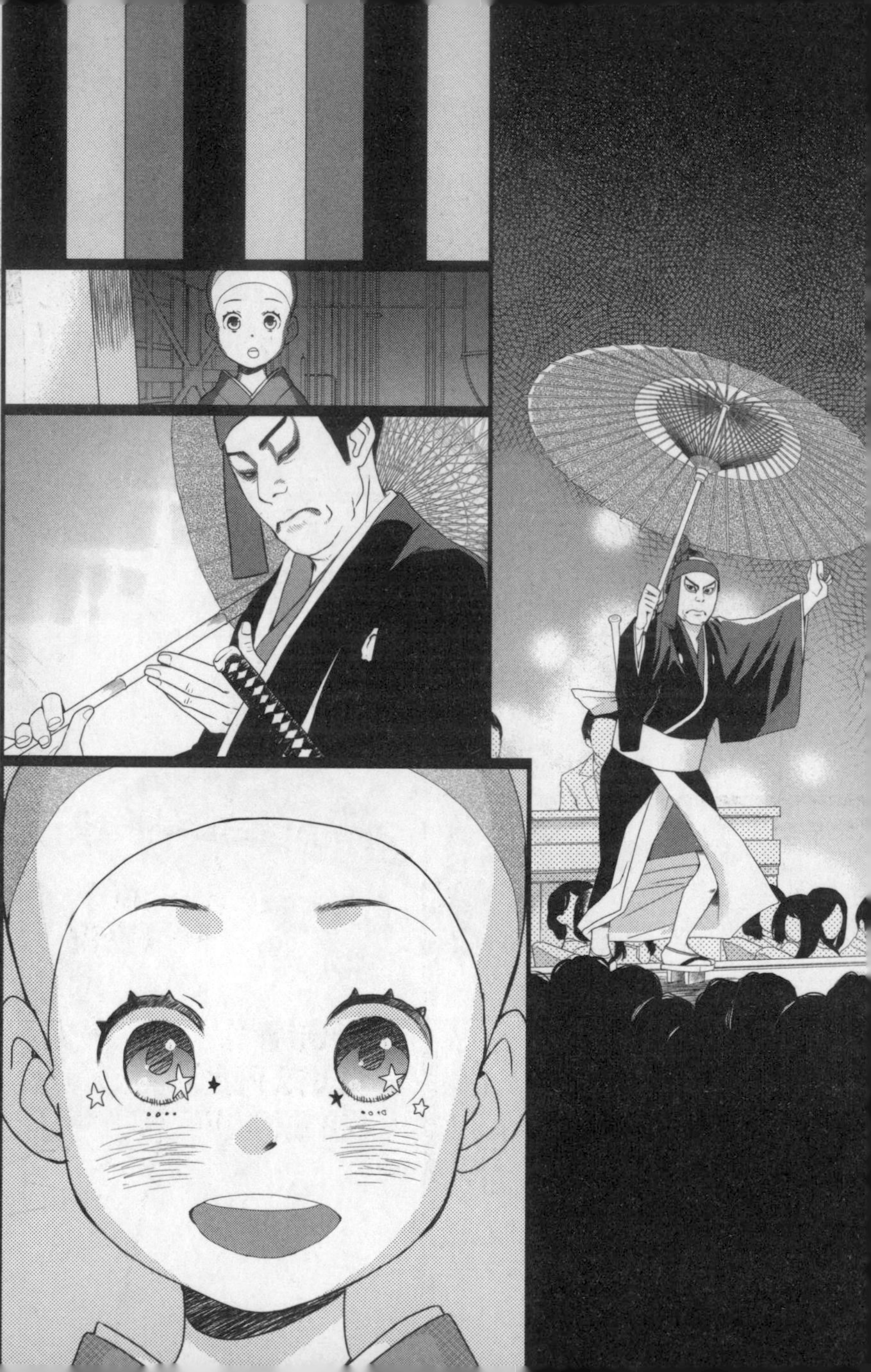

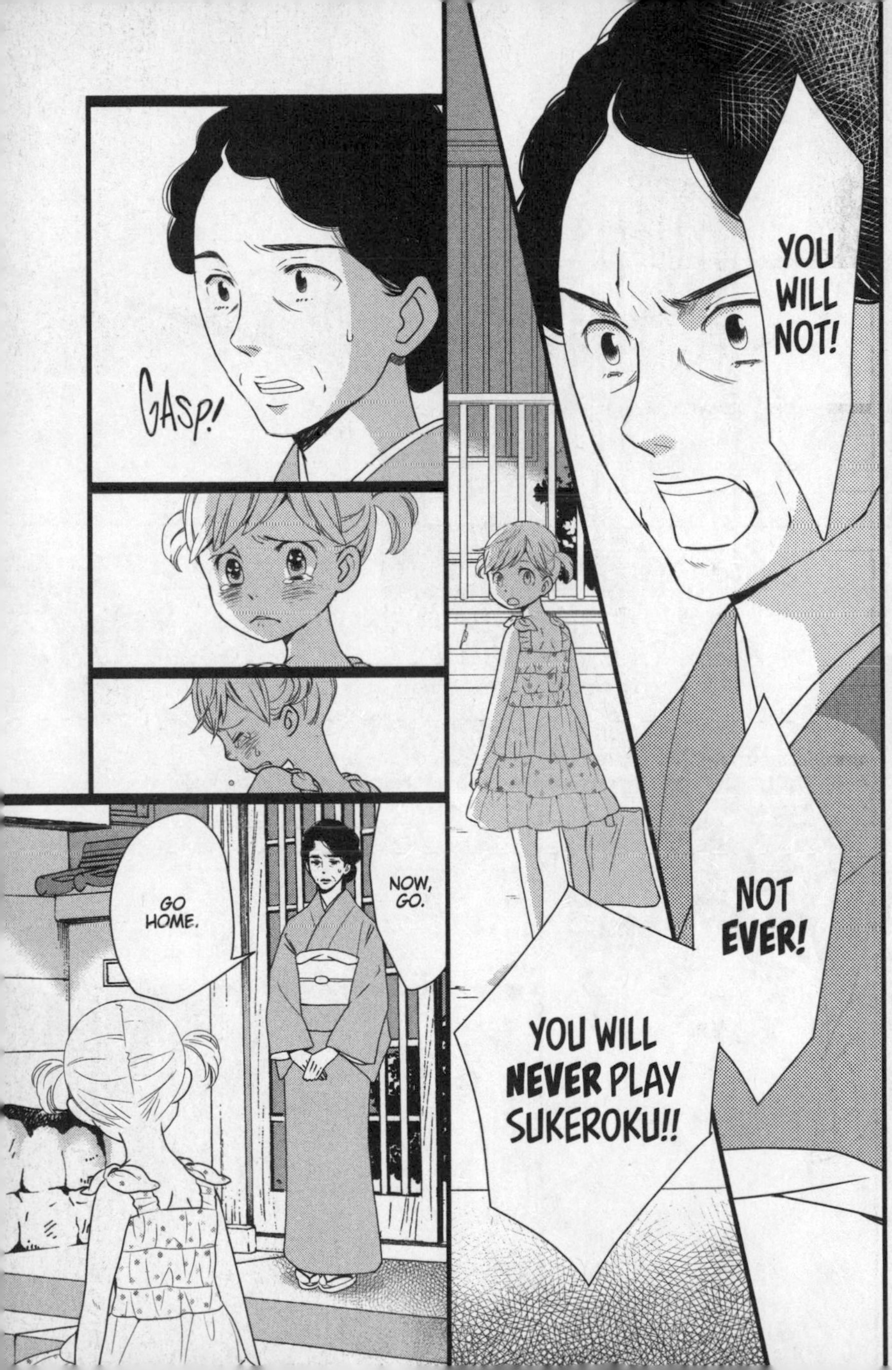
YOU WILL NOT!
NOT EVER!
YOU WILL NEVER PLAY SUKEROKU!!
GASP!
NOW, GO.
GO HOME.

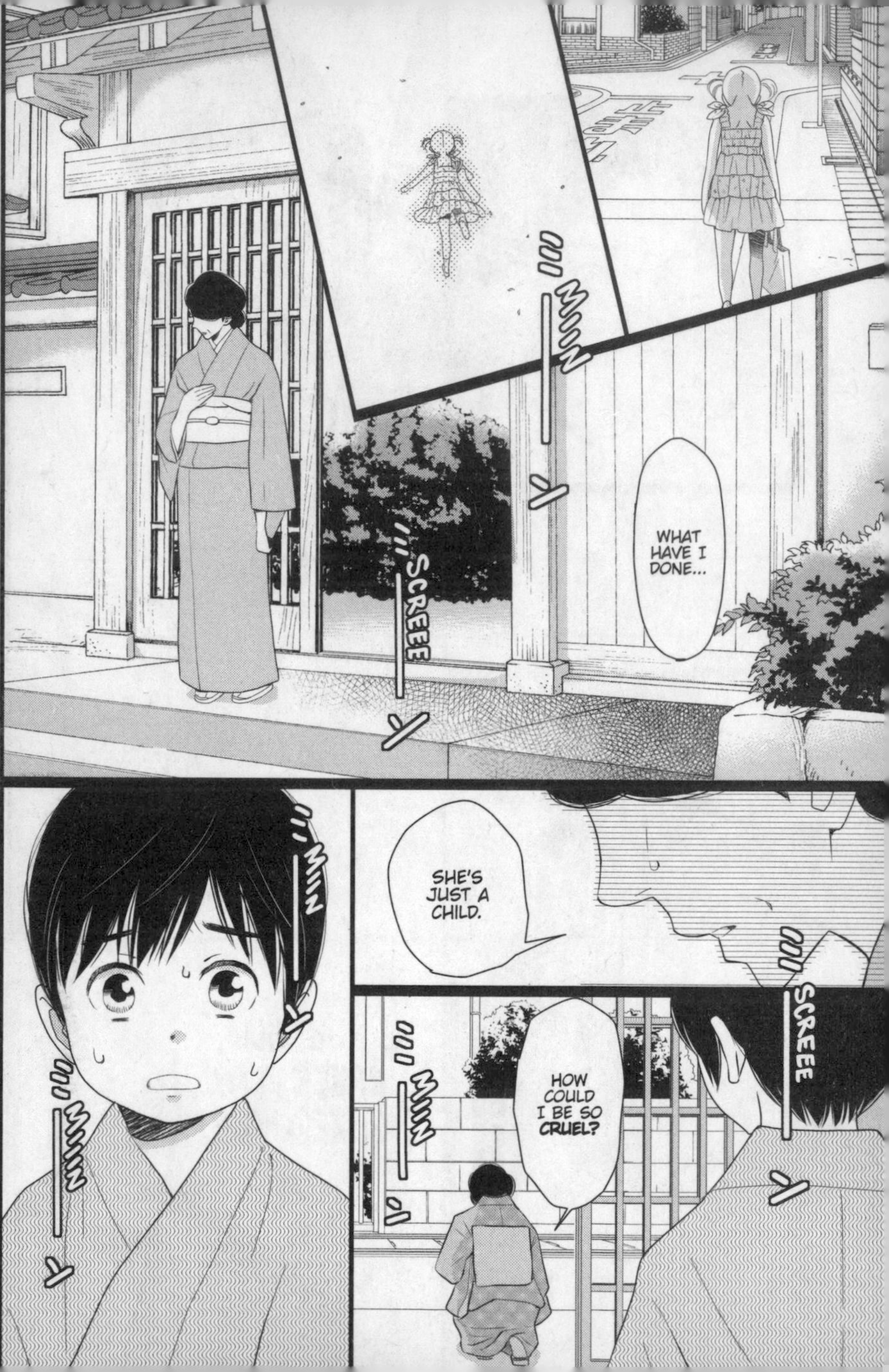

MIIN
WHAT HAVE I DONE...
SCREEE
SHE'S JUST A CHILD.
SCREEE
HOW COULD I BE SO CRUEL?
MIIN
MIIN
MIIN

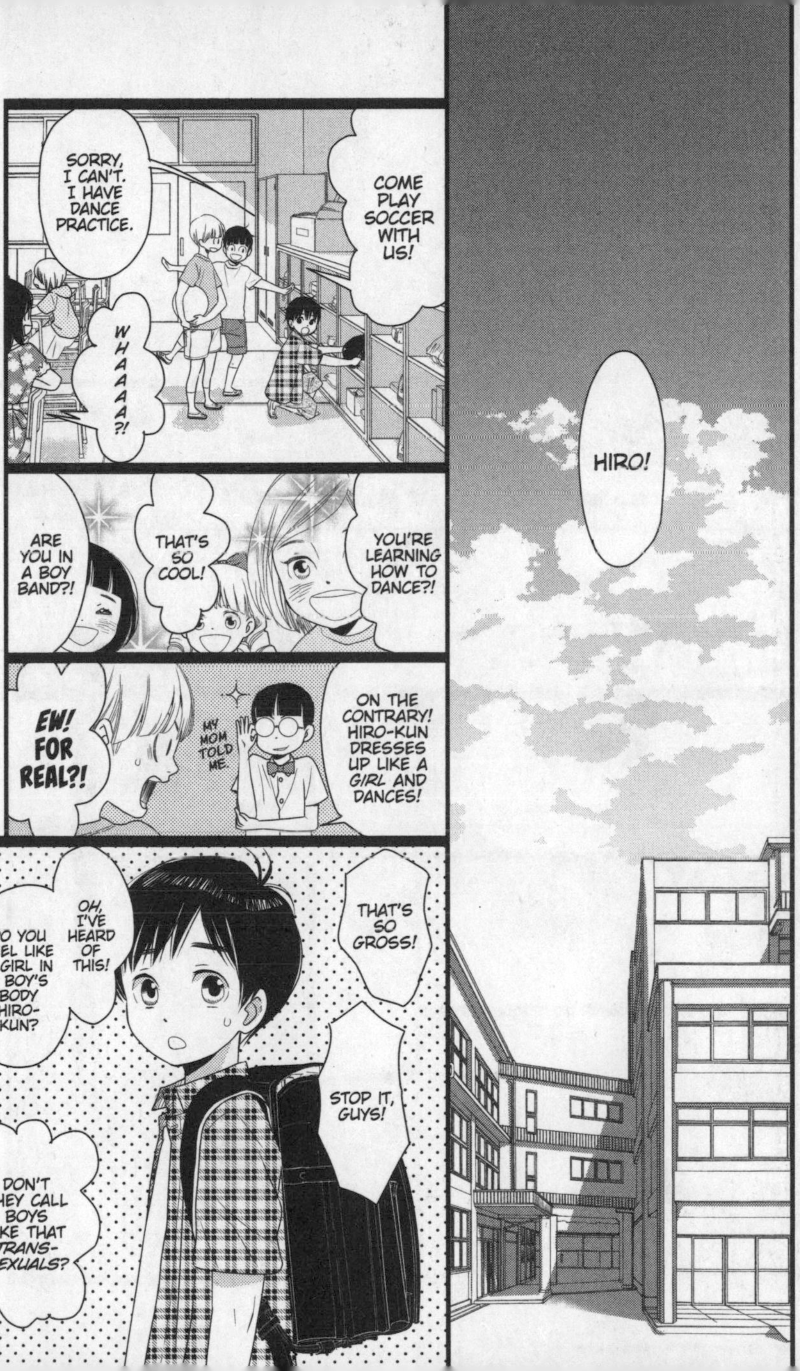
HIRO!
COME PLAY SOCCER WITH US!
SORRY, I CAN'T. I HAVE DANCE PRACTICE.
WHAAAAA?!
YOU'RE LEARNING HOW TO DANCE?!
THAT'S SO COOL!
ARE YOU IN A BOY BAND?!
ON THE CONTRARY! HIRO-KUN DRESSES UP LIKE A *GIRL* AND DANCES!
MY MOM TOLD ME.
EW! FOR REAL?!
THAT'S SO GROSS!
OH, I'VE HEARD OF THIS!
DO YOU FEEL LIKE A GIRL IN A BOY'S BODY HIRO-KUN?
STOP IT, GUYS!
DON'T THEY CALL BOYS LIKE THAT *TRANS-SEXUALS*?

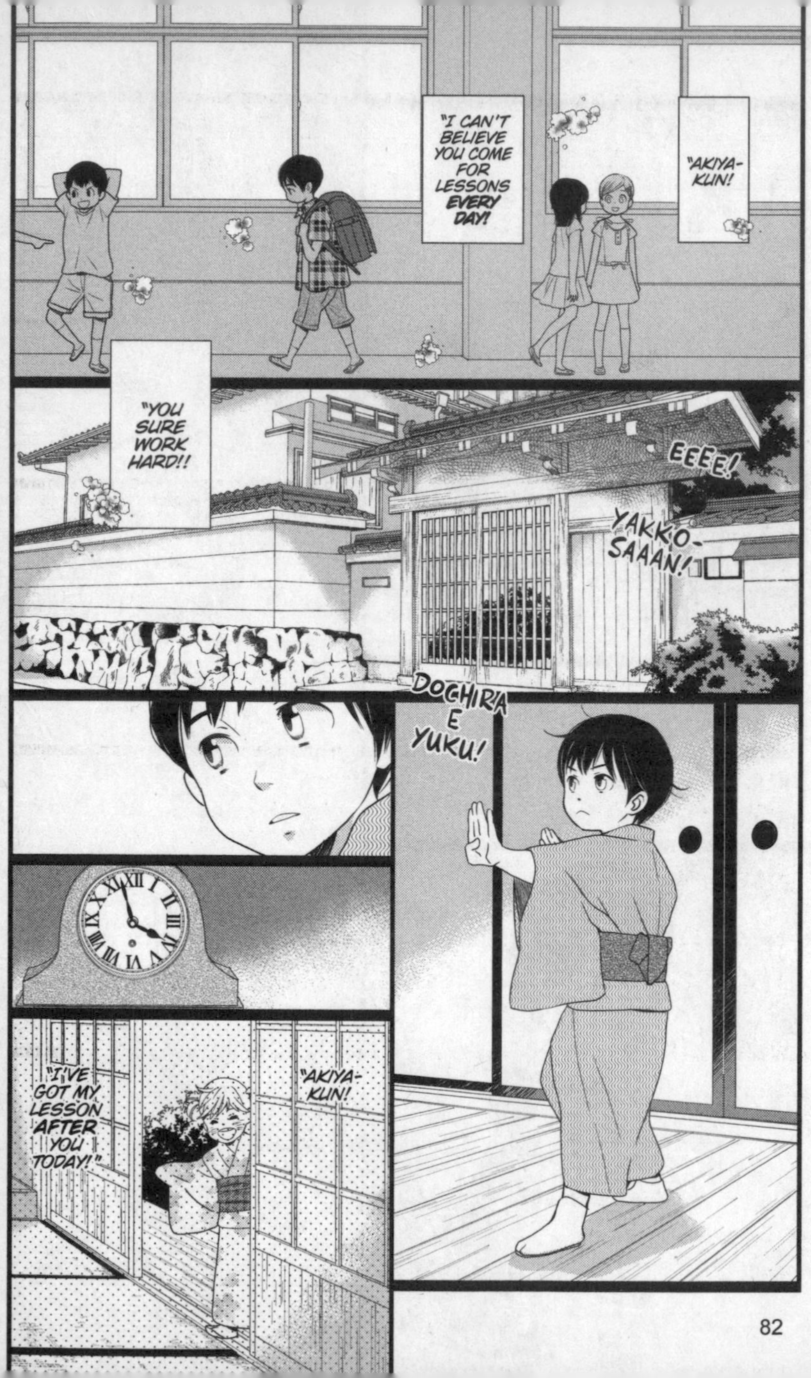
"AKIYA-KUN!
"I CAN'T BELIEVE YOU COME FOR LESSONS EVERY DAY!
"YOU SURE WORK HARD!!
EEEE!
YAKKO-SAAAN!
DOCHIRA E YUKU!
"AKIYA-KUN!
"I'VE GOT MY LESSON AFTER YOU TODAY!"

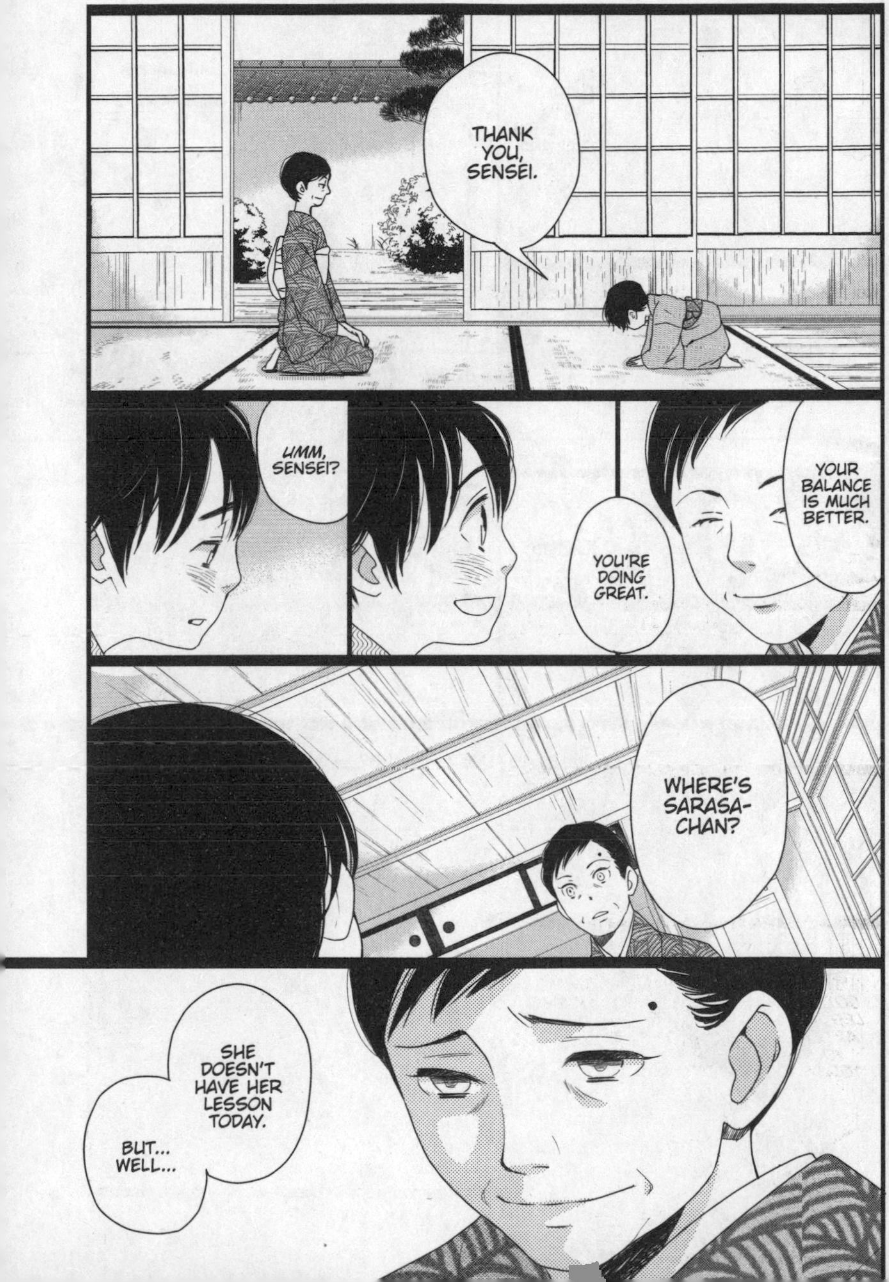
THANK YOU, SENSEI.
YOUR BALANCE IS MUCH BETTER.
YOU'RE DOING GREAT.
UMM, SENSEI?
WHERE'S SARASA-CHAN?
SHE DOESN'T HAVE HER LESSON TODAY.
BUT... WELL...

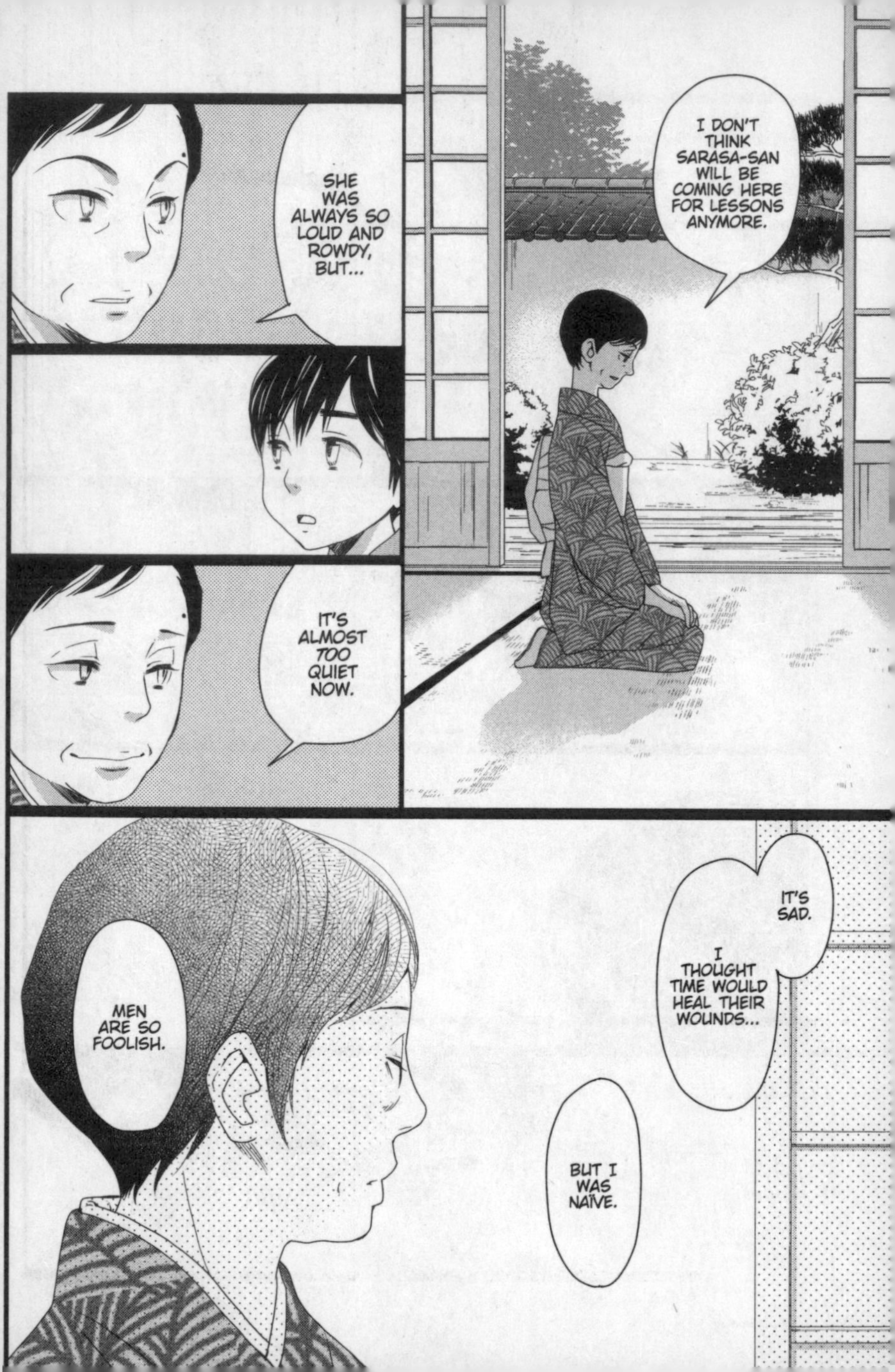
I DON'T THINK SARASA-SAN WILL BE COMING HERE FOR LESSONS ANYMORE.
SHE WAS ALWAYS SO LOUD AND ROWDY, BUT...
IT'S ALMOST *TOO* QUIET NOW.
IT'S SAD.
I THOUGHT TIME WOULD HEAL THEIR WOUNDS...
BUT I WAS NAÏVE.
MEN ARE SO FOOLISH.

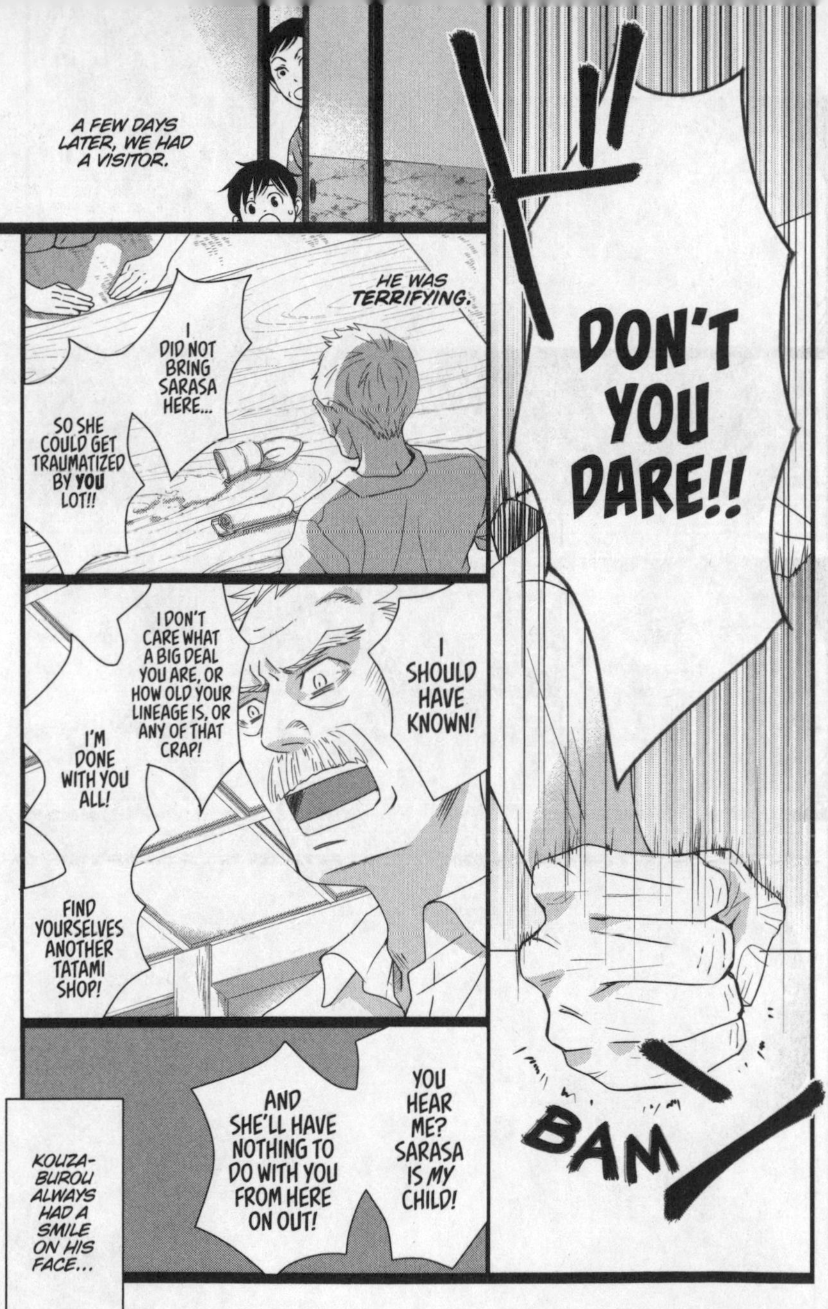
DON'T YOU DARE!!
BAM
A FEW DAYS LATER, WE HAD A VISITOR.
HE WAS TERRIFYING.
I DID NOT BRING SARASA HERE...
SO SHE COULD GET TRAUMATIZED BY **YOU** LOT!!
I SHOULD HAVE KNOWN!
I DON'T CARE WHAT A BIG DEAL YOU ARE, OR HOW OLD YOUR LINEAGE IS, OR ANY OF THAT CRAP!
I'M DONE WITH YOU ALL!
FIND YOURSELVES ANOTHER TATAMI SHOP!
YOU HEAR ME? SARASA IS *MY* CHILD!
AND SHE'LL HAVE NOTHING TO DO WITH YOU FROM HERE ON OUT!
KOUZABUROU ALWAYS HAD A SMILE ON HIS FACE...

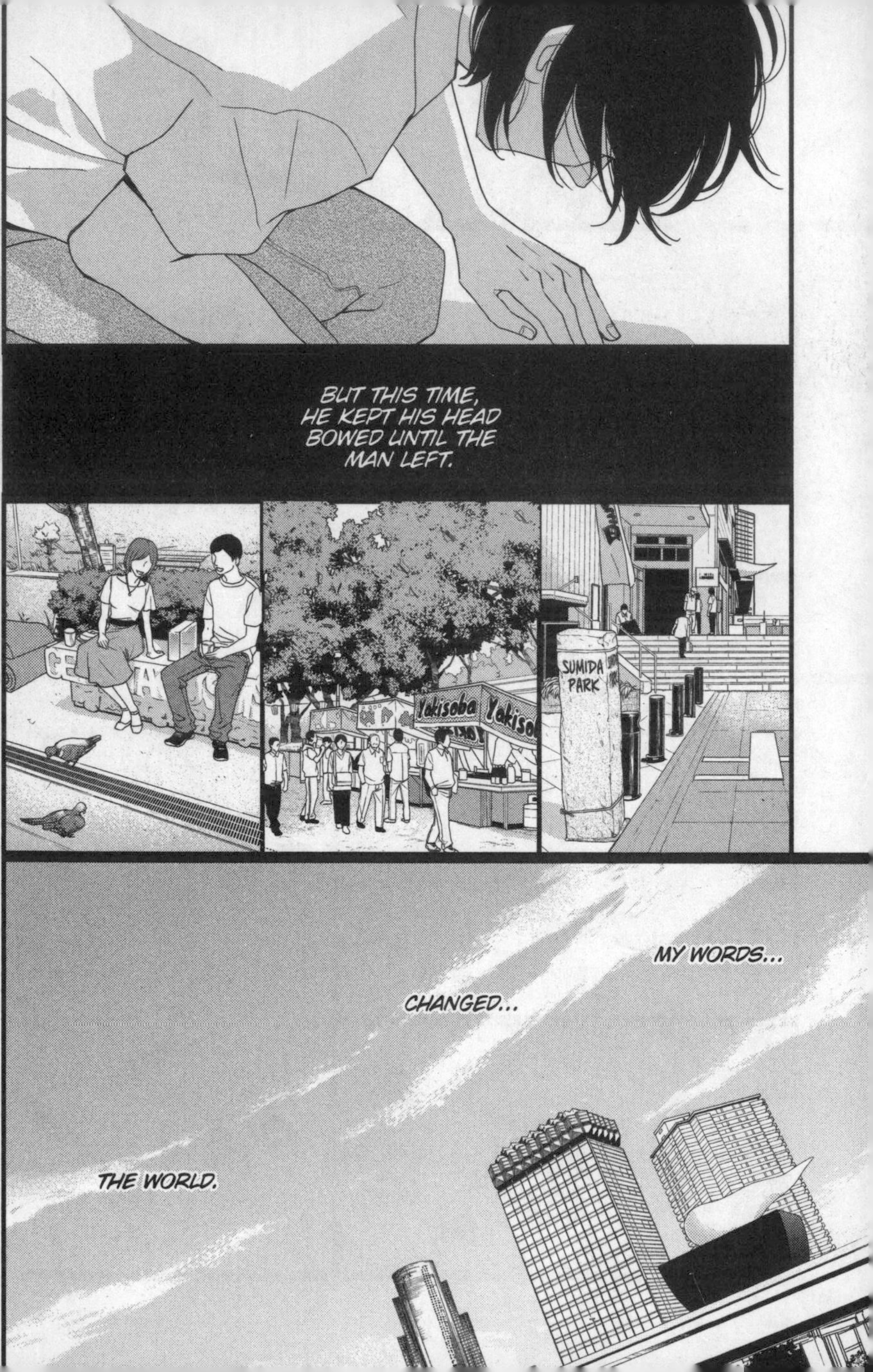
BUT THIS TIME, HE KEPT HIS HEAD BOWED UNTIL THE MAN LEFT.
SUMIDA PARK
Yakisoba
MY WORDS...
CHANGED...
THE WORLD.

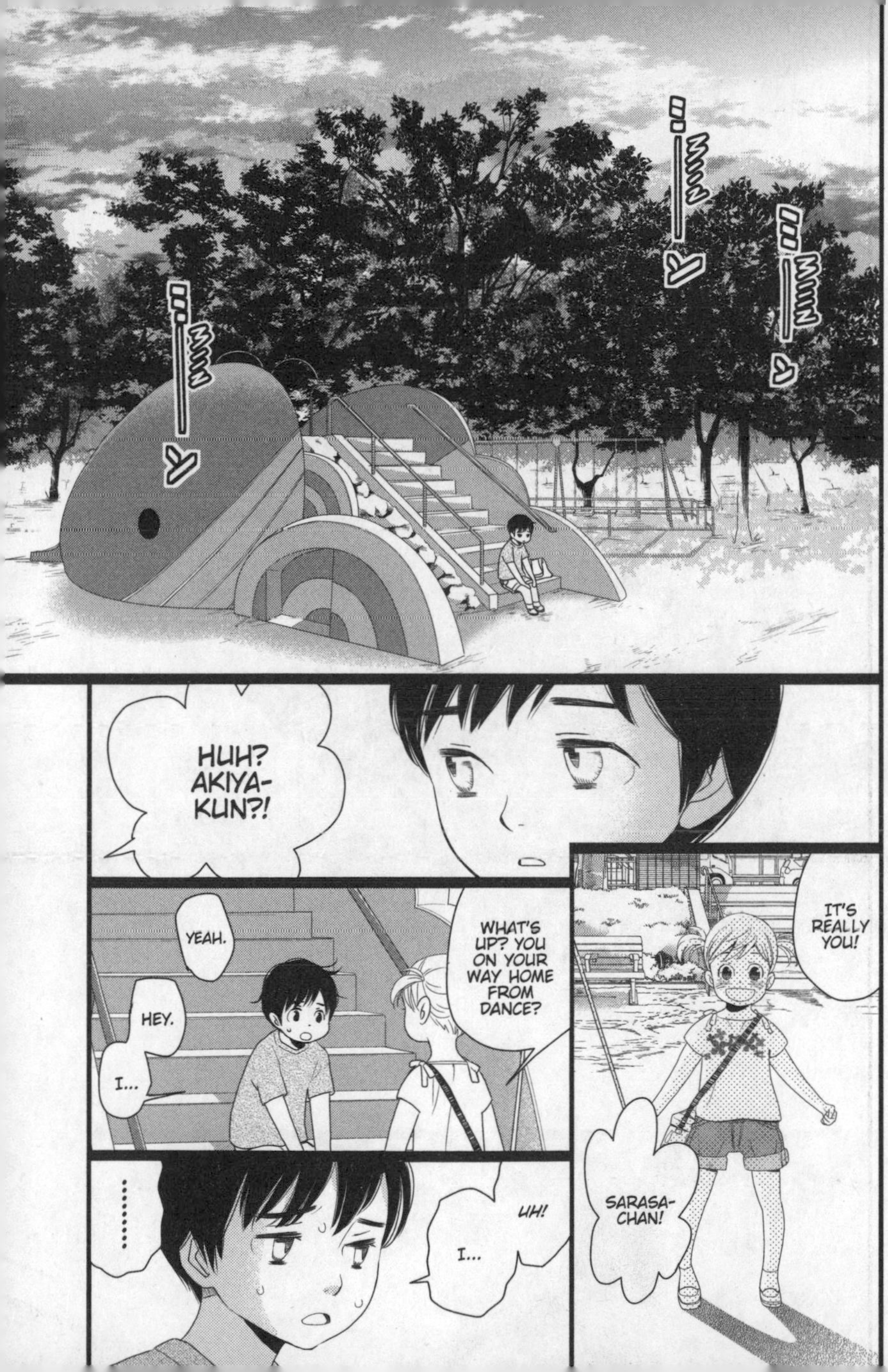
MIIN—...
MIIN—...
MIIN—...
HUH? AKIYA-KUN?!
IT'S REALLY YOU!
SARASA-CHAN!
WHAT'S UP? YOU ON YOUR WAY HOME FROM DANCE?
YEAH.
HEY.
I...
UH!
I...
......

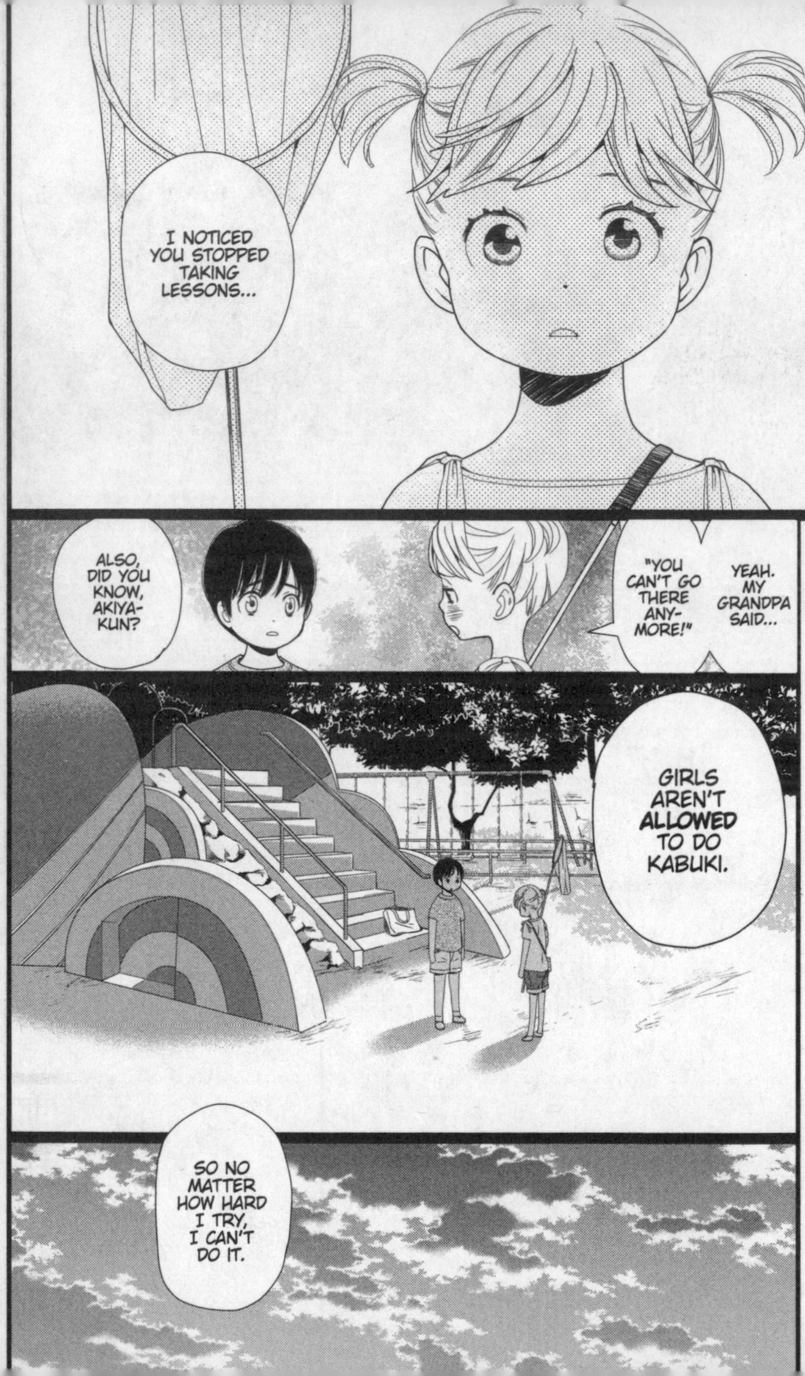
I NOTICED YOU STOPPED TAKING LESSONS...
YEAH. MY GRANDPA SAID...
"YOU CAN'T GO THERE ANYMORE!"
ALSO, DID YOU KNOW, AKIYA-KUN?
GIRLS AREN'T **ALLOWED** TO DO KABUKI.
SO NO MATTER HOW HARD I TRY, I CAN'T DO IT.

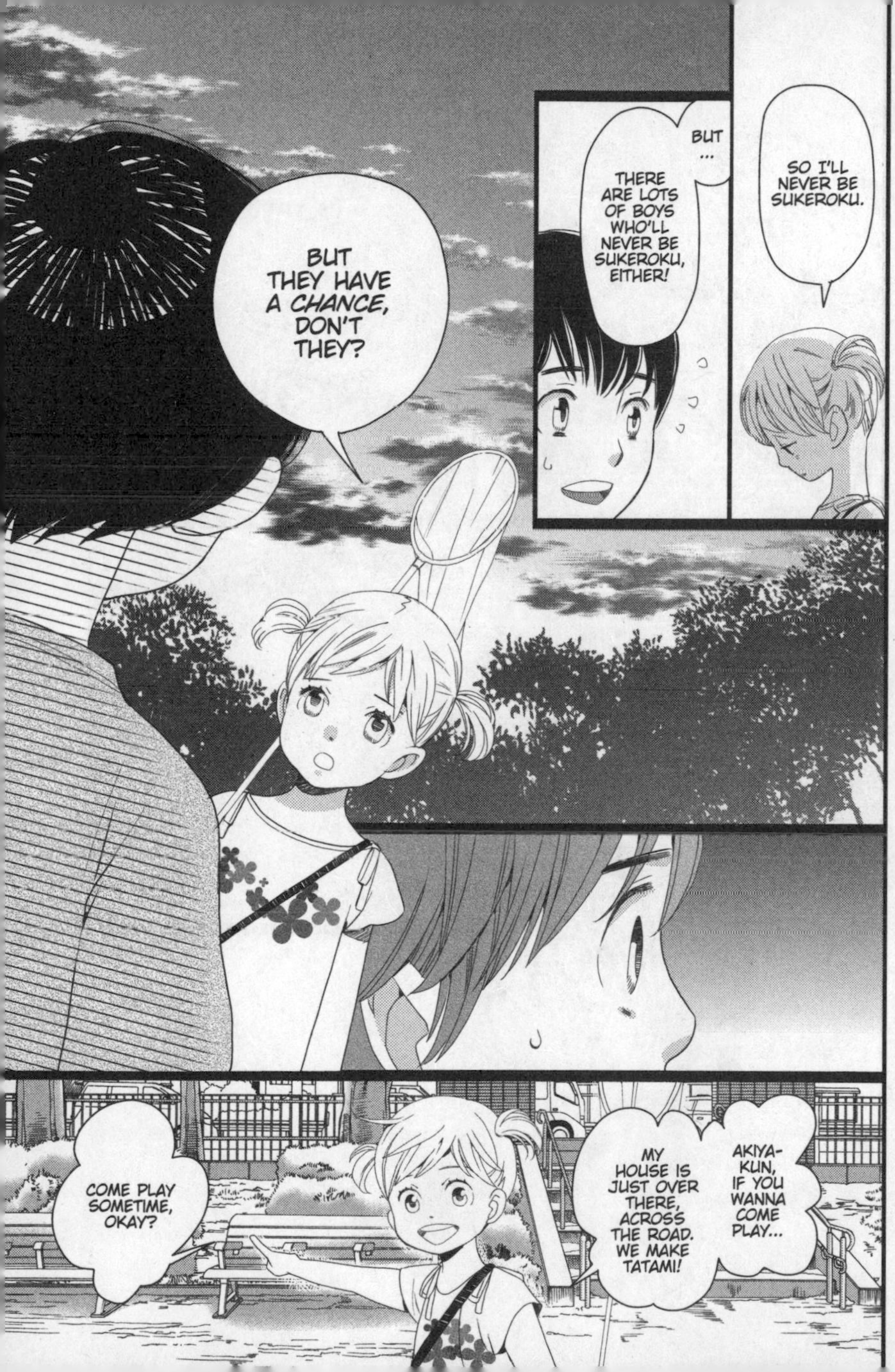
SO I'LL NEVER BE SUKEROKU.
BUT ...
THERE ARE LOTS OF BOYS WHO'LL NEVER BE SUKEROKU, EITHER!
BUT THEY HAVE A *CHANCE*, DON'T THEY?
AKIYA-KUN, IF YOU WANNA COME PLAY...
MY HOUSE IS JUST OVER THERE, ACROSS THE ROAD. WE MAKE TATAMI!
COME PLAY SOMETIME, OKAY?

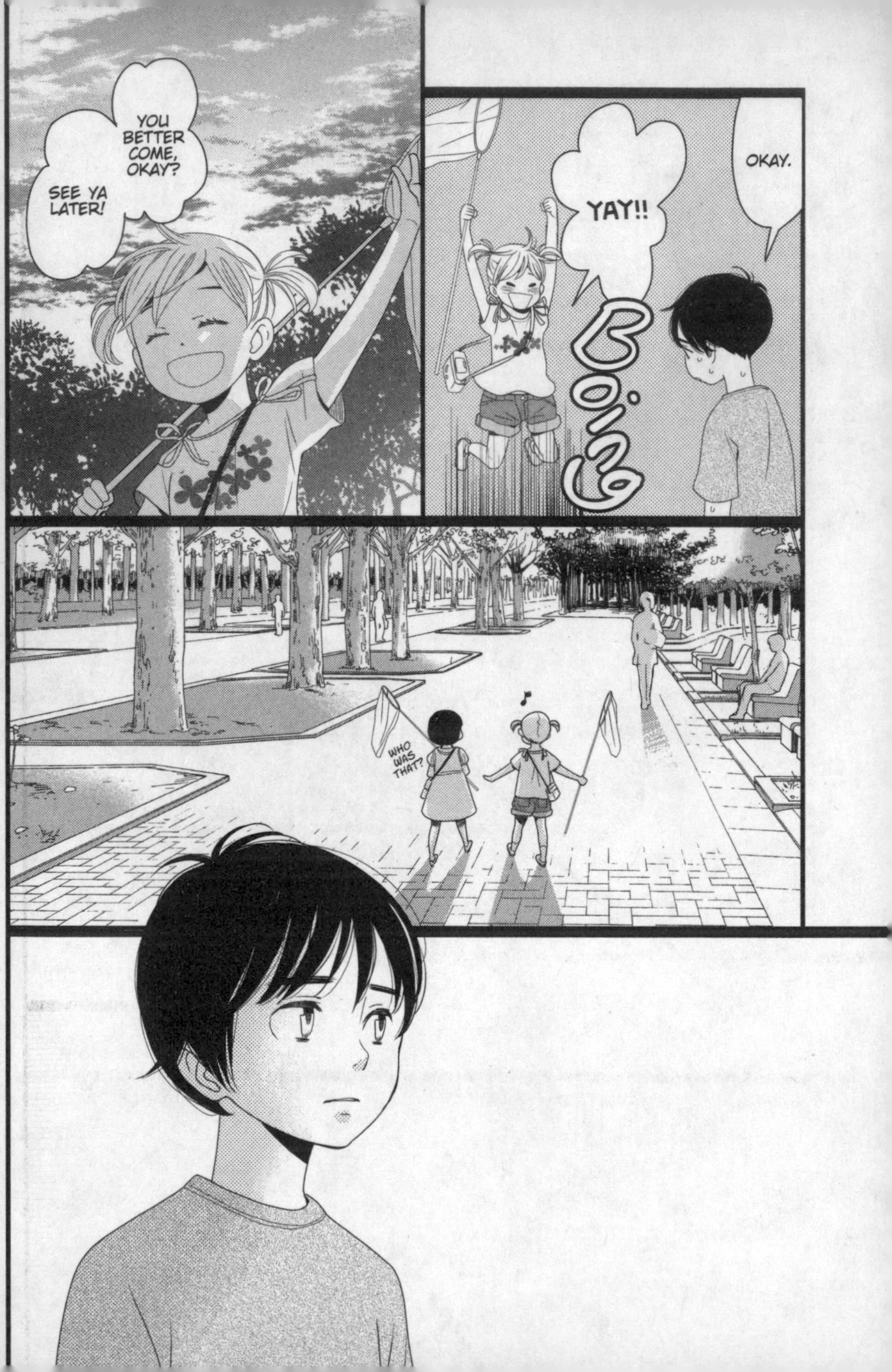
OKAY.
YAY!!
BOING
YOU BETTER COME, OKAY?
SEE YA LATER!
WHO WAS THAT?

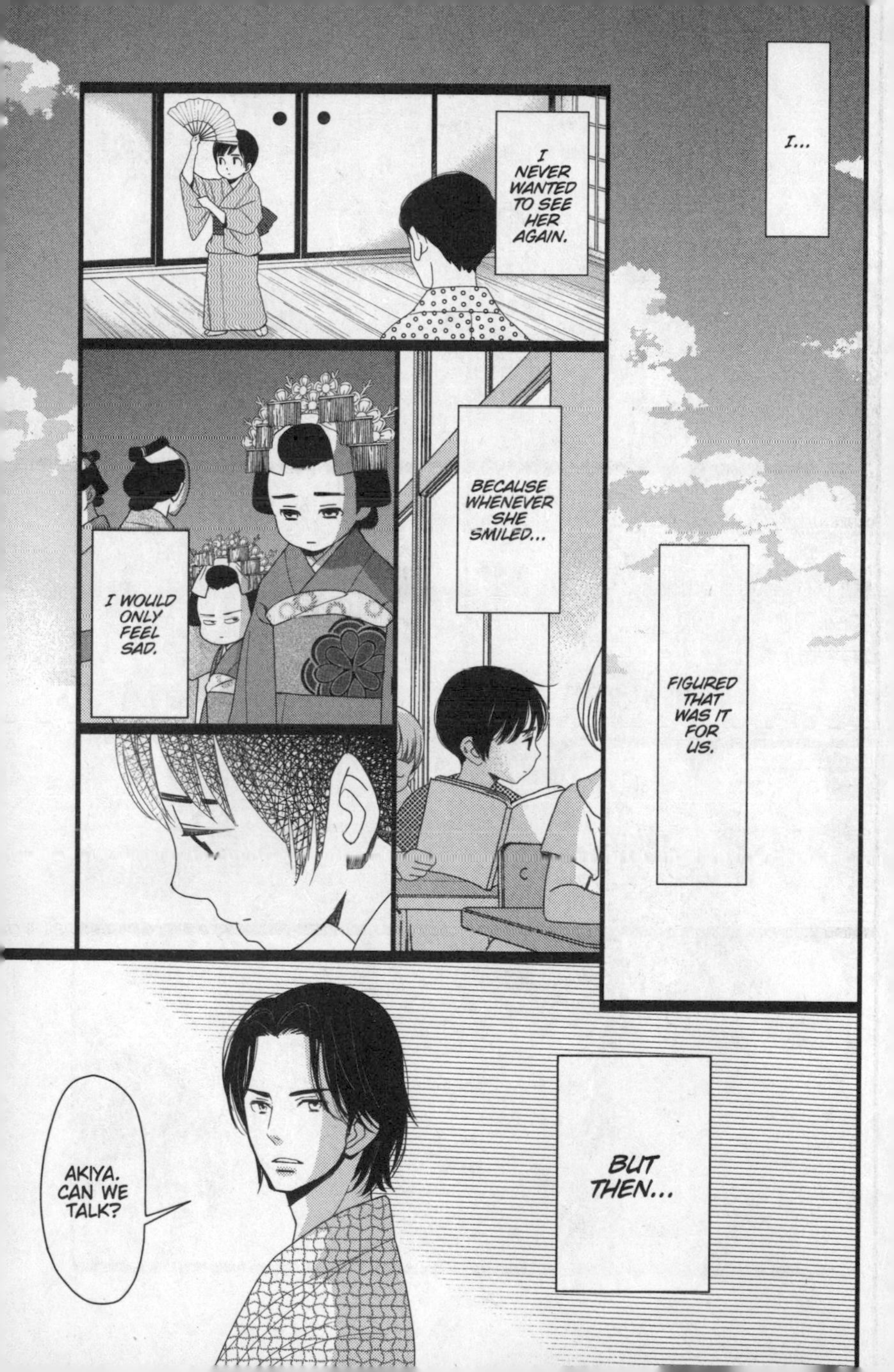
I...
FIGURED THAT WAS IT FOR US.
I NEVER WANTED TO SEE HER AGAIN.
BECAUSE WHENEVER SHE SMILED...
I WOULD ONLY FEEL SAD.
BUT THEN...
AKIYA. CAN WE TALK?

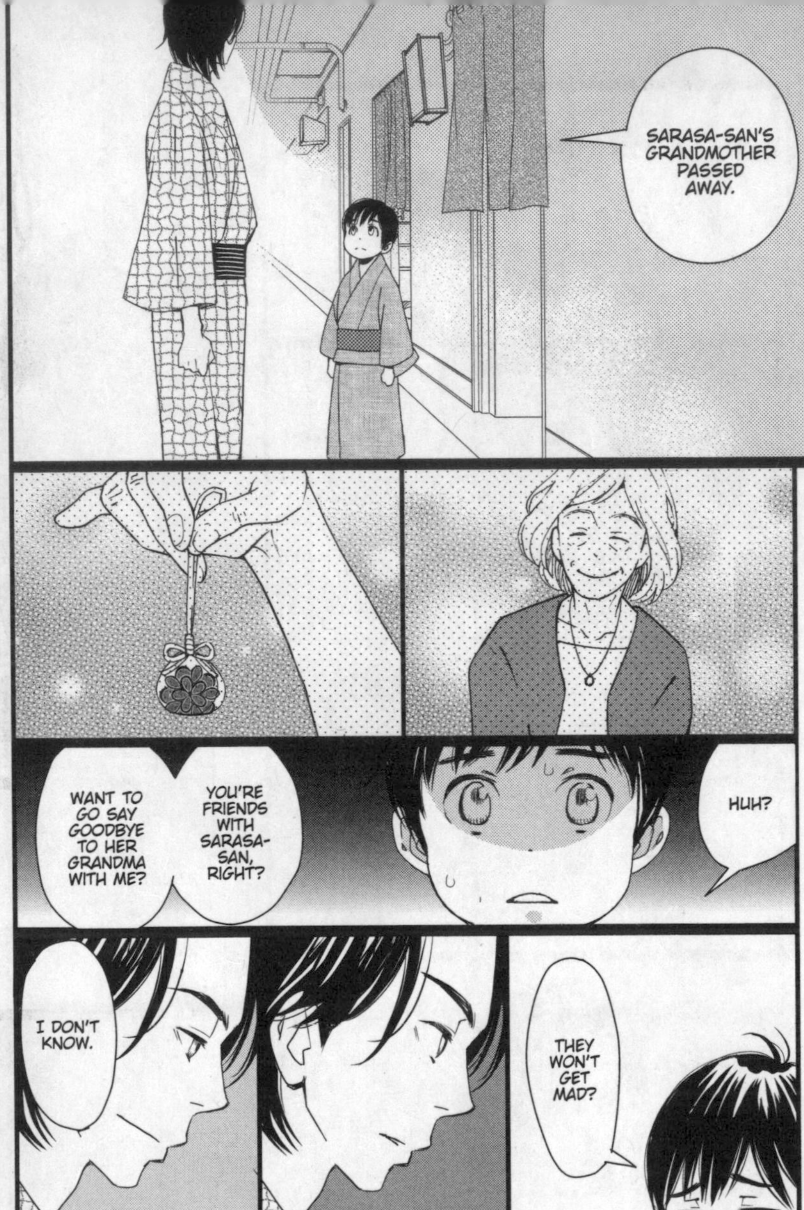
SARASA-SAN'S GRANDMOTHER PASSED AWAY.
HUH?
YOU'RE FRIENDS WITH SARASA-SAN, RIGHT?
WANT TO GO SAY GOODBYE TO HER GRANDMA WITH ME?
THEY WON'T GET MAD?
I DON'T KNOW.

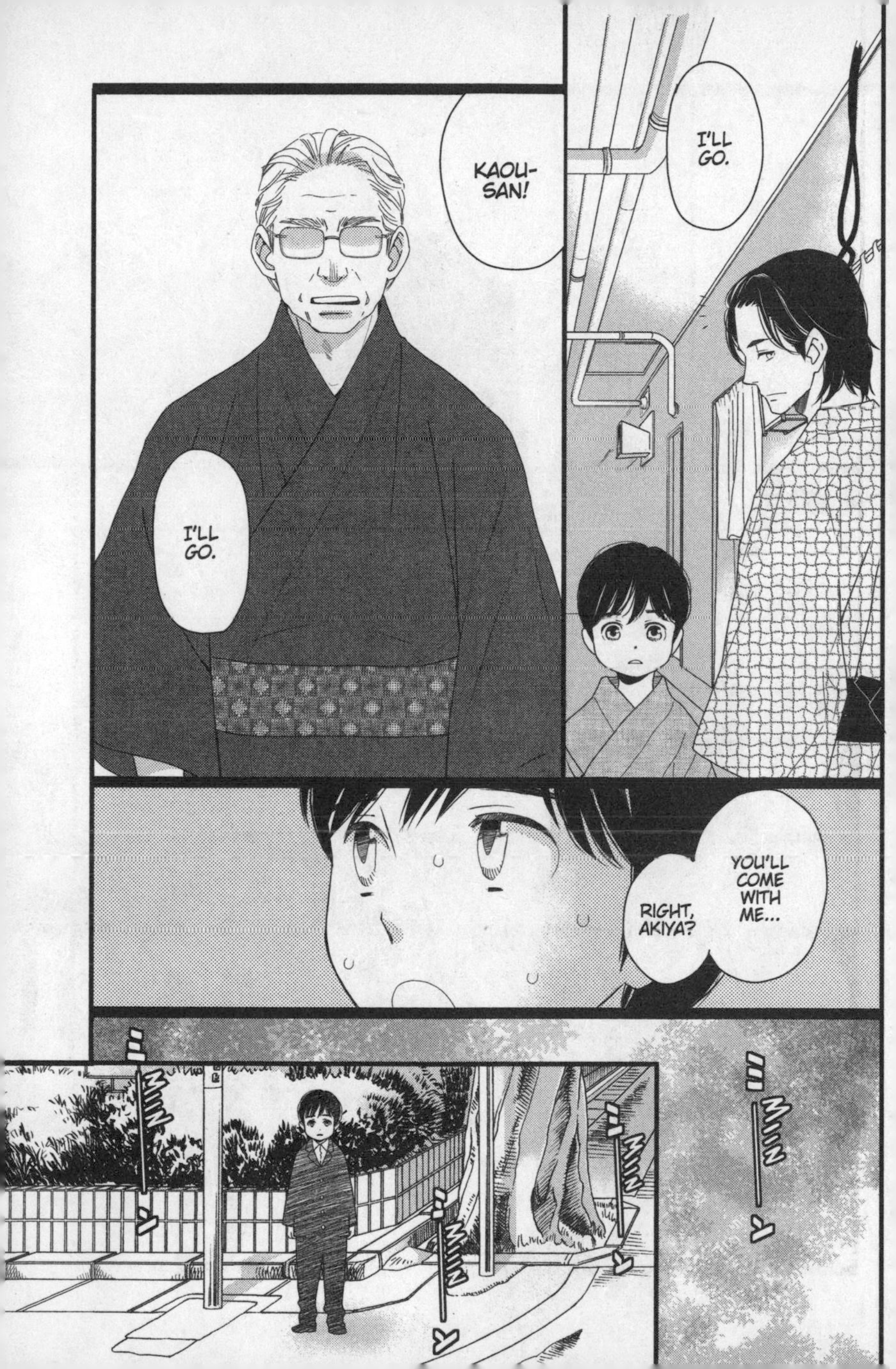
I'LL GO.
KAOU-SAN!
I'LL GO.
YOU'LL COME WITH ME...
RIGHT, AKIYA?
MIIN—N
MIIN—N
MIIN—N
MIIN—N

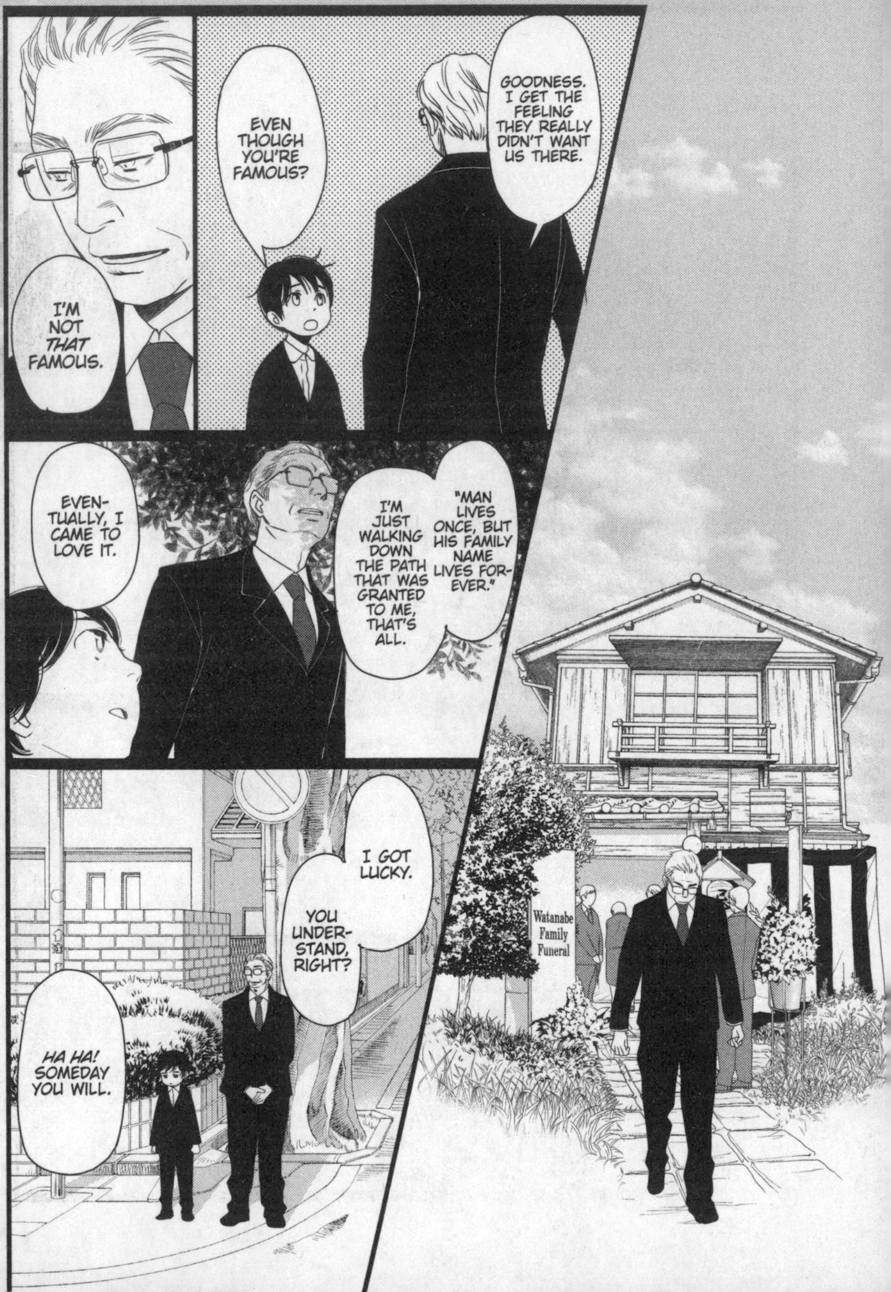
Watanabe Family Funeral
GOODNESS. I GET THE FEELING THEY REALLY DIDN'T WANT US THERE.
EVEN THOUGH YOU'RE FAMOUS?
I'M NOT *THAT* FAMOUS.
"MAN LIVES ONCE, BUT HIS FAMILY NAME LIVES FOREVER."
I'M JUST WALKING DOWN THE PATH THAT WAS GRANTED TO ME, THAT'S ALL.
EVENTUALLY, I CAME TO LOVE IT.
I GOT LUCKY.
YOU UNDERSTAND, RIGHT?
HA HA! SOMEDAY YOU WILL.

Lantern text: "Mourning." It is put up at funerals to honor the dead.

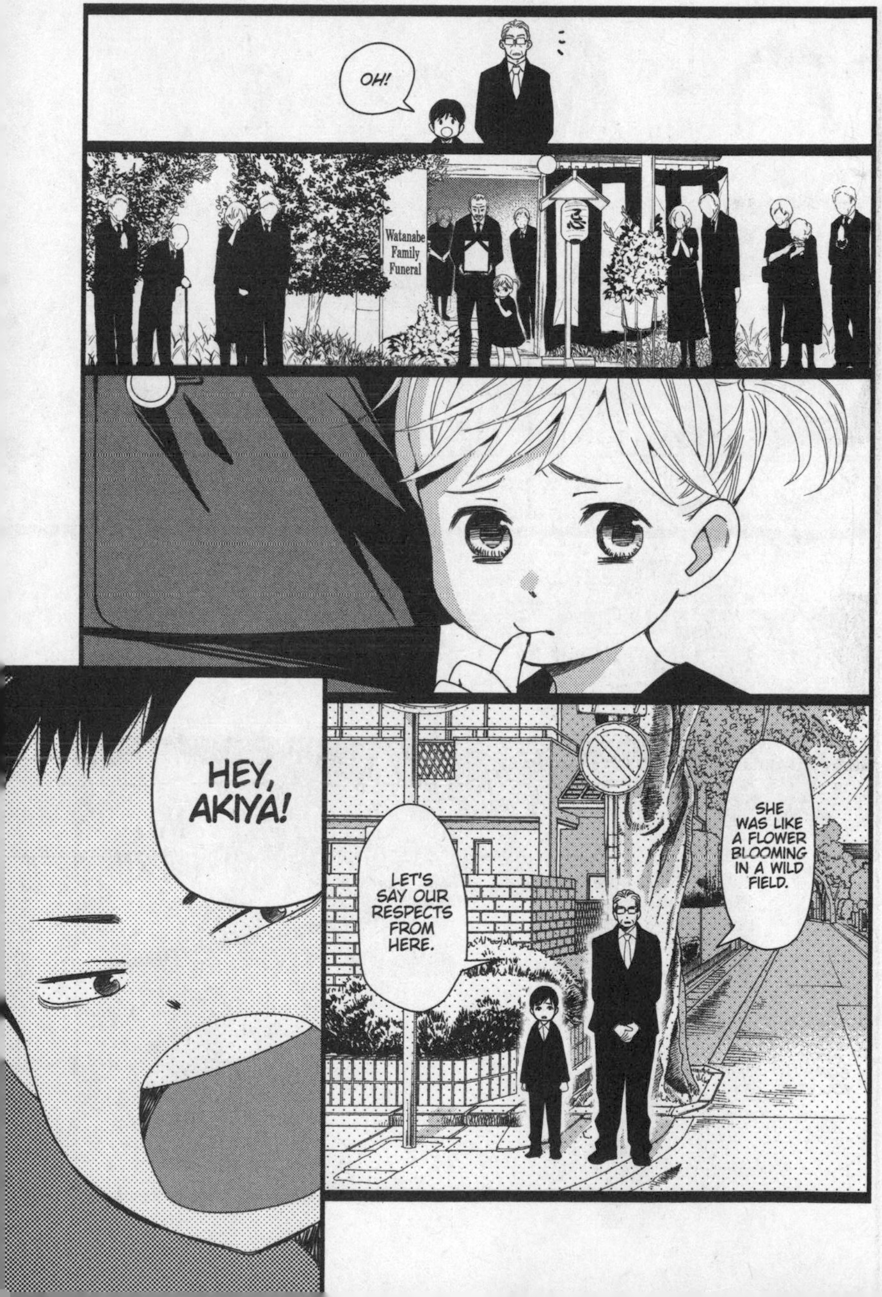
OH!
Watanabe Family Funeral
SHE WAS LIKE A FLOWER BLOOMING IN A WILD FIELD.
LET'S SAY OUR RESPECTS FROM HERE.
HEY, AKIYA!

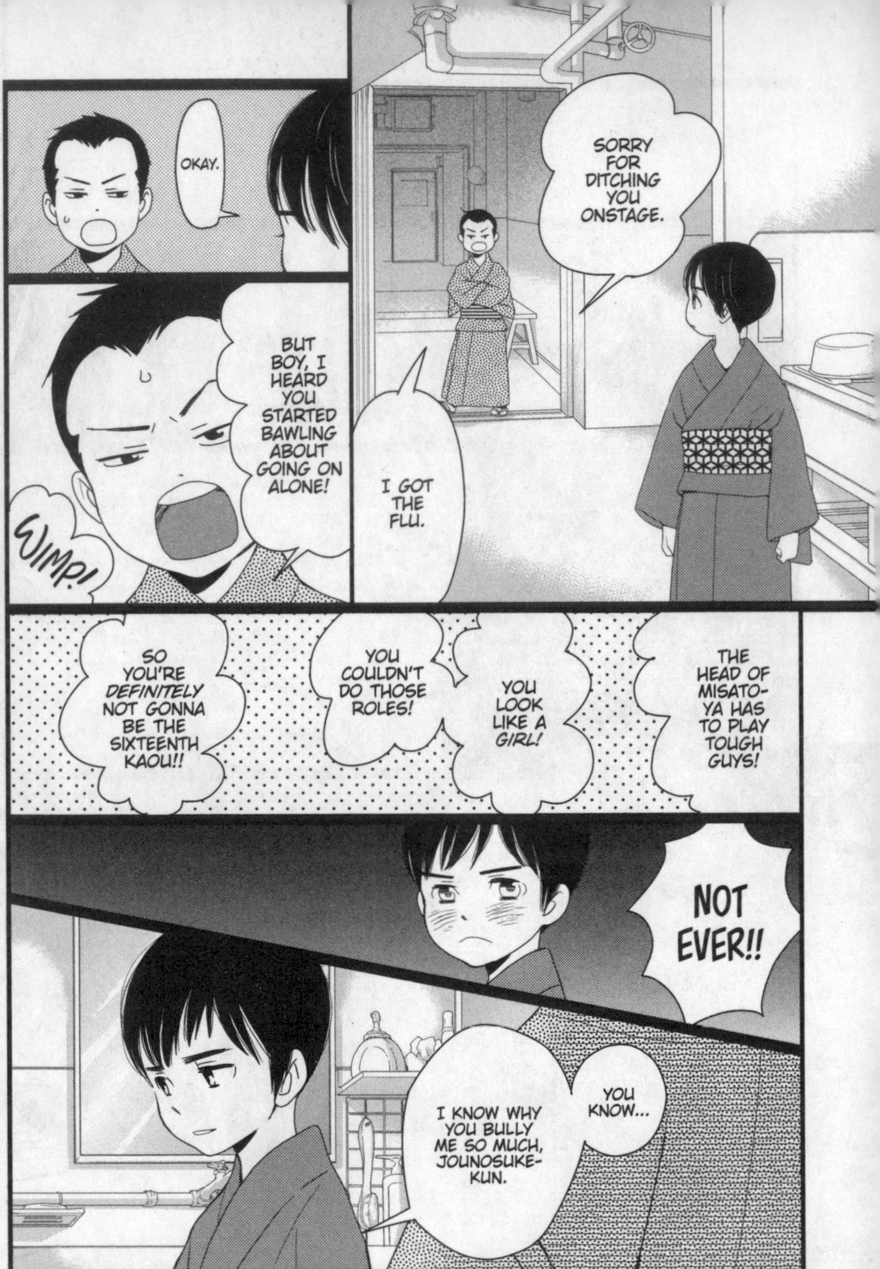
SORRY FOR DITCHING YOU ONSTAGE.
I GOT THE FLU.
OKAY.
BUT BOY, I HEARD YOU STARTED BAWLING ABOUT GOING ON ALONE!
WIMP!
THE HEAD OF MISATO-YA HAS TO PLAY TOUGH GUYS!
YOU LOOK LIKE A *GIRL!*
YOU COULDN'T DO THOSE ROLES!
SO YOU'RE *DEFINITELY* NOT GONNA BE THE SIXTEENTH KAOU!!
NOT EVER!!
YOU KNOW...
I KNOW WHY YOU BULLY ME SO MUCH, JOUNOSUKE-KUN.

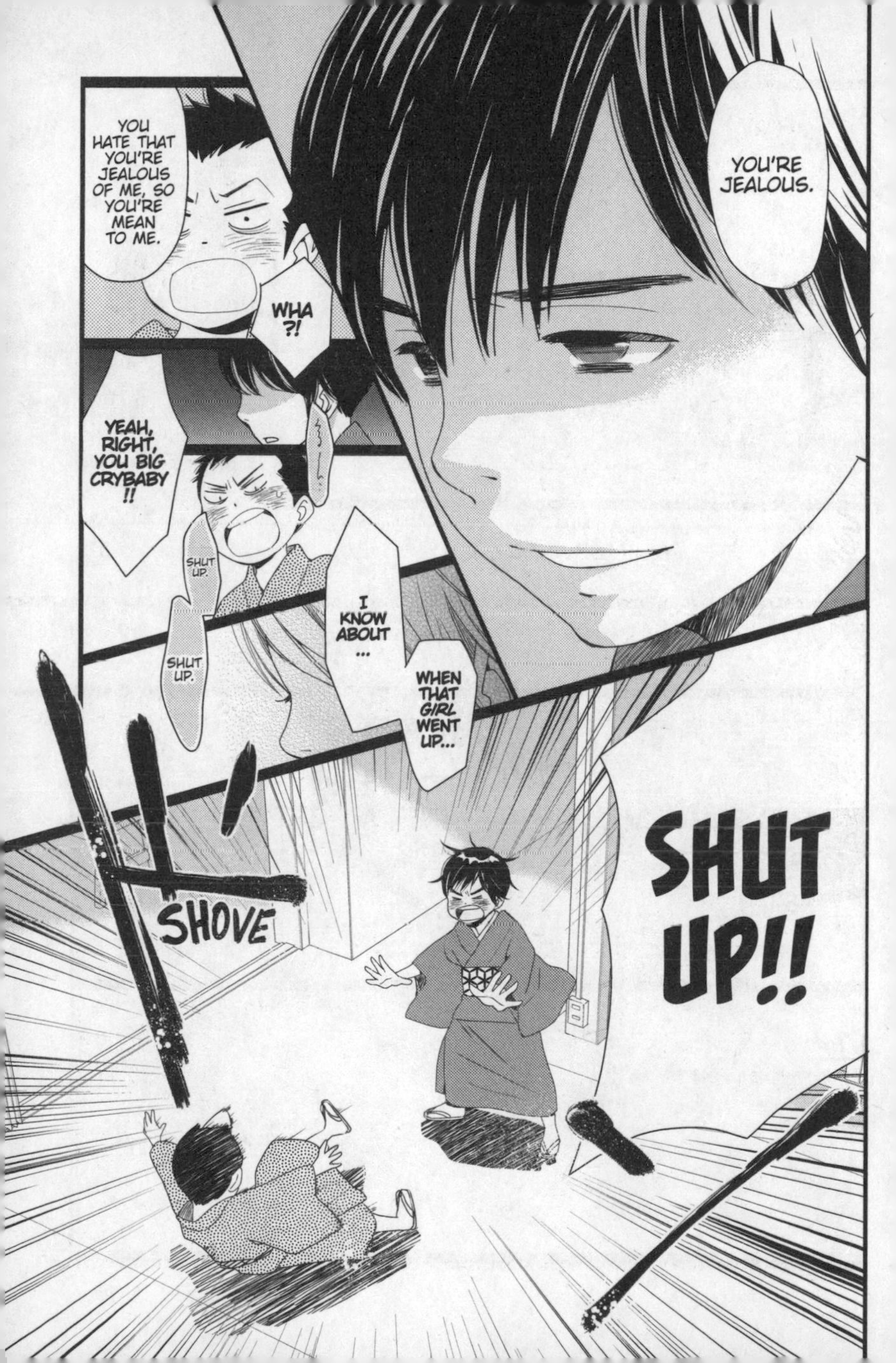
YOU'RE JEALOUS.
YOU HATE THAT YOU'RE JEALOUS OF ME, SO YOU'RE MEAN TO ME.
WHA ?!
YEAH, RIGHT, YOU BIG CRYBABY !!
I KNOW ABOUT ...
WHEN THAT GIRL WENT UP...
SHUT UP.
SHUT UP.
SHUT UP!!
SHOVE

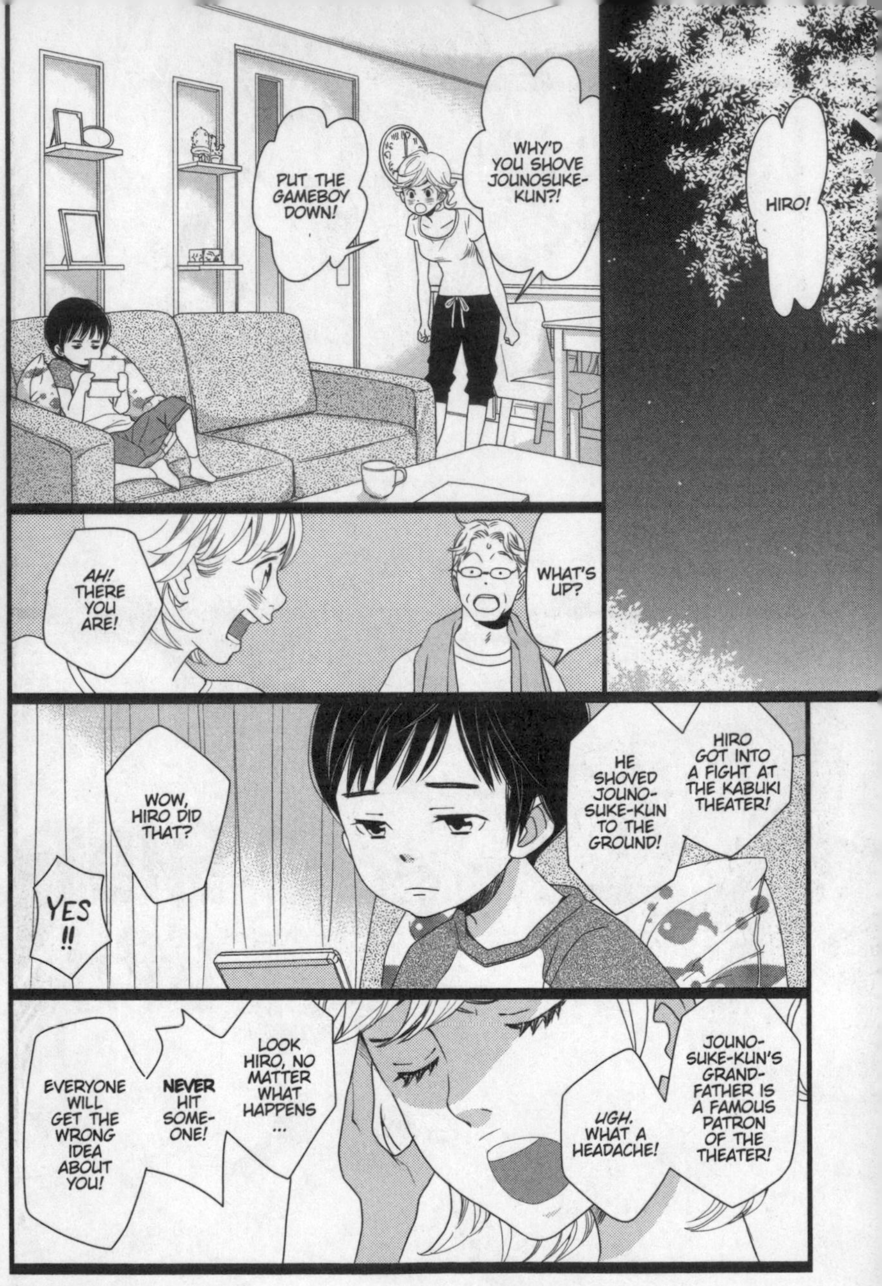

HIRO!
WHY'D YOU SHOVE JOUNOSUKE-KUN?!
PUT THE GAMEBOY DOWN!
WHAT'S UP?
AH! THERE YOU ARE!
HIRO GOT INTO A FIGHT AT THE KABUKI THEATER!
HE SHOVED JOUNO-SUKE-KUN TO THE GROUND!
WOW, HIRO DID THAT?
YES !!
JOUNO-SUKE-KUN'S GRAND-FATHER IS A FAMOUS PATRON OF THE THEATER!
UGH. WHAT A HEADACHE!
LOOK HIRO, NO MATTER WHAT HAPPENS ...
NEVER HIT SOME-ONE!
EVERYONE WILL GET THE WRONG IDEA ABOUT YOU!

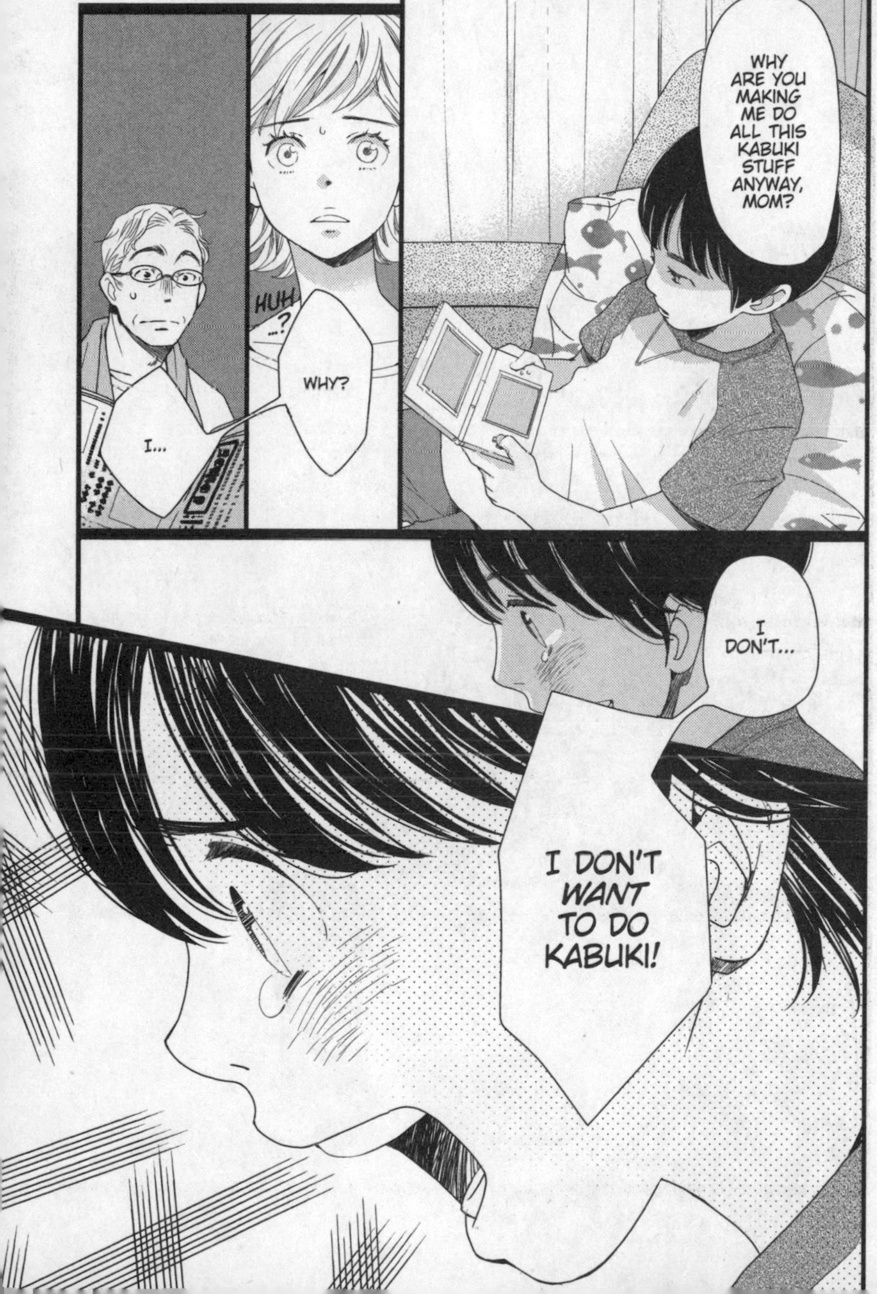
WHY ARE YOU MAKING ME DO ALL THIS KABUKI STUFF ANYWAY, MOM?
HUH ...?
WHY?
I...
I DON'T...
I DON'T *WANT* TO DO KABUKI!

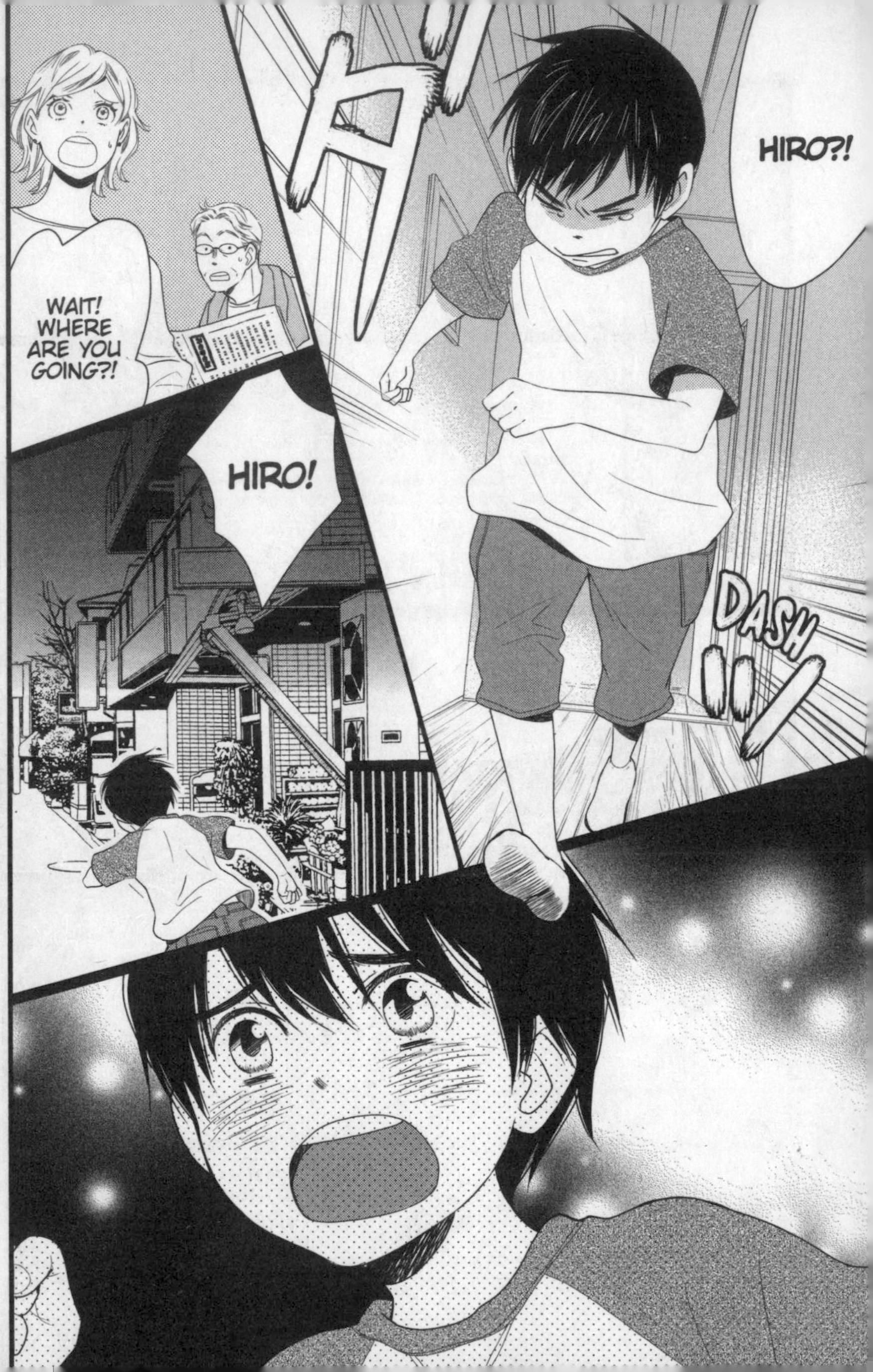
HIRO?!
DASH
WAIT! WHERE ARE YOU GOING?!
HIRO!

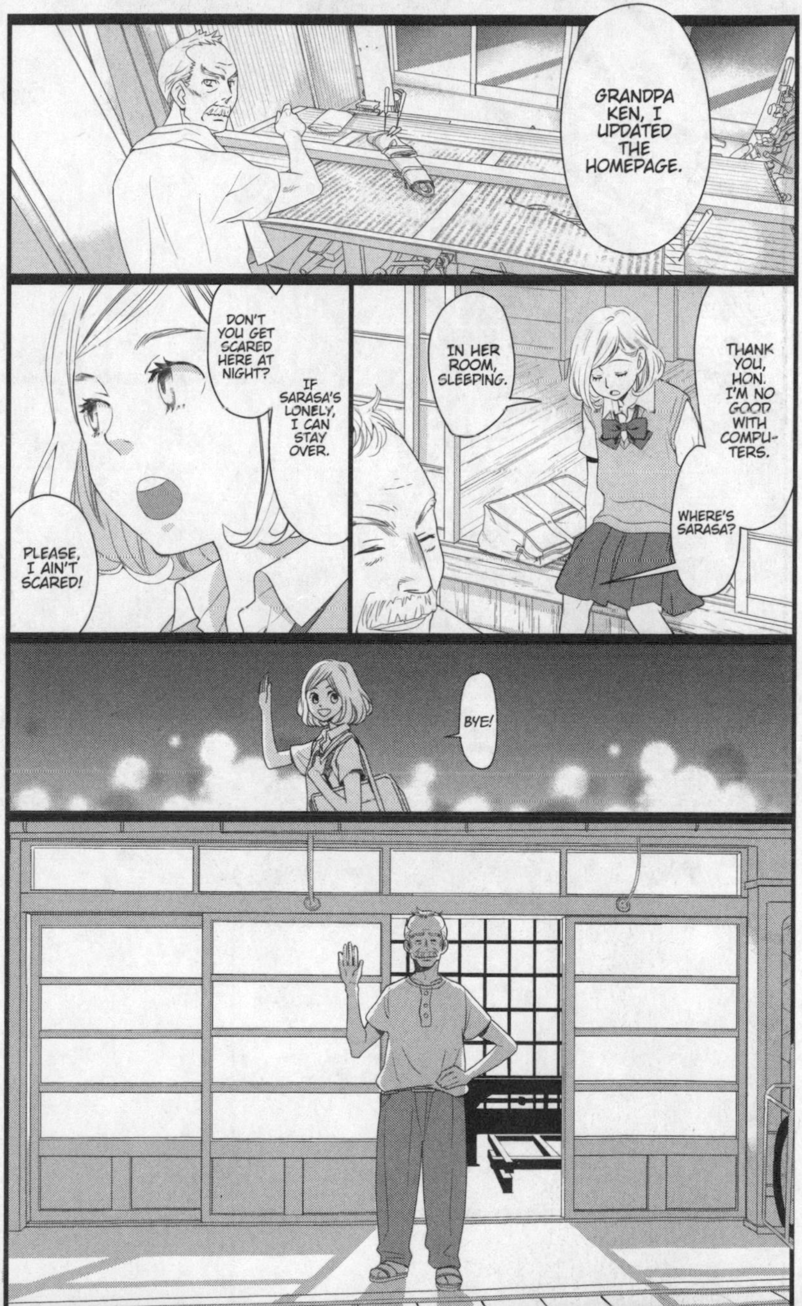
GRANDPA KEN, I UPDATED THE HOMEPAGE.
THANK YOU, HON. I'M NO GOOD WITH COMPUTERS.
WHERE'S SARASA?
IN HER ROOM, SLEEPING.
DON'T YOU GET SCARED HERE AT NIGHT?
IF SARASA'S LONELY, I CAN STAY OVER.
PLEASE, I AIN'T SCARED!
BYE!

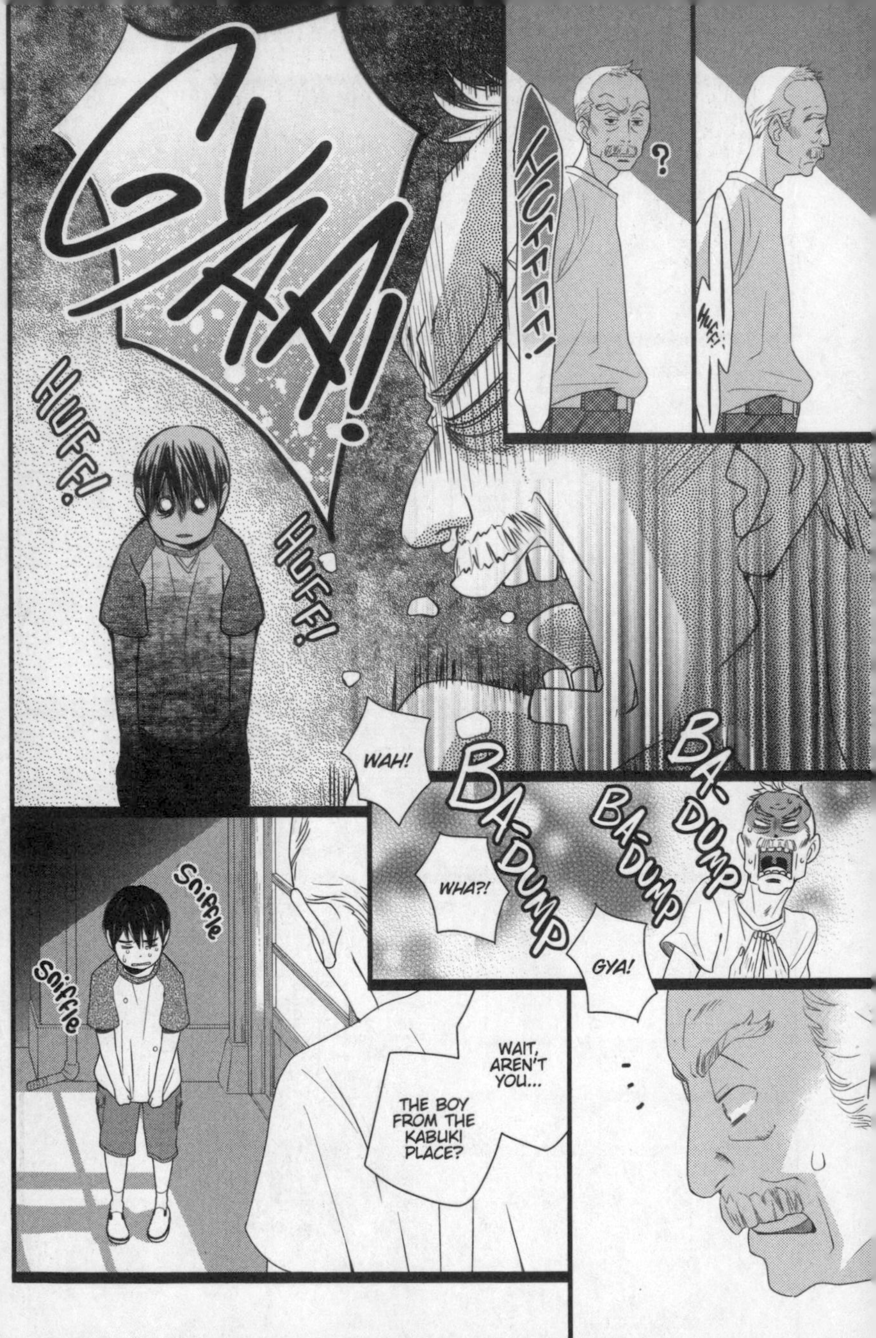
HUFF!
HUFFFFF!
?
BA-DUMP
BA-DUMP
BA-DUMP
WHA?!
GYA!
GYAA!
HUFF!
HUFF!
WAH!
WAIT, AREN'T YOU...
THE BOY FROM THE KABUKI PLACE?
Sniffle
Sniffle

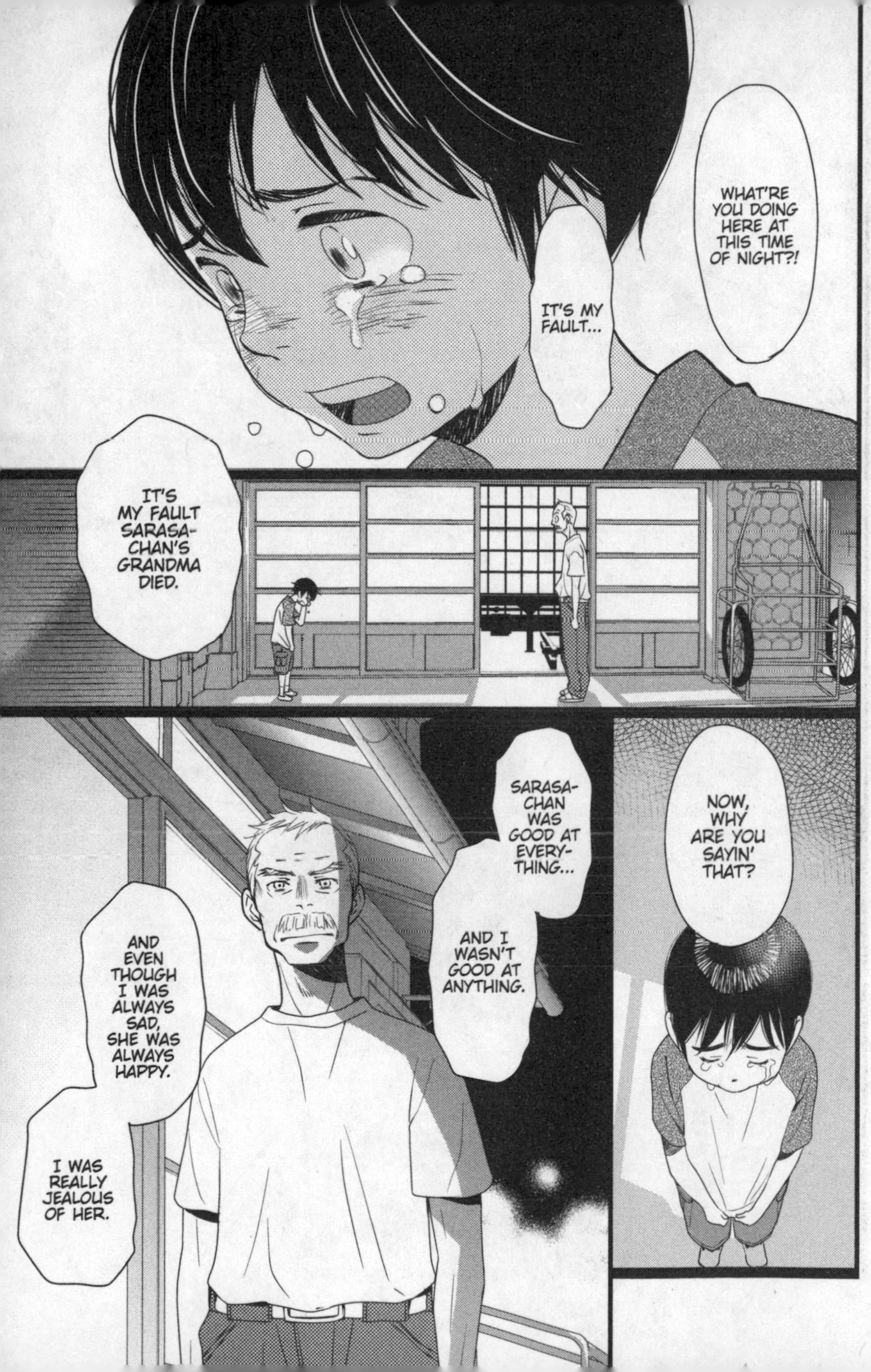
WHAT'RE YOU DOING HERE AT THIS TIME OF NIGHT?!
IT'S MY FAULT...
IT'S MY FAULT SARASA-CHAN'S GRANDMA DIED.
NOW, WHY ARE YOU SAYIN' THAT?
SARASA-CHAN WAS GOOD AT EVERY-THING...
AND I WASN'T GOOD AT ANYTHING.
AND EVEN THOUGH I WAS ALWAYS SAD, SHE WAS ALWAYS HAPPY.
I WAS REALLY JEALOUS OF HER.

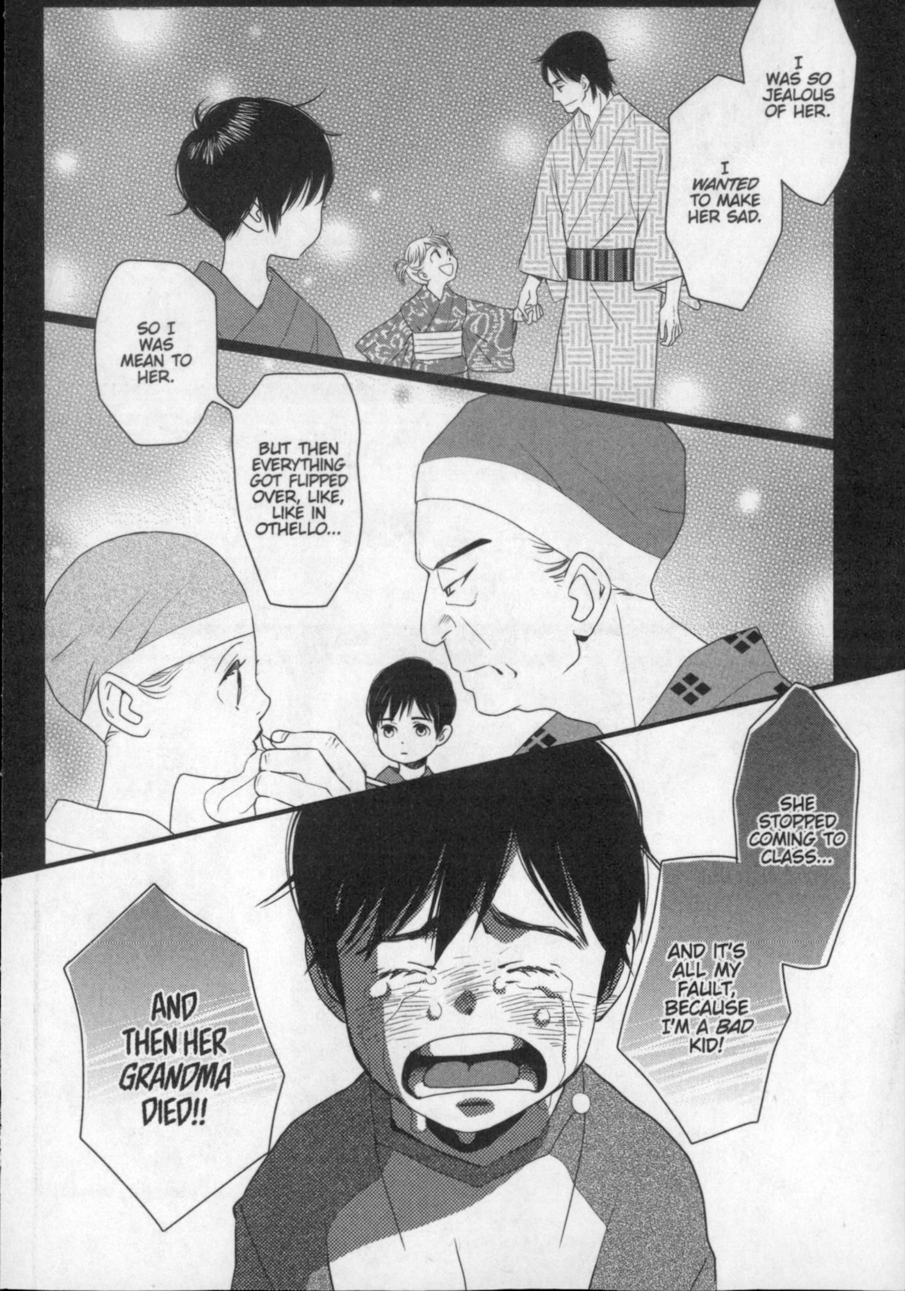
I WAS SO JEALOUS OF HER.
I WANTED TO MAKE HER SAD.
SO I WAS MEAN TO HER.
BUT THEN EVERYTHING GOT FLIPPED OVER, LIKE, LIKE IN OTHELLO...
SHE STOPPED COMING TO CLASS...
AND IT'S ALL MY FAULT, BECAUSE I'M A BAD KID!
AND THEN HER GRANDMA DIED!!

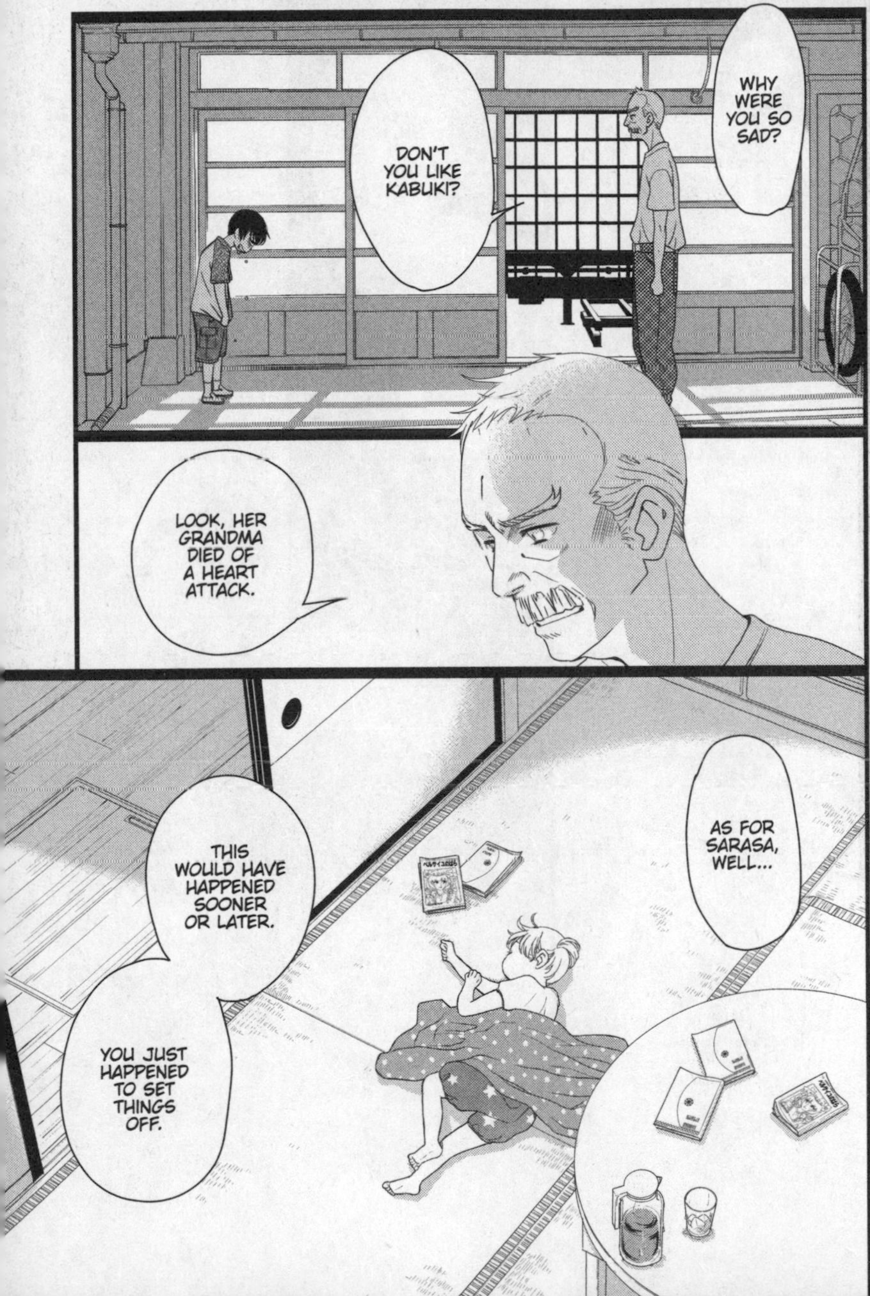
WHY WERE YOU SO SAD?
DON'T YOU LIKE KABUKI?
LOOK, HER GRANDMA DIED OF A HEART ATTACK.
AS FOR SARASA, WELL...
THIS WOULD HAVE HAPPENED SOONER OR LATER.
YOU JUST HAPPENED TO SET THINGS OFF.

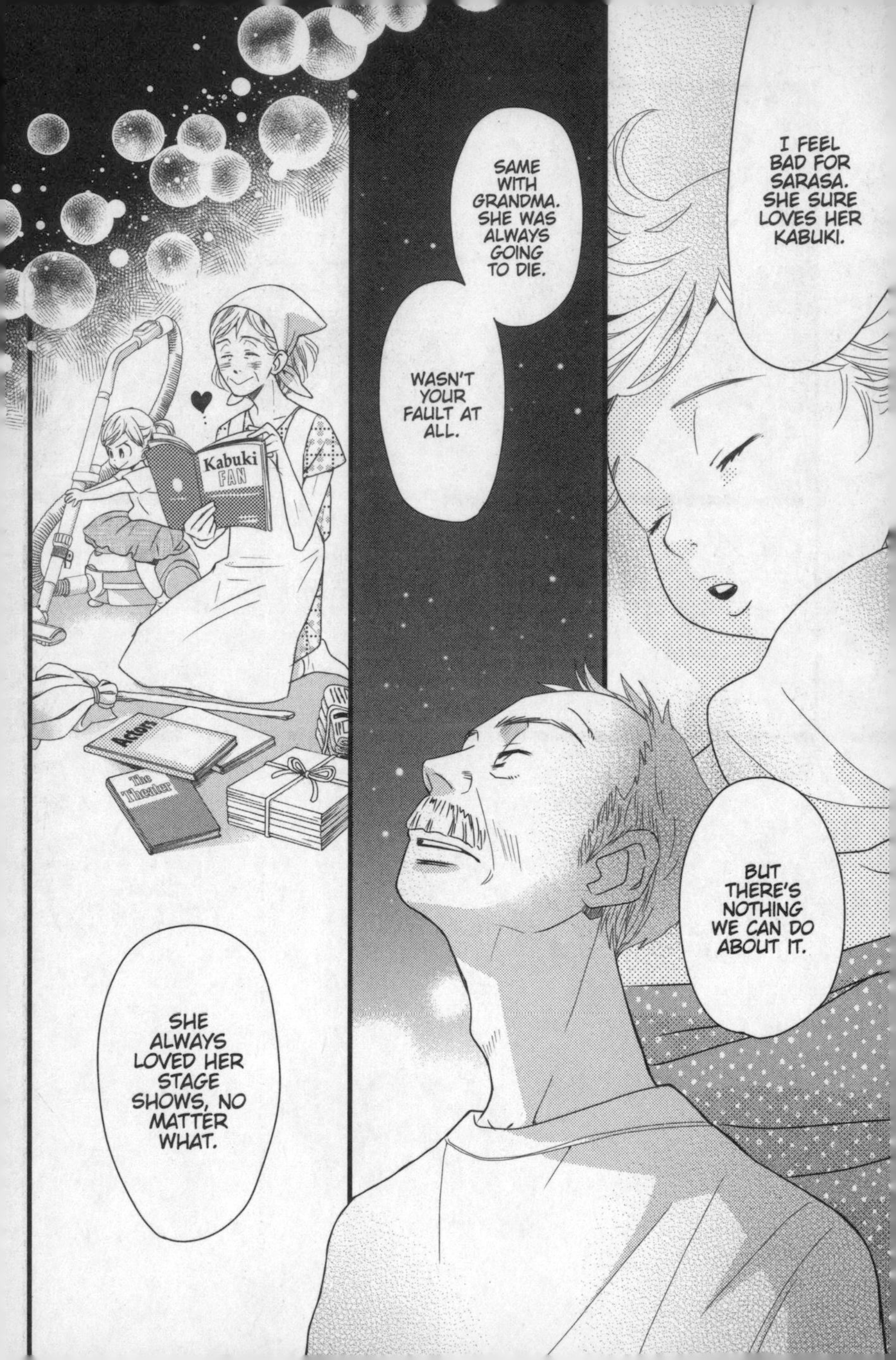
I FEEL BAD FOR SARASA. SHE SURE LOVES HER KABUKI.
BUT THERE'S NOTHING WE CAN DO ABOUT IT.
SAME WITH GRANDMA. SHE WAS ALWAYS GOING TO DIE.
WASN'T YOUR FAULT AT ALL.
Kabuki FAN
Actors
The Theater
SHE ALWAYS LOVED HER STAGE SHOWS, NO MATTER WHAT.

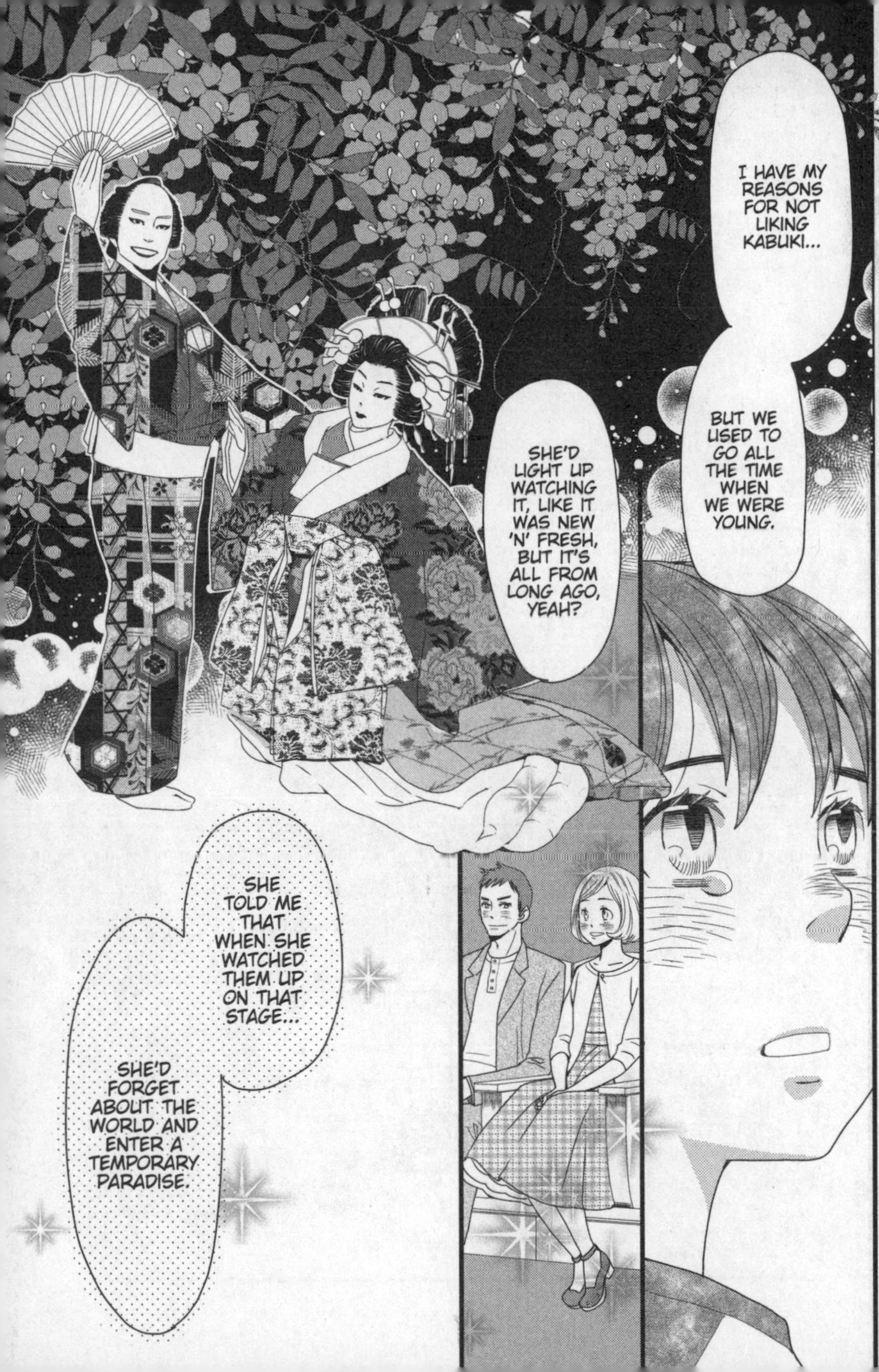
I HAVE MY REASONS FOR NOT LIKING KABUKI...
BUT WE USED TO GO ALL THE TIME WHEN WE WERE YOUNG.
SHE'D LIGHT UP WATCHING IT, LIKE IT WAS NEW 'N' FRESH, BUT IT'S ALL FROM LONG AGO, YEAH?
SHE TOLD ME THAT WHEN SHE WATCHED THEM UP ON THAT STAGE...
SHE'D FORGET ABOUT THE WORLD AND ENTER A TEMPORARY PARADISE.

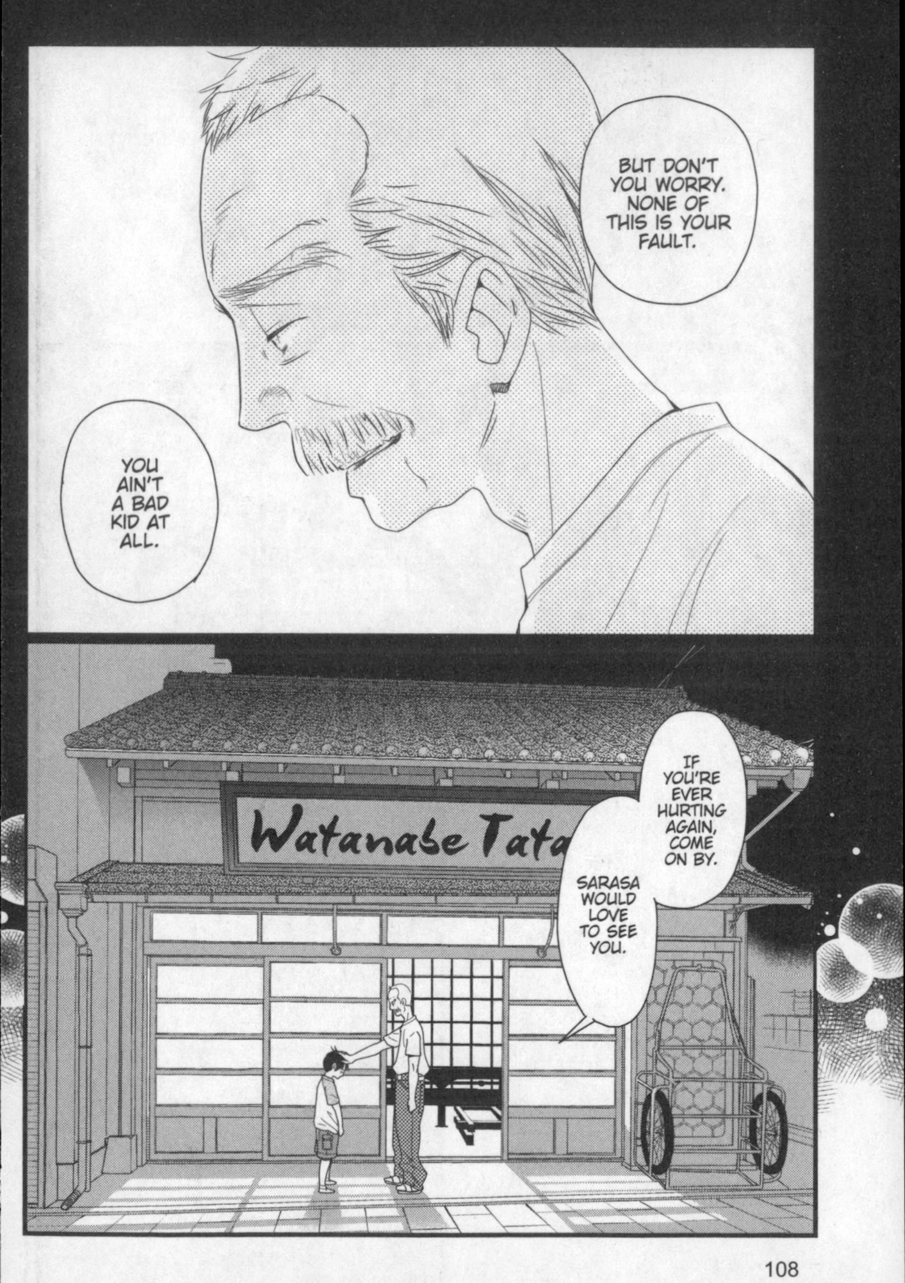
BUT DON'T YOU WORRY. NONE OF THIS IS YOUR FAULT.
YOU AIN'T A BAD KID AT ALL.
IF YOU'RE EVER HURTING AGAIN, COME ON BY.
SARASA WOULD LOVE TO SEE YOU.
Watanabe Tata

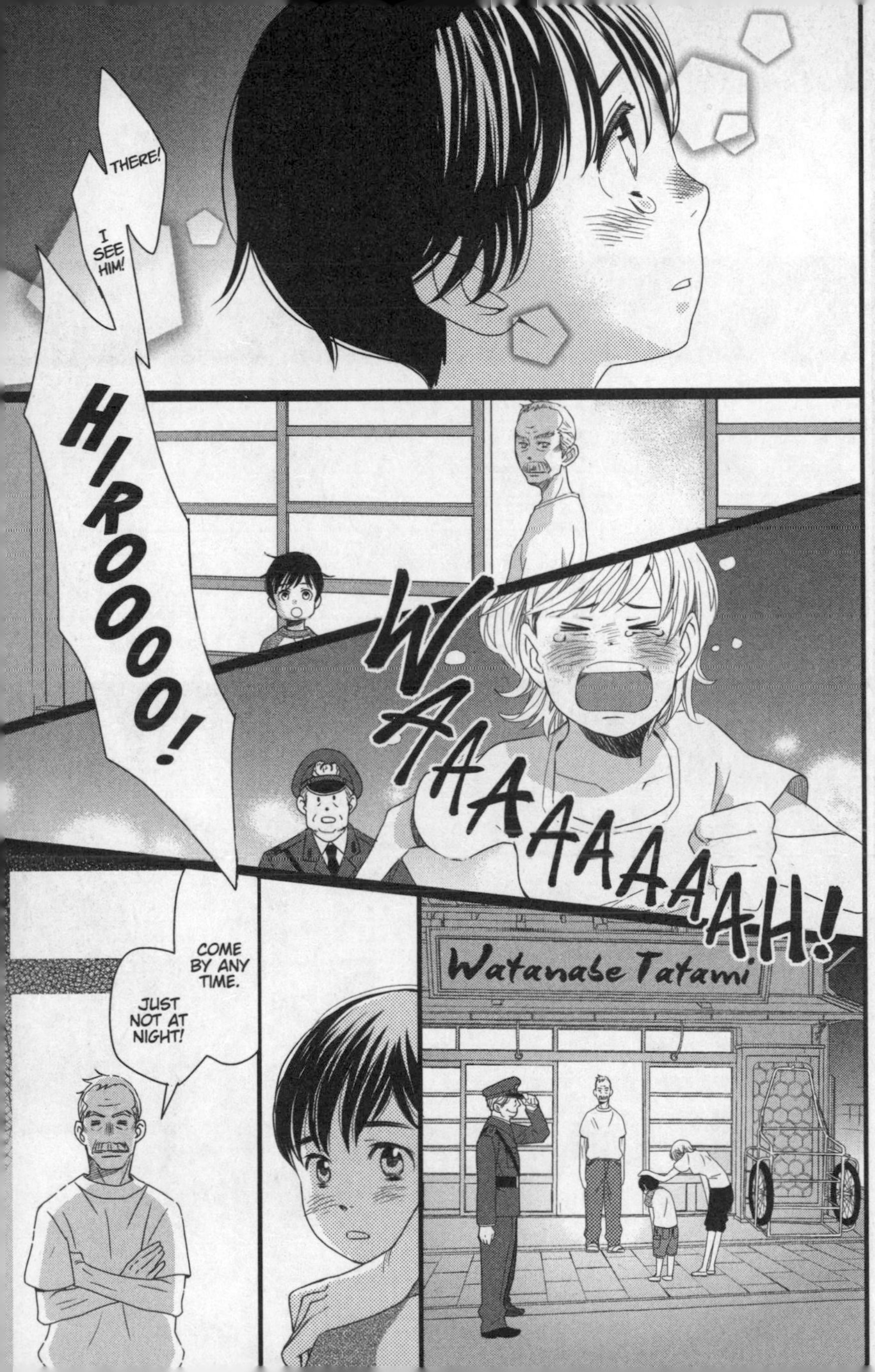
THERE!
I SEE HIM!
HIROOOO!
WAAAAAAAAH!
Watanabe Tatami
COME BY ANY TIME.
JUST NOT AT NIGHT!

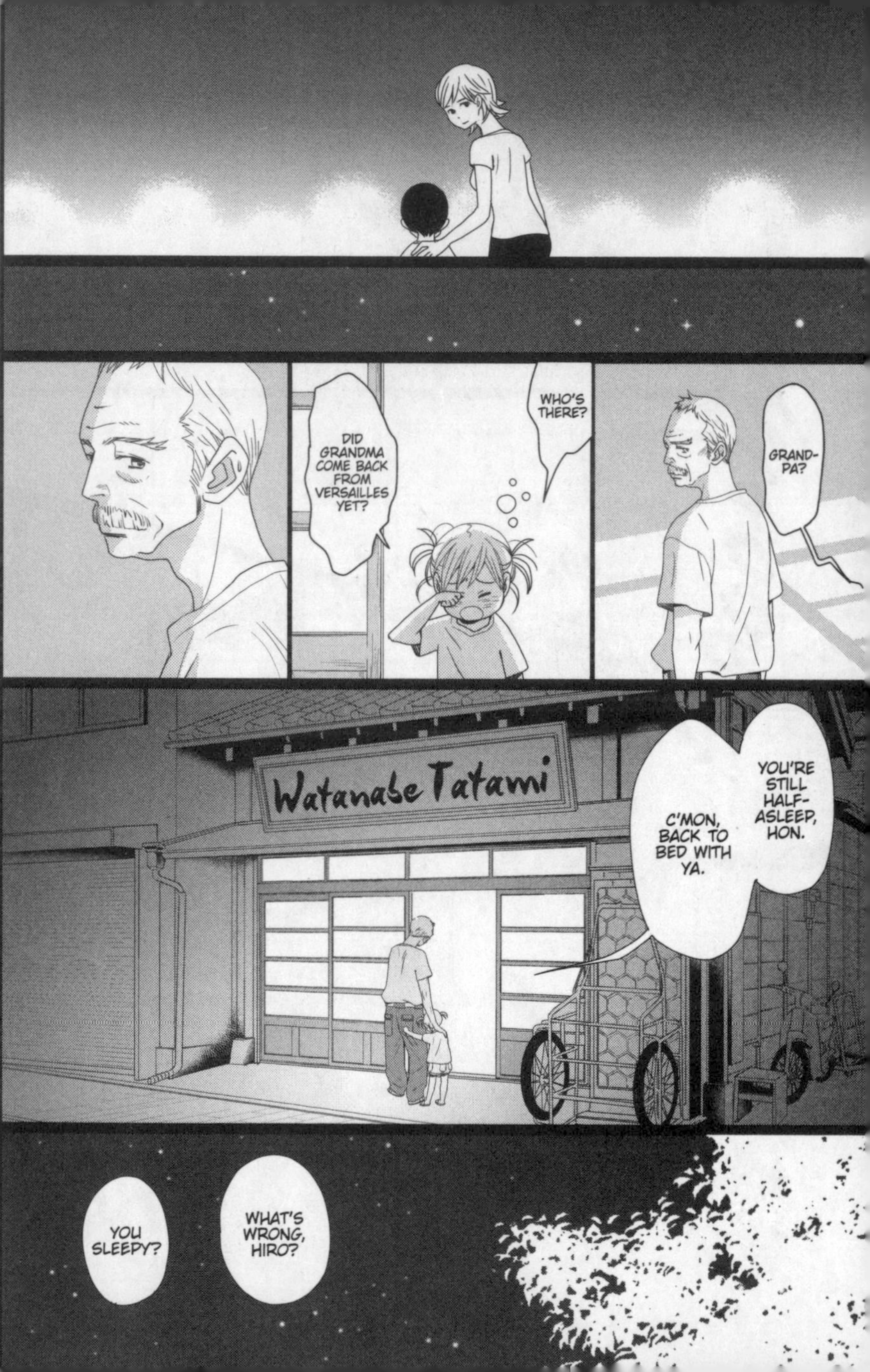
GRAND-PA?
WHO'S THERE?
DID GRANDMA COME BACK FROM VERSAILLES YET?
Watanabe Tatami
YOU'RE STILL HALF-ASLEEP, HON.
C'MON, BACK TO BED WITH YA.
WHAT'S WRONG, HIRO?
YOU SLEEPY?

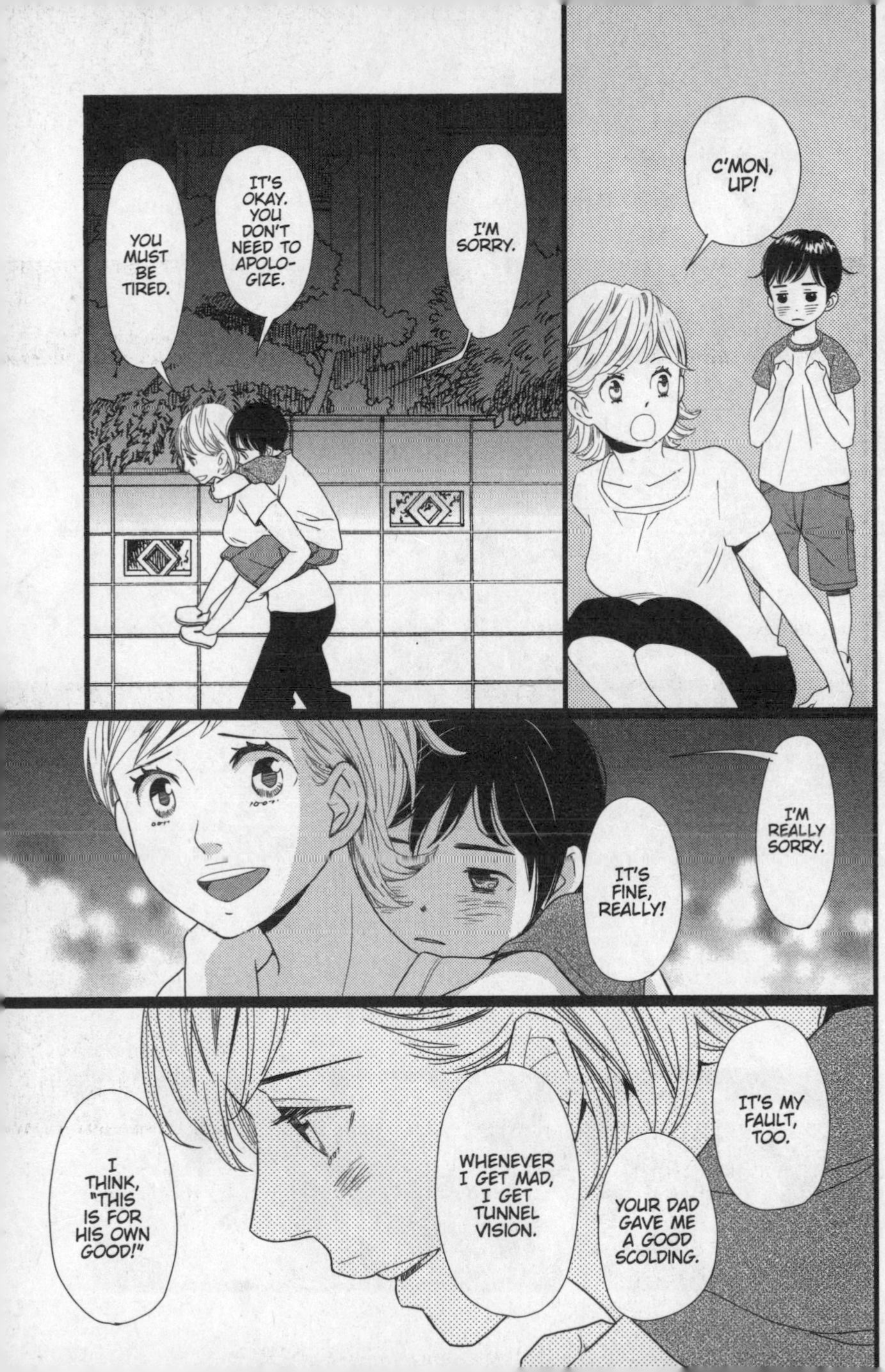
C'MON, UP!
I'M SORRY.
IT'S OKAY. YOU DON'T NEED TO APOLO-GIZE.
YOU MUST BE TIRED.
I'M REALLY SORRY.
IT'S FINE, REALLY!
IT'S MY FAULT, TOO.
YOUR DAD GAVE ME A GOOD SCOLDING.
WHENEVER I GET MAD, I GET TUNNEL VISION.
I THINK, "THIS IS FOR HIS OWN GOOD!"

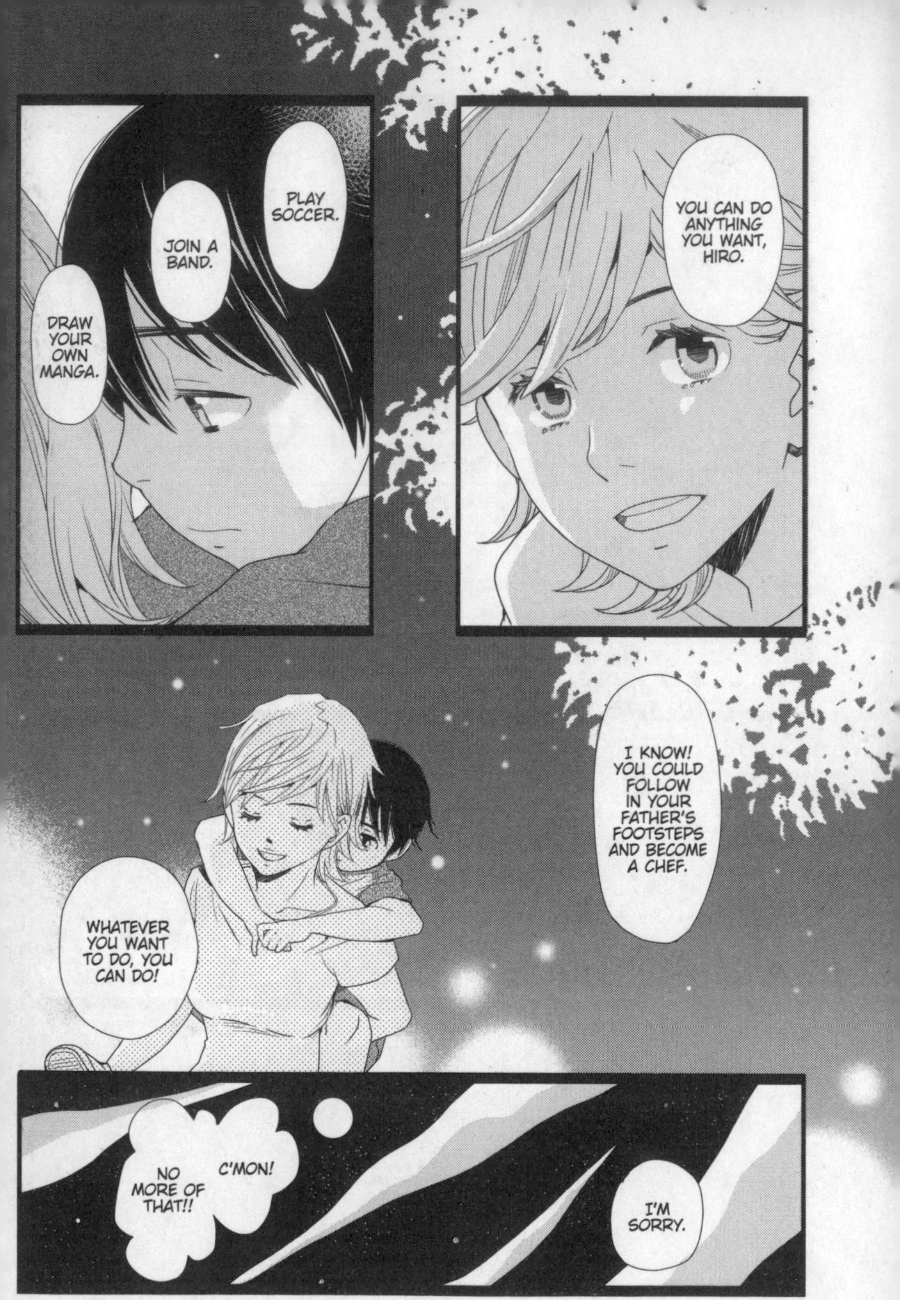
YOU CAN DO ANYTHING YOU WANT, HIRO.
PLAY SOCCER.
JOIN A BAND.
DRAW YOUR OWN MANGA.
I KNOW! YOU COULD FOLLOW IN YOUR FATHER'S FOOTSTEPS AND BECOME A CHEF.
WHATEVER YOU WANT TO DO, YOU CAN DO!
I'M SORRY.
C'MON!
NO MORE OF THAT!!

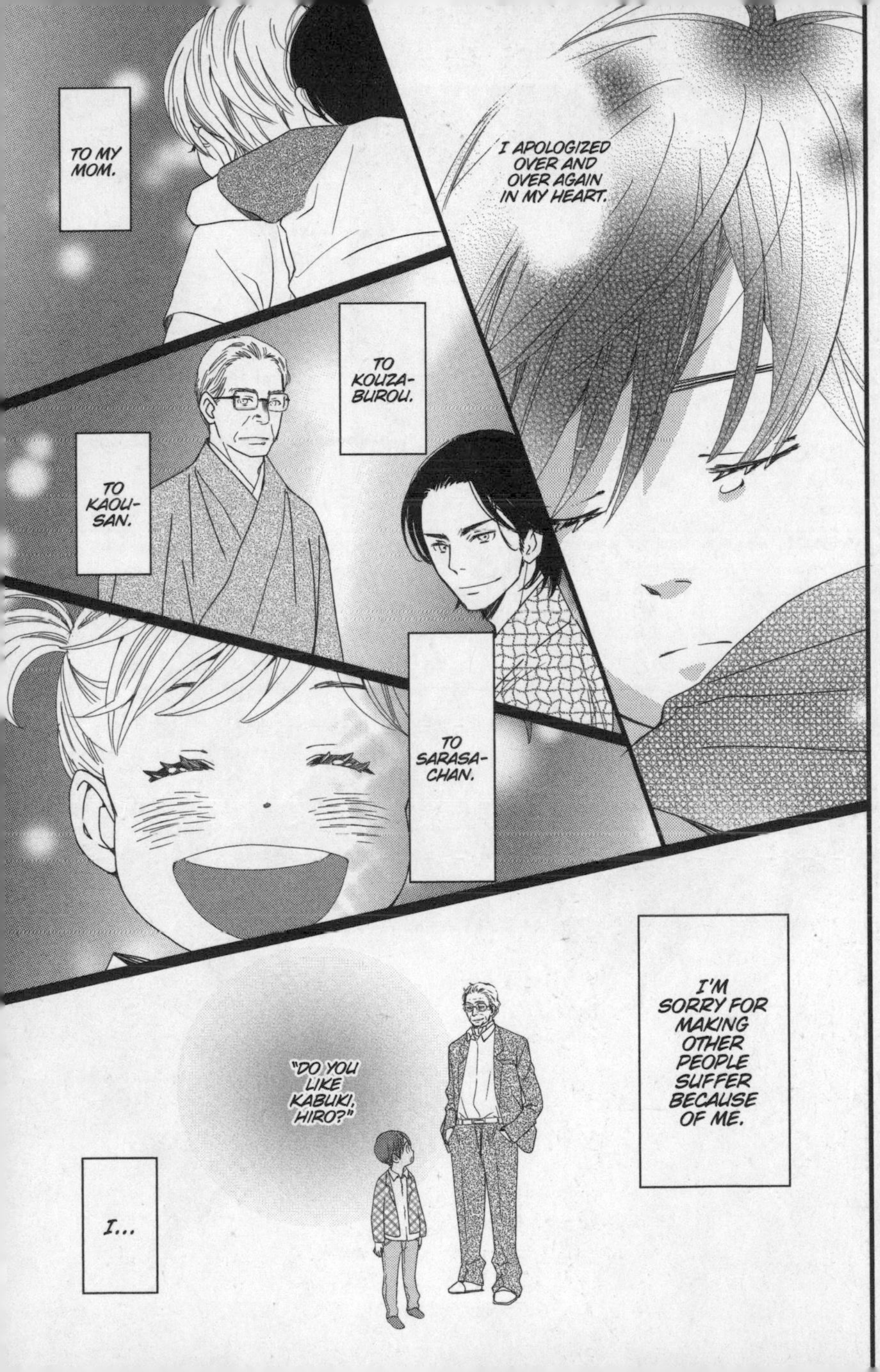
I APOLOGIZED OVER AND OVER AGAIN IN MY HEART.
TO MY MOM.
TO KOUZA-BUROU.
TO KAOU-SAN.
TO SARASA-CHAN.
I'M SORRY FOR MAKING OTHER PEOPLE SUFFER BECAUSE OF ME.
"DO YOU LIKE KABUKI, HIRO?"
I...

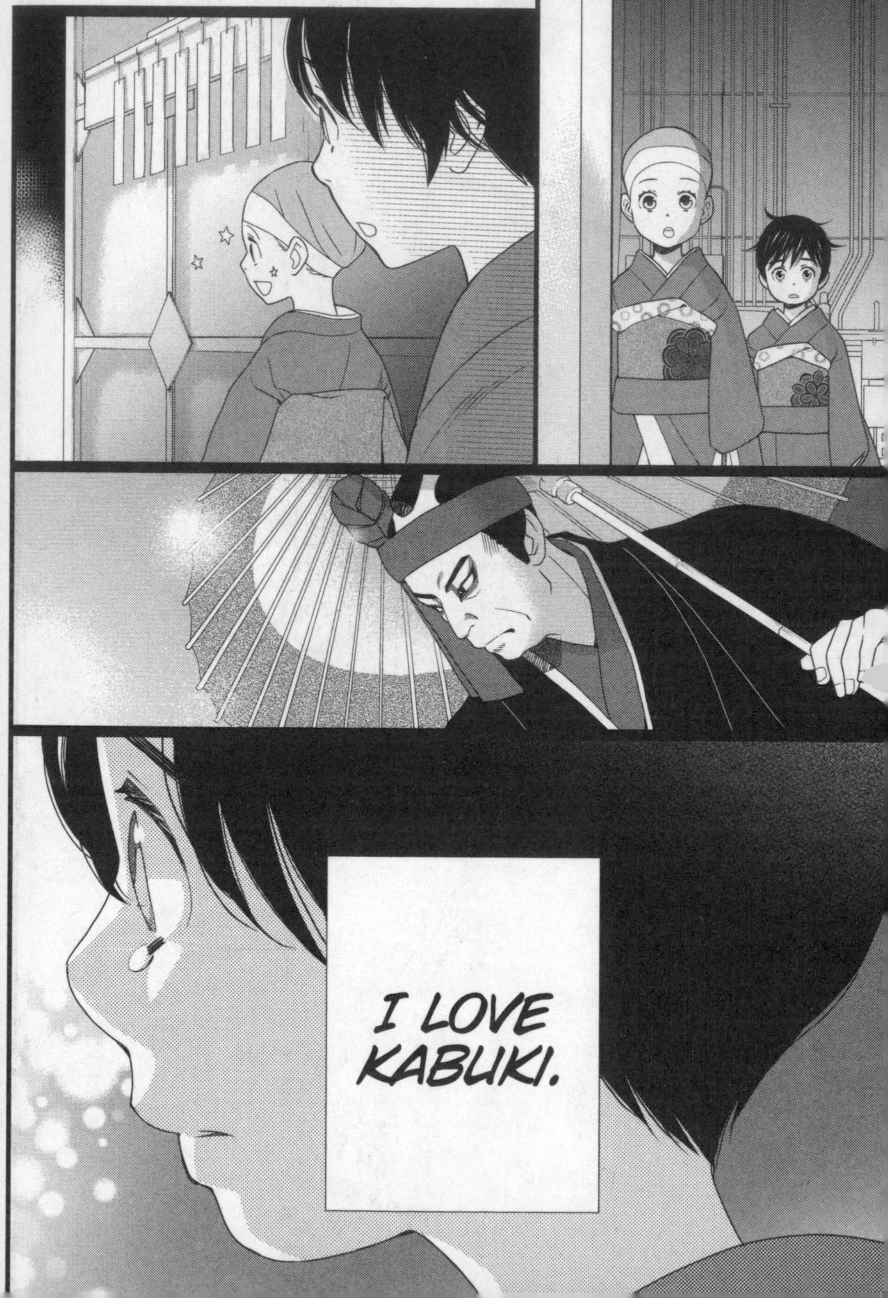
I LOVE KABUKI.

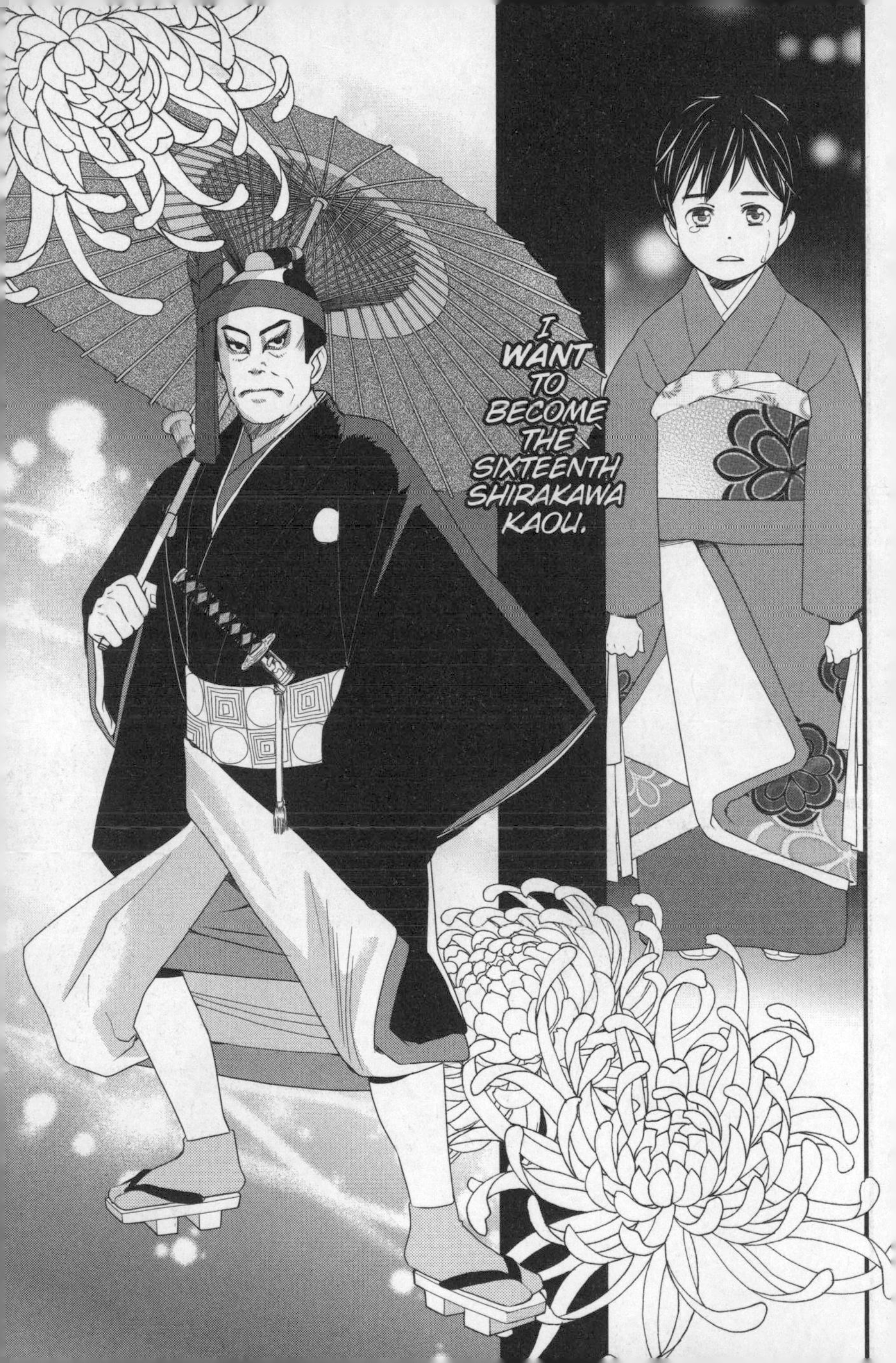
I WANT TO BECOME THE SIXTEENTH SHIRAKAWA KAOU.

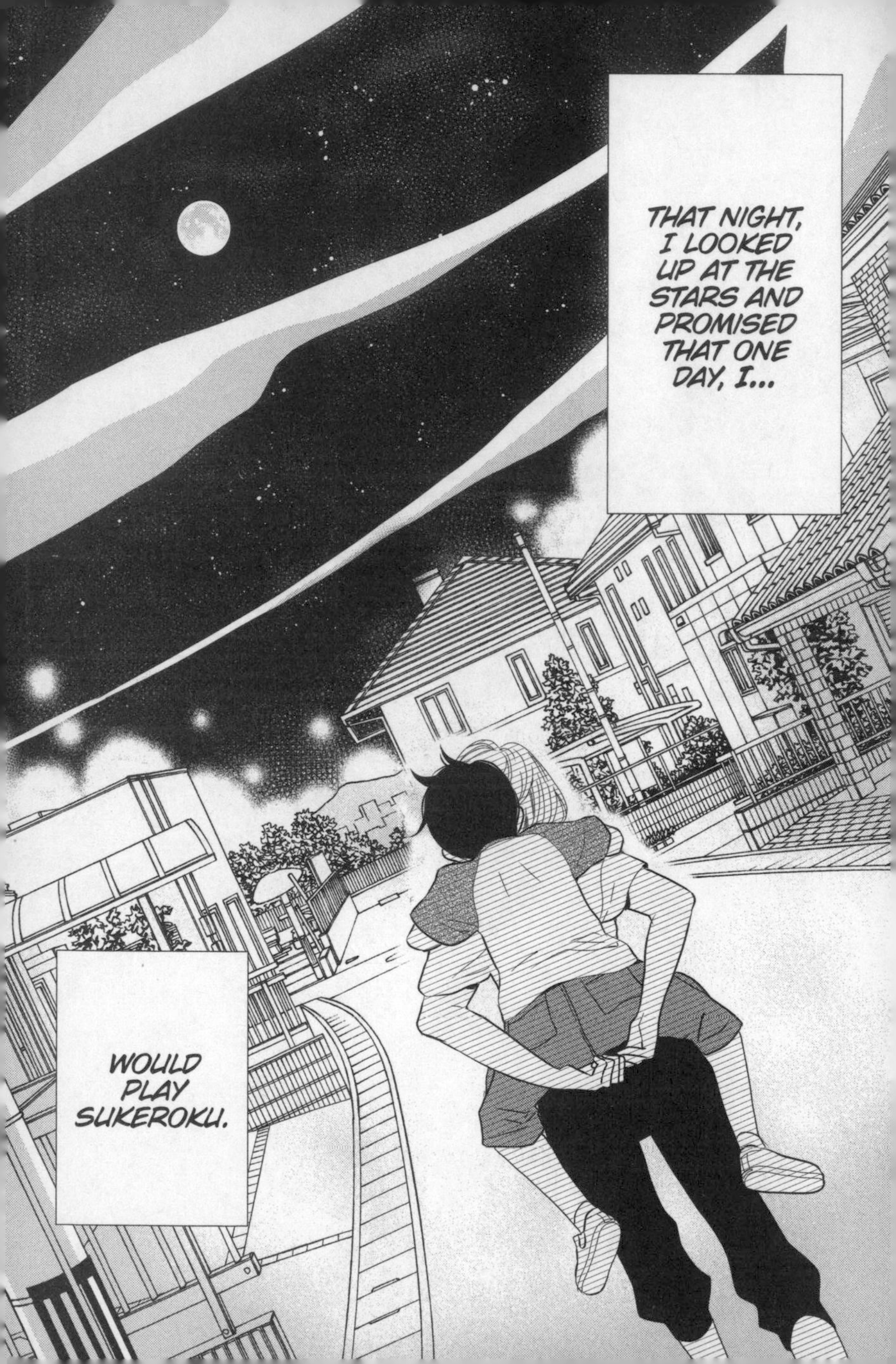
THAT NIGHT, I LOOKED UP AT THE STARS AND PROMISED THAT ONE DAY, I...
WOULD PLAY SUKEROKU.

KAGEKI SHOJO!!

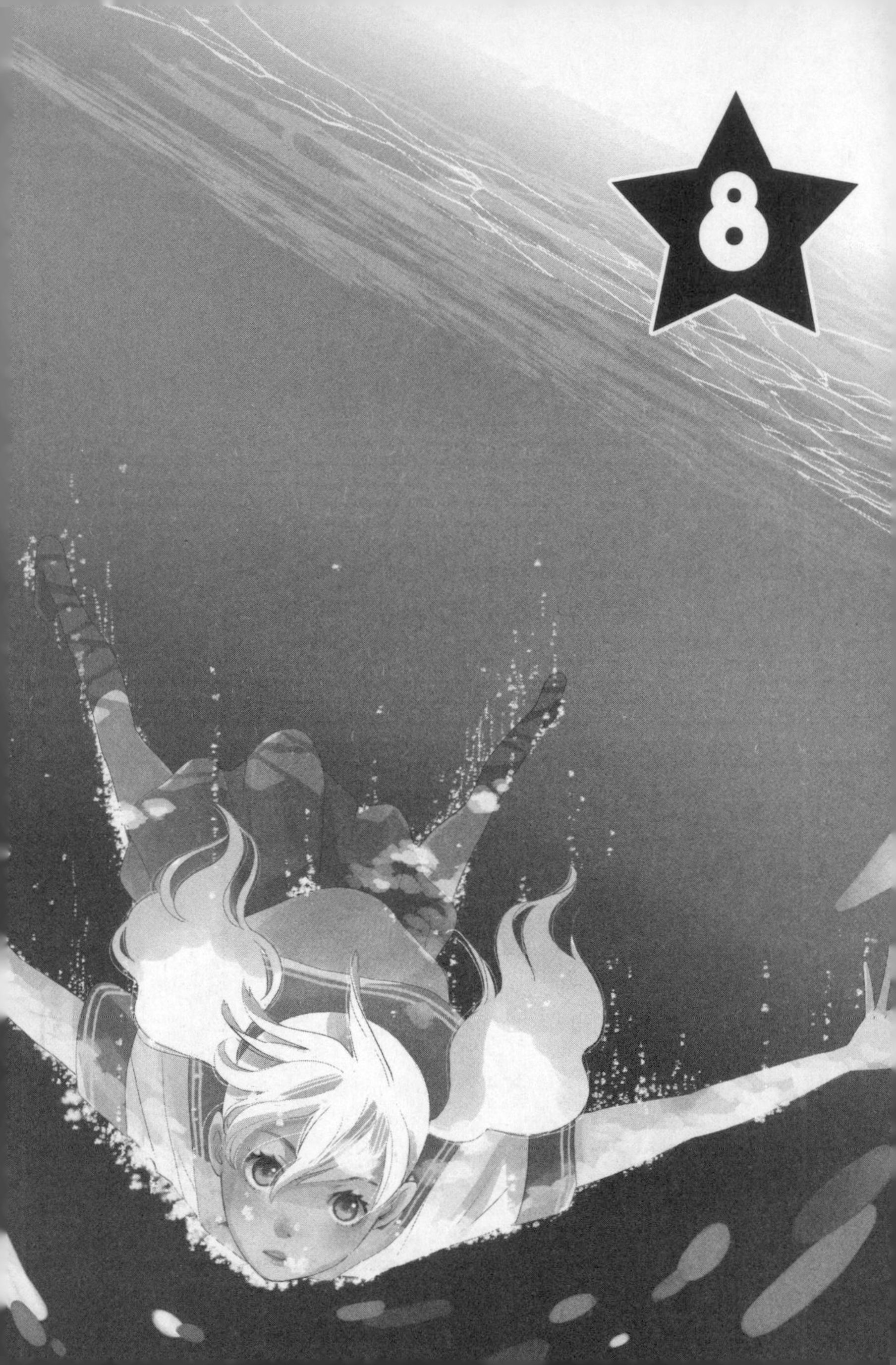
8

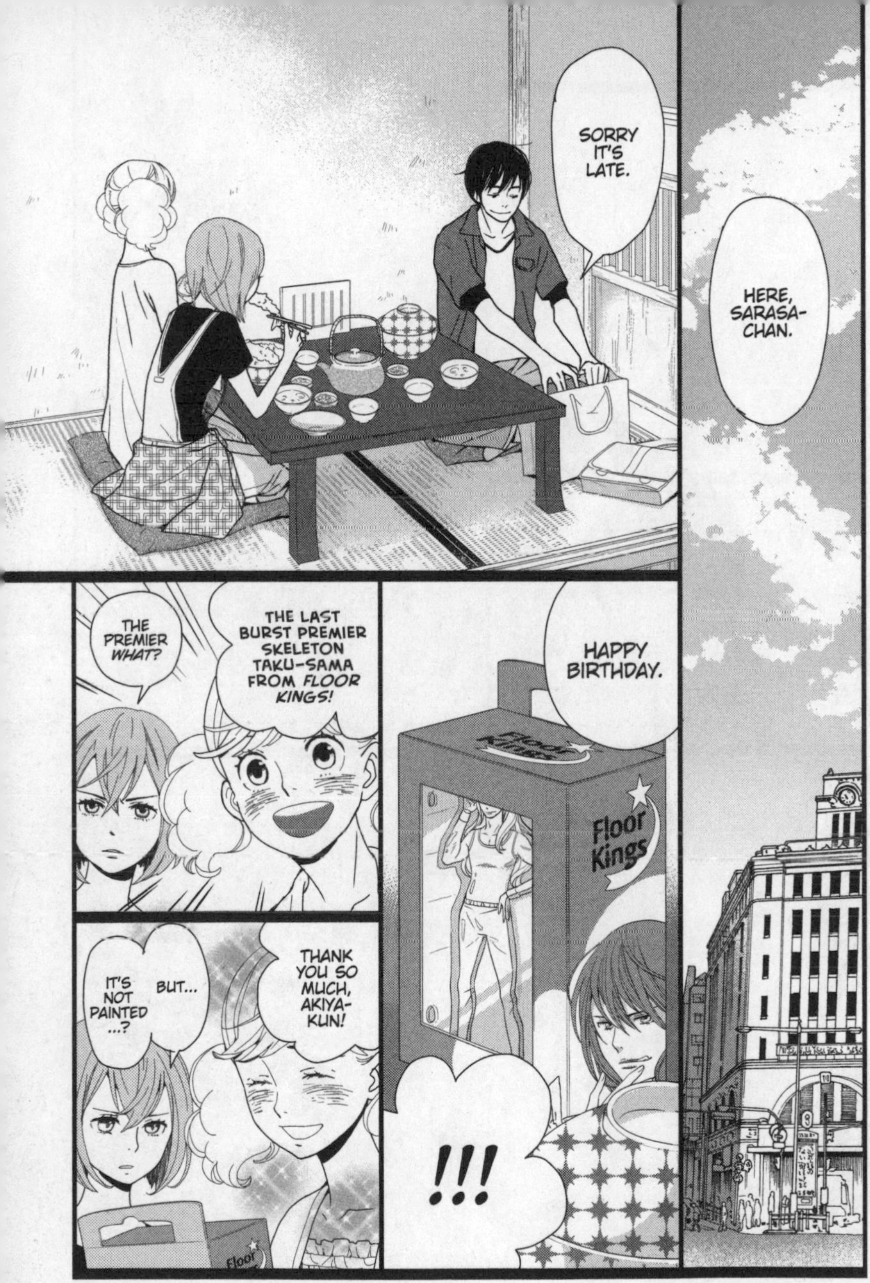
HERE, SARASA-CHAN.
SORRY IT'S LATE.
HAPPY BIRTHDAY.
Floor Kings
Floor Kings
!!!
THE LAST BURST PREMIER SKELETON TAKU-SAMA FROM *FLOOR KINGS!*
THE PREMIER *WHAT?*
THANK YOU SO MUCH, AKIYA-KUN!
BUT...
IT'S NOT PAINTED ...?

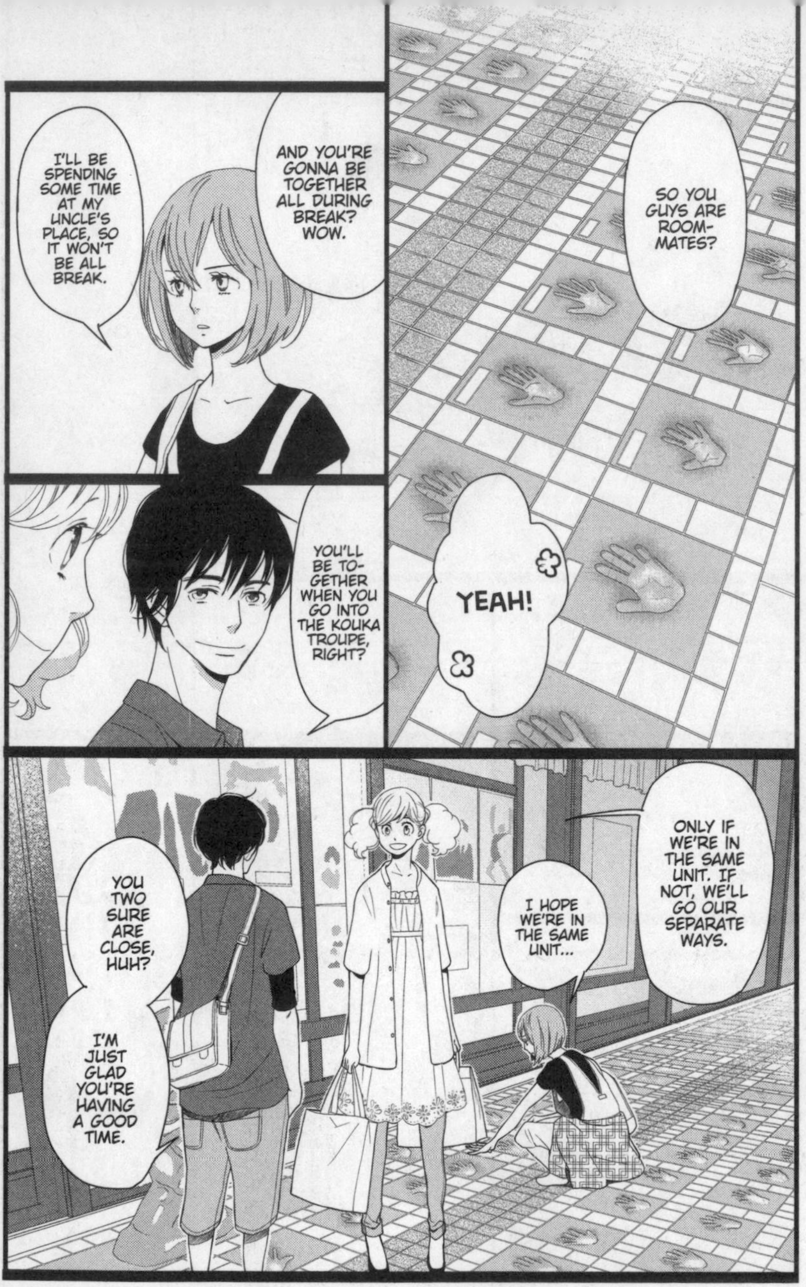
SO YOU GUYS ARE ROOMMATES?
YEAH!
AND YOU'RE GONNA BE TOGETHER ALL DURING BREAK? WOW.
I'LL BE SPENDING SOME TIME AT MY UNCLE'S PLACE, SO IT WON'T BE ALL BREAK.
YOU'LL BE TOGETHER WHEN YOU GO INTO THE KOUKA TROUPE, RIGHT?
ONLY IF WE'RE IN THE SAME UNIT. IF NOT, WE'LL GO OUR SEPARATE WAYS.
I HOPE WE'RE IN THE SAME UNIT...
YOU TWO SURE ARE CLOSE, HUH?
I'M JUST GLAD YOU'RE HAVING A GOOD TIME.

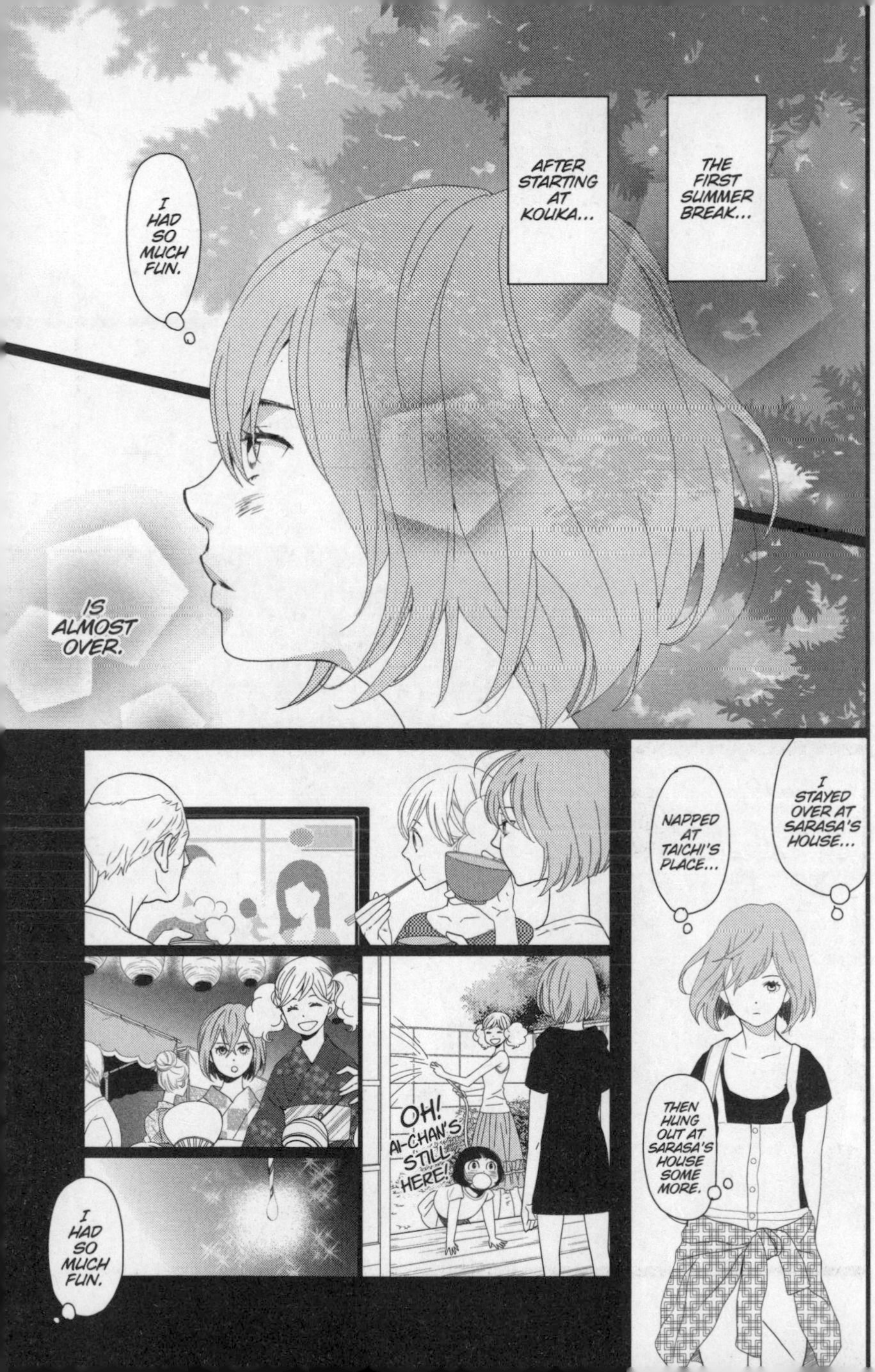
THE FIRST SUMMER BREAK...
AFTER STARTING AT KOUKA...
I HAD SO MUCH FUN.
IS ALMOST OVER.
I STAYED OVER AT SARASA'S HOUSE...
NAPPED AT TAICHI'S PLACE...
THEN HUNG OUT AT SARASA'S HOUSE SOME MORE.
OH! AI-CHAN'S STILL HERE!
I HAD SO MUCH FUN.

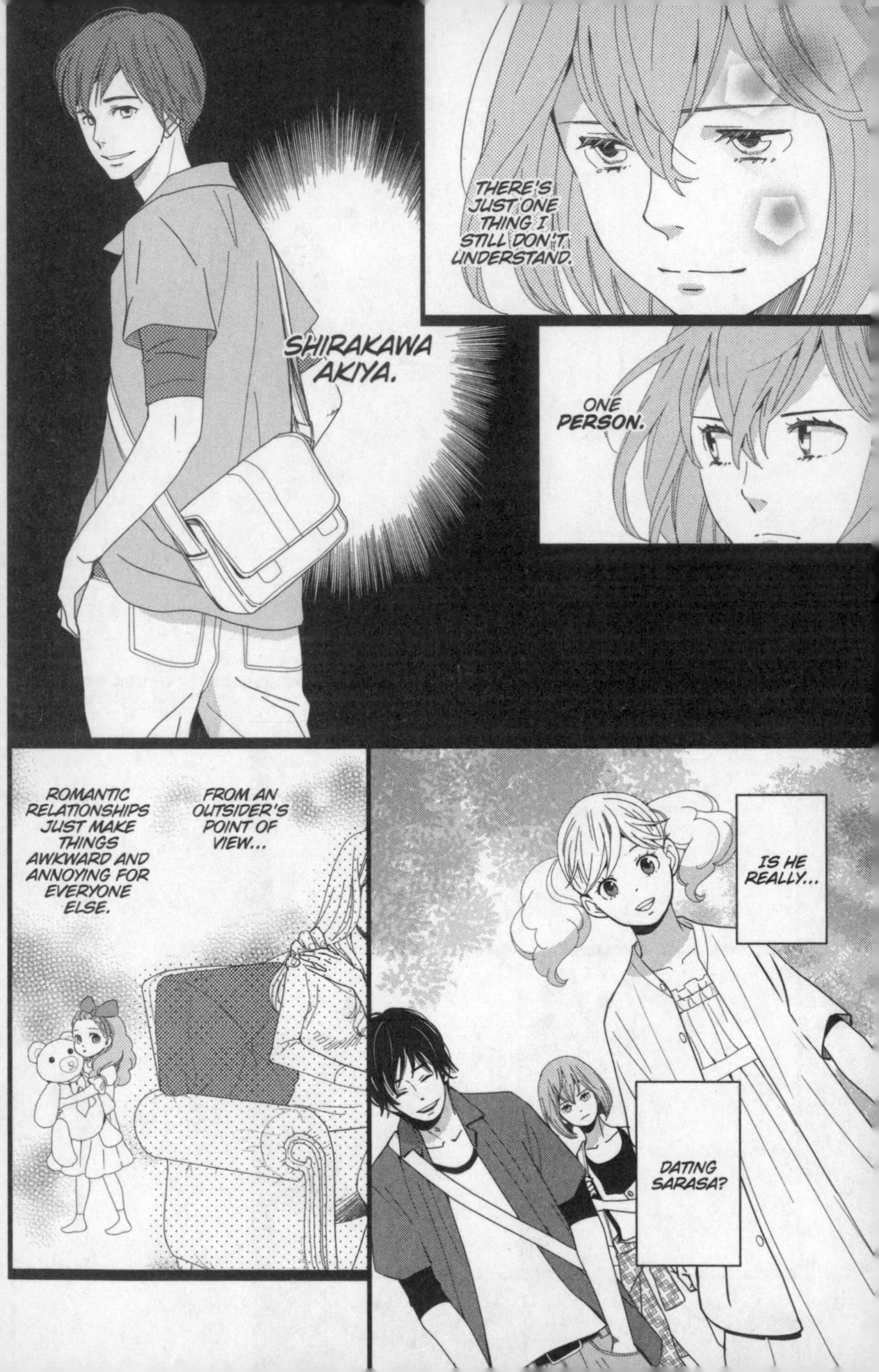
THERE'S JUST ONE THING I STILL DON'T UNDERSTAND.
ONE PERSON.
SHIRAKAWA AKIYA.
IS HE REALLY...
DATING SARASA?
FROM AN OUTSIDER'S POINT OF VIEW...
ROMANTIC RELATIONSHIPS JUST MAKE THINGS AWKWARD AND ANNOYING FOR EVERYONE ELSE.

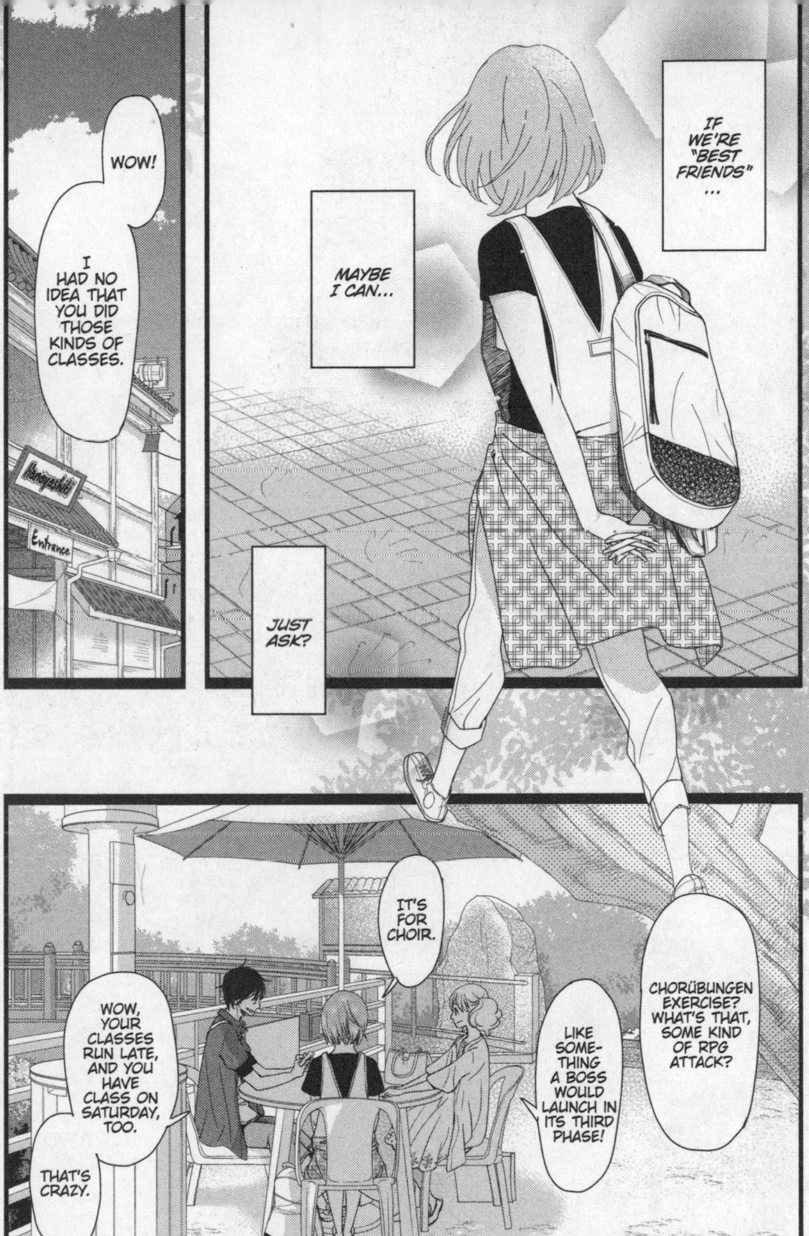
IF WE'RE "BEST FRIENDS"...
MAYBE I CAN...
JUST ASK?
WOW!
I HAD NO IDEA THAT YOU DID THOSE KINDS OF CLASSES.
Entrance
CHORÜBUNGEN EXERCISE? WHAT'S THAT, SOME KIND OF RPG ATTACK?
LIKE SOME-THING A BOSS WOULD LAUNCH IN ITS THIRD PHASE!
IT'S FOR CHOIR.
WOW, YOUR CLASSES RUN LATE, AND YOU HAVE CLASS ON SATURDAY, TOO.
THAT'S CRAZY.

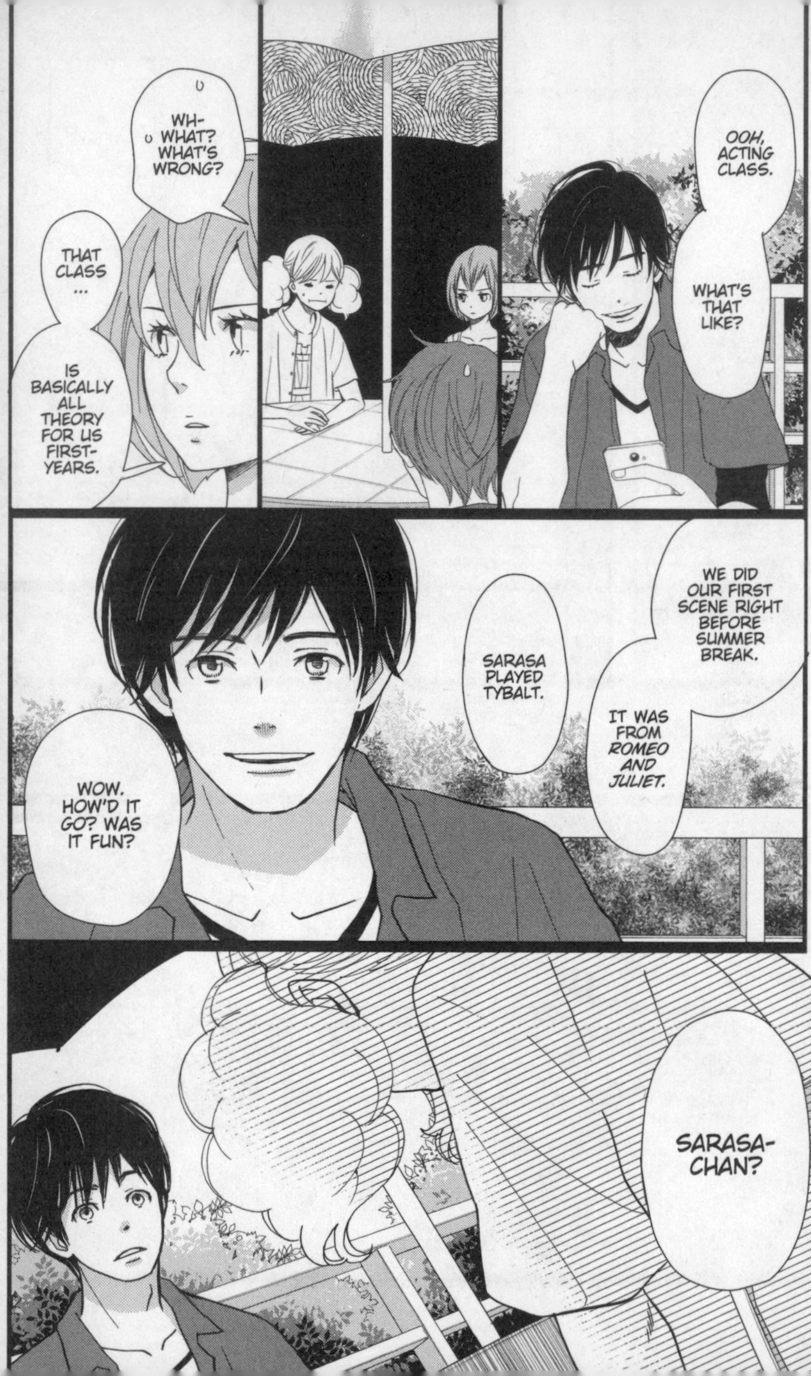
OOH, ACTING CLASS.
WHAT'S THAT LIKE?
WH-WHAT? WHAT'S WRONG?
THAT CLASS ...
IS BASICALLY ALL THEORY FOR US FIRST-YEARS.
WE DID OUR FIRST SCENE RIGHT BEFORE SUMMER BREAK.
IT WAS FROM *ROMEO AND JULIET.*
SARASA PLAYED TYBALT.
WOW. HOW'D IT GO? WAS IT FUN?
SARASA-CHAN?

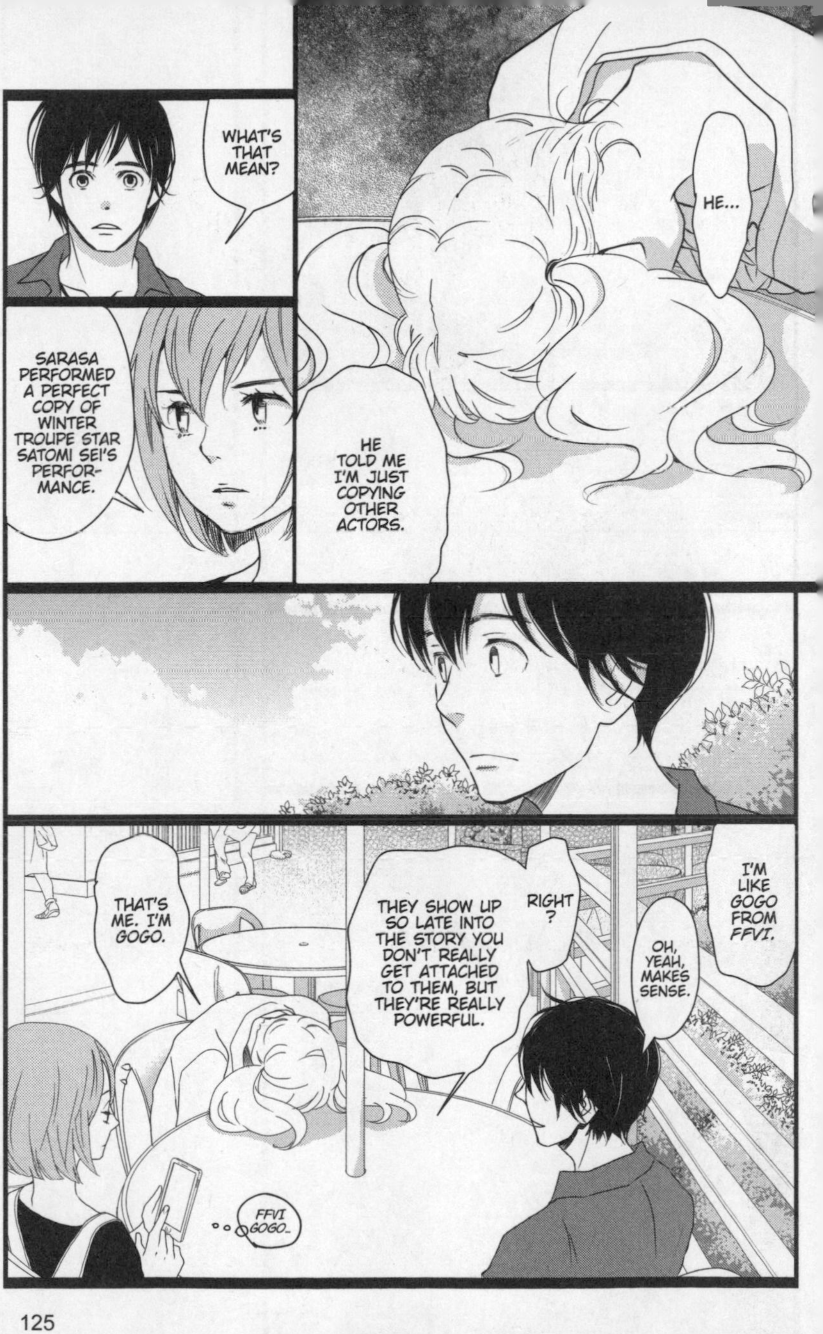
HE...
HE TOLD ME I'M JUST COPYING OTHER ACTORS.
WHAT'S THAT MEAN?
SARASA PERFORMED A PERFECT COPY OF WINTER TROUPE STAR SATOMI SEI'S PERFOR-MANCE.
I'M LIKE GOGO FROM FFVI.
OH, YEAH, MAKES SENSE.
RIGHT?
THEY SHOW UP SO LATE INTO THE STORY YOU DON'T REALLY GET ATTACHED TO THEM, BUT THEY'RE REALLY POWERFUL.
THAT'S ME. I'M GOGO.
FFVI GOGO...

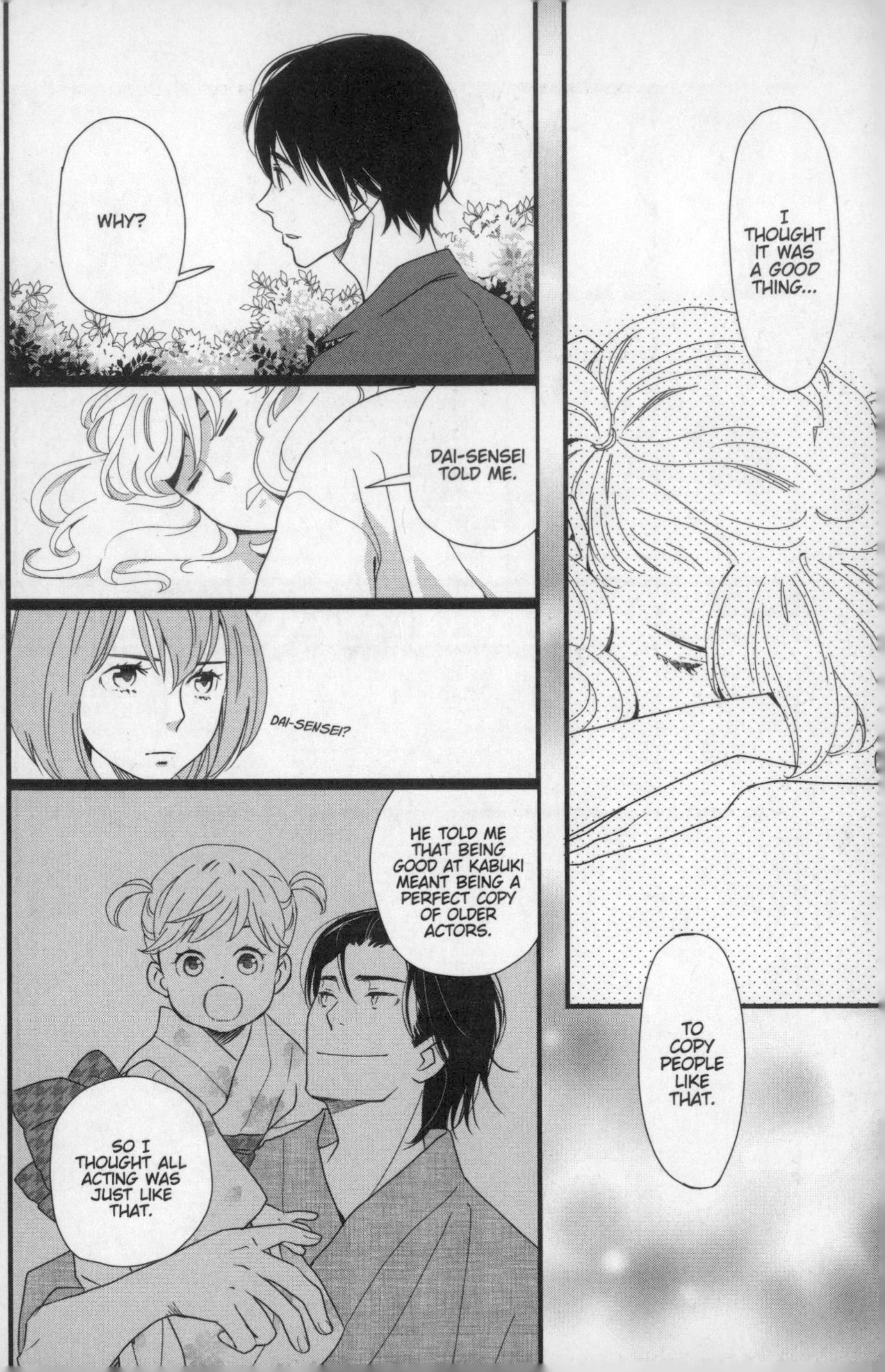
WHY?
DAI-SENSEI TOLD ME.
DAI-SENSEI?
HE TOLD ME THAT BEING GOOD AT KABUKI MEANT BEING A PERFECT COPY OF OLDER ACTORS.
SO I THOUGHT ALL ACTING WAS JUST LIKE THAT.
I THOUGHT IT WAS A GOOD THING...
TO COPY PEOPLE LIKE THAT.

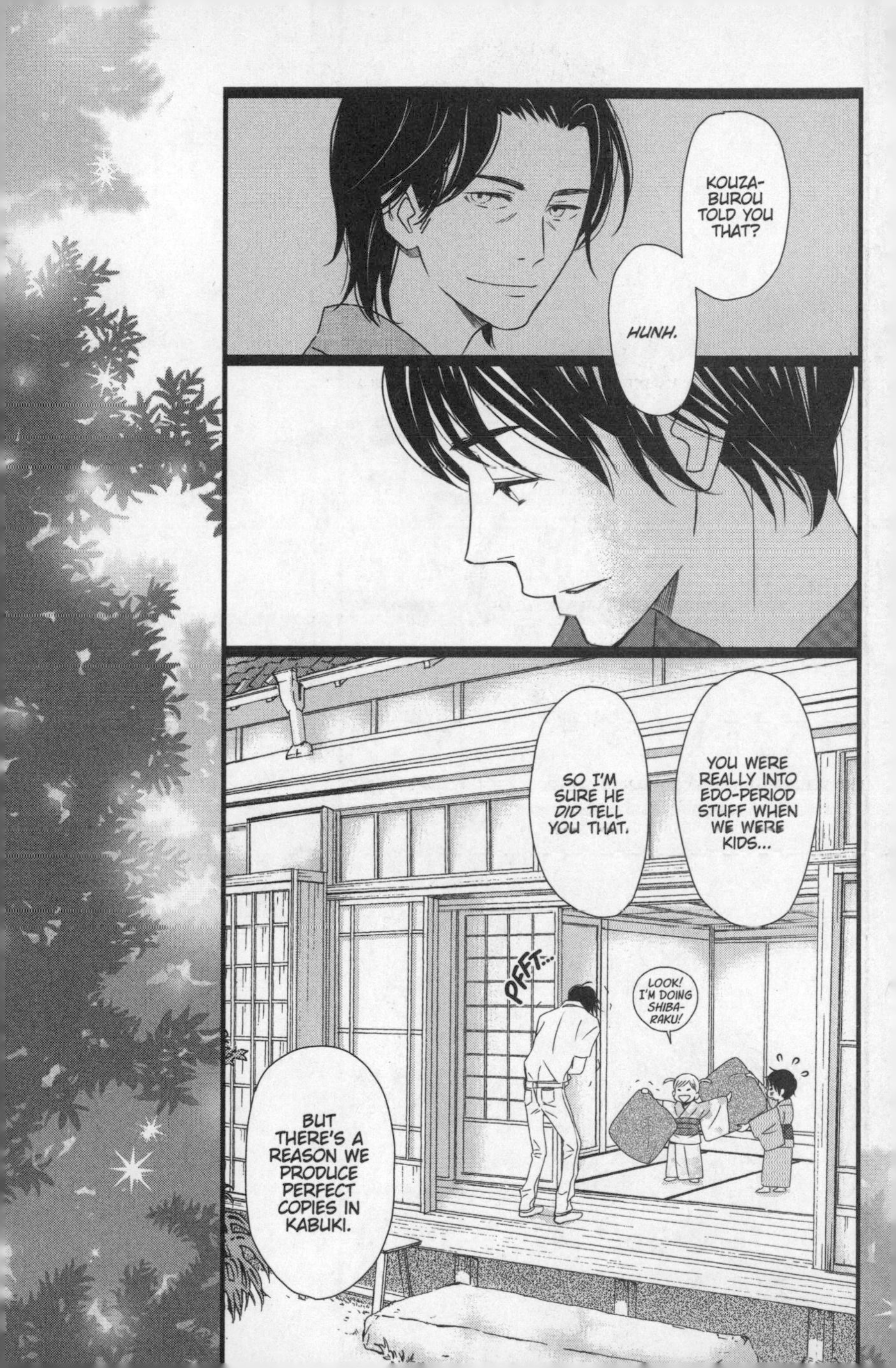
KOUZA-BUROU TOLD YOU THAT?
HUNH.
YOU WERE REALLY INTO EDO-PERIOD STUFF WHEN WE WERE KIDS...
SO I'M SURE HE *DID* TELL YOU THAT.
LOOK! I'M DOING SHIBA-RAKU!
PFFT...
BUT THERE'S A REASON WE PRODUCE PERFECT COPIES IN KABUKI.

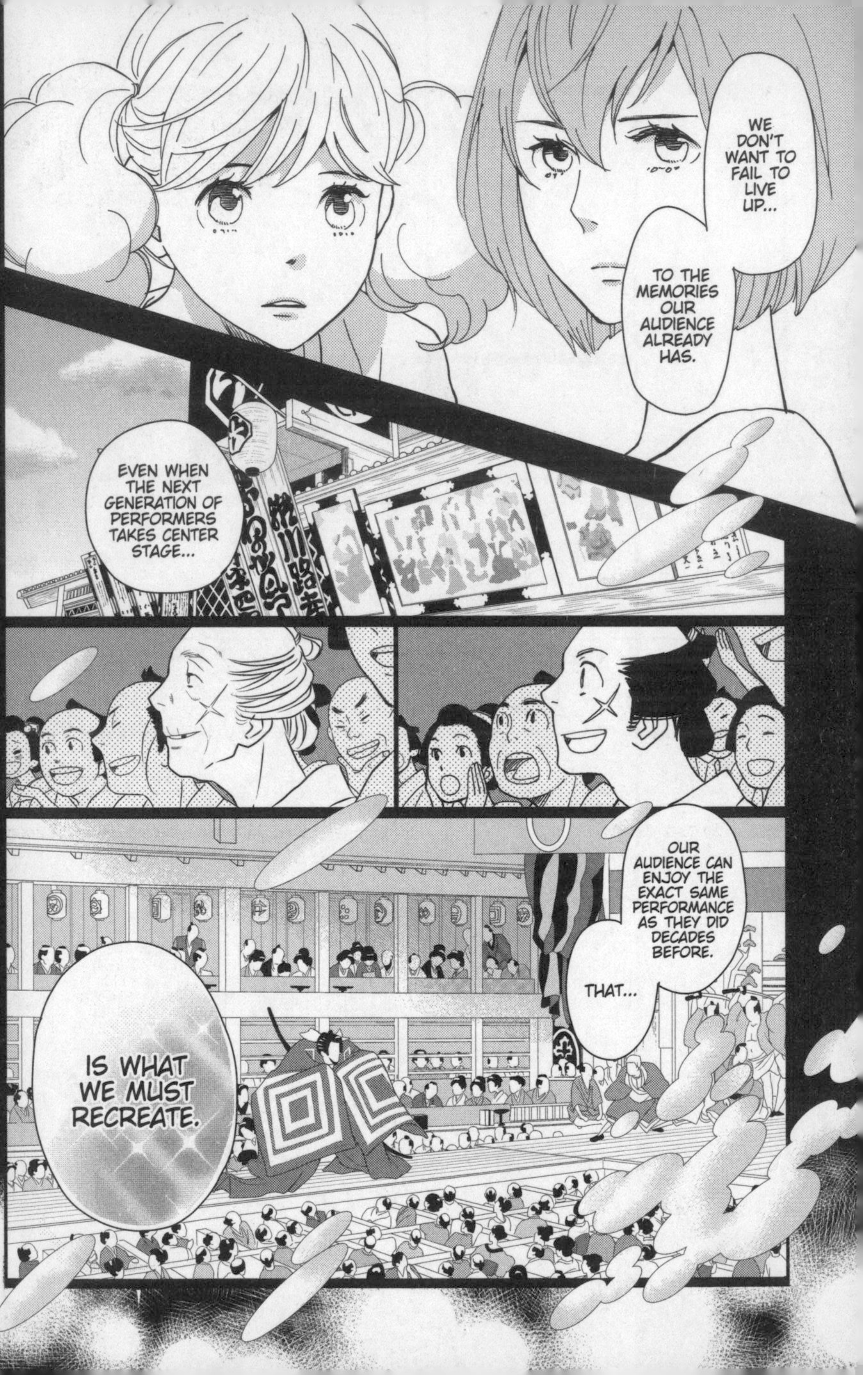
WE DON'T WANT TO FAIL TO LIVE UP...
TO THE MEMORIES OUR AUDIENCE ALREADY HAS.
EVEN WHEN THE NEXT GENERATION OF PERFORMERS TAKES CENTER STAGE...
OUR AUDIENCE CAN ENJOY THE EXACT SAME PERFORMANCE AS THEY DID DECADES BEFORE.
THAT...
IS WHAT WE MUST RECREATE.

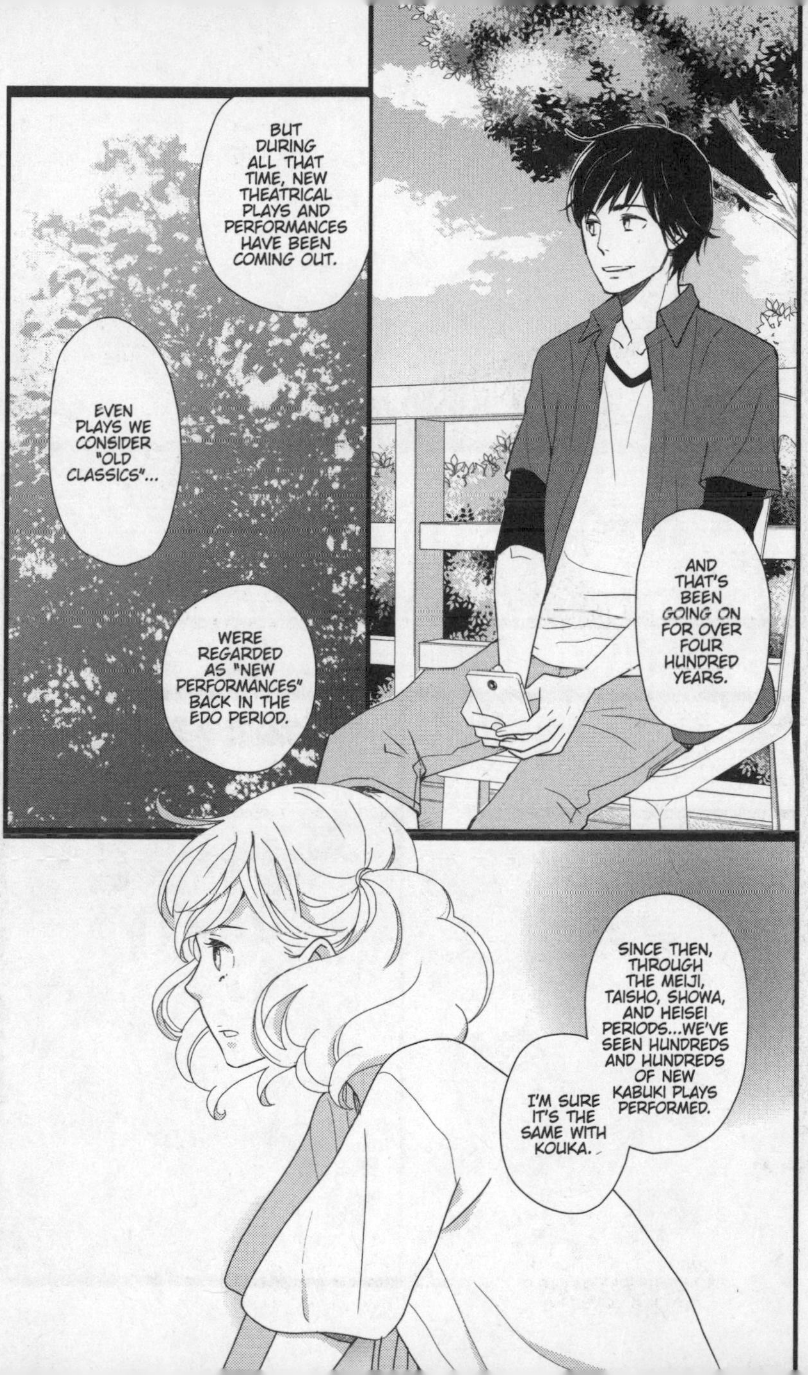
AND THAT'S BEEN GOING ON FOR OVER FOUR HUNDRED YEARS.
BUT DURING ALL THAT TIME, NEW THEATRICAL PLAYS AND PERFORMANCES HAVE BEEN COMING OUT.
EVEN PLAYS WE CONSIDER "OLD CLASSICS"...
WERE REGARDED AS "NEW PERFORMANCES" BACK IN THE EDO PERIOD.
SINCE THEN, THROUGH THE MEIJI, TAISHO, SHOWA, AND HEISEI PERIODS...WE'VE SEEN HUNDREDS AND HUNDREDS OF NEW KABUKI PLAYS PERFORMED.
I'M SURE IT'S THE SAME WITH KOUKA.

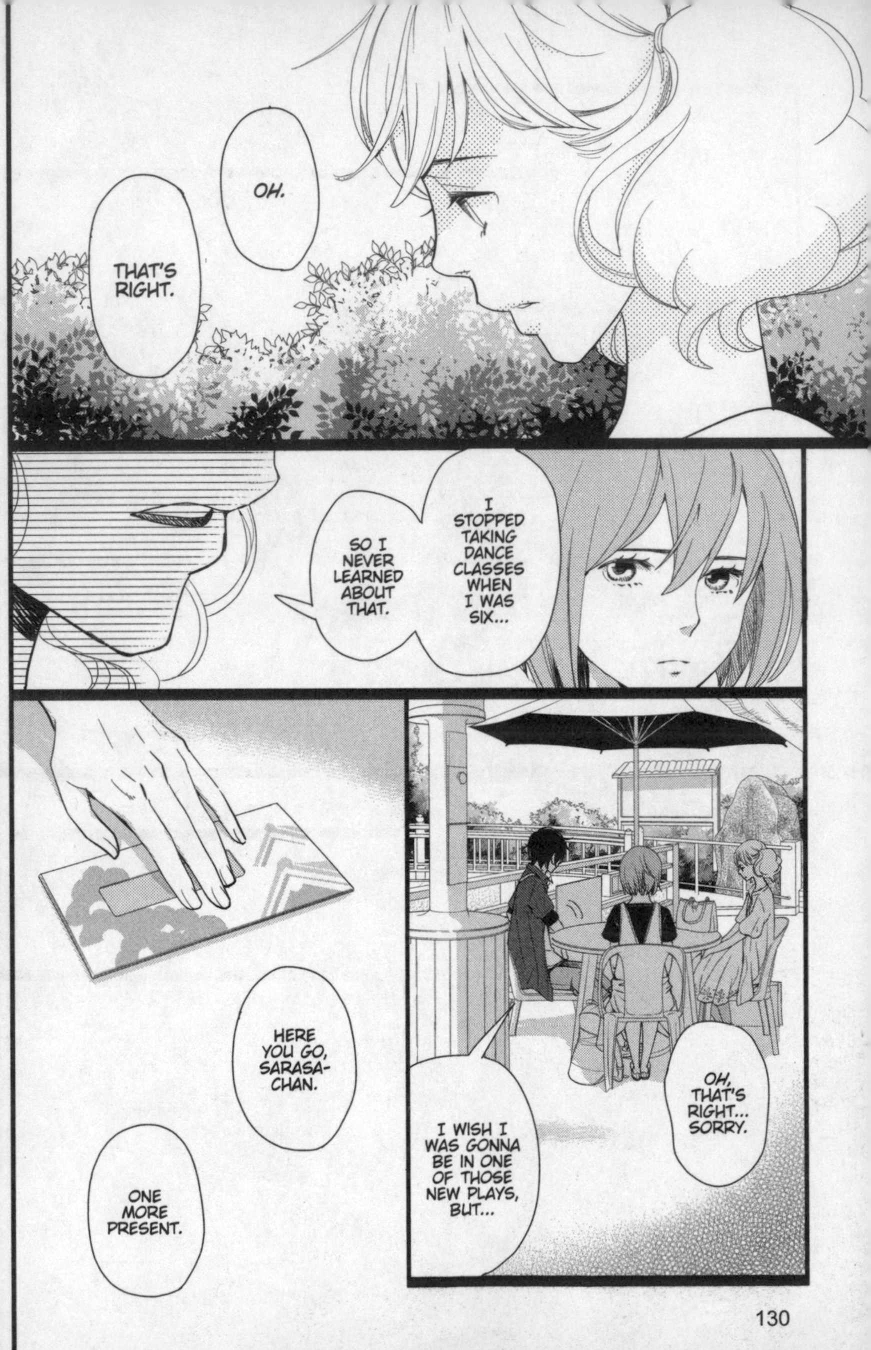
OH.
THAT'S RIGHT.
I STOPPED TAKING DANCE CLASSES WHEN I WAS SIX...
SO I NEVER LEARNED ABOUT THAT.
OH, THAT'S RIGHT... SORRY.
I WISH I WAS GONNA BE IN ONE OF THOSE NEW PLAYS, BUT...
HERE YOU GO, SARASA-CHAN.
ONE MORE PRESENT.

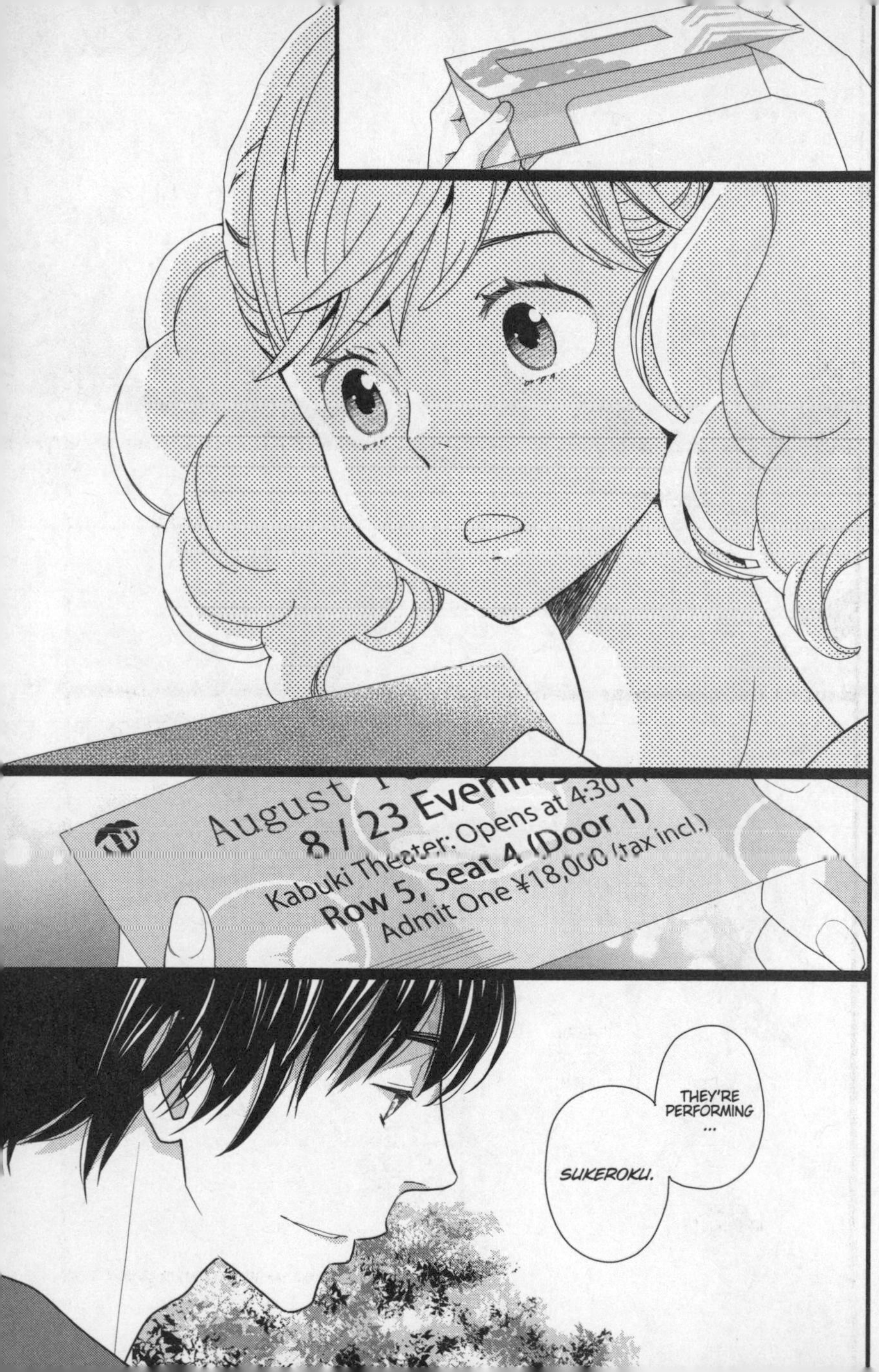
August
8 / 23
Kabuki Theater: Opens at 4:30
Row 5, Seat 4 (Door 1)
Admit One ¥18,000 (tax incl.)
THEY'RE PERFORMING ... SUKEROKU.

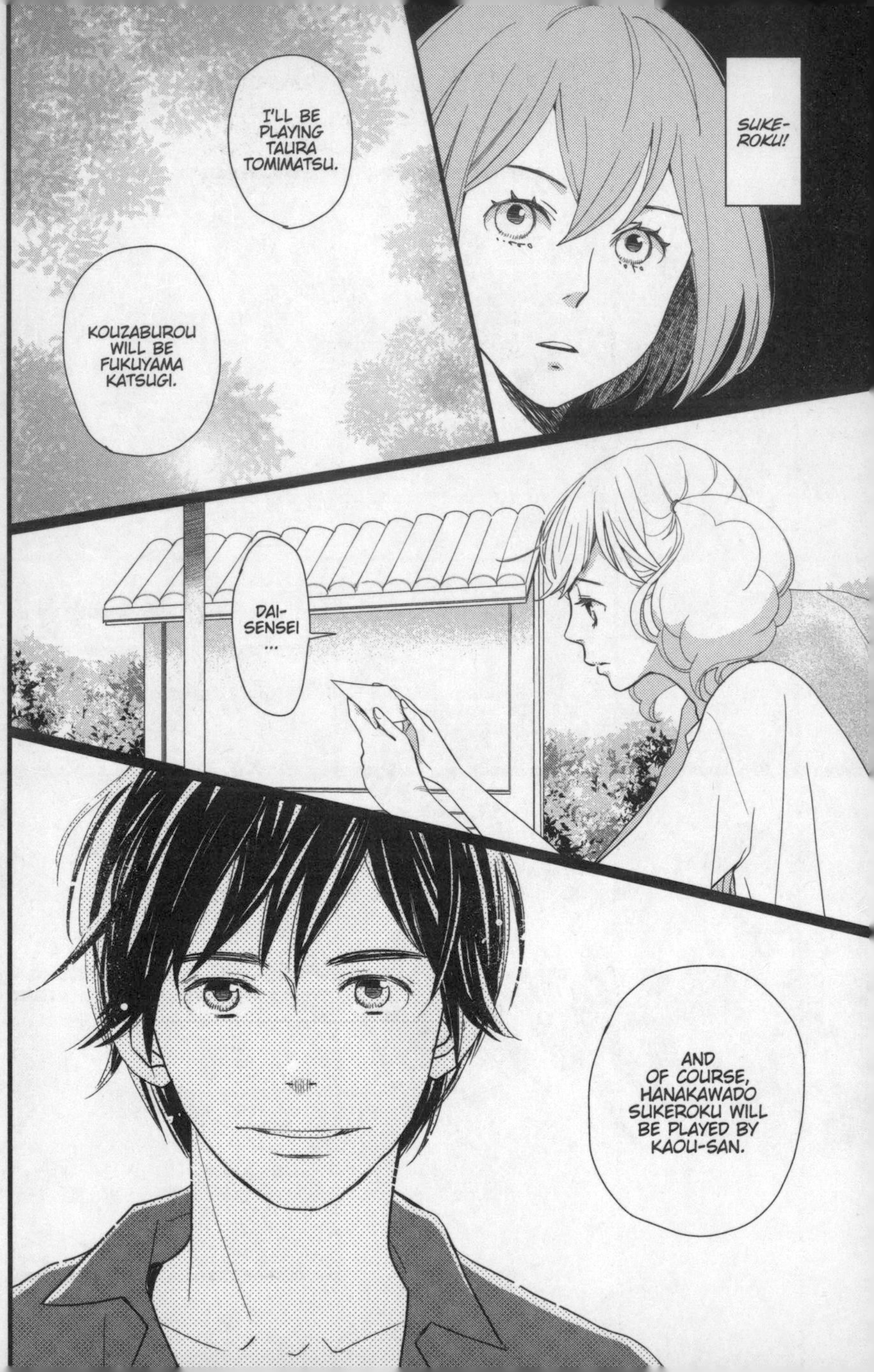
SUKE-ROKU!
I'LL BE PLAYING TAURA TOMIMATSU.
KOUZABUROU WILL BE FUKUYAMA KATSUGI.
DAI-SENSEI ...
AND OF COURSE, HANAKAWADO SUKEROKU WILL BE PLAYED BY KAOU-SAN.

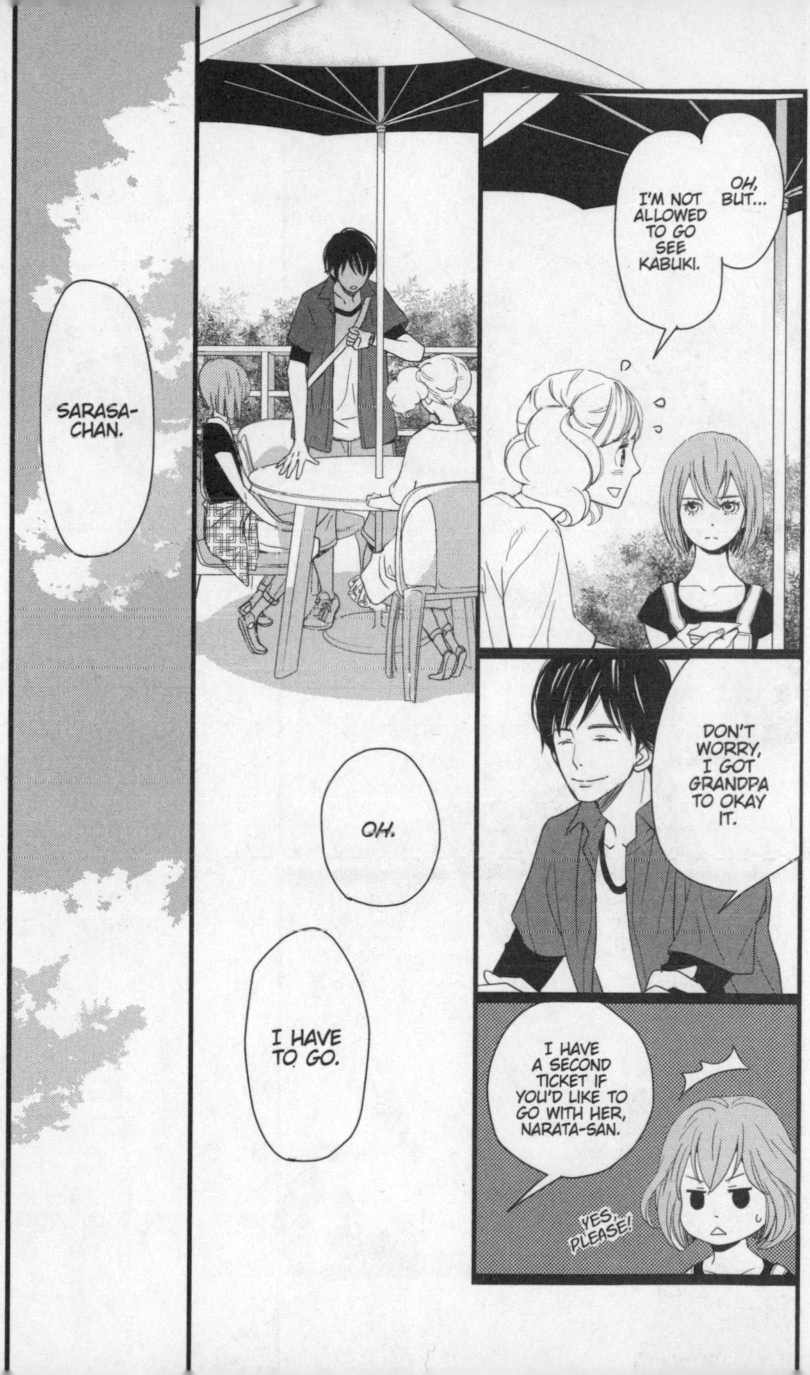
OH, BUT... I'M NOT ALLOWED TO GO SEE KABUKI.
DON'T WORRY, I GOT GRANDPA TO OKAY IT.
I HAVE A SECOND TICKET IF YOU'D LIKE TO GO WITH HER, NARATA-SAN.
YES, PLEASE!
OH.
I HAVE TO GO.
SARASA-CHAN.

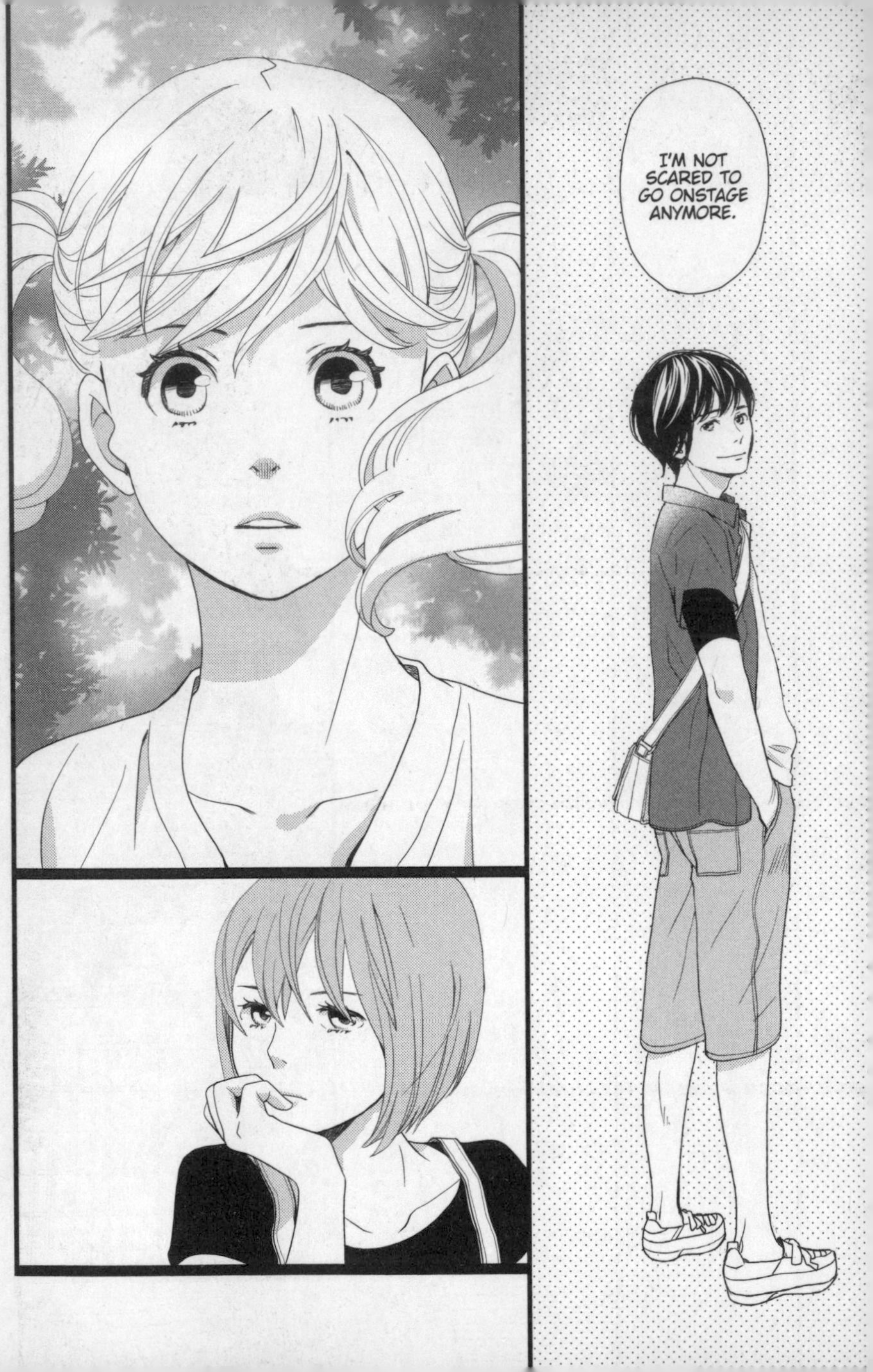
I'M NOT SCARED TO GO ONSTAGE ANYMORE.

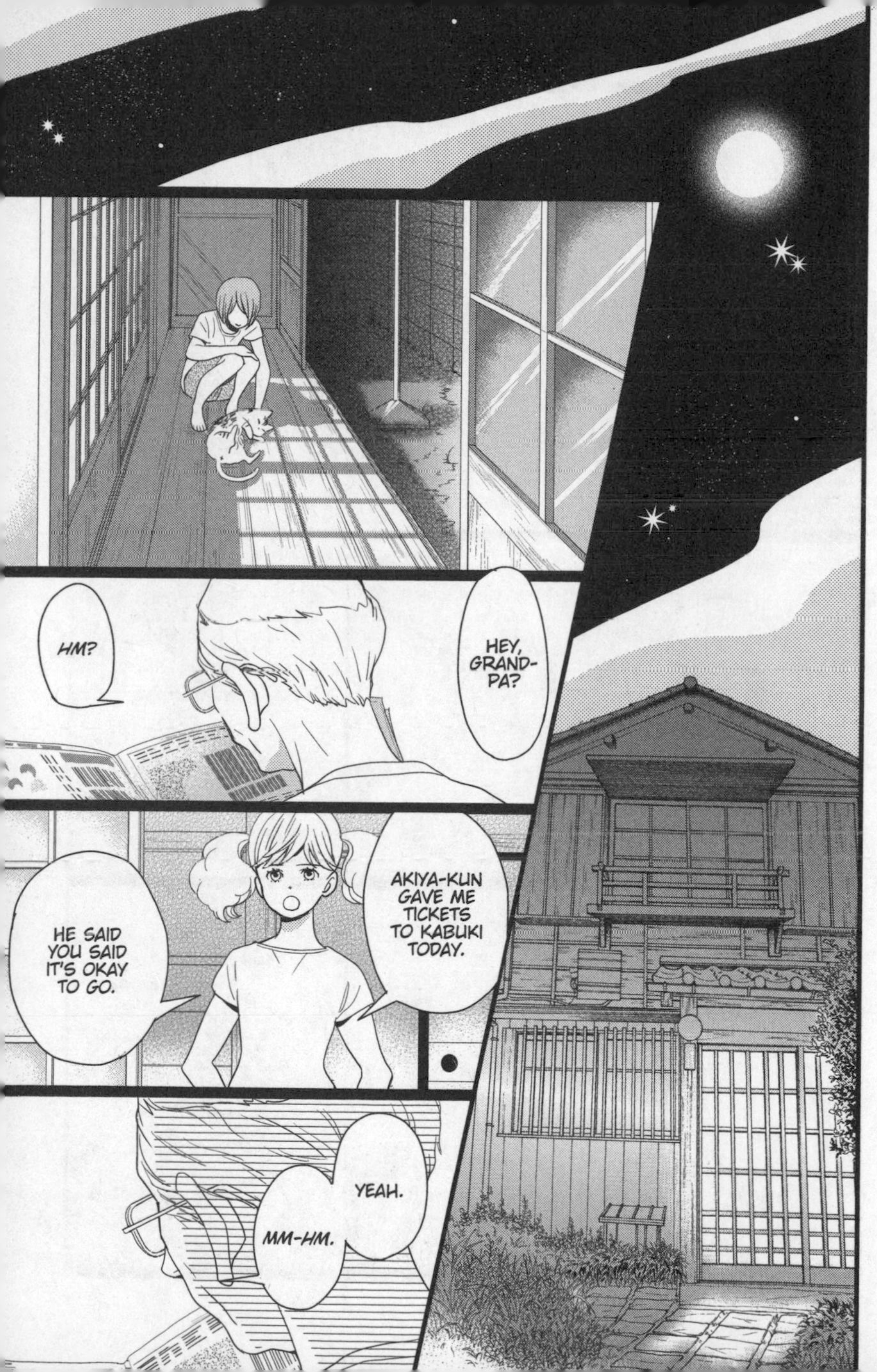
HEY, GRAND-PA?
HM?
AKIYA-KUN GAVE ME TICKETS TO KABUKI TODAY.
HE SAID YOU SAID IT'S OKAY TO GO.
YEAH.
MM-HM.

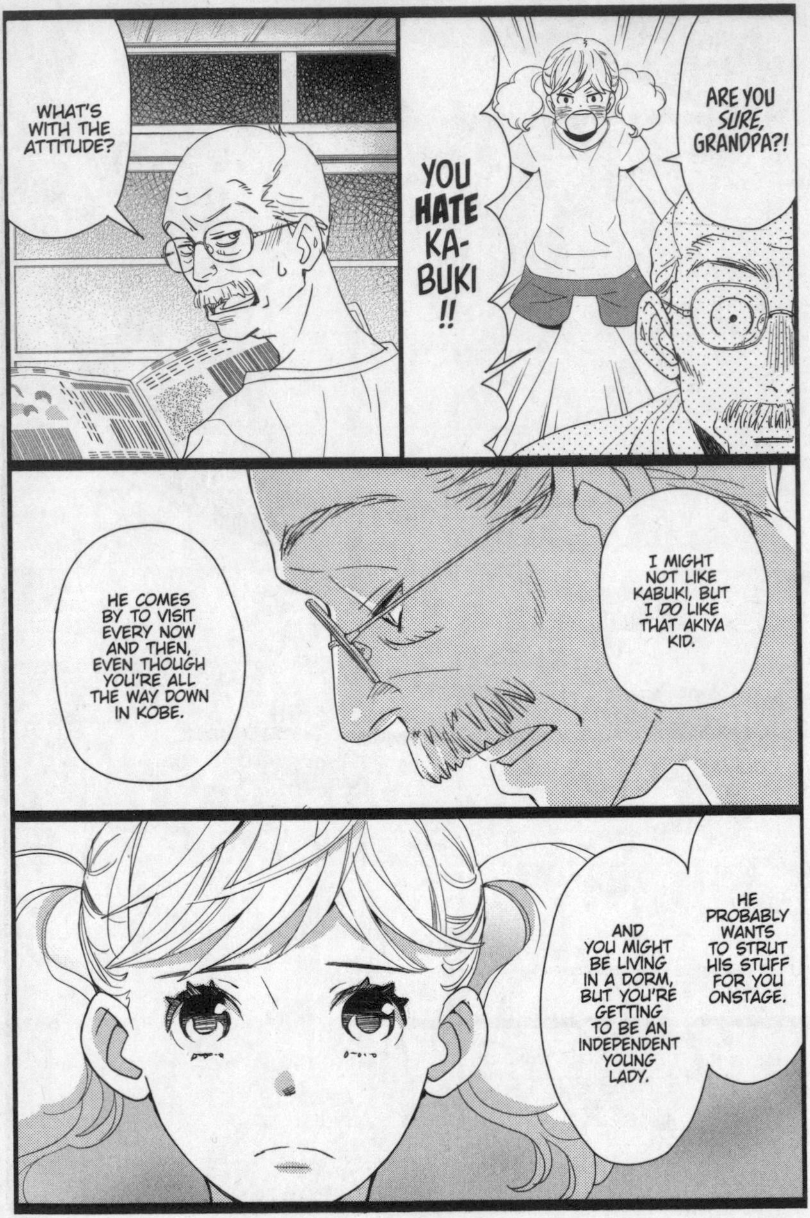
ARE YOU SURE, GRANDPA?!
YOU HATE KA-BUKI!!
WHAT'S WITH THE ATTITUDE?
I MIGHT NOT LIKE KABUKI, BUT I DO LIKE THAT AKIYA KID.
HE COMES BY TO VISIT EVERY NOW AND THEN, EVEN THOUGH YOU'RE ALL THE WAY DOWN IN KOBE.
HE PROBABLY WANTS TO STRUT HIS STUFF FOR YOU ONSTAGE.
AND YOU MIGHT BE LIVING IN A DORM, BUT YOU'RE GETTING TO BE AN INDEPENDENT YOUNG LADY.

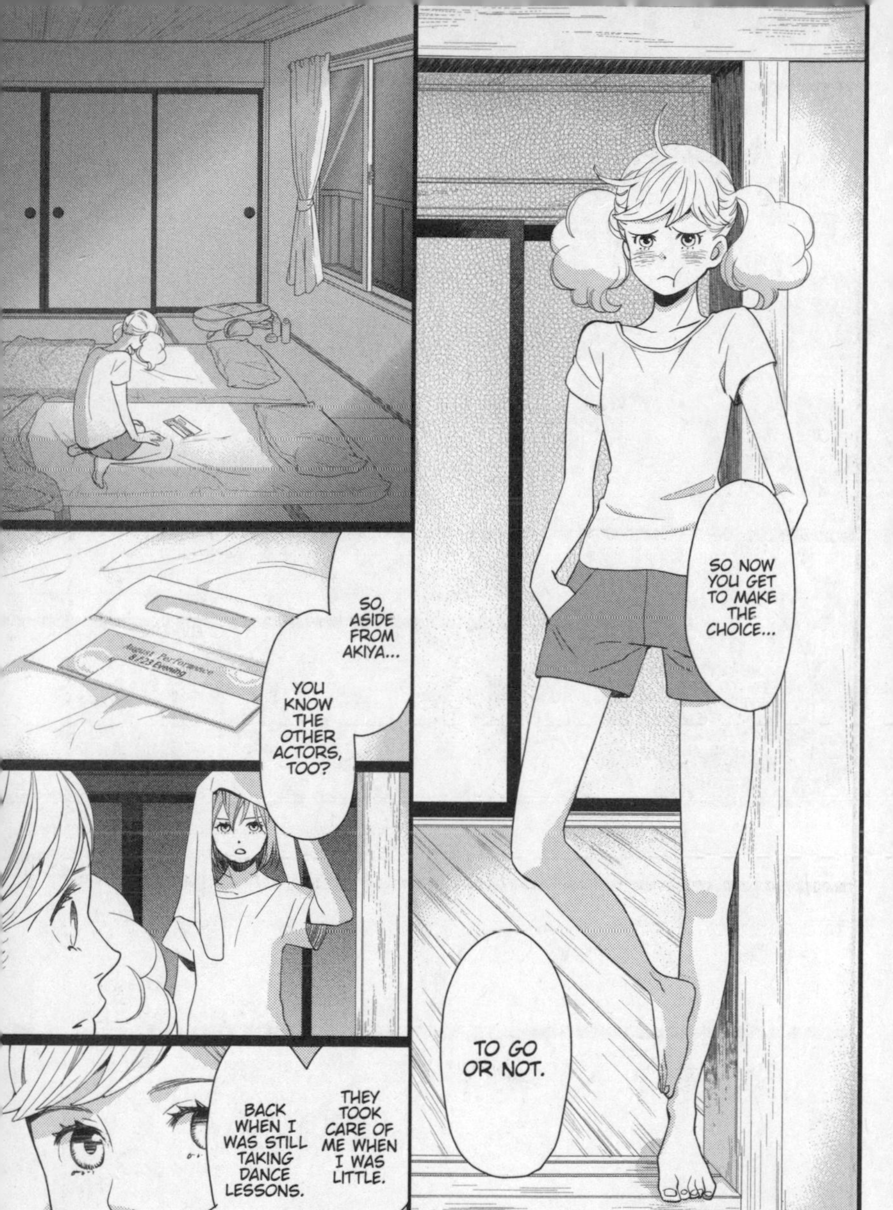
SO NOW YOU GET TO MAKE THE CHOICE...
TO GO OR NOT.
August Performance
8/23 Evening
SO, ASIDE FROM AKIYA...
YOU KNOW THE OTHER ACTORS, TOO?
THEY TOOK CARE OF ME WHEN I WAS LITTLE.
BACK WHEN I WAS STILL TAKING DANCE LESSONS.

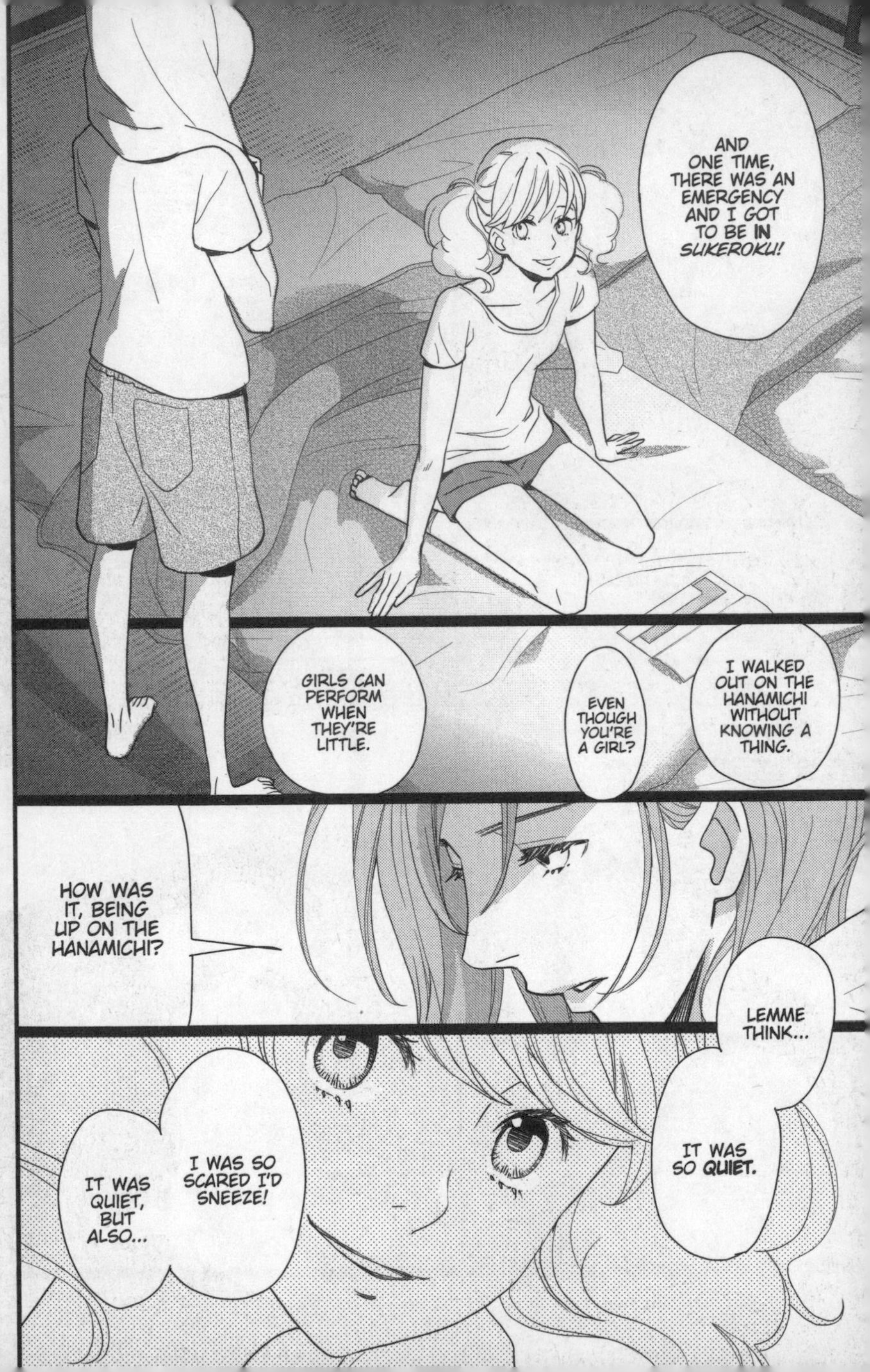
AND ONE TIME, THERE WAS AN EMERGENCY AND I GOT TO BE **IN** *SUKEROKU*!
I WALKED OUT ON THE HANAMICHI WITHOUT KNOWING A THING.
EVEN THOUGH YOU'RE A GIRL?
GIRLS CAN PERFORM WHEN THEY'RE LITTLE.
HOW WAS IT, BEING UP ON THE HANAMICHI?
LEMME THINK...
IT WAS SO **QUIET**.
I WAS SO SCARED I'D SNEEZE!
IT WAS QUIET, BUT ALSO...

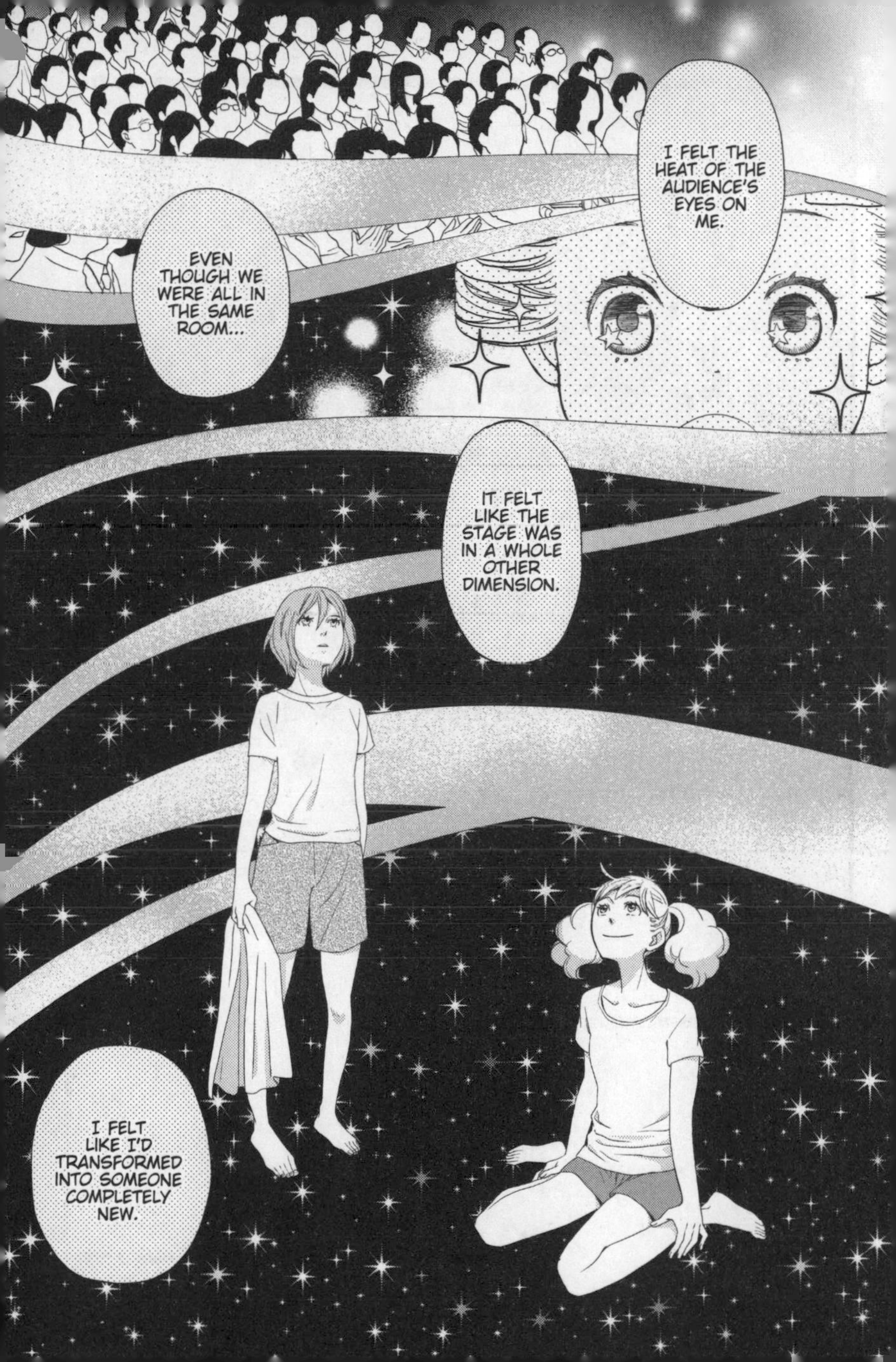
I FELT THE HEAT OF THE AUDIENCE'S EYES ON ME.
EVEN THOUGH WE WERE ALL IN THE SAME ROOM...
IT FELT LIKE THE STAGE WAS IN A WHOLE OTHER DIMENSION.
I FELT LIKE I'D TRANSFORMED INTO SOMEONE COMPLETELY NEW.

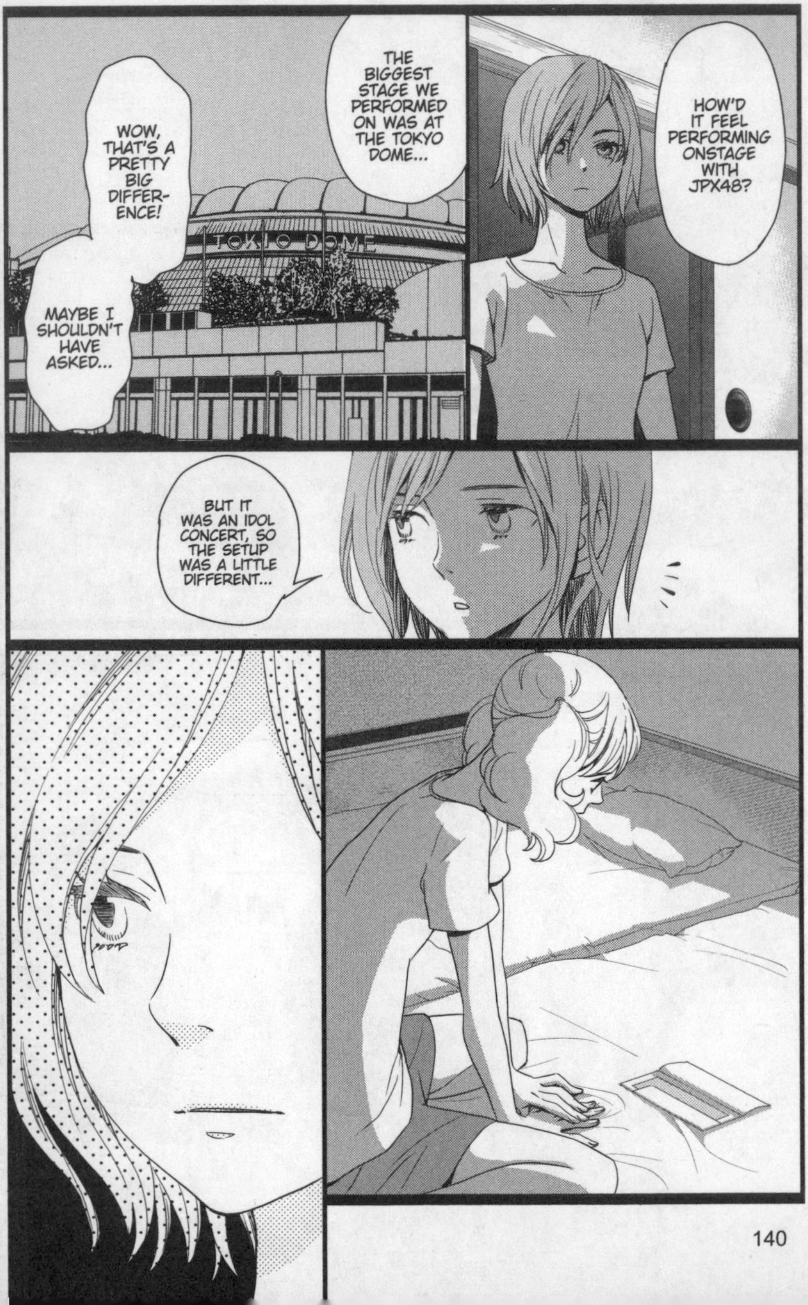
HOW'D IT FEEL PERFORMING ONSTAGE WITH JPX48?
THE BIGGEST STAGE WE PERFORMED ON WAS AT THE TOKYO DOME...
TOKIO DOME
WOW, THAT'S A PRETTY BIG DIFFERENCE!
MAYBE I SHOULDN'T HAVE ASKED...
BUT IT WAS AN IDOL CONCERT, SO THE SETUP WAS A LITTLE DIFFERENT...

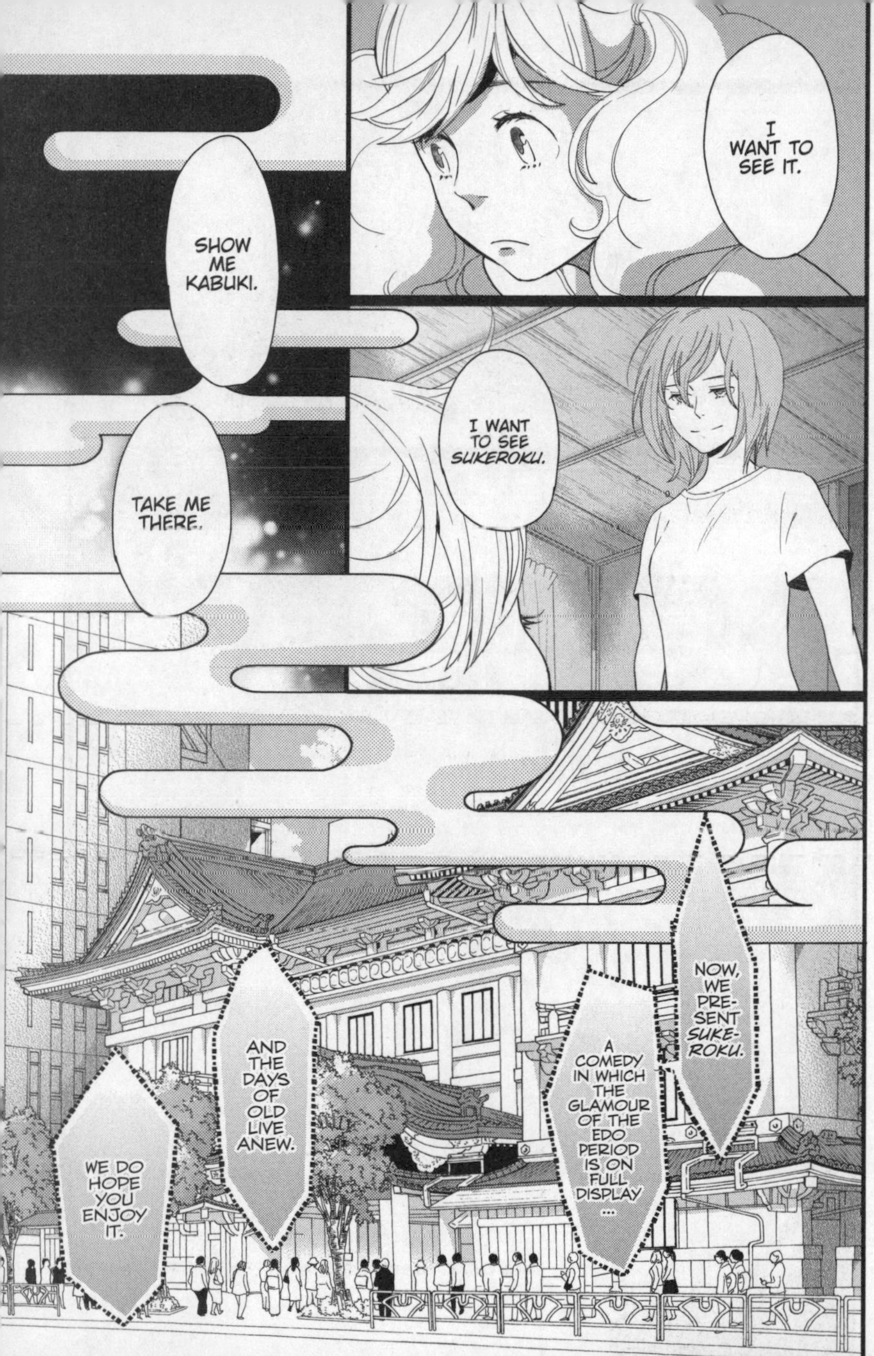
I WANT TO SEE IT.
I WANT TO SEE SUKEROKU.
SHOW ME KABUKI.
TAKE ME THERE.
NOW, WE PRESENT SUKE-ROKU.
A COMEDY IN WHICH THE GLAMOUR OF THE EDO PERIOD IS ON FULL DISPLAY...
AND THE DAYS OF OLD LIVE ANEW.
WE DO HOPE YOU ENJOY IT.

Sign: Water

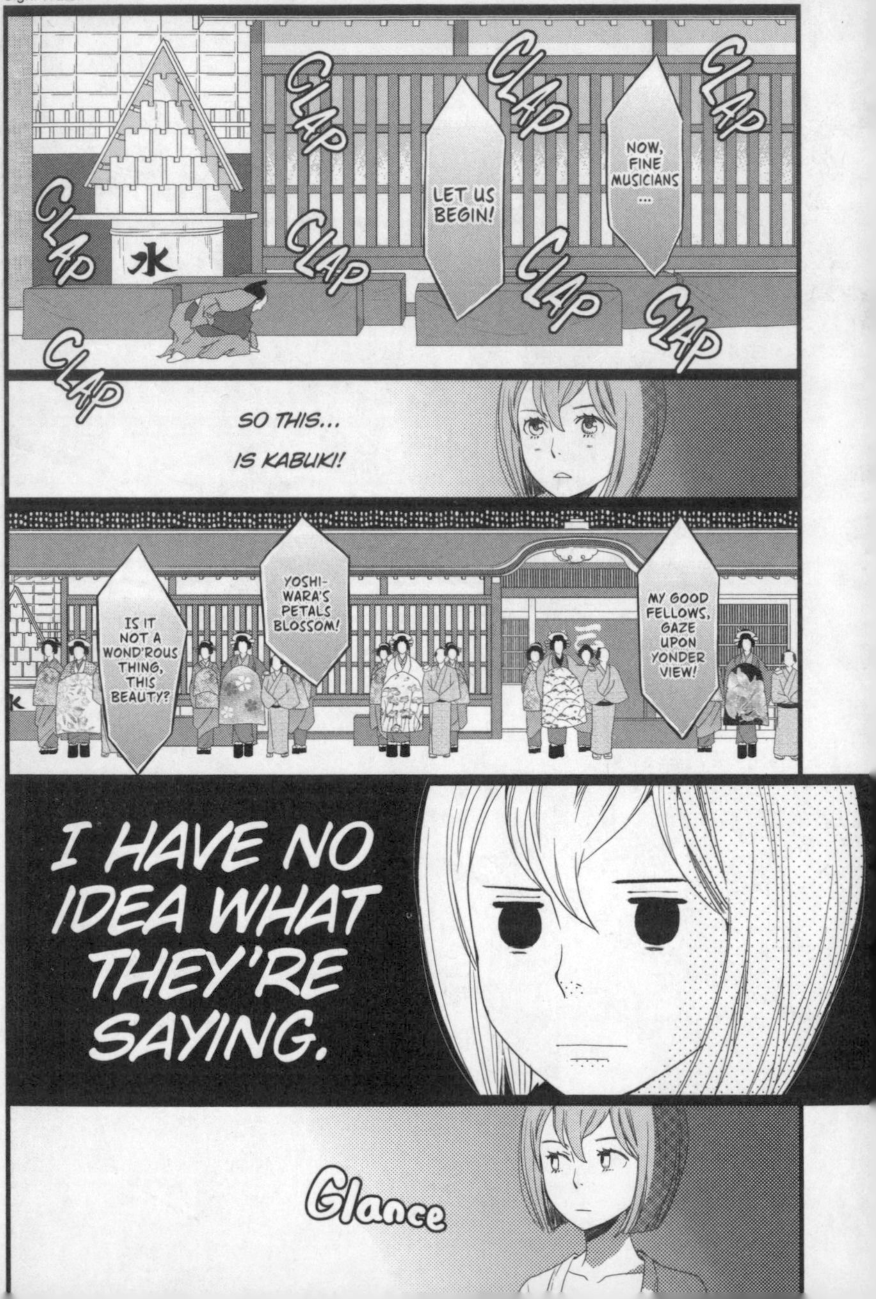
CLAP CLAP
CLAP CLAP
NOW, FINE MUSICIANS...
CLAP CLAP
LET US BEGIN!
CLAP CLAP
CLAP CLAP
SO THIS...
IS KABUKI!
MY GOOD FELLOWS, GAZE UPON YONDER VIEW!
YOSHI-WARA'S PETALS BLOSSOM!
IS IT NOT A WOND'ROUS THING, THIS BEAUTY?
I HAVE NO IDEA WHAT THEY'RE SAYING.
Glance

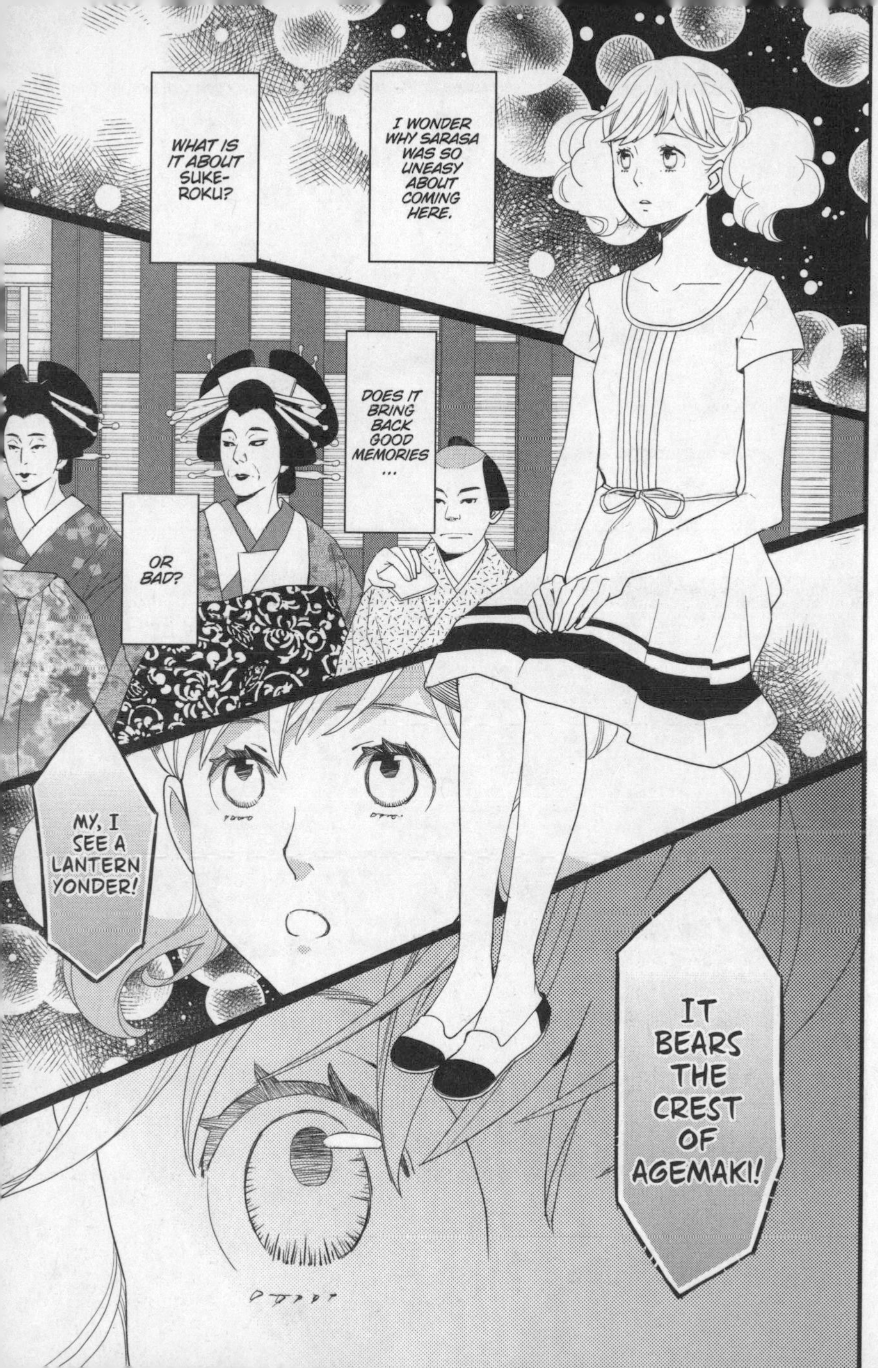
I WONDER WHY SARASA WAS SO UNEASY ABOUT COMING HERE.
WHAT IS IT ABOUT SUKE-ROKU?
DOES IT BRING BACK GOOD MEMORIES...
OR BAD?
MY, I SEE A LANTERN YONDER!
IT BEARS THE CREST OF AGEMAKI!

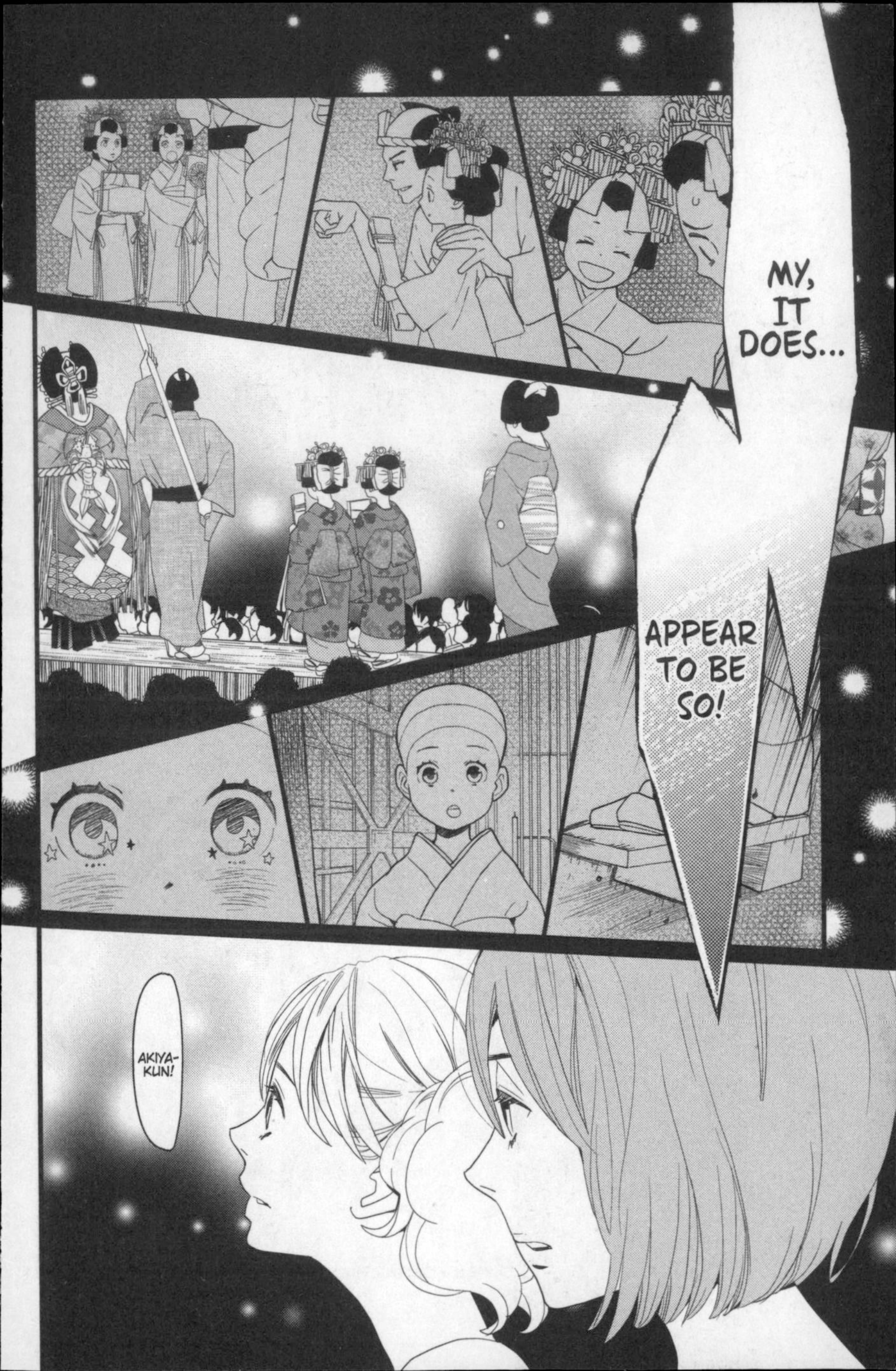
MY, IT DOES...
APPEAR TO BE SO!
...
AKIYA-KUN!

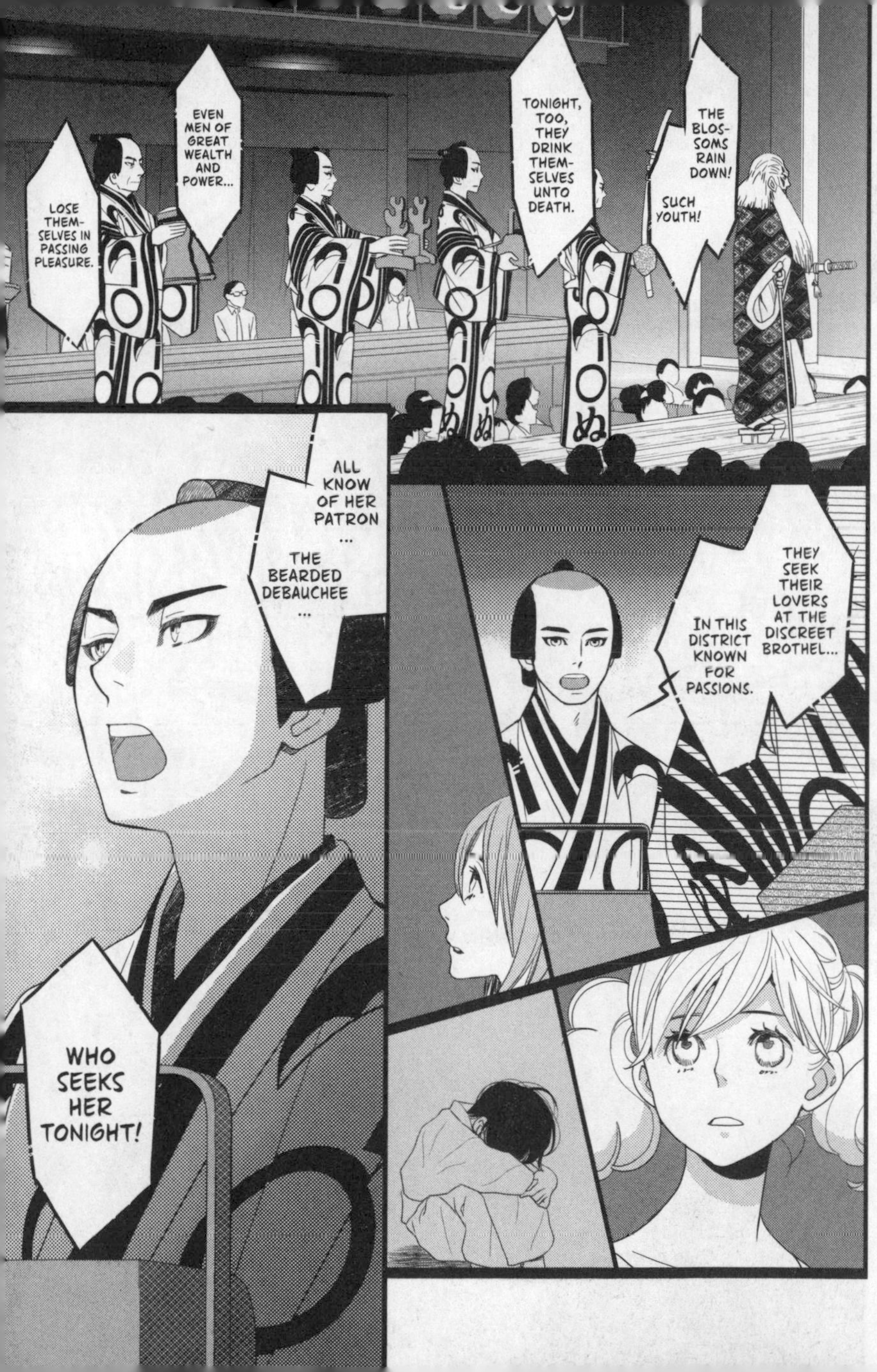
THE BLOSSOMS RAIN DOWN!
SUCH YOUTH!
TONIGHT, TOO, THEY DRINK THEMSELVES UNTO DEATH.
EVEN MEN OF GREAT WEALTH AND POWER...
LOSE THEMSELVES IN PASSING PLEASURE.
THEY SEEK THEIR LOVERS AT THE DISCREET BROTHEL...
IN THIS DISTRICT KNOWN FOR PASSIONS.
ALL KNOW OF HER PATRON...
THE BEARDED DEBAUCHEE...
WHO SEEKS HER TONIGHT!

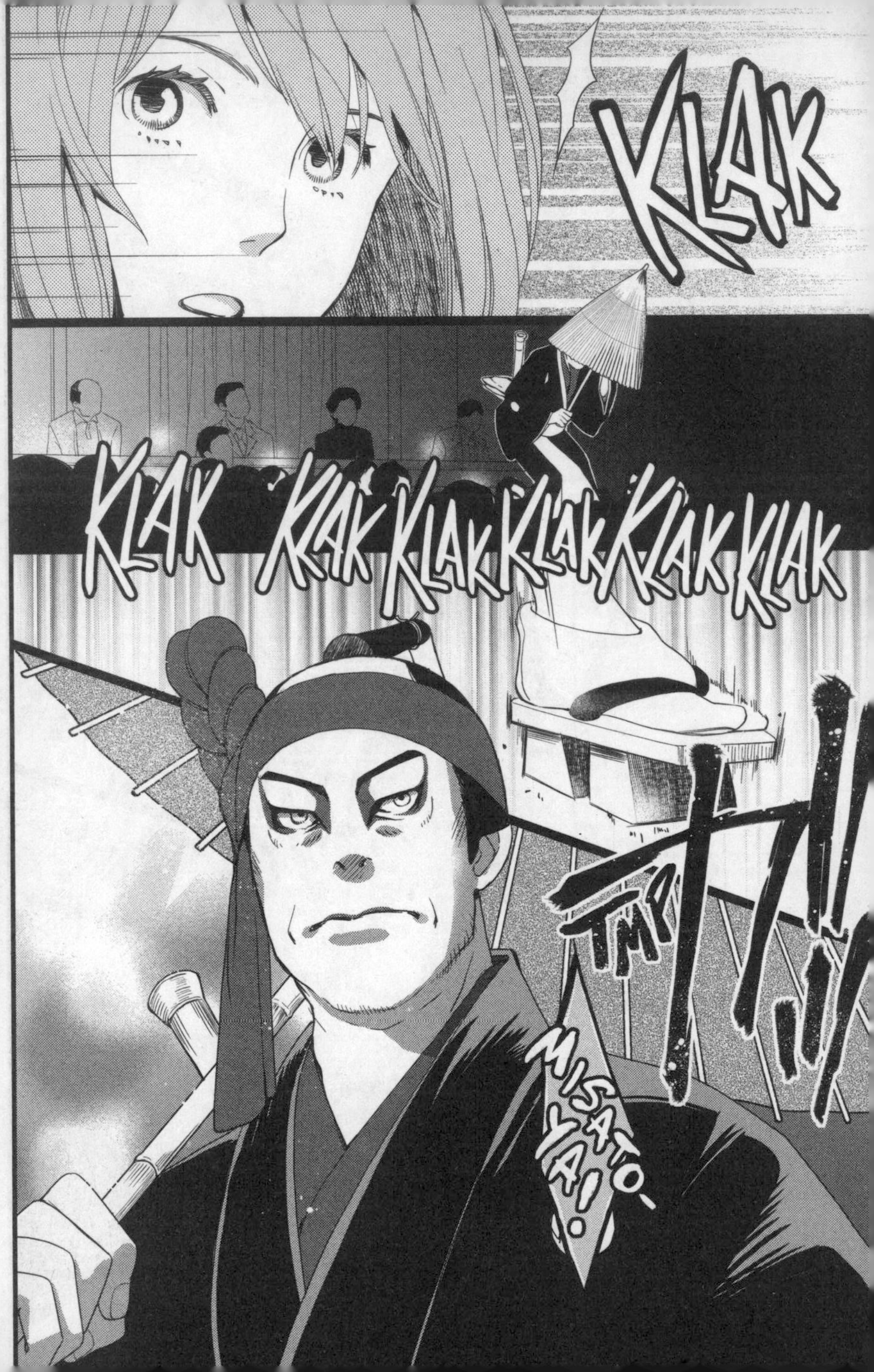
!
KLAK
KLAK KLAK KLAK KLAK KLAK KLAK
TMP
MISATO-YA!

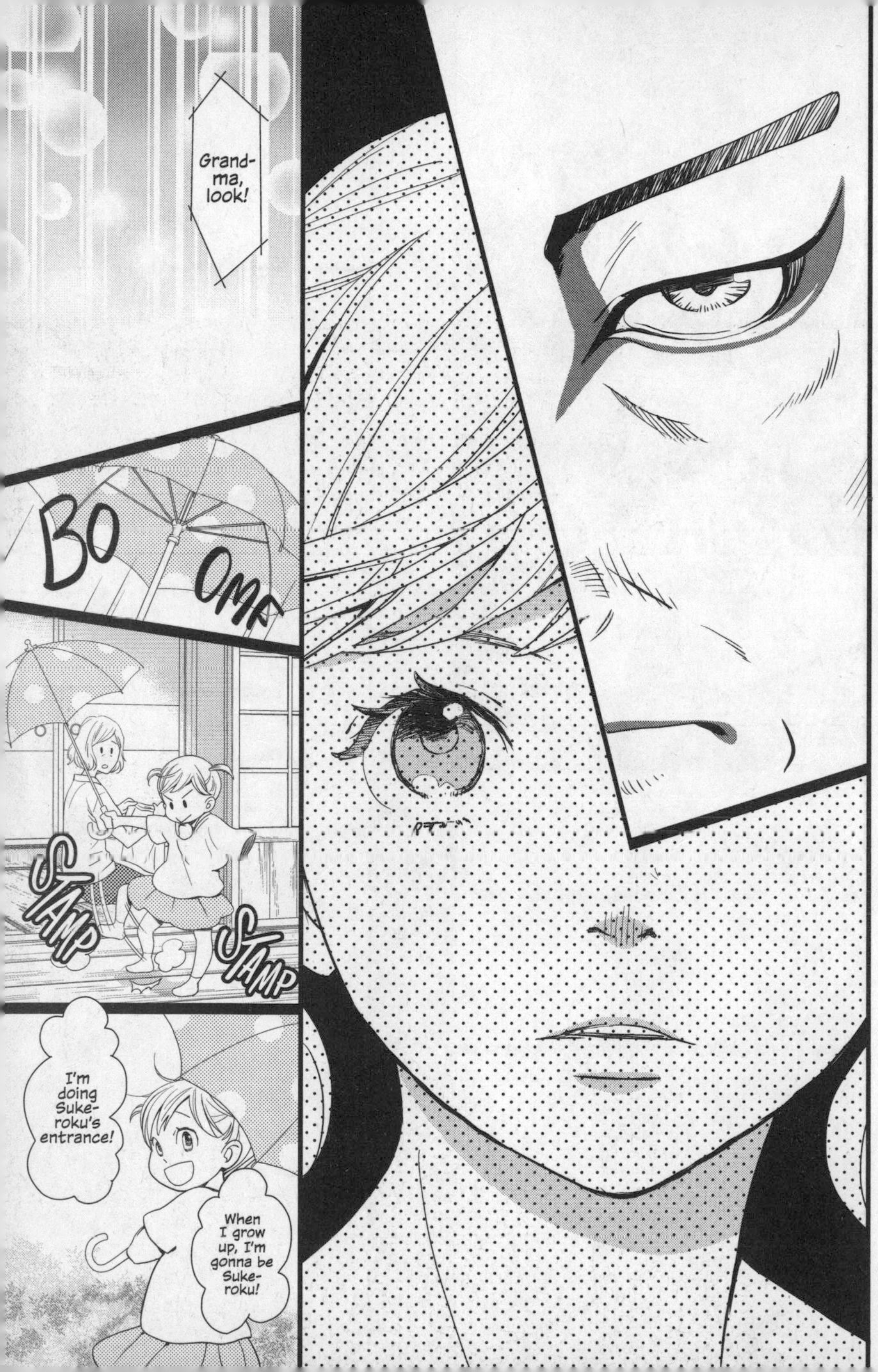
Grand-ma, look!
BO OMF
STAMP
STAMP
I'm doing Suke-roku's entrance!
When I grow up, I'm gonna be Suke-roku!

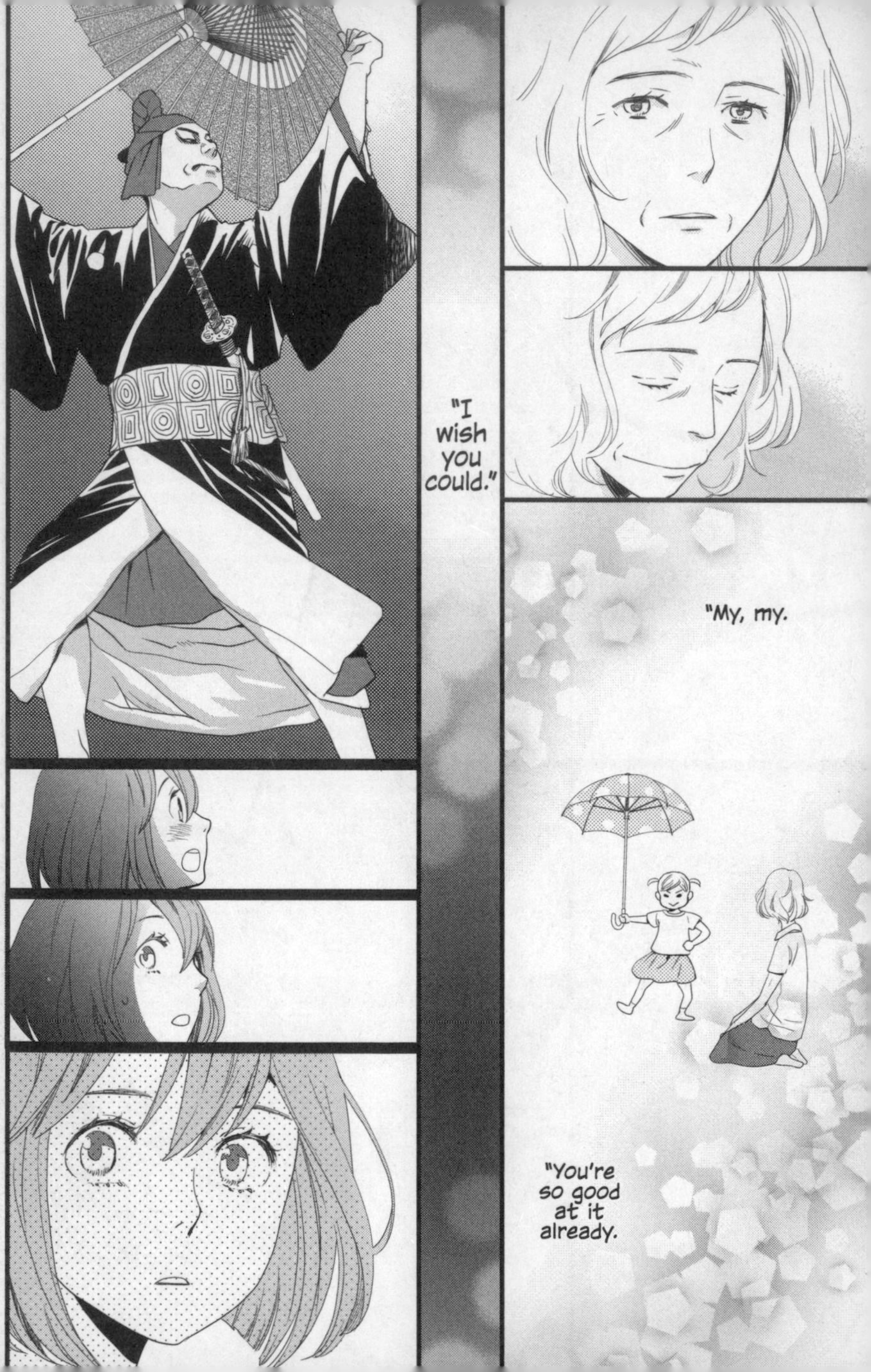
"My, my.
"You're so good at it already.
"I wish you could."

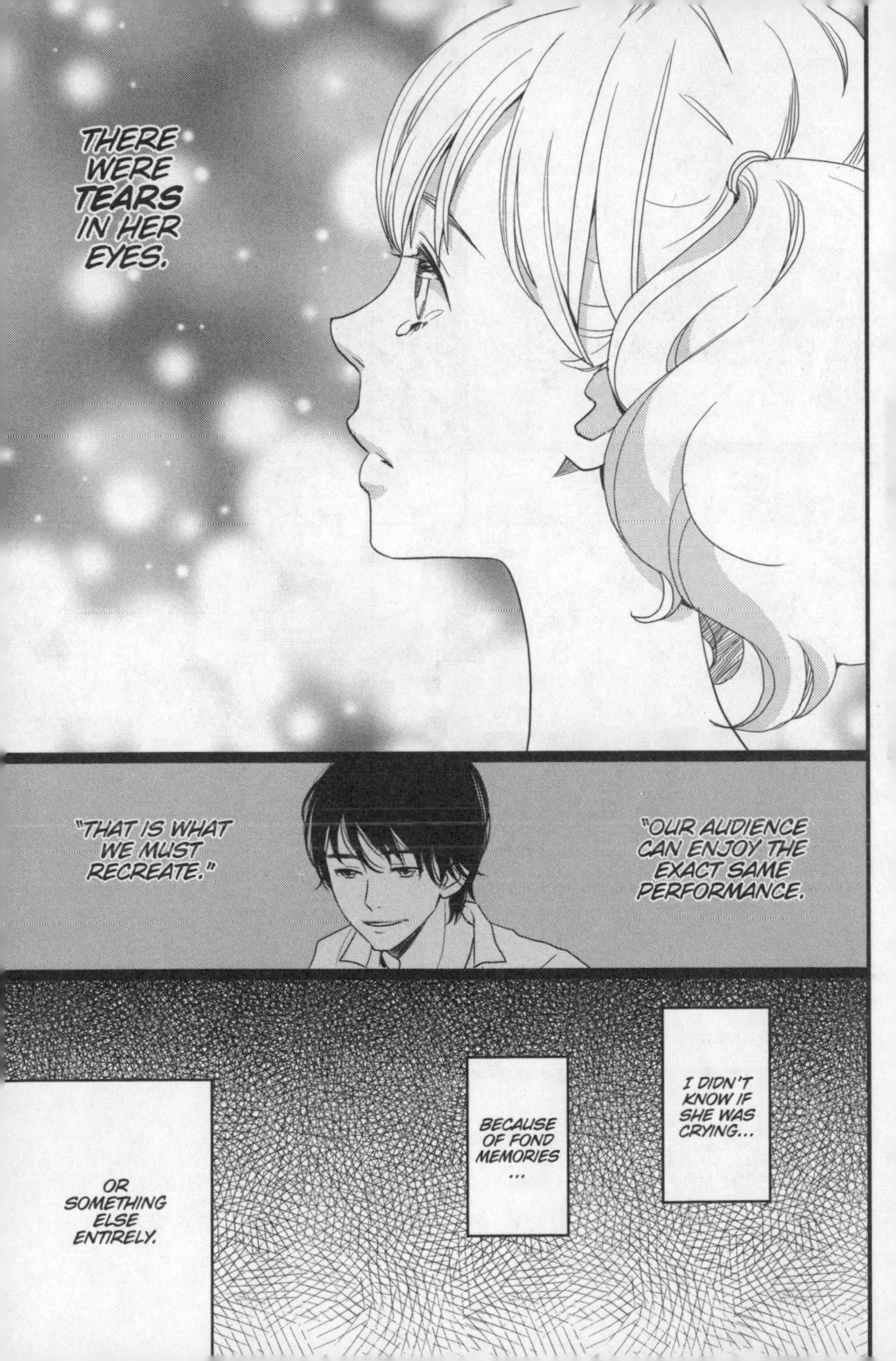
THERE WERE TEARS IN HER EYES.
"OUR AUDIENCE CAN ENJOY THE EXACT SAME PERFORMANCE.
"THAT IS WHAT WE MUST RECREATE."
I DIDN'T KNOW IF SHE WAS CRYING...
BECAUSE OF FOND MEMORIES...
OR SOMETHING ELSE ENTIRELY.

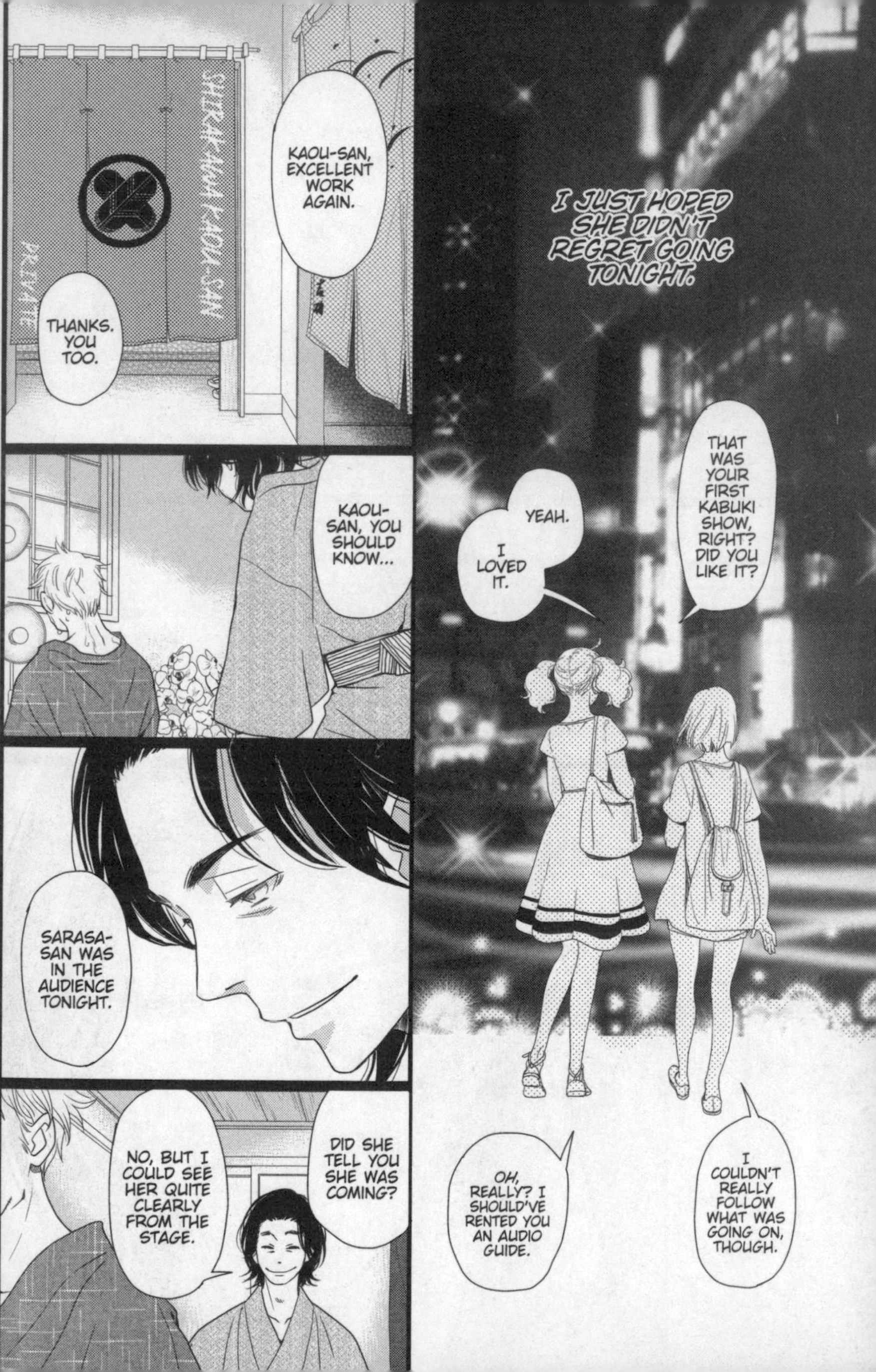
I JUST HOPED SHE DIDN'T REGRET GOING TONIGHT.
THAT WAS YOUR FIRST KABUKI SHOW, RIGHT? DID YOU LIKE IT?
YEAH.
I LOVED IT.
I COULDN'T REALLY FOLLOW WHAT WAS GOING ON, THOUGH.
OH, REALLY? I SHOULD'VE RENTED YOU AN AUDIO GUIDE.
SHIRAKAWA KAOU-SAN
PRIVATE
KAOU-SAN, EXCELLENT WORK AGAIN.
THANKS. YOU TOO.
KAOU-SAN, YOU SHOULD KNOW...
SARASA-SAN WAS IN THE AUDIENCE TONIGHT.
DID SHE TELL YOU SHE WAS COMING?
NO, BUT I COULD SEE HER QUITE CLEARLY FROM THE STAGE.

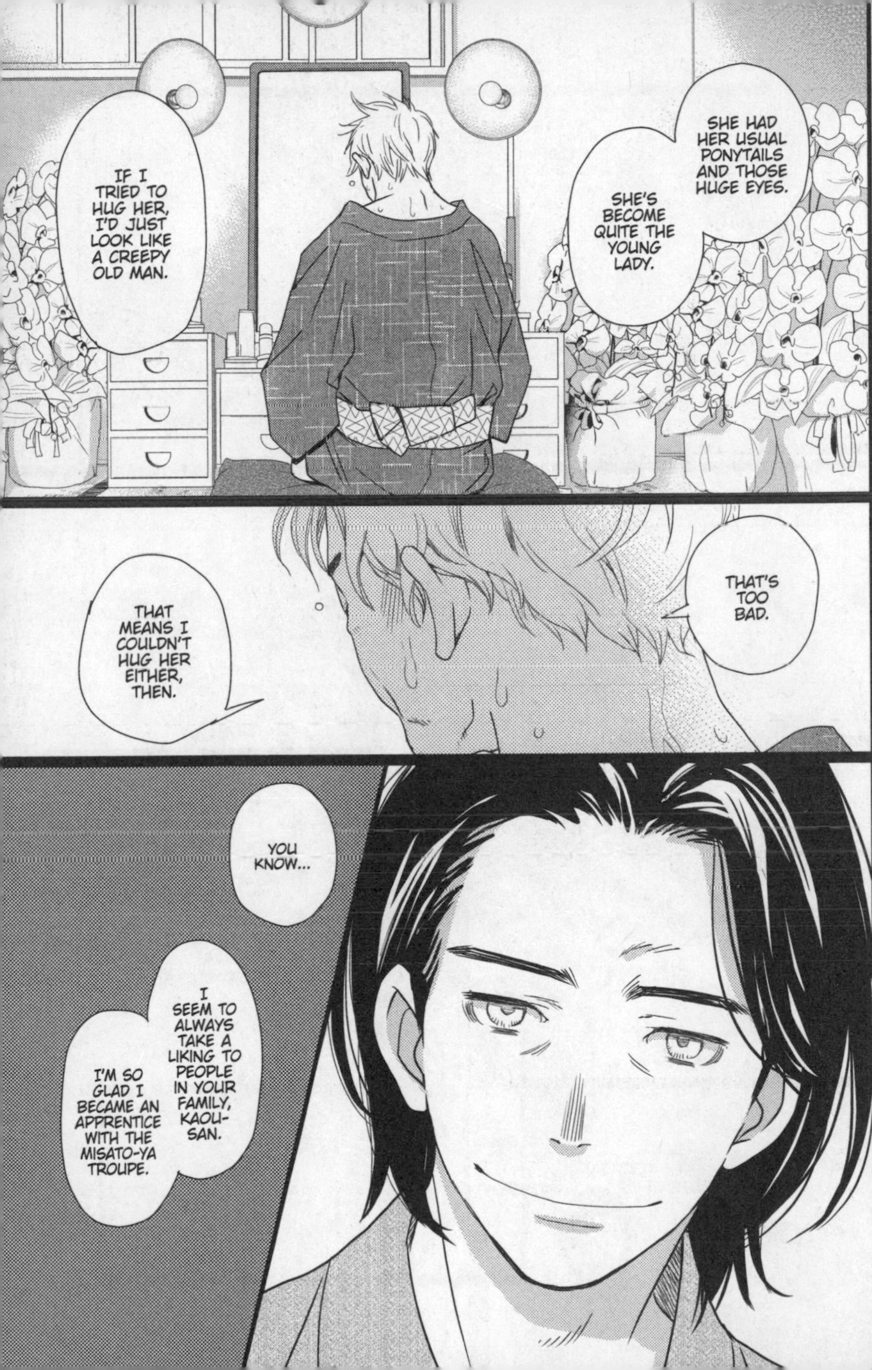
SHE HAD HER USUAL PONYTAILS AND THOSE HUGE EYES.
SHE'S BECOME QUITE THE YOUNG LADY.
IF I TRIED TO HUG HER, I'D JUST LOOK LIKE A CREEPY OLD MAN.
THAT'S TOO BAD.
THAT MEANS I COULDN'T HUG HER EITHER, THEN.
YOU KNOW...
I SEEM TO ALWAYS TAKE A LIKING TO PEOPLE IN YOUR FAMILY, KAOU-SAN.
I'M SO GLAD I BECAME AN APPRENTICE WITH THE MISATO-YA TROUPE.

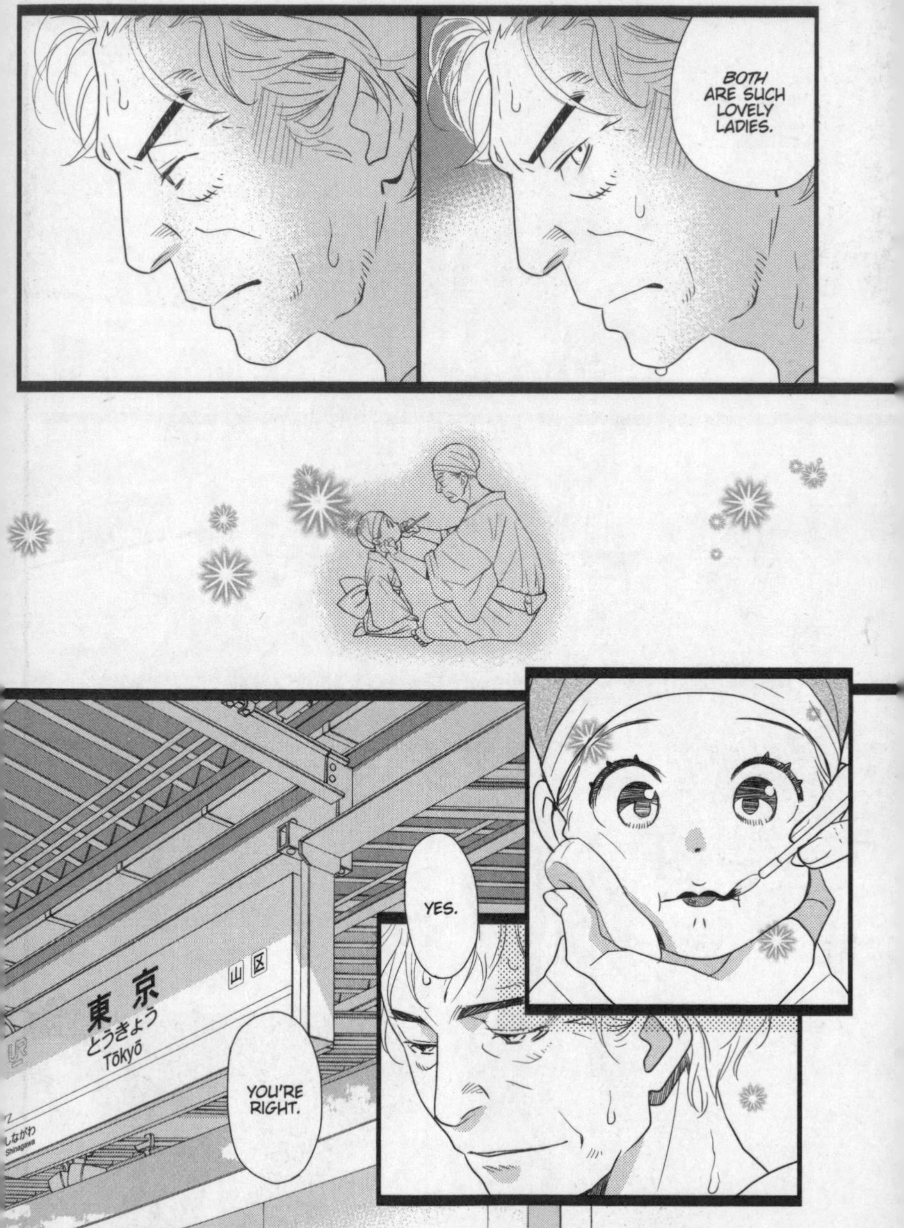
BOTH ARE SUCH LOVELY LADIES.
YES.
YOU'RE RIGHT.
東京
とうきょう
Tōkyō
山区
しながわ
Shinagawa

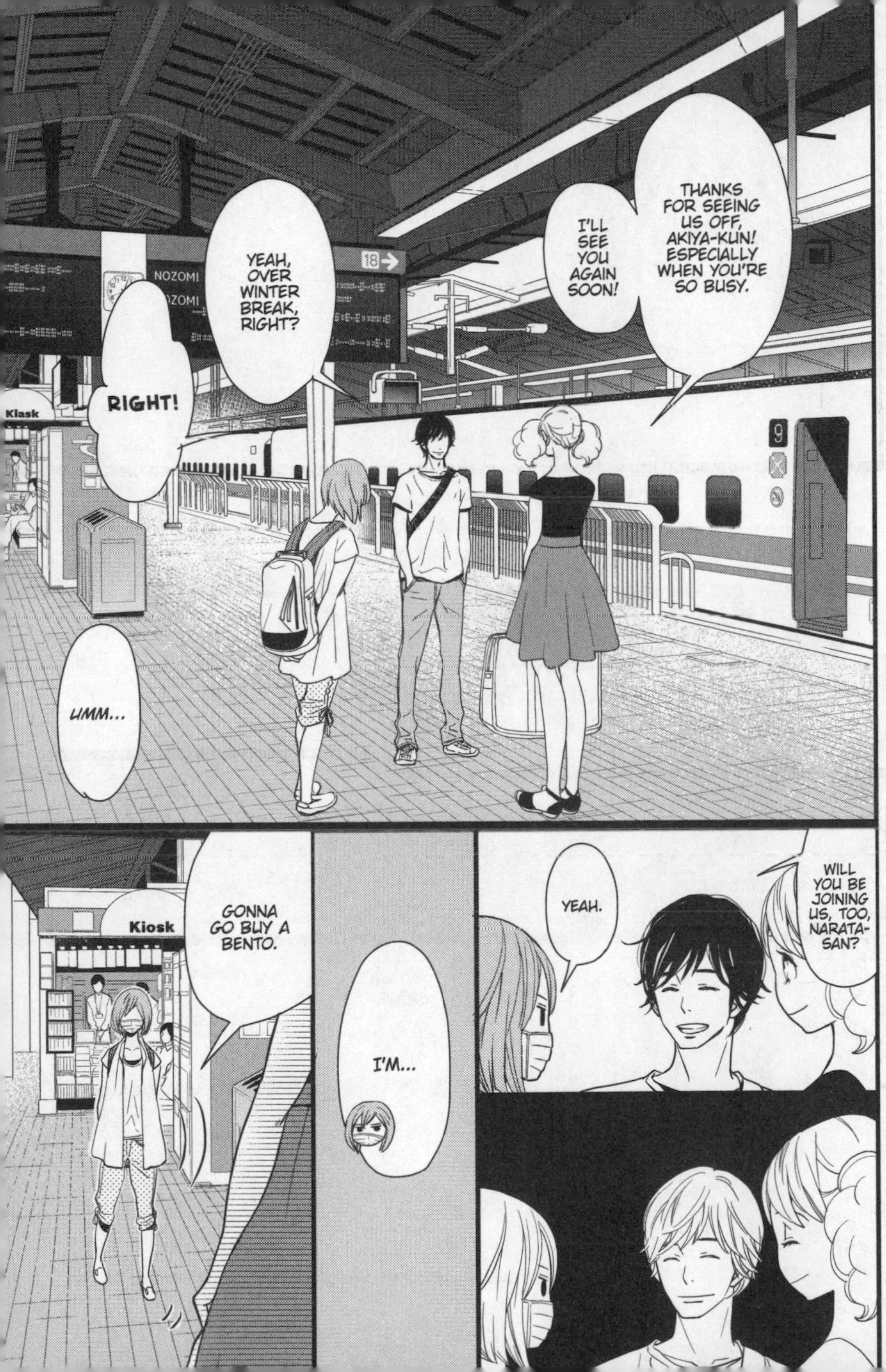
THANKS FOR SEEING US OFF, AKIYA-KUN! ESPECIALLY WHEN YOU'RE SO BUSY.
I'LL SEE YOU AGAIN SOON!
YEAH, OVER WINTER BREAK, RIGHT?
NOZOMI
NOZOMI
18
RIGHT!
Kiask
UMM...
WILL YOU BE JOINING US, TOO, NARATA-SAN?
YEAH.
I'M...
GONNA GO BUY A BENTO.
Kiosk

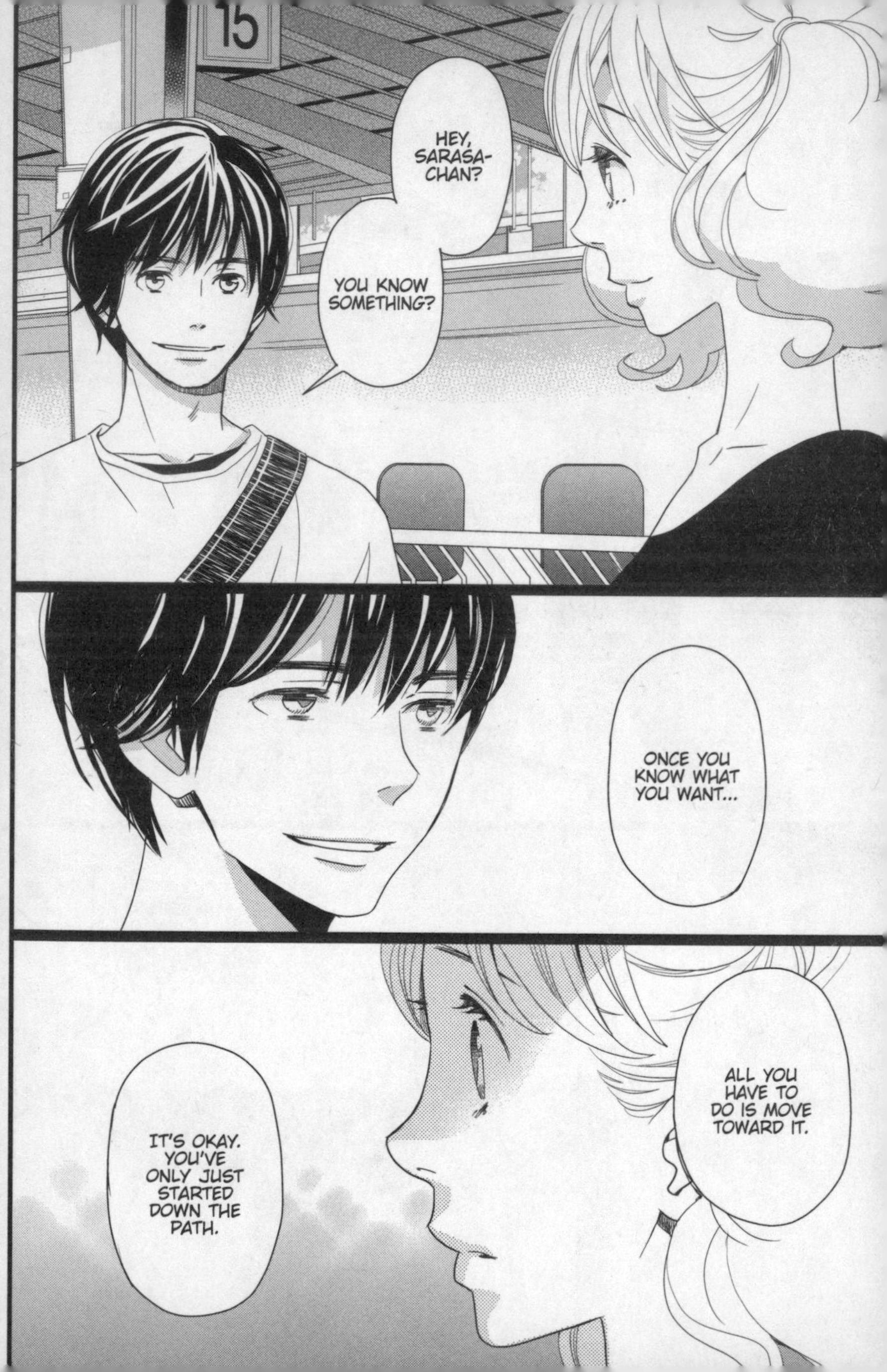
15
HEY, SARASA-CHAN?
YOU KNOW SOMETHING?
ONCE YOU KNOW WHAT YOU WANT...
ALL YOU HAVE TO DO IS MOVE TOWARD IT.
IT'S OKAY. YOU'VE ONLY JUST STARTED DOWN THE PATH.

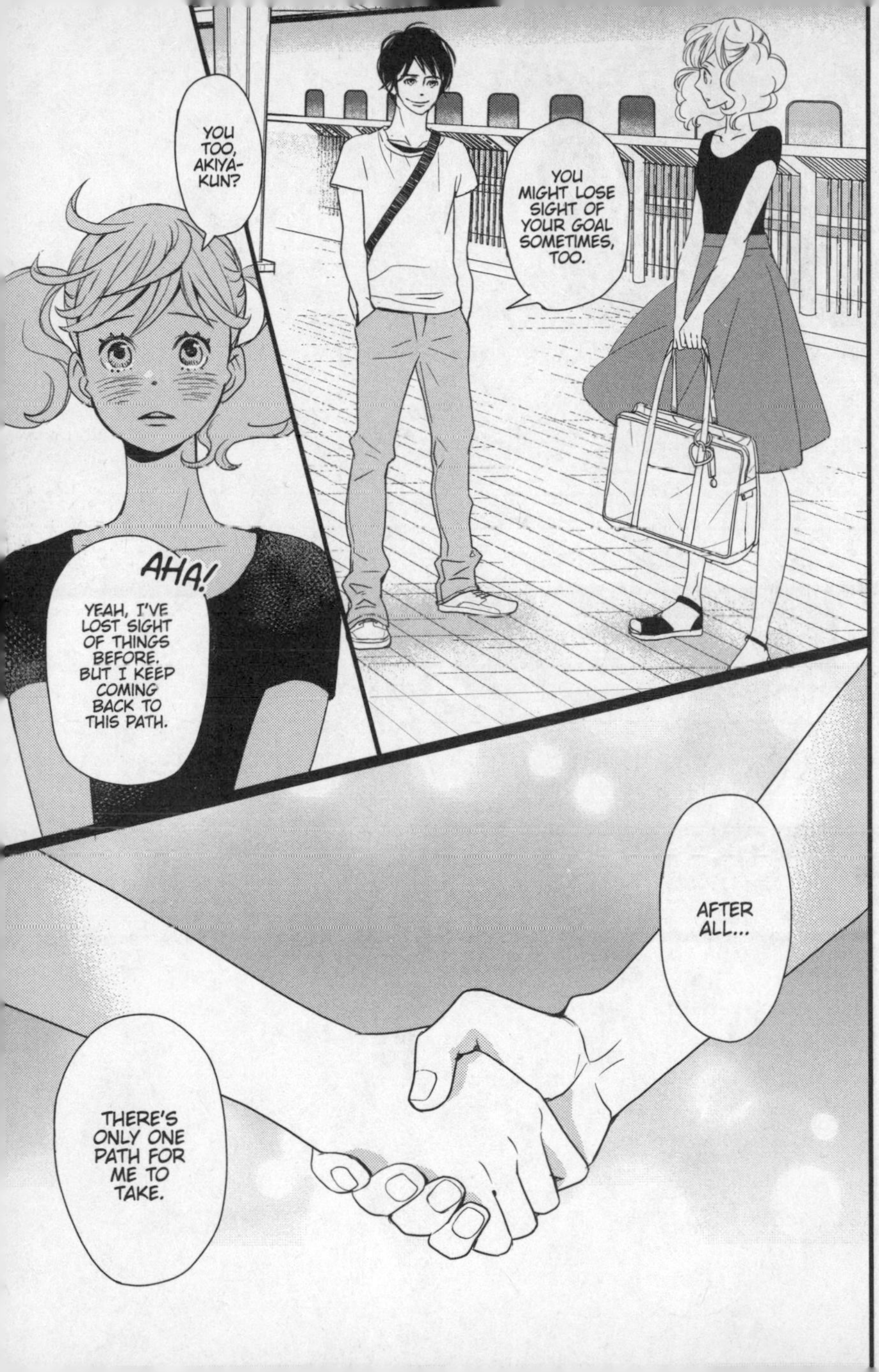
YOU MIGHT LOSE SIGHT OF YOUR GOAL SOMETIMES, TOO.
YOU TOO, AKIYA-KUN?
AHA!
YEAH, I'VE LOST SIGHT OF THINGS BEFORE. BUT I KEEP COMING BACK TO THIS PATH.
AFTER ALL...
THERE'S ONLY ONE PATH FOR ME TO TAKE.

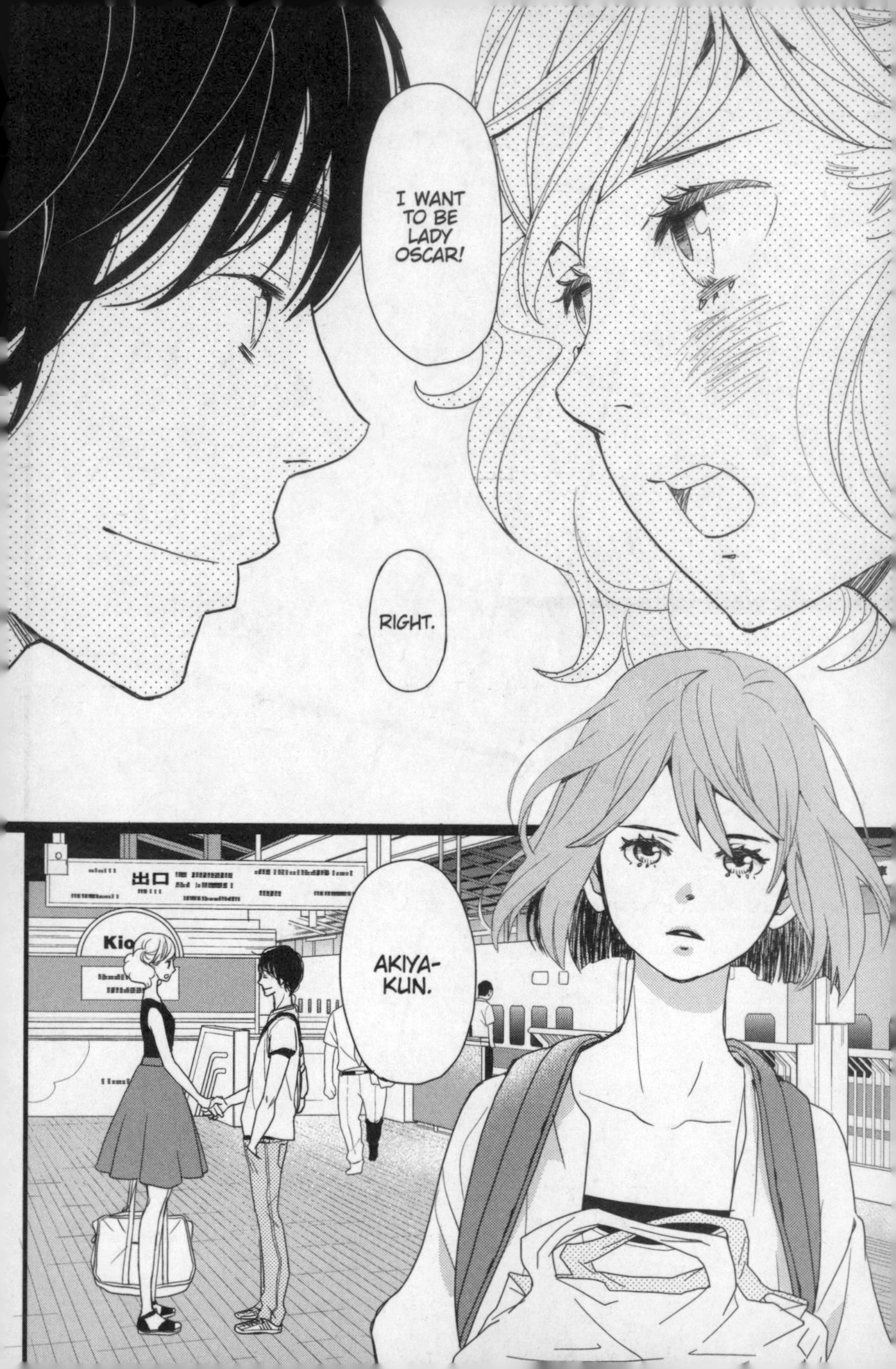
I WANT TO BE LADY OSCAR!
RIGHT.
出口
AKIYA-KUN.

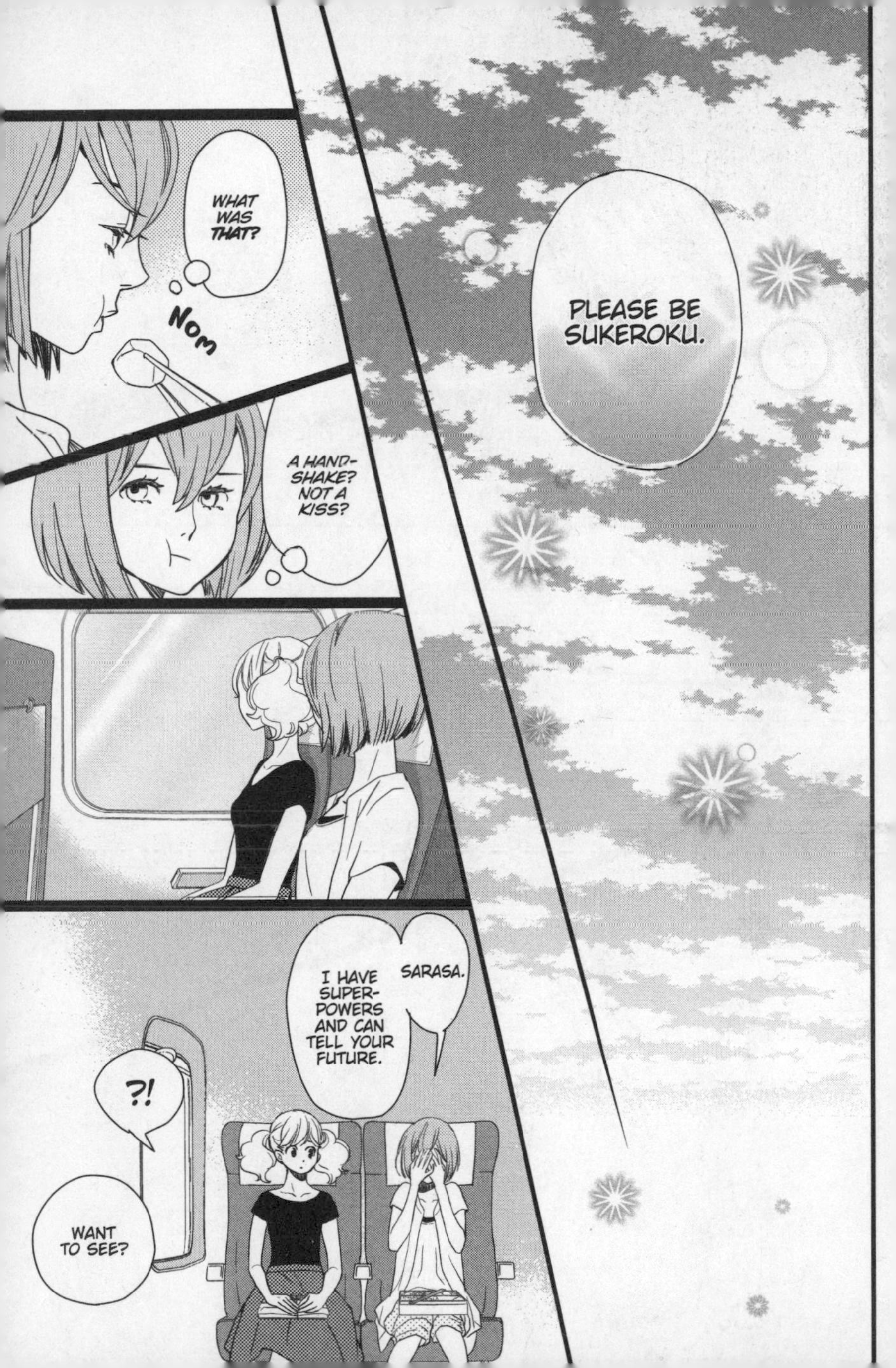
PLEASE BE SUKEROKU.
WHAT WAS THAT?
Nom
A HAND-SHAKE? NOT A KISS?
SARASA.
I HAVE SUPER-POWERS AND CAN TELL YOUR FUTURE.
?!
WANT TO SEE?

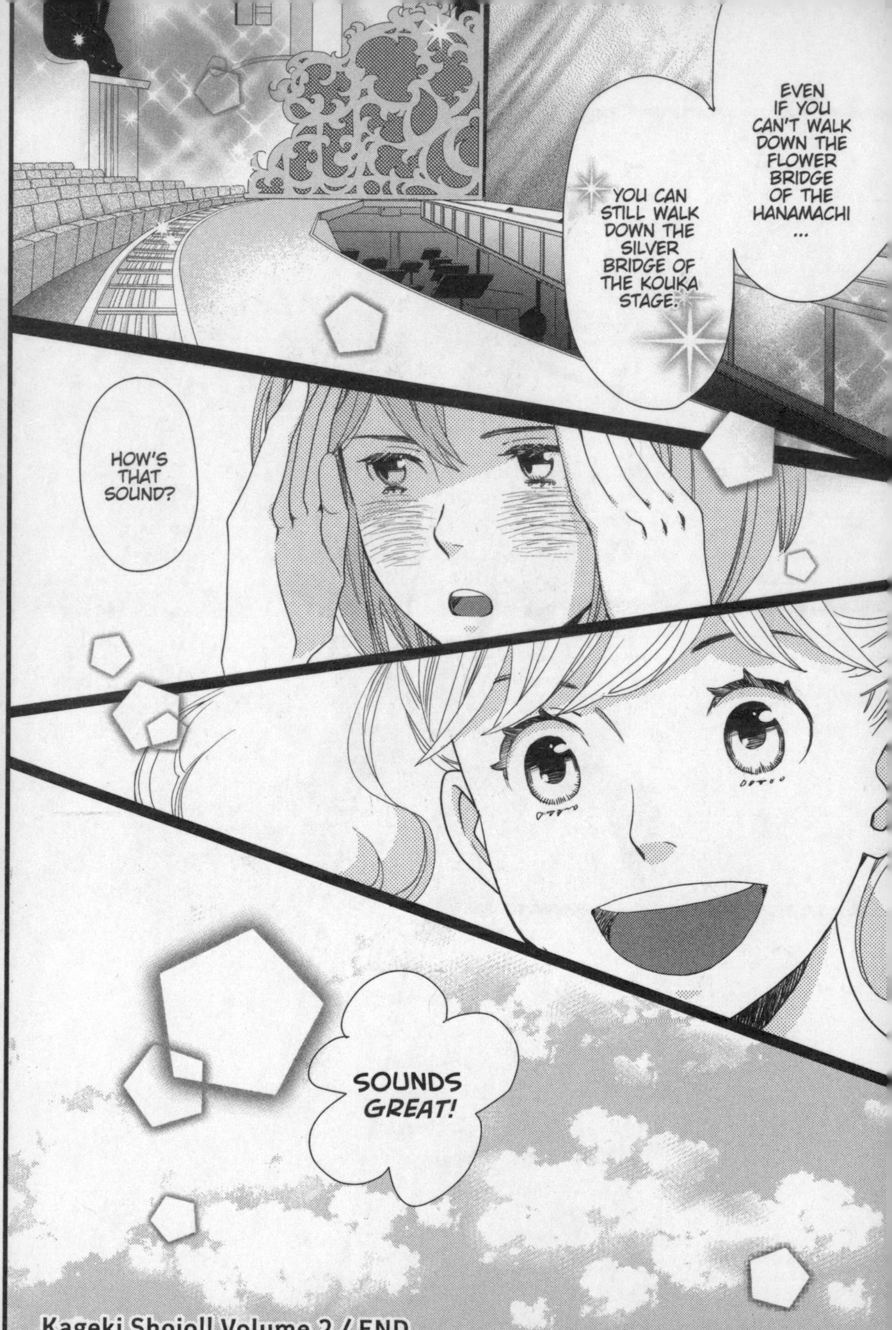
EVEN IF YOU CAN'T WALK DOWN THE FLOWER BRIDGE OF THE HANAMACHI ...
YOU CAN STILL WALK DOWN THE SILVER BRIDGE OF THE KOUKA STAGE.
HOW'S THAT SOUND?
SOUNDS GREAT!

Kageki Shojo!! Volume 2 / END

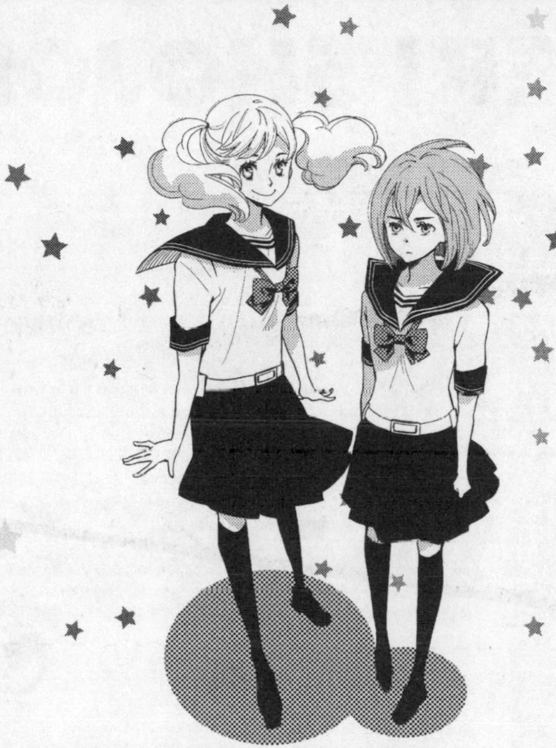

Special Thanks

Tara-chan,
Asai-san,
Kazami-san,
Takato-san,
Miyashita-san,
Nagata-san,
Ishigaki-san,
Kuroki-san,
NonoJill,
&
♡all my readers♡

SEVEN SEAS ENTERTAINMENT PRESENTS

KAGEKI SHOJO!! ★

Vol. 2

story and art by KUMIKO SAIKI

TRANSLATION
Katrina Leonoudakis

LETTERING
Aila Nagamine

COVER DESIGN
Hanase Qi

LOGO DESIGN
Courtney Williams

PROOFREADER
Rebecca Schneidereit

EDITOR
Shannon Fay

PREPRESS TECHNICIAN
Shannon Rasmussen-Silverstein

PRODUCTION ASSOCIATE
Christa Miesner

PRODUCTION MANAGER
Lissa Pattillo

MANAGING EDITOR
Julie Davis

ASSOCIATE PUBLISHER
Adam Arnold

PUBLISHER
Jason DeAngelis

Seven Seas press and purchase enquiries can be sent to Marketing Manager Lianne
Sentar at press@gomanga.com. Information regarding the distribution and purchase of
digital editions is available from Digital Manager CK Russell at digital@gomanga.com.

Seven Seas and the Seven Seas logo are trademarks of
Seven Seas Entertainment. All rights reserved.

ISBN: 978-1-64827-616-3
Printed in Canada
First Printing: September 2021
10 9 8 7 6 5 4 3 2 1

▨▨▨ READING DIRECTIONS ▨▨▨

This book reads from *right to left*,
Japanese style. If this is your first time
reading manga, you start reading from
the top right panel on each page and
take it from there. If you get lost, just
follow the numbered diagram here.
It may seem backwards at first,
but you'll get the hang of it! Have fun!!

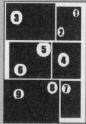

Follow us online: www.SevenSeasEntertainment.com